Dawnsearlylite

Dawnsearlylite

Arvind Kumar

Copyright © 2013 by Arvind Kumar.

Library of Congress Control Number: 2012923743
ISBN: Hardcover   978-1-4797-6869-1
                Softcover   978-1-4797-6868-4
                Ebook   978-1-4797-6870-7

All rights reserved. No part of this book may be reproduced or transmitted in any form or by any means, electronic or mechanical, including photocopying, recording, or by any information storage and retrieval system, without permission in writing from the copyright owner.

This is a work of fiction. Names, characters, places and incidents either are the product of the author's imagination or are used fictitiously, and any resemblance to any actual persons, living or dead, events, or locales is entirely coincidental.

This book was printed in the United States of America.

Rev. date: 02/21/2013

To order additional copies of this book, contact:
Xlibris Corporation
1-888-795-4274
www.Xlibris.com
Orders@Xlibris.com
122017

Where there's beauty

find me.

Where there's beauty

walk with me.

Where there's beauty

Take me.

Cause I cannot get there

on my own.

There shall be no whore of the daughters of Israel, nor a sodomite of the sons of Israel.
Thou shalt not bring the hire of a whore, or the price of a dog, into the house of the LORD thy God for any vow: for even both these are abomination unto the LORD thy God.

—DEUTERONOMY 23:17-18

Pleasure is the Object, the Duty and the Goal of All Rational Creatures . . .
—VOLTAIRE, 1716

1

Dawn's heart pumped faster than usual. Maybe it was from the *luxe* surroundings of the Hyatt Downtown Montréal, the exotic sequined jacket she had just purchased that afternoon on the Rue Saint Laurent, or just plain adrenaline. She wasn't sure, but it didn't matter. Stepping into the elevator, Dawn pressed the button for the main lobby, which, unlike most Montréal hotels, was on the fifth floor. She walked across the huge salon glittering with Swarovski crystal chandeliers, taking care not to bring attention to herself. Dawn knew upscale hotel staffs can recognize a hooker from a mile away, even one whose days were spent instructing the city's youth in reading, writing and mathematics.

Not that Dawn disliked being a schoolteacher. She just needed some extra excitement to liven up her nights. Turning tricks accomplished that. And the money, which was great, helped feed her appetite for luxurious *accoutrements*. Tom, her boss, made sure she had plenty of those. He had also forked over the exorbitant fee to Dawn's favorite plastic surgeon, a man who declared his most fervent desire was to make the world a more "beautiful" place, for her breast implants.

Tom's brainchild, Passion Escorts, provided the cream of the Montréal crop of gorgeous young women to the elite sector of the city's male population. It was a service, he always emphasized to Dawn, and he was proud of it. He treated her well, perhaps better than the other girls, for she was his favorite. She brought a lot of business to the agency, more than any of the others did, and happy clients always called back to see her again and again. She didn't even have to split her tips with him. Clients who requested sessions of one hour always ended up keeping her for two or three. She could afford to be blasé, and she wasn't impressed by his deep, masculine voice when he called earlier that evening.

"I have a nice client for you."

"Yeah? Nice enough to interrupt 'Friends'? Rachel and Ross just got it on in the Natural History Museum."

Tom ignored her casual attitude. "He's at the Hyatt Downtown. Anglophone."

"He damn well better be." She didn't serve Francophones.

"A doctor, Indian accent. Very nervous on the phone, so put on the kid gloves, okay?"

"Yeah, whatever." She yawned.

"When can you be ready?"

"Take it royally easy. I'll be downstairs when you get here."

Dawn switched off the TV and shuffled to the bedroom. She was not going to rush through her make-up routine just because Tom was pressuring her.

If he has to light more than one cigarette waiting for me in the car . . . Well, tant pis.

She was just putting the finishing touches on her blonde mane when the downstairs buzzer jolted her. She grimaced with aggravation but put on her most cheerful voice to respond.

"I'll be right down."

It was going to be a long night.

*

When Dawn emerged from the front entrance of her brand-new condo building on Avenue Victoria, Tom was puffing away as she had expected. She peered into the back seat, where Jeanne-Marie and Claudette were taking the last drags on their cigarettes. Sliding into the front seat next to Tom, Dawn suppressed a smirk and tossed a glance at the two women.

"Tough night, girls?" She turned to Tom. "Sometimes I wonder why you're in this freaking line of work, driving around all night."

Tom flashed a disapproving look at Dawn and murmured under his breath. "What else would I do? I'm an entrepreneur. Besides, it's fun."

"Yeah, right." Dawn cranked open her window to defend herself from the cigarette smoke.

Tom shivered from the icy air coming into the car. "And by the way, how come you were late?"

"Since when are you worried? They're always willing to wait. As long as they get what they want, right?"

He sighed. She knew how to butter her bread—and burn the clients' toast.

Despite the usual Friday night downtown traffic congestion, they managed to reach the Hyatt in record time. Tom pulled up in front and dialed his cell. "She's at the front door." He clicked off and gave Dawn a determined look. "Remember my instructions, okay?"

"You're the boss."

Yeah, right.

2

Dawn crossed the lobby to the elevators accessing the upper floors and realized her excitement stemmed from the prospect of sleeping with a rich married doctor. Married was her preference. With a few exceptions, married men treated her the best and were less demanding, probably because they had long since been able to get anything at all from their wives. But a married doctor was capable of generous tips if she performed to his satisfaction, and money thrilled her more than anything else in life. That, and the anticipation of the unknown.

You never know whom you might meet behind those doors.

The danger and anonymity thrilled her, took her to an extraordinary high every time. It was an addiction, she knew that well, and she fed off of it. Sex, money and intrigue. It didn't get any better.

The elevator stopped at the 19th floor. Dawn rambled down the hallway, searching for room 1912. She forced her body to relax, but her face glowed and her heart galloped as soon as she knocked on the door. She saw her client peering through the keyhole viewer. She certainly couldn't miss his jaw dropping when he opened the door and took a look at her. Dawn smiled. As a child in New Brunswick, she had always enjoyed being admired. In adulthood, she was a package worthy of awe. Shoulder length blonde-auburn hair, small, soft chin, high cheekbones, tiny pixie nose, blue eyes you could get lost in and a body that didn't quit always mesmerized anyone who came within view of her. Not to mention her clients.

"I'm from the agency." The warmth of her smile enveloped him. The tinkling of her voice hypnotized him. After a moment, he came to his senses.

"Oh. Yes. I'm sorry, do come in." He blushed. "I thought you were an angel."

Dawn acknowledged his compliment with a soft laugh. "You can call me that if you like."

She slipped into the room, taking a moment to admire the view. The careworn but historic buildings, the commercial centre of Montréal at the turn of the 20th century, came alive in the soft glow of the setting sun. For her the world ended here, at the basin of the St. Lawrence River, where earth interfaced heaven. She was in love with her city.

"Before I forget, Doctor—"

"Sanjay."

"Sanjay. Nice name."

He blushed again. "What's yours?"

"Dawn."

She checked out his attributes. He wasn't hard to look at. Nice face, wavy hair, dark complexion and athletic build, but slender. Just the way she liked them.

"I need to collect two hundred dollars, up front. Then I need to call my boss. Agency rules, you understand."

"Yes. Of course."

He picked up his wallet from the bureau, pulled out two hundred dollar bills and handed them to her. She slipped them into her purse.

"Thank you. May I use your phone?"

Sanjay nodded towards the phone on the night table next to the bed. Then he undressed and sank onto the luxurious coverlet, watching as Dawn dialed and spoke in a soft murmur. After she hung up, she approached him, her efficient business expression softening, and laid her purse on the night table.

"You're a handsome man. Married?" He nodded. "Handsome married men turn me on." Again his face flushed. She liked that.

Different from my usual. Maybe.

Dawn removed her sequined jacket. "Let's not waste any time. I like to give you your money's worth."

She unbuttoned her pink silk blouse and black skirt, revealing a bright red lace teddy that hugged the arches of her body like a racing car making love to a curvaceous track. She could see by the not so subtle changes in his anatomy that her lingerie was having the desired effect. Now started the high she was so addicted to. She let the straps fall. Then, allowing the teddy to drop to the floor, she milked the striptease for all it was worth, showing off attributes that mesmerized him as they had done so to countless others: long neck, slender shoulders, well-toned arms, tiny waist, perfectly proportioned thighs and breasts, smooth, silky buttocks.

His eyes followed the flow of her torso, all the way down to her delicate feet, more provocative looking than any he had ever seen, then back up to her nipples, pink and prominent, standing to attention. She caught his gaze and knew he ached to touch them. Kneeling before him, she started with his chest, kissing and fondling his nipples, licking each centimeter of his body until a tortured groan escaped his throat. By the time she got to his penis, he was screaming with desire, his heart pounding with the blood coursing through his veins.

She reached into her purse and pulled out a condom. He spoke in short gasps.

"Do it . . . without."

"Not on your life."

But, really, is he nuts?

She could see he was disappointed.

"Maybe . . . Once I get to know you better."

She obeyed and let him caress her. She noticed at once how delicate his hands felt, a physician's hands, which knew where to find the most responsive places on her body. He stroked and probed, at first gently, then with more intensity, her sensitive areas, from her forehead to her breasts. He fondled her nipples with his lips, teasing and licking, massaging her clitoris with his finger. His adeptness startled her. From his blushing, she had expected a novice, or at least a man who was more self-conscious about showing his expertise. That he certainly was not.

"You have beautiful eyes, angel."

This brought her back to reality. She couldn't afford to luxuriate in pleasure. She had a job to do. She pulled his face back from her breasts.

"Fuck me."

Now she could show her own skillfulness. A consummate actress in the bedroom, she lay back and let him enter her. But her frenzied screams came from deep within, and not from a need to put on a performance. Within seconds she was out of control, filling the room with the sounds of her pleasure. A voice inside told her to hold back, but she didn't care who heard her.

"Harder, Sanjay. Faster. Give me everything. I want to be your fantasy."

He needed no further urging. His body contorted, letting go of his pent-up passion. She closed her eyes, taking in the sound of his cry of release, and waited for him to relax. He gave one last shudder and collapsed next to her, exhausted. She glanced at his tranquil face, wondering what he was thinking about.

His fellow conferees, his boardroom meetings, his family at home?

"You know, I almost cancelled you tonight. I'm a stickler for punctuality."

"I'll bet you are."

"I've been known to cancel a patient if he or she is late by five minutes."

She nestled up to him, her head perched on his shoulder. "And are you glad you didn't cancel?"

He locked his arms around her, pulling her to him. "It was well worth the extra 45 minutes' wait."

She grinned her appreciation. "I knew that."

Extricating herself from his embrace, Dawn rose from the bed and headed to the bathroom. After that explosive workout, she decided she deserved a nice shower. When she returned, wrapped in a luxurious Egyptian cotton towel, she found Sanjay stretched out on the bed, eyes closed, his athletic body exposed to her eyes. She smiled to herself.

A satisfied customer is the best kind.

She turned her back to him, the towel falling to the floor, and began to gather her clothing. Then she felt hands wrapping around her waist, caressing her buttocks, burning lips kissing her neck, scorching fingers massaging her nipples. Dawn tried to turn around, but he stopped her, his swollen penis hard against her back. She knew what he wanted.

"That'll cost you extra."

Without a word, he took her from behind. Evidently money was no object.

3

They had been huddled in a tight embrace for a long time—Dawn had no idea how long, she just knew he didn't want her to leave anytime soon—when Sanjay planted gentle kisses on her eyes and lips. "Let's wash up and go out for a dinner."

"Great." She was famished.

"Just . . ." He hesitated.

"What?"

"We can't walk out together."

"Ah." She'd been there before. "Too many people know you here?"

He was impressed by her savvy. "Yes."

"No problem. You can make up for it by tipping me. Generously."

She had noticed the ATM machine in the lobby on her way up. Nothing passed her by. She was too smart for that.

*

"You're not like the others."

"Hmm?" She was lost in the seductive taste of her Indian beer, which she had never tried before, and in the atmosphere of the Maharajah Restaurant, a popular haunt for Indian food aficionados.

"You know, the bait and switch, the hot models on the websites. As a rule, when someone looks too good to be true, she usually is."

"Right." She wondered if he had gotten to the cash machine.

"I'm too experienced for that. Not that I do research. I hate it, at least on that topic."

She raised her eyebrows but decided not to comment on his insensitivity. Still, maybe it had been a mistake to go out to dinner with him.

"But I'm not one of those poor slobs who believe the photos and are too drunk to turn a girl away."

"And since you didn't send me packing, you were not feeling suckered?"

"As I said, you're not like the others."

"Okay. Whatever." She sipped her beer. "I like this stuff."

He nodded with approval. "Back home in India they only serve large bottles."

"Whatever. Did you get to the ATM?"

"It was out of order."

She tried not to let her disappointment show. Sanjay chuckled and withdrew a wad of bills from his wallet.

"I was kidding."

He rose, pulled her up from her seat and steered her towards the buffet, where lettered signs distinguished the "Vegetarian" side from the "Non-Vegetarian." Sanjay headed for the rice and curried carrots, stopped and turned to Dawn.

"I can help you pick some meat dishes."

"Thanks, but I've got my favorites. I even tried cooking Indian food once, but it was a real bust. I guess that's something you've got to learn from your mother."

Dawn eyed the tantalizing array of dishes. The smell of spices was erotic. She had a sudden urge to pile a sample of every offering on her plate. By the time Sanjay had filled his with chickpeas, bhartha, okra and a variety of vegetables and salads, Dawn's mound of tandoori chicken, curried beef and chicken curry was threatening to topple from the plate. When they returned to their seats, she attacked her tender chicken with a vengeance.

"My dad wouldn't let me be a vegetarian. He always worried I wouldn't get enough protein. Do you do it for religious reasons?"

"No, I'm an atheist."

Dawn's hackles went up. She had had a strict Catholic upbringing, and the loose principles of non-believers put her on the defensive.

"Vegetarianism is a philosophy for me. I abhor making other beings suffer, whether animal or human."

Hearing this, Dawn reconsidered her assessment of him. "You're very noble, Sanjay."

"No, I'm not. You don't know me. I have many weaknesses. One of them is beauty." He took her face in his hands, gazing at her. "In the presence of such an angel, I could die happy."

She couldn't remember the last time she felt embarrassed, but his adoration made her squirm. Nonetheless something about her made her want to trust him, and she took a leap of faith.

"I . . . I'd like you to see this."

Sanjay accepted the newsletter Dawn pulled from her purse and began to read it aloud. "Canadian Women Participate in Opus Dei International Development Project."

He paused, raising his eyebrows at her. She nodded. He continued.

"Several young *Canadiennes* from the *Fonteneige* residence hall at Montréal University recently spent two weeks in *Sierra de Querétaro*, Mexico, initiating social development programs for poverty-stricken Mexican children. Among them was Mlle. L'andry . . ." Again, he looked at her. Again, she urged him on. "Who was quoted as saying, 'this unforgettable experience has helped me deepen my own faith. It has given me the opportunity to better understand people of a different culture, to selflessly give them love and spiritual guidance through catechism classes . . . '" He stopped. "What is catechism?"

Dawn was astounded. How could he possibly not know this? Nonetheless, her passion for the religion into which she had been born surpassed all others, earthly or not.

Thrilled at the chance to hold forth about a subject she knew as well as or better than any priest, she sermonized about the Church's efforts.

"To help people, both children and adults, believe in Jesus as the Son of God, thus creating disciples. To awaken their faith and get instruction in the wonders of His life. To celebrate the sacraments and integrate in the ecclesiastical community." Carried away by her purpose, she felt her skin flush as it had when she knocked on Sanjay's door.

Dawn's fervor impressed Sanjay. "Wow, you sound so convincing, you could be a priest. That trip must have been a great opportunity for you."

She sighed, gratified. "I 'work' so I can do God's work." Her face flushed with an ecstasy he had not seen when they had made love. "I have a deep love for Opus Dei. Without them, their coaching and encouragement, I would not capable of being faithful to prayer. I would have given up by now."

Dawn searched Sanjay's face. If he held the common opinion, that Opus Dei was tooting its own horn rather than provide the altruistic aid that she espoused, he was being subtle about it. She liked that.

"They give people a means to finding God in ordinary life." She clasped his hands, holding his gaze. "Underneath the turmoil, way down at the bottom, there's this really still stream, so that no matter what happens, you know your Father God . . . Well, that you're in His hands."

What she didn't know was how astonished Sanjay was at what he had found in her: a girl full of surprises.

And no ordinary hooker.

4

A blast of wind coming off the St. Lawrence chilled Dawn and Sanjay as they made their way out of the Maharajah. Her jean jacket and his thin blazer were no match for Montréal's legendary frostiness. Her intense shivers told him she was feeling its effect to the max. He tried to distract her by making light of it.

"Where I live, we renamed our city 'Winterpeg' instead of Winnipeg."

This brought not even a faint smile, so he wound his arm around her tightly and attempted to hail a cab. No luck.

"Let's walk back to the hotel. I'll warm you up when we get there."

Dawn wasn't having it. Her grimace motivated him to heighten his motions, until a taxi finally screeched to a halt in front of them. She whipped open the door and vaulted inside, scrunching into a corner to keep warm. Within minutes, they were back in the hotel lobby. Sanjay no longer felt self-conscious about being seen with her. A flush of desire colored his face when they passed by the pink flowering orchids, their sensuous lips parted to resemble a woman's genitalia, displayed by the elevator. When the elevator door opened he lost no time in locking his lips with hers as the two of them soared up to the 19th floor. He was hooked.

The warmth of Sanjay's room, its fluffy upholstered furniture and feathery down comforter, were a welcome respite from the frigid air outside. Dawn lost no time in lighting a Matinée.

"Try one?" She offered the cigarette to Sanjay.

His grunt and disgusted facial expression were her answer.

"No matter. This is my dessert."

Sanjay thrust her down on the bed, his breath hot and heavy. "And now it's time for mine."

Too turned on to look for an ashtray, he seized the cigarette from her grasp and choked it out on the night table. Then he kissed her forehead, her long swan's neck. She closed her eyes. When he covered them with kisses, she moaned.

"Kiss them again. I love that."

"It's how we do in India."

"Yes. Yes, it must be. Undress me, Sanjay."

He needed no invitation. With one swift motion he unzipped her blouse, liberating her breasts, swollen with desire, and caressed them with a soft touch.

"They're magnificent. More beautiful than I've ever seen."

His lips moved over the nipples, sending a cascade of shivers through her torso, as he pulled off her skirt and teddy. She had never felt a want as powerful as this. Forgotten were the phone calls, the ride in Tom's car, the other hookers. This was an encounter unlike any other. It wasn't just sexual. It was earth shattering, spiritual. And it was completely reciprocal.

"Make love to me. I want to be loved." Reluctantly pulling away from his grasp, she stretched her now naked body onto the bed. "Sanjay."

His name undulated from her lips, unleashing in him a groan of longing familiar to her. But this time the yearning was mutual. They both knew it.

She thought he would take her that instant, but he decided to surprise her. Starting with her toes, he kissed each inch of her, working his way up through her feet, her calves, until he was licking her thighs. Then his tongue was inside her, with gentle strokes, finding her most intimate spots. Between his medical training and his natural instincts, he knew how to create a craving so deep and unfathomable as to make her explode. The licking, the exploring, the faint tickle of his tongue sent her over the edge. She let out a profound groan, coinciding with the multiple spasms of her body. She wanted to scream at him to make love to her, but her spasms wouldn't allow anything but ecstatic moans to escape from her throat.

The smells of her juices made any further entreaties from her unnecessary. Within seconds Sanjay was thrusting, at first slow and rhythmic, then with more force, as she moved her pelvis in response. Then he pulled out of her, causing her to scream with frustration, until, lifting her buttocks, Dawn heaved him into her from behind. She tightened his grip on her, her knuckles white from tension, her screams uncontrollable, as they both gave into their passions with animalistic violence and climaxed with total abandon. No thoughts, no mind involvement, just sheer ecstasy. Now they were united, bonded to each other, in an almost supernatural way. It was blissful. And terrifying.

Spent, Sanjay turned over on his back and drew Dawn onto his chest. Inhaling her sweet smell, he caressed her buttocks and thighs with a gentle massaging motion. Still blissful from her heightened orgasms, she couldn't believe how his movements brought her body again to the brink.

He sighed into her ear. "I love you."

Stunned out of her bliss, Dawn readied herself for the inevitable demurring. Love had no place in this situation. She was not going to allow herself one minute second of feeling, no matter what heights Sanjay had just brought her to. The ringing phone prevented her from having to respond. It had to be Tom. In an instant, she was out of heaven and back in business. Reality had a way of doing that to you.

Wriggling out of Sanjay's grasp, she reached for the phone. "Yeah. I'm almost done."

Dawn heaved a sigh. She knew Tom didn't want any of his girls out of his sight for too long. Not that he cared about them. Both his desire for financial security, and his overwhelming need to be controlling, drove his fanatical attention towards them. Better to keep up the quick turnover than to be stuck with one client.

"Yeah, no sweat, okay?" Dawn hung up the phone, leaned over Sanjay and kissed him. "That was my boss. He—"

Sanjay stopped her with a wave of his hand and grabbed for his wallet. Dawn dressed with her usual expertise, watching as he counted out eight one-hundred-dollar bills, then extracted two more, and slipped them all into her purse.

"You're a very generous man, Sanjay." She smiled. "Could you give me twenty dollars for the cab, too?"

He handed over a crisp, new bill and accompanied her to the door, not saying a word. She kissed him again, closed the door behind her and sighed with relief. Talk of love made her uncomfortable.

Love is blind.

Dawn had gained enough knowledge of science to know the true meaning of the saying. In the case of Sanjay, it meant his brain circuitry had been altered, causing his serotonin levels to be artificially lowered, the same as people with Obsessive Compulsive Disorder. At least that's what the scientists she had studied liked to say. Oxytocin, that seducer, the false pretender to the throne of true emotion. Who needed it? It just fooled people into an unreal sense of warmth and calm and tenderness after the act. A long sweep of physiological activity, all that heart pumping, sweating, and shallow breathing for a few seconds of pleasure. What a rip-off. If Sanjay thought he was in love, his hormones had just made him blind to her faults.

Oh well. It could be worse.

5

Sanjay felt guilty about not writing in his journal before bed that night. Bedtime was his usual time for journaling, free of constraints or inhibition. That was the beauty of journaling, to be at liberty to write anything that came to mind and not reveal it to anybody. There were no rules. It was like a mental enema, and it always put him right into the arms of Morpheus. Every time.

Before long, however, his mind turned to his work, as it always did. People's ignorance of critical care or intensive care as a specialty, even those in his own field, amazed Sanjay. No one understood how much greater are the special skills involved in critical care medicine. No one acknowledged how vital it was to closely observe people in a critical or unstable condition after major trauma, life-threatening illness, coma, surgery, or the failure of a major organ. He was always awed at how ill a person could become, precariously lingering between life and death, before passing on or recovering. Considering critical care medicine in Canada accounted for more than 14% of the national health care expenditure, and the life-or-death aspect of it, Sanjay expected more recognition for being the one who determines which patients have the potential to survive, not to mention treating them. Thankfully, his hospital had finally recognized the need to train Intensivists. It was slow in coming about, however, and his patience was starting to wear thin.

But his patience with Dawn was infinite. He replaced his musings about medicine with a meditation about his new beloved.

My Dawn . . . My Love . . . My Angel . . . My apocalyptic beauty . . . When I am with her, nothing matters . . . Famine, le feu, dévastation, la mort . . . Ah, mon ange . . . What pleasure, what infinite pleasure I derive from giving her pleasure! I would make it last forever if I could. She is my beacon of love in a loveless world. My Dawn's Early Light . . . No. No journal that night. The only written material in his hands was the paper on which she wrote her phone number, which he kissed and folded and placed in his wallet with great care. After that, he slept like a babe sated with its mother's milk.

6

Fingering the crisp bills, Dawn made her way through the entrance and spied Tom waiting in his white LTD. She thought he should have driven something more impressive. But she knew he considered the car useful for ferrying as many as three girls in the back seat, and even one in the front on the rare occasions when he was willing to scoot over his three cell phones, pager, notebook, maps and other accoutrements of his business.

When she was new, she had asked him why he needed so many phones. He grudgingly explained it was because he used so many names to advertise in the yellow pages, even if they all fit under the umbrella of Passion Escorts. Dawn thought Garden of Eden, Young and Restless and especially A Piece of Tail were all really lame. But the fourth name, VIP Escorts, sounded classy to her. It didn't take her long to realize what a savvy businessman he was. The accountant's nightmare of having so many monikers served to confuse the Taxman, and to protect Tom from the prying eyes of the Police. Eventually he appreciated her questions, her natural curiosity, and her intelligence. Those special qualities set her apart from the others. He didn't know, however, that Dawn was close friends with his common-law wife, Marie, and that Marie had shared her intimate personal history with Dawn.

Before he hooked up with Marie, Tom had always kept his work and personal life separate. If one of his girls caught his fancy, he went out of his way to find satisfaction with a past lover rather than become involved with an employee. One of the reasons he kept his distance was to save as much time as possible to be with his eight-year-old son, Bobby, from a previous marriage, whom Tom's ex had left with him when the boy was a toddler.

She'd absconded with as many of their common possessions as she could and ditched the poor kid instead.

Devastated by the loss, Tom overcame his alcoholism to be there for Bobby. Raising the boy as a single dad changed his perspective on life. Everything he did to make his business succeed was driven by his commitment to his son. But he recognized, too, that he couldn't do it alone forever. That's when Marie happened.

Marie had been down-and-out when she joined Tom's business, but she soon became his favorite escort. Tom took Marie to his best clients, and never asked for a cut of her tips. But Marie was smart. She knew Tom was gone on her. She gave him an offer he couldn't refuse. And since she and Dawn had been friends since their waitressing days at Ristorante Da Vinci, she made sure to fill Dawn in on the details.

"I told him I was fed up with being an escort, that we both needed each other, and I could take care of him and his son, so he should take me in."

"You're outrageous, girl."

"Yeah, aren't I? And you know what?"

"He said yes?"

Dawn and Marie high-fived. It was a straightforward business deal, Dawn was sure of that. She often wondered what would happen when Bobby became old enough to understand what his father did for a living. Right now, though, Tom had enough hungry customers, and sufficient girl-candy to feed them, to dispense with any money issues caused by adding another member to his household.

Dawn was lost in thought when Tom turned to her and asked if she was ready for another customer.

"No, just drop me at my condo."

She knew he would consider this strange, her being a workaholic in general and turning down work, but she didn't care. Sanjay had depleted her of any desire to turn another trick that night, and of her energy as well. No need to explain this to Tom. There was so much he didn't know about her, and that was fine with her. He had no concern with her real life, least of all the fact that both her family, and her colleagues at her day job teaching school, knew her only as Renée.

Dawn said a quick good night to Tom and hurried past her living room, where her dentistry student boarder Lindsay was glued to a TV "Bachelor" episode. She was in no mood to greet Lindsay and went straight to her bedroom, exhausted. When she tried to sleep, she couldn't stop herself from thinking about Sanjay. His dark good looks, his powerful lovemaking. And for some reason, that brought her thoughts back to her childhood and a fateful conversation with her father, Pierre.

Dawn worshipped her father. To her, he was the embodiment of what love was all about. That summer in Halifax, when her dad was finishing up his medical studies before the family moved back to their hometown of Bellesable in New Brunswick, she often stayed at a friend's house. One particular humid night, Pierre picked up his daughter and they drove along downtown George Street towards the bridge for Dartmouth, the bedroom community where they lived. It was there that five-year-old Dawn first saw the women in their high heels and scanty, low-cut outfits.

"Are they going to a party, Dad?"

"Who, *mon ange*?"

"The women over there, dressed in pretty clothes. Why are they waving at the men in their cars?"

Pierre glanced over in the direction Dawn was pointing and frowned. "They're hookers, *mon trésor*."

"What are . . . hookers?"

"They are . . . women who give love to people, *ma petite*, people who are not loved by anyone."

"Not loved? But why?" Dawn pouted, confused. "Why would a person not be loved?"

"I don't know, *mon amourette*."

Dawn paused to reflect. "Do you love me, *Papa*?"

"Yes, *ma chérie,* of course. We all love you very much."

"Then I want to be a hooker when I grow up."

Pierre could not hide his shock. "But what are you saying? Are you out of your mind? Hookers are bad women."

"Bad? How can they be bad, if they give love to people not loved by anyone?"

"You don't understand, *ma petite ange*. They sell their love. For money."

"Okay. Then when I grow up I want to give love, to all. But not—"

Pierre interrupted her abruptly. "You already give love to all who love you, my darling."

"I just want to give it to everyone, *Papa*, but not for money. I will not sell love."

He pulled over and banged on the steering wheel, shaking with anger. Dawn jumped, startled.

"*Tais-toi!* You will not speak of this again."

She refused to be silenced. "But *Papa*, no one should be without love."

Dawn turned over in bed and shook off the memory. That long-ago event had been buried, deep in her subconscious.

Why on earth is it surfacing now, like the rerun of a bad movie?

Distressed, she shifted her thoughts again to Sanjay and wondered what was he doing. She hoped he was Googling Opus Dei on the Internet. He was so intelligent, so curious. Surely he had something of the spiritual in his atheistic soul. He disdained the organization but didn't know a thing about it. There was no lack of information: two million, two hundred-seventy thousand results in 0.15 seconds when Dawn had last checked Google. She giggled.

Still didn't beat "fuck" at twenty-five-plus million, or "sex" at two hundred-seventeen million . . . Sex. Men. Orgasm was easy so for them. It was almost cheap, attainable in theory within two minutes of the first initiation of foreplay, according to Kinsey, whereas a woman really had to work for hers. It wasn't fair.

Why even bother cohabiting with someone if you can, well, take care of your own needs? And why do most women insist on falling in love?

Dawn considered the pursuit of love a useless exercise. Men and women had different sexual experiences, different goals. Why ruin things by bringing love into the mix?

Lust is where it all happens.

Her mind wanderings didn't help her to fall asleep, however. Turning over on her other side, she thought of the Organization and allowed her stream of consciousness to overrun her wide-awake brain.

She had read "The Da Vinci Code" and been mortified by its premise and the nerve of its author to thrust Opus Dei in the harsh glare of public censure. Aware her anger over this was not conducive to sleep, she went back to her contemplation.

Mary Magdalene . . . Now there's someone I can identify with . . . Women as domestic workers . . . No, I won't go there. Thank goodness for prostitution. At least that allows a woman to make a decent, if dishonest, living.

Finally feeling the tug of Morpheus, Dawn gave in to his seduction. She was tired, so very tired. She drifted off, smiling to herself, glad she'd planted the seed in Sanjay's brain about Opus Dei but wondering how wise it had been to slip him her phone number. The music to "Angels and Lovers" lulled her to sleep.

In fitful fantasies,
Replaying memories,
Logging torture between . . . We are caught as a deer,
Deep in the sight,
Of one unbearable light.

A crack in the door,
The sunlight pours in;
The warmth of the glow
Turns to passion.

The spark takes hold,
The crackling is heard,
The flame within breaks out;
Unto the whole world the heat is felt . . .
In fitful fantasies . . .
Do you dare to see a woman
Walk a changing maze?
The Goddess herself seated
Forever ready for play.

Her sole purpose, to lay herself down
At the source, with the King and his crown.
She can't be controlled, nor be figured out
Don't take her for granted, she'll slay you cold.

In fitful fantasies . . .

7

The sky was overcast, a slate grey, when Dawn pulled her Tercel out of the heated garage of 6354 Avenue Victoria the next morning. Driving southeast toward Avenue Isabella, she lit a Matinée Jackson and cracked open a window. She felt a blast of frigid air slam her cheeks.

Montréal. You have to love it in the depths of winter.

Dawn squirmed in her seat, still sore from the past evening's escapades. The discomfort pulsed from deep inside her vagina, not unusual for an active night. But this morning her whole pelvis throbbed. This guy was a maniac. Nonetheless, memories of her spasms of pleasure, the ones he had drawn out of her, came flooding back, and suddenly she was enveloped in ecstasy.

To bring her focus back to reality, she contemplated the long day ahead. 6:45 was too early, in this sleepy French *quartier* of the city, to see much sign of life on the Autoroutes. But Dawn liked it that way. The tranquility was conducive to preparation for her math class, which was complex and intricate. It was a strain on her abilities to make geometry understandable to the students. Still, she liked to be on her toes for them.

Just as well. Sunday nights are hectic, and the clients are so unpredictable.

Tom always insisted she work on those nights, since other agencies were either closed or short on staff. Most prostitutes, she learned, either had family responsibilities or boyfriends, or they were enduring a nasty divorce.

Good thing I have none of that to contend with.

Glancing at the clock, she shook off all thoughts of escorting. She wanted to focus on the bumper-to-bumper traffic ahead of her. But as she sat on the choked *Autoroute*, she couldn't avoid thinking of her work—both kinds. She certainly didn't want the line between them to obscure, but she sometimes felt foggy about the difference.

Am I a hooker or a schoolteacher?

Suddenly she wasn't sure. She loved sex and loved getting paid for it. The fancy restaurants, expensive wines, and the wild, crazy sex—at least those times when it was wild and crazy. She wanted to love and be loved.

Is that so bad?

But at school Dawn was a respected citizen, even if she didn't respect herself. She had worked five long, hard years at the University to earn her high-powered teaching position and was expected to act accordingly to satisfy everyone's expectations of her.

By the time she turned onto Boulevard Crémazie East, she had lit her fourth cigarette, sucking it hard to finish it before arriving at school. No one there knew she was a smoker, and she wanted to keep it that way. A teacher smoking in front of her students and colleagues conveyed a bad impression. She on the other hand, wanted to set a perfect example: the consummate *enseignante,* even if it was only Junior High.

Soon the landscape had morphed from cold, grey apartment buildings and condo units to the middle class single-family suburban dwellings of Saint Leonard. Those houses on Rue Jean-Nicolet with no garages had makeshift plastic covers positioned over their driveways to keep the cars from freezing. Families had lived in this enclave for generations, though the latest influx of immigrants had insisted their children learn French as a second language, with an emphasis on English. Thus, the face of Saint Leonard was slowly transforming from Québecois to Cosmopolitan.

Before long Dawn was pulling her car into a space in front of St. Paul Junior High School. She could tell by the cars sprinkled through the lot that the principal and a few of her teaching colleagues had already arrived. She sprayed herself with Opium, a gift from a well-heeled client, to cover the stench of her smokes, and made her way to the entrance. With her head held high, she left her less savory persona behind her in the frosty air.

I am a schoolteacher after all. She shivered. *It's colder than shit.*

Once inside, Dawn greeted the school principal.

"Good morning, Mrs. Nelly."

"Bright and early as always, Renée." The older woman smiled, nodding her head. "So dedicated, such a role model. If only my other teachers were as hard-working as you."

"I do my best, Mrs. Nelly."

If you only knew, Mrs. Nelly. If you only knew.

Waving her farewell to the principal, Dawn strode down the hall to the Staff Room, took a quick look at her email on the staff computer and found two email messages from regular clients. Business was good.

Praise the Lord.

Dawn looked up at the clock. 8 am, barely an hour to prepare her lessons for the first class, grade seven Statistics. She had last week's eighth grade quiz on properties and geometric to correct, too. But still, she adored teaching Math.

If only it paid well.

At the very least she had an excuse to skip the morning assembly. The last thing she wanted was to listen to Mrs. Nelly's discourse on morals and ethics and rules.

Again Dawn's thoughts turned to Sanjay. He had mentioned in passing his plans for a long day of meetings in the Acadia boardroom, something about a research group that held forums to improve the lot of critically ill patients in the ICUs. The top academics and researchers, the cream of the crop from around the country, attended these meetings. Dawn couldn't relate to any of that. She was young, vibrant and healthy. What need had she for intensive care? She couldn't help being impressed by the important work Sanjay was doing, but it was no more important than her own work, that of forming and challenging young minds. These kids were the wave of the future.

Let Sanjay have his stuffy clinicians and scientists, his new ideas and protocols, his presentations.

Dawn chuckled to herself. She just hoped he could come back from his fantasies of her long enough to hear his name being called, give his presentation and be on his plane at 3 pm. She had no idea he had already decided to stay another night.

8

Sanjay was feeling the fallout from a long, tiring day. Ungodly morning start time, 7:30 am, but by then the Acadia boardroom was so full that any additional clinicians and scientists would have had to hang from the rafters. Most of them looked hung over, too. Sanjay himself hadn't yet returned to the land of the living. Those sensuous lips, perfect breasts. He really had to force himself away from thoughts of . . . her. Not the best behavior for the incoming chair of Canadian Critical Care Research, a.k.a. CCCR, trying to state his vision for the group's progress over the next year.

It was the first time he hadn't rehearsed his PowerPoint presentation, too. He looked over the audience: mostly middle-aged men, a few women, a couple of younger males. The youth quotient was not well represented, though that morning he felt even younger than his usual. 20 years old instead of 25, not bad for a 45-year-old. He almost missed his name being called. Visions of her enchanting face, her high cheekbones, her sensuous lips, not to mention her statuesque "goddess" body, drove him to distraction. *A mourir pour mourir.*

Freezing cold in this place. Doesn't the prestige associated with this highly acclaimed research group have any clout with the decision makers in the boiler room? If it doesn't, it certainly should.

No other consortium provided a national forum to improve the care of critically ill patients through research and education about research comparable to theirs. They were cutting edge in clinical trials. But with oil prices what they were these days, even CCCR couldn't write its own ticket anymore.

Nonetheless, it was the cream of the crop at today's meeting, the top academics and researchers throughout Canada. No better way existed to present new ideas and have them criticized without mercy. Their method of peer research and review was based on that principle. But they did manage to conduct meetings in an amicable and friendly atmosphere. Ideas were fair game, not the people presenting. Sanjay admired that.

The most pressing issue, how much the patient and family should be involved in decisions regarding withdrawal of care in cases where the patient is a lost cause, was left unsettled. Should it be done abruptly, gradually, or not at all? Sanjay thought that God, if He existed, might have provided some answers. Mere humans were only capable of subjective judgment, which is unscientific to say the least.

If only computers could treat the patients instead of mere mortals.

And how was it that people come up with the most absurd, unanswerable questions afterwards? The ones who weren't rushing away to catch their flights home, that is.

By the time he climbed into the cab to the airport, he was suffering. It was as if he were leaving his heart and soul in Montréal with that girl. What was this illness, this mental torture he called love? And what was there about the intensity of these emotions that could turn a brilliant physician with a core of iron into a feeble weakling? He hated his weakness, but he also agonized about staying another night. After all, Dawn had given him her phone number. She must have wanted to see him again. But his wife Vinita had her heart set on taking the kids out for dinner that night at Ivory's. How could he disappoint them? His mind reeled with possibilities.

Maybe they'd be willing to put it off until the next weekend. For her birthday celebration.

In the end he couldn't come up with the courage to tell the driver to turn around and head back to the hotel. That was a shame, too, because after landing in Winnipeg he walked, zombie-like, back to the Rapid Air counter and booked himself on the next flight to Montréal. And as he winged his way back, there was only one thought on his mind, one goal in his entire being. To get back to Dawn.

9

"Good morning, class."

Dawn surveyed her classroom, the neatly dressed seventh-grade students with their eager faces turned up towards her. Unlike Dawn, they looked as if their weekends had refreshed them. And with the exception of the usual couple of bullies who preferred doing any other activity over sitting in a classroom, the kids looked ready for anything.

"We're learning simple statistics today, so stop me if you don't understand something. Otherwise, we've got a lot to cover, so fasten your seat belts."

She liked the way the children tittered when she made a joke. The class was evenly divided between girls and boys, so tittering outweighed sniggering. At least Dawn preferred to think of it that way.

"I'll try to make it as simple as possible. Here's an easy example."

Dawn wielded her chalk like a master violinist with violin and bow.

"Statistical mean is synonymous with average. Thus adding 7 plus 4 plus 11 equal 22. Divide by the number of digits, 3, and use the nearest whole number. *Et voilà*, the answer is 7. Here's another example . . ."

She solved the problem on the blackboard. Then she glanced over the faces, making sure at least a modicum of the students understood before she went on.

"Now let's talk about mode. To find the mode of a group of numbers, arrange in order of size, then determine the number of instances of each numerical value."

This was more complicated, and she knew she would start to lose some students, but she pressed on. "Now find the median of 6, 9 and 4. If you arrange these in increasing value—"

"Miss L'andry?" Raymond, Dawn's favorite student, raised his hand. Dawn nodded, pleased as usual, smiling her encouragement. "Why would you use mean versus the medium?"

"Good question, Raymond." She could always depend on him for that. "Mean is used when there is equal distribution of a group of numbers. If there is unequal distribution, median is a more valid indicator."

Dawn launched into a lengthy explanation of mean vs. median, illustrating with examples on the board. She hoped most of the students understood the difference. Some, of course, never did, and she often wondered how those kids advanced to the next grade. She and Derek O'Neil, who taught grade eight English directly across the hall, had discussed this phenomenon on more than a few occasions.

By the number of glazed-over faces before her, however, Dawn realized it was time for something a bit different. "Okay, guys, here's something to challenge you." She paused to write a title on the board, "Man Seeks Order and a Pattern in Odd Things," then a sequence of numbers: "1-1-2, 6-24-120—?" She turned to look at her charges. They showed a small degree of interest. "Whoever solves this puzzle will receive a musical Christmas card from me. So take a few minutes and then I'll ask for your answer."

As the students contemplated, Dawn gazed out at the horizon. The clouds had dissipated, replaced by a brilliant sun, which illuminated the roofs of the Arts Academy to the east and Wilfred Laurier Secondary School to the west. Spying her Tercel parked in her own school's lot, her mind wandered to thoughts of something better.

If only some client would give me a shiny, fast new sports car. To go with my fast men.

Forcing herself back to reality, Dawn turned back to the class. "So. Who's getting the Christmas card?" Most of the faces were blank, but Dawn noticed the little red headed girl's hand waving frantically. "Rhonda?"

"720?"

"That's correct, Rhonda. Good job. Would you please explain to the class how you figured it out?" Dawn gestured to the girl to rise.

Rhonda hesitated, and then she inched out of her seat. "To get the next number from the previous number, you multiply by 1 then 2 then 3, then 4, then 5. Since the last number is 120, multiplying it by 6 equals to 720."

Dawn beamed. "Exactly! Well done."

She reached into her desk drawer, pulled out a large envelope and strode over to Rhonda's desk. The girl, quaking with excitement, accepted her teacher's affectionate hug and the proffered envelope and took her seat, flushing with pleasure. Then Dawn returned to the front of the room.

"Good work, everyone. Class dismissed."

Satisfied she had made her contribution to the education of humanity, Dawn left the students to do whatever they were to do next and made her way down the hall towards the Staff Room. She planned to use the free time at hand to check emails and prepare for her next class. The schedule really worked for her. Done with school at 3 pm, home by 4, ready for clients at 5. Tom was under her strict instructions not to call her before 4, since school policy prohibited the use of cell phones during school hours. But she kept hers on vibrate mode just in case some VIP client was in too much of a hurry to wait for the evening. That usually happened on Fridays, though, and today was only Monday. The school week loomed long in front of her. She tried not to think about it.

Once inside the Staff Room, Dawn headed for the mailbox where each teacher had his or her own rectangular slot to receive school memos and other communications from the school board. Occasionally a personal letter showed up there, but Dawn made sure that never happened in her case. Finding only a couple of brief notes in her slot, she moved past the desks where Mrs. Nelly's and the Vice-Principal's personal secretaries fielded phone calls and memoranda, grabbed a mug of coffee from the machine on the counter and pulled an apple from the mini-fridge next to it. Most teachers brought a lunch and kept it in the Staff fridge, but some went over to the Laurier Academy for a hot meal if they had enough time.

Munching on the fruit, Dawn headed to the Dell flat panel computer on the desk in the opposite corner from the food and drink station. She made an effort to catch up on her emails during her school breaks to save valuable time she needed for herself once she got home at the end of the day. The recent model computer, compliments of the School Board, resided there for the teachers to download lessons from the Internet, thus staying at the cutting edge of contemporary education. Dawn knew most teachers used the desktop for emails, just as she did.

Other than that, Dawn had little in common with her colleagues and spoke with them only on rare occasions. The younger ones obsessed about their social lives. The older ones chatted about their kids, their experiences as hockey moms or dads. Often, as she listened to their conversations, Dawn ached to have kids of her own.

Someday.

10

When she got the call from Tom, Dawn was wandering through Côtes des Neiges. She had a warm spot in her heart for this, the most ethnically diverse Montréal neighborhood. The shops there were fun to explore, with their array of tasty foods and colorful goods, and the people were friendly and spoke an assortment of languages. She also loved taking long walks in Parc Mont Royal. Most of all, Dawn enjoyed strolling through the *Notre-Dame-des-Neiges* cemetery, where she could be alone with her thoughts. She often stopped at the *Oratoire* St. Joseph just outside the park to say a brief but heartfelt prayer.

The cell phone vibration interrupted her musings. She answered with an edge to her voice. "Oh, man, this is too much. I really needed a night off, Tom."

"He sounded insistent. Well, obsessed, actually." Tom paused to let this sink in. "He practically exploded when I told him you weren't on tonight."

"Which guy is it?"

"The Indian doctor guy. He said he . . ." He took a breath. "He said he flew all the way home to Winnipeg and then got on the next plane back here. Frankly, I don't like the sound of it."

Dawn shook her head. Sanjay. He thought he was in love. She would have to set him straight. "Don't worry, he's harmless. Okay, I'll see him."

"Thanks, kid, I owe you."

"Yeah, right."

If I only had a dollar for every time he said that.

*

Dawn strode through the Hyatt lobby, beset with a feeling of *déjà vu*. Same hotel, same client. It almost felt like the same night. She waited at the front desk while the concierge made the call to Sanjay, her thoughts turning to the subject of love.

She had never allowed herself to fall in love, in part because her University education had afforded her an objective look at the phenomenon. To her it was a mental illness that caused irrational behavior in people. Compulsive phone calls, impromptu serenades, yelling from rooftops, it all sounded like the diagnosis for psychosis. Amidst all the euphoria, the craving, the obsessive drive, there was also the gamut of emotion, from anger to anxiety to fear of rejection. What other human sentiment had the potential to cause stalking, homicide, suicide?

Dawn's father, an MD who specialized in reading x-rays and scans, had shown her the studies chronicling scientific efforts to explain the overwhelming impact of love on humans. MRI scans that revealed changes in neural activity when a person was shown a picture of a true love. Cells deep in the brain that produced dopamine, which circulates when desire comes into the mix. All of this activity occurred in the area of the brain that handles the most basic human functions like eating, drinking and eye movement, and all at an unconscious level.

I'll leave that kind of action to men. And sentimental females.

When she spied Sanjay striding towards her, she recognized his excitement, as if she had a finger on his racing pulse. He looked flushed with the joy of a man possessed, a man about to be enveloped in the arms of his true love. His intensity made her uncomfortable, and she was determined to calm him down, but her face showed only pleasure at seeing him again.

Once the elevator door had closed, he lost no time in kissing her cheeks, then her eyes. The memory of how she'd felt when he last did so flooded her being, and she felt a warming sensation throughout her body.

"You're so special, Dawn."

"So my father tells me." Then she noticed the bandage around his hand. "What happened?"

With a self-conscious gesture, he withdrew his hand and placed it behind his back. "Nothing."

"It doesn't look like nothing." She took his hand. Faint traces of blood oozed through the bandage. "Tell me, Sanjay."

The sound of his name from her lips turned his athlete's body into jelly. "I cut it."

"How?"

He hesitated, watching the lit numbers move up the wall indicator, listening for the familiar ding as the door opened on 24. He ushered her out of the elevator and guided her up the hall.

"I'll tell you later."

When they entered the room, Dawn scanned the view from the window, this time of the slopes of Mont Royal and McGill University. She sensed the labs at McGill were not uncharted territory to him, and from the shape his body was in, the trails there and on Mont Royal were familiar terrain as well.

Sanjay read her thoughts. "I've visited Royal Victoria Hospital and worked at Meakins-Christie Labs." He chuckled. "I once did a CBC radio interview while jogging on Mont Royal in 10 degrees Fahrenheit. And then . . ."

He spoke slowly, his gaze never leaving her. The sight of her, stunning as always, interrupted his train of thought. Dawn removed her leather coat and noticed he had seen the one button hanging by a thread, a contrast to the rest of the buttons on the otherwise impeccable garment.

"Sorry about that. You kind of called at the last minute." Uncomfortable, she undid the top button of her pink silk blouse, hoping to distract him from her couture shortcoming.

Mission accomplished. Pulse quickening, he laid her down on the bed, all thoughts of buttons or other accoutrements gone from his consciousness. Still, he managed to finish his previous thought.

"McGill made me an offer. I was impressed with the academic environment there, but . . ."

She reached back to unhook her handmade black bra of Alençon lace, took it off and put her blouse back on. "But?"

"I felt I belonged in Winnipeg."

"Maybe someday you'll belong here."

Her violet mini-skirt slid to the floor. She kicked off her shoes and saw him gulp.

So much for small talk.

He leaned over her and caressed her nipples through the soft fabric of the blouse. She could tell from his stilted breathing, and the bulge in his pants, he was ready.

"I need to make love to you. Now." Then his expression turned from demanding to pleading. "I want you. Oh, please, Dawn."

But there was a problem. "We have to wait, Sanjay. I didn't have time to . . . to get any—"

"No. I can't wait." He ripped her blouse open, freeing her breasts, the nipples now hard and inviting to his lips. He licked one nipple, sucking it into his mouth, squeezing it with his tongue.

She gasped, her words coming in short breaths. "But I didn't . . . have time to get . . . to get . . . condoms."

Now his hand was probing her vagina, his mouth enveloping the other breast. "Let's do it without."

"That's not an option. I would never—"

Yelping in frustration, Sanjay jerked away from her. "Don't move."

"I won't. I promise."

He stalked out of the room, and within minutes he had returned. She was in the same position on the bed. Without a word, he tore off his shirt and pants and thrust inside of her. She cried out, taken aback by his hardness, his sudden violence. But that didn't prevent her body from going into abrupt spasms, and soon she was gyrating with him until they were moving together, kissing, screaming, twisting, moaning, as if they had never been apart for one moment.

"You're tight, so tight." His moans grew louder. "Oh, Dawn, so tight."

"Yes. Yes, Sanjay." She squeezed hard with the muscle she knew would enhance his pleasure.

"I love you, I love you!" Only his climax, loud and intense and abrupt, could drown out his screams.

Her own orgasm obliterated her unease at hearing that phrase, which made her so uneasy. But she sat up in one sudden movement when he bit her on the chin.

"Hey, cut it out! That's not part of the package."

"I'm sorry, I . . . You just make me do things I've never done before." He rubbed her chin in an effort to eradicate his indiscretion.

She couldn't help grinning. "I'm that tasty, huh?"

He laughed. "Did you know I moved heaven and earth to be with you?"

Extricating herself, she lay next to him, catching her breath. All was forgiven. "Oh? Now you mention it, I thought you were going home yesterday."

He caressed her with gentle movements. "I went to the airport. I couldn't get you out of my mind. I thought if I tossed away your phone number—"

"Oh, so that's why Tom called me and not you." She didn't know whether to be offended or amused.

"I threw it in a trash bin at the airport. I felt better, for a few moments. I kicked myself for it later."

She smiled to herself at the image of the impeccable MD kicking himself in the pants.

"I got on the 2 pm to Winnipeg. I didn't want to. I was miserable." He paused, drinking in the beauty of her in warm afterglow. "As soon as we took off, it was as if an eight point earthquake erupted in my mind. I was barely alive. There was only one thought on my mind. You."

Dawn swallowed hard. He was not only in love. He was possessed. The danger of it excited her. She stroked his shoulder with tenderness. His anxious expression softened.

"As soon as I got to Winnipeg, I booked myself on the next plane back here." He turned away, ashamed. "I didn't know what I was doing. I didn't want to be weak, to go back. I couldn't stop myself. You. You bewitched me. You ensnared me."

She turned his face back to her and held his gaze. "Is that so bad?"

"Yes, it's horrible. It's agony. It's . . ." He pulled her tightly to him. "Paradise."

Dawn was beginning to feel a tug, one she had not experienced before. His ardor was infecting her, like a virus that takes hold of one's body and won't let go. She shivered in his arms. He breathed a sigh of relief, rocking her with gentle motions, trying to capture every shred of the ecstasy he was feeling while she was still within his grasp.

After a moment, he whispered to her. "Dawn, how . . . How do you feel about me?"

She squirmed, uncomfortable. "How do I feel about you?"

"Do you love me, the way I love you?"

She couldn't bring herself to respond, to tell him he really didn't love her, that he was just besieged with lust. Instead, she took his wounded hand and caressed it.

"You still haven't told me how this happened."

Sanjay was silent for a minute. Dawn felt his distress.

"When I got to the airport in Montréal, I swore at myself for throwing out your phone number. But I remembered exactly where I'd tossed it, in a trash bin near the departure security gate. I thrust my hand inside the bin, carelessly, without thinking. There was some kind of plastic toy in there that was broken. It sliced right through my hand."

"Poor baby." She kissed his hand like a mother consoling her child.

"It was a bloody mess, and I still couldn't find the paper. I didn't care about the blood, but a security guard started to question me. Rather than arouse suspicion, I just went to the bathroom to clean up. Then I realized I still had the number for Passion Escort in my cell phone. I called immediately and begged the guy to contact you for me."

"Hmm . . . Yes, I heard."

He smiled. "You should have heard me screaming at the taxi driver. The *Autoroute* was jammed, and I was worried I wouldn't get to the hotel in time to be there for you. The rest, you know. I hope I didn't cause trouble for you with your boss."

She stretched, catlike, the tips of her breasts thrusting in the air. "Not a problem. I'm his favorite employee."

Sanjay felt his passion welling up again, both in his heart and in his groin. He reached to pull her back down on the bed, but she was too quick. Leaping up off the bed, she fixed her gaze on him.

"I'm starving. Let's go somewhere. Somewhere nice."

Once dressed, they walked out of the hotel room as a couple, he with his arm wrapped around her waist, she with one hand on his left buttock.

"Nice buns." She grasped the other cheek. "Nice and tight. Nothing turns me on like a firm, good-looking ass."

Sanjay was secretly pleased, but he didn't let on how flattered he was. "If you say so. As long as you don't grab it in public."

"Oh no? Just watch me."

While they were in the taxi, Dawn caressed his buns again, making Sanjay squirm with pleasure. He was barely able to stand up straight when the cab deposited them in front of Gibby's in old Montréal. He did manage to hand the driver a ten-dollar bill for the $7.50 fare and tell him to keep the change. But for some reason the driver rolled down his window and shouted at Sanjay as he drove off.

"*Connard!*"

"What did he say?" Sanjay's French was minimal at best.

"You don't really want to know."

But he was insistent, and finally she acquiesced. "'Asshole.' That's what he said. I guess he didn't like your tip."

Embarrassed, Sanjay's lips contorted. "He's just jealous." Then he shouted at top volume in the direction of the cabbie, who had long disappeared.

"Fils de chienne!"

Dawn smiled. "Oh. You do know French after all."

Sanjay responded with a grin. "Just a few well chosen words."

11

Steeped in old Montréal charm and romantic ambience, Gibby's had a long tradition of attracting both tourists and locals. 200-year-old décor, mouth-watering steak specialties, impeccable service, and linen-clothed tables arranged around an immense stone fireplace, helped to make the restaurant a place where patrons returned again and again. The tables were dimly lit, but each was festooned with its own hanging lamp.

"To make sure patrons eat only what's edible?" Dawn chuckled.

Sanjay didn't reply. He was focused on how beautiful Dawn appeared in the soft lighting, even more so when the hostess lit the small votive in the middle of the table.

Dawn pointed to her companion. "He's Vegan."

"No problem." The hostess made a discreet exit while the couple looked over the menu.

After a moment, a waitress came over to take the order. She spoke with a French accent, pronounced but charming, and shared some details of the restaurant's history. Dawn was especially interested in the fact that Gibby's stood on the former banks of the Little St. Pierre River, and was once part of stables belonging to the Sisters of Charity—the Grey Nuns—in the 17th century.

"I love knowing stuff like that. Whets my appetite even more."

She looked at Sanjay, who regarded her thoughtfully for a long minute, then spoke.

"Tell me more about yourself."

She hesitated, reluctant to reveal too much about her life to this man, who was still a complete stranger to her and was likely to remain so. "Well if you insist . . ."

"I insist."

"Okay. I was born in New Brunswick, I'm a fourth-year physiotherapy student at the University of Montréal—"

He interrupted. "Is that why you do this . . . this 'work'? To pay for your education?"

"Yes, but I also want to help Opus Dei, to do God's work. Don't you remember?" She frowned. "Besides, I like to travel, too. I already told you that." She tried to restrain her impatience. After all, he was being nice.

"Aren't there are other ways to accomplish your goals? A loan, perhaps, from your family?"

On the subject of family, she remained silent. "I like adventure, to meet people. And honestly, I'm not really a hooker. I'm a 'GFE.'" From his puzzled look, she knew she was venturing into uncharted waters. "It means—"

The arrival of the waitress with two plates of appetizers interrupted Dawn's explanation.

"Compliments of the house, sir." She walked away.

"I'm starved." Dawn tucked into the plate of fried *escargots* before Sanjay could manage to look at his spinach salad. "'GFE' means 'girlfriend experience.' You know, sex with a girl who enjoys the experience and not just the mechanics of it."

"Oh." Sanjay had never heard of GFE, but it was clear Dawn embodied the definition. "You mean, having an emotional and intellectual connection with a 'provider' like you would with a real girlfriend."

"Exactly."

An encounter with a GFE was more intimate, more mutually satisfying on a human, rather than commercial, level than a "normal" encounter. No clock watching, no rushing to get done and out the door. Treating the client in a relaxed, human and not mechanical manner was important and, most of all, being responsive to his needs beyond the physical. Dawn knew she could elaborate about the subject, but something told her Sanjay already understood this. She waited for him to process what she had said and let him take the next step in the conversation.

"I see. And who am I?"

"A doctor, I knew that." She peered at him. "Is there something you're not telling me?"

Sanjay laughed. "Well, yes and no. 'Doctor' is only a part of my persona. What else would you guess?"

"Well, you have that 'professor' look, too."

"Do I look that old? I don't wear wire-rimmed glasses, after all."

He laughed again, and she felt a bit self-conscious.

"But you're right, I am both doctor and professor."

Dawn polished off the last of her *escargots*. "Can you do that? Be both, I mean. My dad's a doctor, and—"

"If you work in a university, you can see patients and teach as well. But you also have to do research."

"But is there a medical university in Winnipeg?" Dawn's lack of advanced educational background was beginning to show. "I didn't think there was."

"Yes, there is. It's your New Brunswick that doesn't have one."

"Oh."

She was dying for more food. The waitress fulfilled her desire. Dawn wolfed down her seafood platter as if she hadn't eaten for days but ignored the expensive red wine the waitress had uncorked. Then she noticed Sanjay had not touched his vegetarian pasta.

"Aren't you hungry?"

Sanjay tasted a morsel and sipped his wine. "When I have you, I have no other earthly desire."

Dawn was not prone to blushing in general, but this time she felt the color mounting on her cheeks. Uncomfortable, she hid her expression in the plate before her.

"What kind of doctor is your father?"

She stopped chewing and frowned. "I can't tell you that. There are only so many doctors around, know what I mean?"

"And I can't really tell you who I am, either. "Sanjay held her gaze. "But that doesn't prevent me from wanting to know you. The real you."

Dawn thought for a moment. "If you knew the 'real' me, we couldn't see each other. But I do have an idea."

"An idea?"

She hesitated, watching his eager, besotted expression. "Here's the deal. I become your GFE, or your mistress, whichever you prefer. In exchange, you don't ask about who I really am, about my life outside of 'us.' Not even my real name."

He raised his eyebrows in surprise but said nothing. She eyed him, wary, and continued.

"By the same token, I don't want to know about you, your wife, or your kids. Is that doable for you?"

Sanjay gasped, unable to believe his luck. What she offered him was beyond his wildest dreams. "Are you real, or am I hallucinating?"

This time, Dawn laughed. "Is my proposition so over-the-top?"

"But you . . . You're so beautiful, so urbane. I can't picture your being anyone's mistress, let alone mine. It just doesn't seem possible."

"Well, believe it, Sanjay."

He put down his wine glass, staring at her in amazement. "You're an angel, my guiding light. Dawn's Early Light." He seized her hand, clutching it so tightly her knuckles turned white. "And I'm in love with you. You know that, don't you?"

She pulled her hand away. "Don't. Don't ever fall in love with me. You don't know me. I'm no angel. And I'm dangerous."

"I don't care." He grasped her hand, covering it with kisses. "It may be inappropriate for me to have fallen in love with you, but—"

"Inappropriate?" She suppressed a laugh. "I don't think so. In fact, I think you're scared. Scared of loving someone like me, and scared of the consequences. Am I right?"

"Perhaps. Loving you frightens me, but the consequences do not."

"Whatever you say, Sanjay. But as far as love goes, you've got to get a grip."

"But if only you would tell me your name, where you work, where you live."

Her eyes narrowed. "What did I tell you about that? No questions about my private life, remember? That's not an option."

"I'm sorry. I know how you feel about it. I just couldn't help myself."

"Then you'll have to learn how."

"But I want to know the real you."

"Well, you can't. Just as I can't know the 'real you.'" She gazed at him, her expression stern. "And if you don't stop asking, I won't see you anymore. I mean it, Sanjay. Do we understand each other?"

He managed a sober nod.

The waitress arrived to clear the table, looked at Sanjay's untouched plate and shot him a glance of mock derision. "You eat like a teenage girl on a diet." Picking up Dawn's immaculate plate, devoid of any remaining morsel, the waitress smiled in approval. "Dessert, Miss? *Crème brûlée*'s our specialty."

"Umm. Sounds perfect." Dawn's mouth watered.

The waitress turned to Sanjay. "Sir?"

"Coffee. Black, no sugar."

"Right away." The waitress moved off, balancing the plates.

Sanjay gazed at Dawn. "Okay. I understand your constraints, and I've heard your proposition. Here is mine." He eyed Dawn's curious face. "I will pay your tuition and expenses, reasonable ones, until you finish school. And in return—"

Her mouth dropped in awe. "You'd do all that for me? You are a very generous man."

Sanjay continued. "And in return, you will immediately cease working as an escort."

Dawn's guard went up. The thought of relinquishing her independence frightened her. "But I really don't think I could—"

"I would insist upon it. I can't bear the thought of you servicing sleazy, ugly men for money."

She frowned in silence. What was he asking of her? Could she give up her life, as she knew it?

The arrival of dessert interrupted her thoughts. She was happy to be distracted by the waitress's deft handling of the flamed chafing dish by the table as she burned the top of the *crème* in a circular motion, causing sparks to fly in all directions. Dawn couldn't imagine any other place on earth where this confection was served in such a way. It had to be uniquely Québécois.

Sanjay watched, amused, as Dawn again cleaned her plate. "Are you just hungry, or is that your favorite dessert?"

"Both," she said, and polished off the last of the crumbs. There was nothing like sugary sweets to obliterate anxiety over a life-altering proposition. She patted the corners of her mouth and looked up at Sanjay. "Why are you doing all this for me?"

He smiled. "What else can I say? I'm completely fucked up."

"Me, too. I guess we deserve each other."

12

The wine circulating in his blood compounding his light-headedness from lack of food caused Sanjay to set upon Dawn without inhibition when they returned to the room. She responded in kind. Gone were the barriers of sex worker and client. Two hungry bodies had found everything in each other and enjoyed the ride, taking their time to slow arousal and gentle, long-lasting lovemaking. Dawn was happy to give Sanjay his money's worth and more. She was beginning to warm to him as a person, not to mention as a lover.

But she was still feeling unsettled. She had no idea who he was, this inscrutable being who agreed her to take her as his mistress. After they had made love, she lit a cigarette and cuddled next to him.

"Do you have any idea how lucky you are to be fucking an Acadian woman?"

"Excuse me?" He blushed. "I thought you were from New Brunswick."

She ignored his discomfort. "Yeah, but I'm from Acadian stock. I guess you didn't know."

"No, I didn't."

"Then you probably don't know why Acadian women are so special."

"Enlighten me. I want to know everything about you."

"Well, I can't tell you everything, just the things I think you should know." She took a drag of her cigarette. "Cool. So to understand, you have to know some Acadian history, too."

"Yes, my darling. 'Fire away,' as you would say."

"Okay. Well, the small NB village I grew up in was a lot like the French settlements in New France from 450 years ago. The origin of the name

'Acadia' is of European and Indian origin. King François I sent Verrazano and his crew to the New World, and he landed in what's now Georgia in the US. The land was so fertile and beautiful and green, and the Indian inhabitants so friendly, it reminded the settlers of the ancient province of Arcadia in Greece and they named it 'Arcadie.' Later they dropped the 'r' and called it 'Acadie, and eventually 'Acadia.'"

"Interesting, but I'm still waiting for you to tell me about the women."

"I knew you would. Just hold on to your pants." She returned his grin. "You see, some people say it was really the French fishermen and fur traders, who came before Verrazano, giving their own pronunciation to the Indian words for 'fertile place.' Thus, 'La Cadie,' or 'Acadie.'"

"And so?"

"And so, that explains why the word is used all over the Maritimes, in Québec, and even in Louisiana in the US."

"I see. And where does your name, L'andry come from?"

"I'm getting to that. It's the second oldest name in France, not a very common one, though. But the origin is actually Germanic, from 'Land-rick,' meaning 'land-powerful.'

"Oh, I like that. So your ancestors came from France?"

"Yes, the Poitou region. René L'andry settled in Acadia in the mid-1600s."

"Are we getting to the good part now?"

"Yeah, you've been patient, so I won't go into any more history. Acadian women played such a great part in the lives of the people that they were revered. Not only could we cook, sew, weave wool and do all the housework, we also worked in the fields."

"I like the way you say 'we.'"

"Well, of course, I am one of them, silly. Anyway, we were responsible for all the socializing, too. Singing, dancing, telling jokes while working at the same time. There was nothing we couldn't do. Plus we tried to impress our families with the values of peace, tranquility and equality."

"Sounds like there was nothing you couldn't do."

"Exactly. So what do you think?"

"I think I'm very lucky to be fucking an Acadian woman." He cuddled closer to her. "But how did the L'andrys come to NB?"

"I think we've had enough boring history for now, don't you?"

"It's not boring, if it's about you. Tell me about your childhood."

"Not now, Sanjay, I prefer you awake." Dawn smiled and changed the subject. "I can't believe you're a doctor, at least a practicing one and not just a professor. You don't act like one."

"I told you, I'm both." He plucked the cigarette from her fingertips and tamped it out in the ashtray. "And just how does a doctor behave?"

"Well, for one thing, you would have noticed I have breast implants."

He gave her a crooked smile. "I was meaning to ask you. Did you get them the same time you had your nose job?"

"My nose job? How did you know about that?"

"I'm a doctor."

They both laughed. Now convinced, she lifted up her breasts with her hands. "Then tell me what you think of these."

He examined the tiny, barely visible scars underneath her breasts. "A master's handiwork. Well done, in my estimation."

Satisfied with his judgment, she squeezed a few drops of milky liquid from her nipples. "Want to taste? It's really sweet."

Dawn was surprised when Sanjay resisted the temptation. "I can't. One lick of your nipple would cause me to ravish you without a moment's hesitation." He paused. "Do you know what galactorrhea is?"

"Sure, it means I'm lactating when I shouldn't be."

"It might indicate a neurological disorder. Are you having any problems with your eyesight?"

His worried expression touched her. "Not to worry, I've had an MRI. I'm fine. But thanks for asking."

Now she was convinced without a doubt he was an MD, and a knowledgeable one. Plus he had a sympathetic soul. He was revealing himself to be a real human being.

Someone I could even fall in love with.

Then she chastised herself. She wasn't falling in love. She just liked to make people happy. Hookers didn't fall in love, especially with customers. She had just lucked out and found herself a good one. A really good one.

The trouble was, Dawn no longer felt sure about her actions and feelings. She had just shared intimate information about her background with a client. She had never done that before. Was she losing her former persona, or was this just a brief fling towards a "safe" relationship for the time being? No matter, as long as Sanjay still thought of her as a "mystery woman," as well as a hooker. She made a mental note to keep her personal history to herself, at least for now.

Tuesday, 9 pm

Now that I'm back home, I spent some time penning a note to Frederick Lupul. Who better than a hypnotherapist to help me gain some perspective on this obsession of mine, to explain my erratic behavior? He didn't tell me anything I didn't already know, but it was good to get confirmation. Millions of years of sexual evolution can't be changed overnight. The patterns of courtship, mate selection, marriage, and even cheating, are as old as the human species itself. He did emphasize, however, the difference between love and lust. The latter is driven by simple chemistry. Casual sex can be dangerous, since it can send oxytocin levels soaring and produce feelings of attachment to someone who is "inappropriate." Romantic love, driven by a whole other barrage of chemicals, can generate obsessive emotions about the sexual partner: a natural addiction that proves indispensable in keeping the partners together when pregnancy occurs. Infatuation goes a step further, causing persistent "intrusive thinking" about the object of affection.

When weighing all of this information, however, I came to the conclusion that I am a victim of infatuation. I think about Dawn at least 90% of my waking hours, and who knows how much of my somnolent ones. Infatuation is riding roughshod over my mind and body, overrunning all rational thought.

No wonder I'm a physical and mental basket case. I'm in pain, in anguish. But the torture is bliss.

13

It was Dawn's turn to help set up for the fourth annual St. Paul's community breakfast. The event was her brainchild, her baby. As a new teacher four years before, she had proposed the idea to fulfill the school's search for a service project. Apart from demonstrating the school's community spirit, the breakfasts raised about $5,000 each year for the Montréal Children's Hospital. It was a win-win. Dawn had no problem convincing the teaching staff and the Parent's Council as to the value of teaching students about the joys of service, a concept familiar to her from her work with Opus Dei.

Thus she was awake by 4:30 am and by 5:30 was ready to present herself to Vice Principal Antoine at the school gym. By 6 am, 1200 people were expected to show up and stuff themselves with pancakes, eggs, sausages, bagels, juice and coffee and continue to do so until 9. At three dollars a head, Dawn considered it a bargain. She had the procedure down to a science: food donated by parents and teachers, cooking and cleanup done by grades seven and eight. She made sure her favorite eighth graders, Ariel and Kevin, had command of the situation. Then she headed to the staff room.

As soon as she spied the email from Sanjay she felt an involuntary heat coursing through her face and her body, settling between her legs. She clicked on the message, her pulse quickening.

> *Dawn, my darling, my love, I can't thank you enough for giving me a weekend to remember and cherish forever. Since leaving Montréal, I feel your presence beside me constantly. Your lovely face haunts me. Your body, your touch, your voice, never leave my consciousness. I am in a never-ending state of agitation. My tranquility is lost forever.*

Please, I beg you, consider my offer. You are too precious to me to allow yourself to work day and night. You have my pledge to support you while you complete your education. And I am a man of my word.

With love forever, Sanjay"

Sanjay's passion and sincerity melted her heart, but she resisted.
How can I give in to him? I'm happy being an escort, a fantasy to other men. How can I let this one invade my life, break down my barriers? This can't happen to me.

Dawn recognized the familiar voices of the science teacher, Mrs. Martin, and the gym teacher, Leblanc. Their entrance interrupted her thoughts.

"I still say the science department should get the bulk of whatever resources are available."

"Physical education is every bit as important. Oh, good morning, Renée."

Both teachers nodded their greeting to Dawn. She returned the gesture. "Good morning." She couldn't help admiring Mr. Carroll's well-built, athletic form and dark skin. Just her type.

No time for chitchat this morning. Too much work to do.

Dawn returned to the computer screen and penned a reply.

My dearest Sanjay,

I had a wonderful time, too. I only wish we could see each other more often, but the miles separating us mean that phone and emails are our only means for keeping in touch. Don't worry about me, I am fine. Classes have started again, and the studies are even more difficult. But you'll be proud of me. I am treating myself to a massage tonight after class.

I look forward to the next time we meet.

Hugs and kisses,

Dawn

Short and sweet was the only way to go. She wasn't about to elaborate on her class load, since the whole issue was a subterfuge. What would he think if he knew she had no knowledge whatsoever of physiotherapy, that the course of study was a complete sham? It was a great cover-up, posing as a student. It made clients feel sorry for her and give her more generous tips. An attractive young woman moonlighting as a hooker to earn money for her education was a sure-fire way to elicit sympathy in an unsuspecting, horny client. For Dawn, it was all about the money. She never had enough of it, and she was willing to do whatever was necessary to accumulate as much of the green stuff as she could get her hands on, for Opus Dei and for herself.

The appearance of Mr. Antoine and the rest of the teachers put an end to Dawn's reverie. Suddenly the school was besieged with commotion, as hordes of donating contributors and breakfast guests descended upon the halls.

Optimism radiated from Mr. Antoine's wide smile. "I feel this year's donations will surpass last year's, don't you, Renée?"

Dawn nodded. "Absolutely, Mr. Antoine."

"Well, shall we?"

He turned and led the entourage from the room. Dawn followed them. It was her show, and the time to perform was at hand. Dawn, the exemplary teacher, was at her best.

14

Sanjay encountered his colleague George, who was sporting his usual tight t-shirt and body-hugging jeans, in the narrow basement passage leading to the cafeteria of St. Baptiste Hospital.

"How come so early?" Sanjay knew George was not an "A" type who showed up at the crack of dawn.

George ignored the question. "Have you checked out Krista in ICU? Hot, hot, hot."

Sanjay nodded his agreement. "She is looking pretty spicy these days."

"Divorcing, they say." George rolled his eyes. "Probably married some dumb prick, right?"

"For the life of me, George, I can't imagine why they marry the brainless, immature simpletons."

"It serves their purpose. Whatever that is."

"I believe God created human beings in three sexes." Sanjay smiled at George's raised eyebrows. "Ugly men, women . . ."

"And the third?"

"Beautiful women." Sanjay sighed. "Seraphs."

The two men shared a sardonic chuckle but were interrupted by the booming, disembodied voice of the ever-present P.A. System.

"Dr. Kaul to the ICU, stat."

Sanjay shrugged. "That's me."

George turned to gawk at an attractive nursing student passing them by. "Krista wants you. Stat, man."

Sanjay grinned and rushed off. He wondered if they were both sharing the same thought.

Yes. Hot and ready.

The ICU isolation room was in chaos. Hordes of people, nurses' aides, ICU nurses, resident doctors and medical students, rushed about. The monitor alarm's constant ringing jarred the atmosphere.

Sanjay glanced at the patient, her face a ghostly white. She was laid out on an expensive ICU bed, which the hospital no doubt obtained for the same inflated prices accorded the military, probably ten times its worth.

Krista spoke in a loud, clear voice. "She's developed sudden disordered heart rhythm, doctor. Supraventricular tachycardia."

Sanjay watched the heart monitor, his eyes narrowing. He had no trouble recognizing the syndrome. "Yes. *Torsade de pointes.*"

He was all too familiar with the malady, in which the heart keeps on rotating on its axis, as if the patient were madly in love. It was a well-known cause of cardiac arrest. He quickly assessed the situation, speaking in a clear voice for the benefit of the observing students.

"Precipitated by certain drugs or electrolyte imbalance, the effect prolongs conduction through the heart to such an extreme the whole heart beats into the organized chaos. The electrical instability of the rapidly beating muscle is unable to pump blood and oxygen into its own muscle, causing yet more turmoil."

Turning to the onlookers, he explained further.

"As a result, the heart becomes completely ineffective. Ventricular fibrillation, or cardiac standstill, develops. If not zapped out with an electric current with dispatch, the next stage occurs, an inevitable agonal rhythm of the dying heart. All in all, not a pretty picture."

In swift succession, Sanjay felt the woman's pulse and barked orders. "Somebody start bagging her and getting her ready for cardioversion. Give amiodarone 150 mg and Magnesium Sulfate 2 gm intravenously to halt the heart rhythm. Stat."

Krista's beautiful behind, made it all the more interesting when she bent over to deliver the shocks, distracted Sanjay's gaze from the monitor, however. Her short blouse lifted, exposing her bright red panties and butt cleavage. He brought himself back to reality. Even after the drugs and two shocks were administered, and the rhythm slowed down, the frequent ectopics looked ominous.

By this time the isolation room was so filled to overflowing it was hard for people to move without stepping on each other's toes. Everyone shouted his own orders simultaneously at the nurses. In the midst of this,

Sanjay, who was aware the effect of the electricity was at transient at best and ineffective at worst, noticed his precocious resident Rick was especially fidgety. Sanjay knew Rick tended to be as hyperactive as a caffeine addict who had drunk an entire carafe in one sitting. He was worried Rick would try to order a sternotomy. His fears were soon realized.

"Bring the sternotomy tray, I'm going to open her chest for open cardiac massage and direct cardioversion." Rick's trembling hands and terrified expression belied his aggressive shouting. "She is post cardiac surgery and has mitral valve prosthesis."

The last thing Sanjay wanted was to open up the patient's chest. It was so messy, and they would lose precious time in the process. "All of you, except me, stop calling the shots!" His voice, akin to a lion's roar, had the desired effect. Every voice hushed in an instant. "Start the CPR and defibrillate with 300 joules of electricity."

"Clear!" Krista's high-pitched voice announced the subsequent pressing of the defibrillator button. The patient's body shook and jerked as the inexpensive hydro was delivered to her chest. Squiggly lines appeared on the monitor, then a regular rhythm.

Sanjay was relieved. "The pulse is strong and bounding." He allowed himself a quick look at Krista's breasts before giving his next order. "Start dual chamber pacing at 120 beats per minute to suppress ventricular ectopy. Amiodarone infusion at 44 mg per hour. Maintain mean arterial pressure at 70 mm Hg or above with norepinephrine, milrinone for cardiac index of 2.2 l/minute or more."

Leaving Rick in command, Sanjay walked out of the room to find the patient's husband.

*

George sauntered into Sanjay's office with a smile on his face. "You practically brought her back from the dead."

"Her family is not going to want her in heaven just yet. But she's not quite out of the woods." Sanjay mumbled, his eyes on the Goldinvestor.com market charts. "Oil prices are going straight up. Go ahead and buy some while there's still money to be made."

Having given George this advice, the doctor/market expert went off on his morning rounds. A hospital, especially a teaching hospital, has an endless succession of rounds: morning rounds, X-ray rounds, teaching rounds, weekly rounds, sign out rounds. Sanjay's duties consisted of endless repetitions of specific medical processes.

Every time he did his rounds it reaffirmed his impression that St. Baptiste's ICU, a spacious unit located on the second floor of the hospital, was the best in the country. Recently renovated and redecorated, its posh atmosphere rivaled New York City's most expensive hotels. Each patient there was admitted to a private room, each room equipped with the latest and the best technology to observe all bodily functions minute by minute, including a large-panel computer screen to instantly demonstrate heart rate, blood pressure, level of oxygenation, respiration and pulmonary arterial pressure. Cardiac output, a measure of forward flow from the heart, was periodically assessed. A state-of-the-art ventilator continuously breathed life into the patient.

In the center of this particular room, Ruth VanHeusen lay sedated, her eyes moving about from time to time. At the age of 65 she had managed to avoid hospitals her entire life. She arrived at the ER that morning, sweating and unable to breathe, after complaining of a nasty heartburn that had kept her up all night. From the cold sweat drenching her body, Sanjay knew her most important muscle was not pumping warm blood through her body.

"Likely cardiogenic shock." He addressed the resident who was leaning over the woman and listening to her heart. "Acute anterior myocardial infraction. Intubate her, place a Swan-Ganz catheter into her heart and start her on inotropic drugs."

In Sanjay's experience, even the ventilator, tubes, drugs and other modalities, though likely to keep her artificially alive, were unlikely to improve her condition. He anticipated having to query the medical team—in this case consisting of the attending physician, three resident doctors, two medical students, dietician, bedside nurse, clinical resource nurse, pharmacist, respiratory therapist and cardiologist—as to the efficacy of continuing this patient's treatment. No improvement in five days meant probable extensive damage from the heart attack. That, along with likely severe coronary artery disease and multiple blockages, seriously decreased her chances of survival. The only recourse was a coronary angiography and possible stent. With such a poor prognosis, a family conference was the next step. Not pleasant, but all in his day's work. It was an enormous burden, and he needed to share it with someone else.

Dawn. He had to see her. His aching heart reflected his patient's agony. In his mind's eye he was planning his next trip back to his beloved. As soon as possible.

Remembering the next conference scheduled to take place in Montréal, he sighed with relief. Medical conferences were not his favorite thing. But this one couldn't come soon enough.

15

Immersed in thoughts of Sanjay, Dawn was so filled with remorse over continuing to see clients after promising him not to, she almost didn't recognize Tom's LTD Ford until he honked. She forked over the $400, but not until she was comfortably burrowed in the back seat of the car. She had finished her one-hour appointment at the Hotel Fairmont much earlier but treated herself to a drink while she waited for her boss. When she noticed they were driving North on Sherbrooke, she sat up and became alert. She wasn't sure where he was taking her, but she could tell by the upscale changes in the neighborhood they were probably headed towards Westmont, one of the most elite areas of the city.

Tom flashed her a quick glance from the front. "How was this guy?"

"Nice enough, I guess, but kind' a strange."

"Like how?"

"He never once looked me straight in the eye. He was awful quiet, too."

"Doesn't matter as long as he paid up."

"He didn't give me any tips, though."

"Yeah, right."

Dawn knew her hunch was correct by the posh buildings coming into view. Westmont was a stomping ground for the well heeled. Politicians, lawyers, judges, businessmen, and other celebrities, not only from Montréal but from all of Canada, lived there. Dawn had been in this neck of the woods a number of times for work. She was eager to know who her next call would be.

Tom solved the mystery. "Judge Vouriot asked for you tonight."

Dawn groaned. "Oh, no, I can't handle him tonight, I'm too tired. I really need some sleep."

"Well he wanted you, and only you. You know what a busy man he is. But for you, he somehow found time."

Thoughts of what she knew the Judge wanted made her squirm. "I'm not in the mood to be spanked, thank you very much."

"You will be after you hear this. He's doubling his usual $500. Just for you and only for tonight." Her silence made him grumble. He got past it. "Anyway, he's expecting you. We already set a time."

Dawn contemplated with dread her imminent encounter, while Tom griped to himself and pulled out a cigarette. The flashing lights and loud sirens of an approaching speeding police patrol car startled them from their thoughts. Tom pulled over and allowed the car to cross their path. The last thing he needed, with a hooker in his back seat, was to arouse the suspicions of the cops.

After the police car had passed them and was out of sight, Dawn decided to change her perspective.

Okay. Yes, what the Judge wants to do to me will hurt, but after awhile it sometimes gets pleasurable. Plus he's paying double.

The vision of the immense, well-kept turn-of-the-century castle cemented her resolve. It was a beautiful picture: long, elegant circular driveway, stone turrets, and a blanket of fresh snow covering the land surrounding the building. Thoughts of fairy tale castles flitted through Dawn's mind. She became flushed with excitement.

Tom parked in the middle of the circular driveway. Staying close behind Dawn, he accompanied her to the double entrance carved mahogany doors and wielded the heavy steel knocker. She felt Tom shroud her eyes with a dark blindfold, obscuring her vision completely. Dawn was familiar with the protocol. The judge did not wish to be seen by the young girls he liked to spank. The door opened, and Dawn could sense Tom had made a quick and silent exit. Then she felt two warm, chubby, leathery hands lead her inside. She recognized the feel of those hands and the deep, commanding sound of the voice.

"Well, well, if it isn't my favorite girl. Always a pleasure to see you."

Dawn tried to visualize the face belonging to the hands. The thought wasn't comforting.

"And how are you this evening, my dear?"

"I'm just fine, Judge, how are you?"

"I don't know what it is about you, but just being in your presence excites me so much I can hardly contain myself."

Dawn was glad the blindfold obscured the terror in her eyes. "I love being here, too. Why you don't call me more often?"

The Judge clicked his tongue. "I wish I could, but I'm too busy. Québec nationalism, language rights issues, the Medicare challenge. You know how it is."

I don't, but never mind that.

"My one pleasurable diversion in life is being with one of you beautiful girls. And only once in a blue moon."

The judge led on, Dawn's high heels clicking on the stone floors, until he ushered her into a room reeking of mahogany and leather. His den, she supposed. She tried to imagine the surroundings. Paneled walls with floor-to-ceiling shelves filled with thick legal books, a leather cushy La-Z-Boy easy chair, a gargantuan desk stacked with important judicial papers, the kinds of documents the best legal minds of Canada pored over on a daily basis.

"Your name is Dawn, isn't it?" The Judge interrupted her reverie.

"Yes. Yes, it is."

"I've been in the mood ever since I found out you were coming. Why don't you get naked?"

Dawn took her time undressing, soothing her nerves with distracting thoughts.

If only I'd known I'd be seeing him, I would have insisted on going back to the condo and changing into something sexier, flashier.

Then she chastised herself. He didn't give a damn what she wore, as long as he hurt her, wounded her tender young flesh. She stripped off her blouse and bra and unzipped her skin-tight skirt, revealing her perfectly shaped buttocks. She thought back to her childhood, when she considered herself ugly. That had all changed by the time she turned 16. Now at age 28, she still had it all. God had been generous in granting her endowments in spades, and she didn't take the bounty for granted. She was happy with her body, with its violin-shaped curves, long thin neck, rounded breasts and narrow waist, curvaceous buttocks, tapered thighs. She sensed the Judge was enjoying the scenery, but she knew inflicting pain on a young girl was his real fetish. That was orgasmic to him.

"Do you want me to take my panties off?" She made every effort to be polite.

"No, my dear. They're so skimpy they might actually enhance my view."

Now seated in his La-Z-Boy chair, the Judge ordered her to hold her hands above her head and walk around the room. Although unable to see, she remembered from previous experience to walk four steps to the right, six steps to the left, and then turn back four more steps. It was hard to keep track of her steps, but she didn't falter.

His voice grew more forceful, more agitated. Her heart raced, whether from fear or excitement she wasn't sure.

"Now get down on the floor on all fours. Lift your buttocks in the air. High."

By now she guessed he was aroused and ready to climax. She heard his steps on the parquet floor walking slowly behind her. The feel of his rough hand, massaging each of her buttocks, drove her into a frenzy. Anticipating pain, she again distracted her mind with other thoughts.

God is punishing me.

He was penalizing her for dancing in the nude and showing her body, for being a go-go dancer at the Crazy Horse club during her undergraduate years at the University de Montréal. For getting off on the loud music, the staring eyes of the ogling patrons, the free alcohol allowed to the dancers. For getting all keyed up from her wild dancing, which revealed every bit of her anatomy, and faking sex acts. The tips were not as good as she was making now, but she reveled in the pleasure. She quit only after she thought she saw her cousin Edmund there from her hometown. Now God was showing her his wrath by subjecting her to the mistreatments she was about to endure. She had tried many times to turn down an encounter with the Judge, but between his lavish tips and the hedonistic ecstasy she enjoyed, she always came back for more.

The violent force of the judge's hand on her posterior wrenched her from her thoughts. The spanking started out gentle and slow but became harder and faster within seconds. Each blow, first on the right and then the left buttock, produced fiery red marks on her pale skin. The sounds of her punishment echoed through the room, like the noises of an animal being slapped by a cruel trainer.

Despite her now-intense pain, she was astonished to find her genitals becoming swollen and engorged from the vibrations of each blow. The pleasure they created traveled to her depths, causing such an intense reaction she could not help rubbing her clitoris to enhance the sensation. All this time, she had been crying and screaming, like a little girl enduring retribution from an enraged parent, begging for forgiveness.

She imagined the Judge always spanked her with one hand so he could play with himself or masturbate with the other. Only once did she see a drop of semen on her skirt when she later changed in her apartment. She knew it had to be his because her other clients always wore condoms. When the spanking stopped, she heard his soft grunts and knew it was over. Even blindfolded, and stiff from pain, she was able to get dressed without hesitating. The judge handed her three bills, a thousand dollar bill for the agency and two hundreds as tips. Once she was dressed, he led her to the doorway. When he saw her appear, Tom pulled the car up to the door.

Dawn climbed into the back seat with great difficulty. Her backside was smarting, on fire. Unable to sit, she had to lie on one side instead.

"Take me to my place, Tom. Now." She spoke through her teeth. "I'm never doing this again. Got that?"

It took her ten minutes, one torturous step at a time, to mount the stairs to her third-floor condo unit. Once inside the spacious apartment, she bolted for the kitchen cupboard, dug out two oxycontins and gulped them down with a glass of chocolate milk. Then she collapsed onto her bed, still in her street clothes, and contemplated her evening's work.

A lucrative night, thirteen hundred dollars. It would take me three weeks to make that much in my day job. Plus all that fun tonight as a fringe benefit.

Within seconds she was fast asleep, avoiding the inevitable self-doubt. Was it really fun? Or was she just kidding herself?

If she hadn't missed Sanjay's phone call, she would have known he wanted to hear her voice, to feel her presence, to know what she was up to that night. But she was dead to the world.

When she awoke the next morning, she saw the red light blinking on her answering machine. It was the message she had missed.

> *My dearest, you must know by now I am hopelessly in love with you. This cannot possibly work. I have thought endlessly about my unrelenting desire for you and have decided to end it between us now, before either one of us gets hurt. I hope you understand.*

Dawn listened to the message several more times. Her disappointment surprised her. After all, romantic love with a client was nothing but a liability. She was much better off putting the whole episode with Sanjay behind her and going back to her former life.

The trouble was, she couldn't.

16

The conference with Mrs. VanHeusen's family did not go well, but that didn't surprise Sanjay. What surprised him was the fact her heart was still pumping. Her angiogram results showed multiple plaques in all her arteries. Her pump function, at 20%, was as low as it gets. He discussed this with the medical team before meeting with the family.

"We need a roto-rooter to open up those blockages." Justin, the ICU fellow, was showing off his limited knowledge and experience, as usual.

"You mean, balloon angioplasty? I don't think that's an option." Sanjay tried not to gape at the beautiful dietician's celestial-blue eyes. "The blockages are too multiple, too distant from the heart."

"Bypass surgery, then?" Justin was still trying.

Sanjay shook his head. "Dr. Cohen doesn't think so. From the images, he and I concurred. She's a very high-risk candidate."

The sober glance between Sanjay and Justin signaled what they both knew. They were out of options.

The family gathered around Ruth's bed. Her daughter Genevieve, a radiology technician in the hospital's X-ray department, was on edge. So were her two friends and their spouses who had come to support her. With a seasoned doctor's patience, Sanjay explained the disturbing prognosis. He was calm and frank. There was no point in offering hope in a hopeless situation.

"The patient's multiple blockages, the kidney and liver damage, the lack of life-saving treatment available to her in her condition. These are all major drawbacks."

Genevieve burst into tears. Sanjay offered her a tissue and placed a comforting hand on her shoulder. "We will make sure she doesn't suffer further, but we need to take her off life support."

She looked up at him, her eyes misted. "Can't we keep her on? Just for a little while longer?"

"There's no point, I'm afraid, in making her endure more distress. When there's no light at the end of the tunnel, it just prolongs her agony." He held the daughter's gaze for a moment and turned to leave. "I'll give you some time and come back later."

Sanjay left them to their anguish. He knew what they were thinking and feeling. He had been through this so many times. Grief at first, then the inevitable disbelief, as they chronicled their bewilderment and pain. The inevitable tape played again and again, each time a patient came to the brink. He knew it by heart.

How could she die so soon? Not a sick day in her entire life. Such a nice person, such a wonderful person. An affectionate mother, a good housewife, a helpful neighbor. A true believer in the Lord. She can't leave us so soon, not like this. It's not true, it can't be happening.

He continued on to his sign-out rounds, stopping to hand over his duties to the resident on call for the night, whose sleep was at the mercy of the nurses and the overall suffering of humanity. Sanjay had been there in his own residency. Trying to keep straight all the day's plans, trying to maintain the cycle of life, trying to keep patients alive through the night. Like all residents, he had learned the tricks of the trade for making the most of the limited, fragmented sleep he could catch in the process, sleep that often made him more tired with it than without it.

*

The next morning Sanjay joined the medical team, now reduced to a fraction of its original size, as they hovered over the patient. She lay awake, her wide-open eyes broadcasting her agony. The pain, the constant poking and prodding, the indignity. Sanjay was familiar with it all.

I don't want to live like this. I'd rather die . . . All these people are making me suffer continuously . . . The tubes coming out of my mouth, my privates, my neck . . . The ones coming out of my neck hurt, the breathing one is so uncomfortable . . . The breathing machine fills my lungs up with too much air . . . I wish I could leave this place and go somewhere nice, my own comfortable bed, and make love to my husband of 45 years one last time . . .

Though I wouldn't mind doing it with the hot orderly who gives me bath every day. Now, he's worth dying for . . . The fantasies, Sanjay knew, were the patient's own, at least until the nurses gave her the sleeping meds. Sedating patients kept them from being too demanding. This was a must for nurses, who preferred to spend their time reading the latest Harlequin romance and then retire to the bathroom to touch themselves.

The nurse in charge interrupted Sanjay's thoughts. "Doctor, should we let her know she's dying?"

Justin flashed her a disapproving look. "What for? It would only cause her more anguish."

Sanjay nodded his agreement. The nurse comprehended. "Yes, doctor. You know what's best."

What and how much to tell a dying patient always poses an ethical dilemma. Sanjay knew this from experience. Human nature forces us to hold out hope, even when circumstances look grim. It was a rare patient indeed who was willing to give in to Death's ultimate specter. In most cases, either the patient's family or the medical personnel made such life or death decisions. Physicians, focused on the disease process, try to stay optimistic. They want their patients to stay alive, even for a short time. Nurses, who spend more time caring for the patients, and inflicting pain and suffering to make them better, are often the ones to persuade doctors to withdraw therapy from a patient. It came down to one last choice. What was in the patient's best interest, living or dying? Ultimately, it was the doctor who gave the death sentence.

Mrs. VanHeusen's eyes fluttered open. She gazed at Sanjay, pulling at the hand restraints that had been placed on her during the night. Sanjay took pity on her and loosened them. He imagined the nurse had misinterpreted the woman's late-night attempts at stimulating herself as trying to pull out her catheter. Though there was no data available on these occurrences in hospitals, Sanjay imagined a large percentage of patients engaged in the pursuit of sexual release, even when dying. He held her gaze, touching her arm gently.

"Mrs. VanHeusen, you've had a second attack, which weakened your heart. We've kept it pumping with medication, but your inability to breathe on your own has made it necessary to hook you up to a breathing machine. We really don't have many options left here other than to make you comfortable."

Sanjay knew from her lack of expression she understood what he had told her, and wanted the agony to end. She turned away from him, closing her eyes.

The nurse tried to keep her voice low so that the patient wouldn't hear. "Doctor, you didn't tell her—"

His deep frown interrupted her. "I'm sure she understands. Fully." He waited for the nurse to acknowledge his truth. "Meanwhile, under no circumstances should her hands be restrained, do you understand? Let her pull on her catheter if she wants to."

Sanjay left the room overwhelmed with sadness.

65 isn't that old. Why can't I make her better? Why can't I heal her?

Only the thought of a cold Molson and a hot session with the new escort he had reserved for the night were enough to ease his melancholy. Yes, Cleo. She was young, blonde, and from what he was told, not a bad performer. At that moment Dawn's face appeared in front of his eyes, and his eagerness to see the escort vanished. His heart ached for his beloved, but the thought of her comforted him.

His anguish over the dying patient soothed, Sanjay headed back to the ICU, where the technicians were removing Mrs. VanHeusen's life support. The breathing tube and machine were disconnected. The meds were stopped. The morphine and sedative were taking effect, slowing her respiration and helping her to fall into a coma. Without medication, the heart would weaken and cease its pumping. It was soon over. Sanjay wondered if in reality she had died that day or if she had been dying all along and kept alive by medical intervention. He watched the monitor flat line and imagined seeing her soul depart.

Is there such thing as a soul? Or is there only a human body, with its pleasure and pain?

Sanjay had been through this hundreds of times. Yet he never got used to it. He always found it a painful process to watch and experience.

Yes, indeed. We all come to this end. Death has its common bedfellows.

He wandered off to change. Normal clothes for a normal human being, not the man who had played God today. All the while he thought about Dawn. Would she understand his thoughts, his feelings about life and death and souls?

Someday, I'm sure to find out.

17

At 7:30 the next morning, Sanjay awoke with a start. His usual habit was to be up at least three hours earlier, but after the previous night's labors he decided he deserved fifteen minutes of idleness. The problem was, moments of inactivity brought thoughts of Dawn. There was no denying that. He cuddled Vinita, who lay in deep slumber next to him, unaware of his musing. What would his wife of twenty-one years think if she knew where his mind was wandering and whom it was focused on?

Dawn. His beacon, his light, his angel. How could he not be in love with and admire such a beautiful and intelligent woman? How could he not sympathize with her struggle to put herself through physiotherapy school by working nights as a prostitute?

Unable to sleep anymore, Sanjay extricated himself from his wife's arms and shuffled downstairs to make coffee. Blue Mountain Jamaican was his addiction. Its pungent aroma always woke him out of whatever stupor he was in, at any hour. Upon reading the day's headlines in the Winnipeg Free Press, however, he wished he'd stayed in bed.

First-ever elections in Iraq, what a sham. The front-page photo of an Iraqi civilian waving a sign in support of the elections made Sanjay cringe.

Democracy in Iraq? I don't think so.

Vinita padded in, her slippers making a soft sound on the floor. "Good morning, dear." She gave him a gentle kiss on the forehead.

"Look at this headline." Sanjay waved the newspaper in her direction. "'Eight American G.I.'s killed in Baghdad on election eve.' The conceit of this George Bush, to sacrifice young kids' lives in an illegal war to satisfy his outsized, overzealous imperialist ego. It makes me seethe."

"Yes, dear, I agree." Vinita poured herself a cup from the coffee maker.

Sanjay continued his tirade. "And this election. Only Bush's ultra-conservative corporate cronies could tout such a charade as a so-called democratic process. A puppet government backed by the military might of a super power. It's all about oil, profit-making and exploitation."

Vinita's forbearing expression brought his invective to a halt. "What about the local news, dear?" She made an effort to smile. "Is it any better?"

He flipped the pages and grumbled. "A right-wing mayor elected by big business to abolish their taxes in a city with a perennially destitute budget forced to slash civic programs? It's a scenario from hell."

"Yes, dear, I agree. It is a shame."

"The shame is that the lower and middle classes suffer while the elite enjoys well-maintained roads, private schools for their kids and state-of-the-art fitness centers." He got up and poured himself a second cup. "They elected this so-called mayor to protect their interests. It nauseates me."

Sanjay sat down and gulped the steaming brew. He glanced at Vinita's tolerant expression. She was so patient and understanding, never argued with him. How fortunate for him.

"Would you like a bowl of hot oatmeal, dear?"

"No thank you, I have to get ready." He grazed her cheek with a perfunctory kiss, got up and took the newspaper with him.

He didn't tell her about the other headline that had caught his eye: "Twenty-two 'johns' arrested in weekend city-wide sweep operation." He perused the article as he climbed the stairs to get dressed. Repeat offenders faced a possible criminal record, with their cars impounded for one month.

How can these guys be so stupid as to get caught? Their wives must haul them over the coals for months afterward.

Victoria, an escort he had seen on several occasions, once told him only the inexperienced got ensnared. Prostitution was legal in Canada, but solicitation was not.

"How a hooker can get customers without 'communicating' her proposition is beyond me." She shook her head in disbelief.

"So how does it work?" he asked.

"Female cops go undercover on the street and 'solicit.' Like they'll say to a guy in a car, 'Wanna be gloved?' Or 'Want a dip?' If he asks how much, she ticks off the price list. He reaches out to pass her money, and he's toast. Instant handcuffs. 'Course, the whole sweep is so illegal, any conviction can be challenged with no problem."

"But if it's illegal, why do they do it?"

"They're just looking to put the fear of God in these poor slobs. Embarrass them to death. I mean, really, all he wants is for his needs to be met, right? The john'll get a pardon, but he still has to go to 'john school.'"

"I'd like to find out what happens there."

"Can't. Unless you get caught."

Sanjay's natural curiosity about what went on in "john school" got the better of him. Without mentioning anything to Vinita, he signed up for a monthly class. It took a slew of phone calls and a steep fee, but he finally managed to be admitted. He listened to the talks by police officers, social workers and reformed prostitutes. "Prostitution 101," according to his instructor.

"It's a multi-billion dollar industry that lines the pockets of predators and makes whole communities pay for the damage. Medical care for STDs, mental health treatments for PTSD, substance abuse and such. A third of sex workers end up chronically disabled and on welfare."

Sanjay was astonished but skeptical. "'Normal' people experience all the same problems. How do you differentiate?"

"That's a can of worms, Sir. Let's just say a lot of sex workers started out sexually abused and even shared or rented out by their own families. How's that for starters?"

This shocked Sanjay, but the police officer's information on pimps stunned him.

"Prostitution can be viewed as repeated rape, sexual intercourse forced by intimidation from predators, the pimps. They're small-time criminals looking for sadistic gratification by hooking young girls into the trade, the abused and neglected ones who are trying to escape their families, befriending them and then grooming them. Once they've taken money for sex, they're 'identified' as prostitutes, pretty much for life. Not exactly a 'victimless' crime."

Disgusted by what he had learned, Sanjay consulted Victoria again about her own experiences as an escort.

"The difference is, we provide more than just sex to our clients. They feel comfortable enough to drop their pants and talk about their problems, their frustrations at home. They go back to their families relaxed and happy."

Sanjay was puzzled. "But is it worth selling your body to accomplish that?"

"That's ridiculous, when you think about it. We don't 'sell' our bodies. We still have them at the end of the transaction." Victoria grinned. "Plus clients treat us better than most one-night stands you meet at a bar."

"Why doesn't the media focus on the GFE instead of just street prostitution?"

"Good question. Maybe their readers just don't want to hear about us, but who knows? Maybe someone will put it out there someday. Not a bad idea, in fact."

All his "research" made Sanjay's thoughts focus on Dawn more than ever. He was a successful physician, a renowned professor of medicine, and a national and international leader in his field. Despite all this, he was in love with a prostitute. Her name was written on each and every aspect of his world. For three months, she had dominated his thoughts. He was at his wits' end.

When he was speaking to his patients suffering from chronic obstructive lung disease, he saw her radiant smile in place of their cyanosed, pock marked faces. While he examined the clubbed fingers of a patient with pulmonary fibrosis, he felt instead the caress of her long, slender fingers. When giving lectures to students or discussing matters with colleagues and staff, her face appeared before him. This dazzling French-Acadian woman consumed his mind and body and brain. Like cancer cells, breaking off lung tissue along with blood, spreading their poison through the body of a terminal patient and choking the oxygen supply to vital organs, she had metastasized throughout his brain, infiltrated the grey matter, and held it hostage.

Sanjay's mind strayed to thoughts of Dawn throughout each busy day. He lumbered along, checking emails and performing duties, his entire being consumed by daydreams of being with her, what she was doing, what she was thinking.

My sweet, ingenuous, beautiful Dawn. I can't live without her. I have to get back to Montréal.

18

Sanjay jogged down the stairs and into the Montréal Hotel Vogue's lobby. He took a quick glance around and breathed in the ambiance. Here, late empire style and old world European charm mingled with modern urbanity. Elegant, cream-colored marble with brass accents meshed with the fashionable *L'Opéra* Bar nestled under the winding staircase. There, two perfect, arresting pink Phalaenopsis orchids set into a marble stand bent their long stems towards each other like two lovers reaching for a kiss. These "flowers of love," refugees from the 50s, when so many of these plants were cut down to discourage "immorality" in the underbrush of Parc Mont Royal, were some of his favorites. Among flowers, orchids were his passion, not only because they were beautiful and resembled the apotheosis of female sexual apparatus, but for what they represented in certain cultures. To the Greeks, the plants were a symbol of virility. To the Chinese, they were the "plant of King's fragrance." Through the ages, numerous societies considered the flowers to be an aphrodisiac and used them in love potions.

The sight of these flowers in full splendor so early in the morning brought more thoughts of Dawn to his already-saturated consciousness of her. The Greeks, after all, believed when orchids appeared in a dream they symbolized a deep inner need and desire, for tenderness and romance. The structure of this soft, sensuous flower, its middle petal bearing a striking similarity to female anatomy, reawakened his forbidden fantasies. Although not superstitious by nature, he found himself wondering if this early morning encounter with the "perfect pink" was an auspicious symbol of his next meeting with Dawn. Whatever the rationale, Sanjay needed this distraction from his treadmill of tedium, from the high-pressured Intensivist days dealing with life-or-death situations to his nights filled with the struggle to create engaging language out of dry, scientific manuscripts and make it palatable enough to sell to prestigious peer-reviewed publications.

His brain now focused on love, Sanjay jogged onto Avenue Montagne and turned left. Whatever effect the mid-February chill had on his muscular body through his light running clothing dissipated within the first five minutes. He increased his pace, his state-of-the-art Asics runners pounding the pavement, and upped his speed to a comfortable nine-minute mile. He never got tired of admiring this beautiful city at the foot of Mont Royal, with its intriguing mix of post-modern office towers, centuries-old churches, boutiques, art galleries and museums and ornate 19th century Victorian homes. Aware of the fast-approaching hour of his first meeting, he sped past the funky shops, eateries and hip nightclubs on the commercial strip called "The Main", proceeded along Avenue Mont Royal, where the nightlife had just gone to sleep a brief two hours before, and turned into the park. He was conscious of the early morning serenade of the birds but couldn't pay more than a fragment of attention to them. The scientific session of the Canadian Critical Care Society's clinical trials group awaited his chairmanship.

On the dot of 7:45 am, Sanjay was greeting his fellow Intensivists and researchers, a homogenous group of mostly Caucasian-looking men. He was familiar with the demographics. The large Québec contingent was friendly. The professor representing Toronto considered the gathering to be mediocre. And the Vancouver delegation was attempting to blast away their jet lag by mainlining their coffee. Most of the attendees, Sanjay knew, preferred a tony European resort to a hotel in downtown Montréal, but he was used to their attitude.

Tant pis, as they say in Québec.

Sanjay cleared his throat to quiet the hubbub. His loud, commanding voice, with its hint of accent, ensured their attentiveness.

"Good morning, ladies and gentlemen. We have a busy day ahead. Our objective is to review and endorse our clinical research protocols over the next year." He paused, taking in the faces turned towards him. "I'll be especially interested in hearing about the nitric oxide in ARDS Study from Dr. Martin."

Sanjay chuckled to himself, knowing he had interrupted the deep sleep of the doctor from Vancouver. It was going to be a long day, full of ongoing research study evaluations and updates from principal investigators' success or failure. The delicious anticipation of his rendezvous with his angel got him through it.

*

Dawn was surprised how excited she felt at the thought of seeing Sanjay. It had been almost two weeks since they last met, and during that time her nights witnessed a parade of hungry males vying for her attention. Tom did his job well, that was certain. But the work was beginning to wear her out, and she found herself longing for the gentle, soothing touch of her dark-skinned lover. It didn't matter that he had broken up with her. She knew he was hooked, and that he'd come back to her. It was so predictable.

Lover. It was a term she hadn't considered in terms of her own sexuality. Sex was for making money, not for her own gratification. But with Sanjay, sex was different. Making love with him fulfilled her in ways she had never experienced. The increasing intensity of her feelings for him frightened her. If she was falling in love, she had no intention of admitting it to herself or anyone else, least of all Sanjay.

Perhaps her mushrooming emotions had to do with her admiration for him and for what he did. She couldn't fathom how he handled all his professional responsibilities at his hospital, his conferences, and with his family. Yet, in the midst of all this, he managed to make her feel taken care of.

Is this what love feels like, admiration for someone? Respect? Esteem? Is he what they call "Mister Right?"

She wasn't sure. Love was both mystery and anathema to her. What she felt now was impatience. He was late, an unusual occurrence for him. But the excitement welling up inside her when she spied Sanjay emerge from the elevator dispersed all her negative thoughts.

"I'm so sorry I'm late. Those professors, you can't shut them up." Sanjay eyed her impeccable business suit with approval. "I'll make it up to you."

"You will?" She took his arm and flashed him a teasing grin.

Arm in arm, the couple glided across the opulent marble floor to the elevator bank, where they entered an elevator designated for the deluxe level. When they were between floors 9 and 10, Sanjay inserted his credit card into a slot next to the numbered panel, a trick he had learned during his training at Victoria General Hospital in Halifax. The lift halted. The elevator's sudden standstill both startled and excited Dawn.

"You're always full of surprises, Sanjay."

"That's the way I like it." He pulled a small box from his pocket and placed it in her hand. "Open it."

She raised the lid and gasped at the bright gold matching ring and necklace set nestled within. "Oh, they're beautiful."

"Not as beautiful as you." Sanjay placed the jewels on Dawn and stood back to admire the effect.

Her eyes sparkled. The feel of the pure gold made her glow from within. "Do I look Indian now?"

"Very much so. *Bahut sunder.*"

"What?"

He kissed her eyes and face. "It means 'very pretty.'"

"Oh." She smiled, admiring the shimmer of the gold against her skin, and reached up to kiss him. Their lips locked, their tongues tasting each other's with intense hunger.

Sanjay murmured, his voice soft and urgent. "Let's do it here."

"Hmm, is that one of your fantasies?"

"What do you think?" His tongue outlined the curve of her ear.

She demurred. "Let's go to the room. I have something for you, too."

Sanjay's expression revealed his reluctance. He removed his credit card from the panel. The elevator continued its ascent to the 18th floor.

19

Dawn's eyes lit up when she spied the champagne bottle and crystal flutes waiting on the marble-topped table inside the room.

"Ooh, I love *Veuve Clicquot*. It's my favorite."

"Courtesy of Management. For regular guests." Sanjay popped the cork and filled the glasses.

"No doubt." Dawn sipped, enjoying the tickle of the bubbles on her tongue. "For special 'regular guests.'" She gave him a sly smile. "So how was your trip to Montréal?"

"Good for the most part except that in Winnipeg we were almost in an accident driving to the airport. An old geezer nicked the fender of my wife's new Mercedes I bought her for her birthday."

"Awesome, a new Mercedes!" She flashed him a seductive smile. "I want a new Mercedes, too."

"I thought you wanted a shiny new sports car."

"I do."

"You are the devil." Throwing his arms around her, he laughed. "Devil and angel, how is that possible?"

"Life is full of surprises."

"Speaking of surprises, what's mine?"

She gave him a gentle push. "You'll find out. After you treat me to dinner at the Sky Lounge. I haven't eaten all day."

His eyes narrowed. "But why? You poor thing, didn't you have enough money? What about the check I sent you? Did you receive it?"

"Yes, I did. And thank you." Avoiding his penetrating gaze, she changed the subject. "How was your week?"

He was willing to be distracted. "Spent saving lives, as usual. I've hardly had time to sleep."

She tousled his hair with a gentle gesture. "Sorry, I won't be able to help in that department."

His smile of anticipation morphed into a serious expression. "Such suffering on this earth, Dawn, and by innocent people. I don't know why God allows it."

"I thought you didn't believe in God."

"Thanks for reminding me." His smile returned.

"All the pain and suffering came from Eve's original sin. She brought all this misery on the world—"

He tightened his grasp on her. "If you are the embodiment of Eve, then I believe you."

She held him at arm's distance, intent on finishing her thought. "But our prayers are our salvation."

"I'll gladly pray anything to anyone. As long as I can have you."

"You do have me." She pulled him towards the door. "As long as you feed me first."

*

Once her hunger was satisfied, Dawn was eager to fulfill her promise to Sanjay. Back in his room, she excused herself and went to fill the tub, gazing at the expensive marble tile and luxurious gold fixtures in the oversized, exquisitely decorated bathroom.

I could get used to this.

When she returned to Sanjay, Dawn sat him down on the cushy leather sofa and placed an open beer in his hand. "You've been so good to me, now's your turn for a treat." She took down her hair from its up do and shook out her waves. "First the striptease, then the water sports."

In fitful fantasies,
Replaying memories,
Logging torture between . . . We are caught as a deer,
Deep in the sight,
Of one unbearable light.

*And when you discover, in your own royal seat
With honour and pleasure, she'll make you believe
She'll shower and shine you, and set you on fire.
Give you life-blood, never bore or tire.
She'll take you to Heaven, where you belong;
Once and for all, stand tall.*

*In fitful fantasies . . .
The smart one's uncover the secret of love:
To love and be lover
The secret of love
To love and be lover,
The secret of love.*

In fitful fantasies . . .

Sanjay was entranced, his eyes glued to her sinuous form. After the third song, she had divested herself of every thread of clothing. She stopped dancing and sidled over to him, brushing her fingers over her soft tufts of golden pubic hair.

"You see, I haven't been working." She took hold of his hand. "Now let's play."

Sanjay slid into the tub. Dawn slithered between his legs and began caressing him from his feet to his calves to his thighs, massaging with expert strokes. The warm water heightened his sensation of her hand stroking between his legs. He was panting with desire.

"Please. Let me have a turn."

She smiled. "I think I can handle that."

He lifted Dawn onto his thighs and reciprocated her movements, rubbing her legs, her buttocks, kneading her waist, stroking her breasts. They lost track of the time, languishing in each other's moist caresses, their skin burning with the wet heat of their mutual arousal, until she rose and coaxed him up out of the tub. She guided him to the bed and drew him into her arms, where she enfolded him with her passion, and let him love her to his heart's content.

Afterwards, she laid her head on his chest. He stroked her hair. "I love you, Dawn. I just want you all the time."

"I do, too, Sanjay."

"But my desire for you keeps growing. It's stronger than my own will. Can you handle that?"

"Nothing I can't handle." She lied to him. Truth was, she had no idea what to do with his deepening infatuation, but she wasn't about to admit that.

Sanjay thought of the article in the Winnipeg Free Press and his "research" on prostitution and escorts. He was curious about Dawn's take on the subject.

"Tell me why you do this, this work, Dawn?"

She frowned, suspicious. "Why are you asking me that?"

"I was just wondering, now we've gotten to know each other better. I'd like to know more."

Dawn thought for a moment. "Okay, if you must know, I do it for the money, like everyone else. But I want to live in a 'bubble,' to be protected from cops and bad experiences, so I keep my private life to myself."

"And why do you stay with it?"

"Well, I'm still fascinated by men, their stories, their needs and desires and fantasies. It's intoxicating, and also a hobby for me, being able to enjoy intimacy without the entanglements of relationships.

"Clients don't have to worry about me calling them at 3 am at home or undermining their marriages. For them, it's like ordering pizza. They get what they want without fear of being judged for it. No repercussions. For me, it's almost like being a sexual surrogate or sex therapist. But you should know all this, right? You've been seeing escorts for . . . how long?"

"For me, it's like going back to adolescence. I need variety, adventure."

"Spreading the seed, even if it's collected in latex." Dawn grinned. "And getting something that's not on the menu at home."

Sanjay pulled her closer. "Yes, and with a willing and enthusiastic partner."

"I wish more of them were like you, Sanjay."

He blushed. "What do you mean?"

"Well, some guys are into the 'male domination' thing. They want to call the shots. You sometimes just lie back and let me be aggressive. I like that."

"I live for it. What's the point if you can't allow each other to act freely?" He thought for a moment. "But you must have some other motivations, yes? Isn't it about money, after all?"

The mention of money made her sit upright. "You're right, it is. I'm an educated woman, and I want more out of life. What I earn I use to survive, but I try to put aside some as an investment in my future. I want to be rich someday."

"On that subject, Dawn, I just wanted to tell you, if . . ." He hesitated, unsure if the moment was right to bring up the subject. "If you need money, I can teach you how to make a small fortune."

"You can? How?"

"In the stock market. I've been investing for years. It's the only way to become rich."

"You mean you don't make enough being a doctor?"

"I do that to satisfy my intellect and keep my mind sharp. To make real money, you have to invest. I think you're smart enough to learn."

"Of course I am. Adventure is my *forte*. And I love learning new things."

"Good. I'll open up a joint brokerage account and teach you the tricks of trading. All you have to do is study the tutorials on the websites I give you and keep up with the markets on a daily basis."

"You'd do that, for me?"

"I'd do anything for you."

"You're awesome." She leaned over and pressed her lips to his. After a moment, she pulled away. "I'd better take off now."

"So soon?" He was reluctant to let her go. "Stay with me."

"I can't, I have to be at Opus Dei in a few hours. Don't you have early meetings as well?"

"Yes. Another full day tomorrow."

"There. You see?"

Dawn extricated herself from his arms and rose, leaving him bereft on the bed.

She dressed quickly, and when she returned to plant a kiss on his cheek she noticed two foil-wrapped chocolates on the pillow. "Okay if I take these? I'm guessing chocolate is on your 'no' list."

"You're guessing right." He watched her move towards the door. "Choose a restaurant for tomorrow evening. I'll meet you there."

"Whatever you say, Sanjay."

And she was gone.

20

Sanjay strode into the Pimento Rouge on Avenue du Mont Royal that evening to find Dawn waiting for him inside the entrance. He was taken aback to see she had brought along company.

"This is my friend Sophie." Dawn's smile melted his annoyance. "She's finishing up her dietary assistant training at Canuck College in Ottawa. She comes to visit me on weekends sometimes."

Sanjay offered his hand to the girl who, though attractive, was not in Dawn's league in that department. "Nice to meet you."

I hope you don't mind her joining us." Dawn squeezed Sanjay's hand.

"No. Of course not." He decided not to quibble about Sophie's being there. "You both must be hungry. Let's get a table."

Sophie returned Sanjay's friendly smile. Dawn was happy to see them warming to each other. She figured it was worth taking a chance on irritating Sanjay by bringing Sophie along. She knew how to make up for it later. Sophie was recouping from a nasty break-up with her long-term boyfriend. Though she was making plenty of money as an escort, courtesy of Dawn's introducing her to Tom, Dawn knew Sophie was curious about Sanjay. And the girl always jumped at the chance for a free meal.

"So where will you find work once you complete your studies?" Sanjay, who was pouring Sophie a glass of pricey Pinot Noir, wondered why Dawn had brought her along.

"At a hospital, assisting dieticians and kitchen staff in planning nutritious meals."

Sanjay was impressed. "I like dieticians. They're always lean and in shape. To set an example to others, I suppose?" Sophie nodded. He appraised her slender form. "I consult a dietician myself when I'm training hard getting ready for a race."

"He's a Vegan, you know."

Dawn glanced at Sophie, hinting she wanted to score points with Sanjay. He caught the look but didn't get the message. Sophie did.

"You're in great shape, Dr. Kaul."

"Thank you, I like to keep my fat composition low. Right now it's at about 7%."

"Wow, that's really low, maybe too low, Dr. Kaul, don't you think?"

"Please, call me Sanjay."

Dawn was pleased.

Good. They're getting along.

She gave Sophie an approving smile, took another sip of the wine and gazed at Sanjay. "This is awesome stuff."

"It's from Bordeaux, exquisitely aged." He clinked glasses with Dawn. "And by the way, excellent choice. This restaurant is fabulous."

"Award-winning décor and relaxing atmosphere. That's what they say in the ads. It's all good." She signaled Sophie by standing up. "Will you excuse us?"

"Of course." Sanjay rose and watched the sway of Dawn's hips as the two young women retreated out of sight.

Sophie came back alone and sat down opposite Sanjay. He glanced in the direction from which she had come. Noticing his concerned expression, she smiled. "Don't worry, she'll be right back." She studied his face. "You're just as handsome as Dawn told me you were."

"No, I'm not. But thank you for the compliment."

"Seriously, you are." She paused. "Dawn thinks she's falling in love with you, you know."

As pleased as he was to hear this, Sanjay felt an uncomfortable heat spreading to his cheeks. "Let's change the subject."

"What subject?" Dawn arrived and slid in her chair.

"Books." Sanjay exchanged glances with Sophie. "I'm curious about what you're reading, Dawn. I know how you love fiction, as I do."

"Yes, just like you." They grinned at each other. "Right now it's 'The Alchemist' by Paulo Coelho."

"Ah, mysticism, mystery, spirituality. Good choice." He beamed at her in approval. "I just finished reading it. What did you like best?"

"The way he writes prose, it's beautiful. And his message excites me."

Sophie interrupted, confused. "I never heard of it. What's it about?"

Dawn's eyes sparkled. "It's the magical story of a shepherd boy, Santiago, from Andalusia, who—"

"Anda... lusia?" Sophie frowned. "Where's that?"

"In Southern Spain." Dawn continued where she had left off. "He's just dying to travel and look for the most valuable treasure ever found, so he journeys to the market of Tangiers. That's in Algeria, in Northern Africa. And into the Egyptian desert, where he meets the Alchemist." Dawn turned to Sanjay. "Remember that scene where Santiago meets the King of Salem, and the King gives him that sermon on destiny. You know, what you've always wanted to accomplish, ever since you were young?"

Sanjay nodded. "Yes. When you really want something, you have the power to achieve it, as long as it has its roots in the soul of the universe. That 'something' is your mission here on earth. People's happiness, sorrows, envy and jealousy nurture this world. When you truly desire something, the entire universe makes a plan to help you bring it about." He paused, capturing Dawn's radiant face in his gaze. "But I always like to add my own message to this one."

"And that is?"

"'If I like something, I go all the way.'"

Dawn reached over and enveloped his hand in hers. "I like the way you put that."

Sanjay thought of another saying. "'Every person on earth plays a central role in the history of the world. And normally, he doesn't know it.'" The sudden realization of the quote's deeper meaning came to him. He leapt up, leaned over Dawn and kissed her on the cheek, not caring about the stares coming from the patrons at adjoining tables. "Isn't she beautiful, Sophie?"

"Yes, she is." Sophie beamed. "And very special."

"Like little Santiago, I am always dreaming, always fantasizing. Chasing my dreams and fantasies." Sanjay gazed at Dawn.

"Me, too." She returned the kiss. "So, Sanjay, did I tell you Sophie is getting over a nasty break-up?"

"Yes, my angel, you did."

"Well... Do you have any friends for her?"

"'Friends?'"

"Yeah. I mean, you must know some guys at the hospital, right?" Sophie blushed in response to Dawn's knowing wink.

Sanjay thought of George, the only friend he could confide in. "Well, just one, actually."

"One is all we need. Maybe you could fix him up with Sophie." She squeezed Sanjay's elbow in a place she knew was sensitive. "What do you think?"

He considered her request. Sophie was bright and attractive, just George's type. "I suppose so."

"What about it, Sophie?" Dawn looked over to see her friend still blushing.

"Well . . ." She turned towards Sanjay. "Only if he's just like you."

Dawn saw it was Sanjay's turn to blush. "Will you talk to him about her?"

"Yes, darling, I will."

"Awesome." Dawn's eyes sparkled. "First he could fly here so they can meet. Then if it goes well, as I'm sure it will, we can plan a trip for the four of us. Maybe Paris?" She turned her baby blues on Sanjay. "I've been wanting to get back to the Louvre for so long. It's my favorite."

Sanjay hesitated. "I'll think about it, Dawn."

The two young women squealed and joined hands in delight. Sanjay sighed, wondering what he was getting into.

*

While Sanjay paid the bill, Dawn accompanied Sophie to the entrance to wait for Tom to pick Sophie up. Watching for him from the window, the two women whispered to each other.

"Who's your client tonight?" Dawn was always curious about Sophie's activities.

"That gangster guy, Mario."

"Oh, right. I know him. Intimately." She winked at Sophie.

Sophie leaned closer to Dawn, her expression concerned. "Dawn, you don't mind if I give you some advice?" She half-turned her head in Sanjay's direction.

Dawn nodded. "I know what you're going to say, Sophie and—"

Sophie interrupted her. "It's a bad idea to fall for a client. I just wanted to remind you."

"You don't need to worry. Everything's under control."

"You sure?" Seeing Sanjay coming their way, Sophie frowned. "If you let him get too close, it can lead to trouble."

"As long as you don't say anything to Tom, I'm covered. Okay?"

They ceased their conversation when Sanjay sauntered up to them, took Dawn's arm and smiled at Sophie. "Good night. Pleasure meeting you."

"The pleasure was all mine." Sophie caught Dawn's gaze.

Dawn shrugged off Sophie's look and hugged her friend. With a carefree toss of her head, she leaned closer into Sanjay and followed him outside to Sherbrooke, on the edge of the Golden Square Mile, where, at the turn of the 20th century, a few hundred families controlled 70% of Canada's wealth. They strolled by the Musée de Beaux Arts and the upscale galleries, gift shops and antique stores. This time, Dawn had been the one to suggest a brisk walk in the chill night air. This time, the cold didn't bother her. She was intoxicated. And it wasn't just the wine.

21

Dawn and Sanjay walked hand in hand down rue Ste. Catherine, keeping a tight hold on each other. Despite the late hour, the street was alive with activity. The clubs and restaurants were bursting with patrons, all eager to enjoy their evening on the avenue whose nightlife never ceased. Boisterous music throbbed from within two adjacent strip clubs. In front of each of them, attractive young women tried to entice all potential comers.

Dawn pointed out Club Supersexe to Sanjay. "I used to strip there."

Taken aback, Sanjay glanced at the flashing lights of the club's second floor. Was there no end to the surprises this young woman had in store?

"Oh? What was that like?"

"Why don't we go inside so you can see for yourself?"

Sanjay hesitated. "I make a habit of avoiding such places."

"Oh, come on, it's not so bad." She challenged him with a bat of her eyelashes.

"Okay. I suppose it wouldn't hurt."

After they had wound through the crowds three-deep with patrons, Dawn and Sanjay found a corner table from which they could survey the scene. He was uncomfortable, as much from Dawn's apparent ease at fitting into the atmosphere as from his unease at being there.

"I love dancing. It's a lot of fun, and the money is good." Dawn swayed to the music, her shoulders dipping in a provocative "stripper" motion.

"How do they pay you?" Sanjay shouted to be heard above the din. "For dancing on the stage, or for lap dances?"

"They don't pay you for dancing and stripping on center stage. You pay them."

Sanjay was astonished. "What? Paying them for the 'privilege'?"

"You make your money by the table dancing or lap dancing. You can make even more money by selling sex, thought most customers don't know about that."

"Really?"

"Not all dancers do it, but most will. All the customer has to do is tip the Bouncer. The club doesn't take a cut. They make their money from drinks and cover charges." She thought for a moment. "The sex is risky, though. You can get busted."

"Why did you stop?"

"Dancing all night is hard work, trust me. Plus someone you know might show up."

"I've talked to colleagues who have been to these kinds of places. They say it costs $20 for each lap dance. That's $100 for five. And if you touch the girl, when it's allowed, and she rubs you somewhere . . ." He glanced down at his crotch. "It's extra. All those dollars add up."

Dawn glanced at the stage. "The girls earn every penny, believe me."

Sanjay slapped a few bills on the table. "Shall we go?"

"Sure." She tore her eyes away from the gyrating dancer. "Let's get out of here."

*

They walked back to the hotel at a brisk pace, cuddling close to keep warm. Sanjay gazed at her shivering form.

"Would you like a massage when we get back?"

"Oh, I'd love it. But I'm sure the spa is closed at this hour."

"No, I mean, I could give you one."

She stared at him in disbelief. "You know how to do that?"

"Many of us in India study the art of massage." He narrowed his eyes. "In my case, Tantric massage."

"Tan . . . tric?"

"Erotic. It's called '*Yoni*' massage. It's about giving, and getting, pleasure."

Her eyes lit up. "Sounds like a win-win to me."

"'*Yoni*' means 'vagina' in Sanskrit. Loosely translated it means, 'sacred space' or 'sacred temple.'"

"Whatever. Let's do it."

When they reached Sanjay's room, he put Peter Gabriel's "Passion" on the CD player and began to undress Dawn, kissing her softly to make her feel comfortable.

"Lie face down on the bed."

She obeyed. Sanjay placed a soft pillow under her head and another under her stomach. He began by resting his hands on her upper and lower back and stroking her back, buttocks, legs and feet, keeping contact with her yielding flesh. He took his time, massaging with a steady rhythm and sensitive touch.

"The purpose of the Yoni Massage is to create a setting for the woman, the receiver, to relax and enter a state of high arousal and experience great pleasure from her Yoni." As if in response to his description, she let out a blissful sigh. "Her partner, the giver, experiences the joy of being at service and witnessing a special moment."

Proceeding from long gliding strokes to deeper ones, he massaged her aching muscles. "This rejuvenates your muscles with fresh blood and oxygen. Do you like it?"

"It's dreamy, Sanjay. I love it."

"The goal of the Yoni massage is simply to pleasure the vagina without worrying about bringing about orgasm, though that can be a welcome side effect. That way, both the giver and receiver can relax."

"Umm, I love the way you touch me."

"Touch is how humans express and communicate their deepest emotions. I've used it in my work, to calm a distressed family member's reaction to distressing news."

Dawn was puzzled. "What? You mean you use Tantric massage on them?"

"No, my angel." He gave a soft chuckle. He loved her naïveté. "Just putting my hand on their shoulder."

Sensing Dawn was beginning to relax, Sanjay stroked the inner folds of her buttocks and thighs with the tips of his fingers. The suppleness of her skin and the sensuous curves of her body aroused him with such intensity he had to remind himself he was the giver and not the receiver. Her moans of pleasure signaled him he had eased any tension she was holding. He turned her over and massaged her chest, breasts, arms and hands. His light touch, brushing her inner thighs and touching the pubic region as he moved down towards her legs, teased her into submission.

She groaned, trying to pull him closer. "Oh my God, this is almost too much."

He smiled. "Good, Dawn, your erotic energy is building. That means it's time to get more explicit."

Knees bent, legs spread apart, Dawn was able to see her genitals and look up at Sanjay at the same time. He sat cross-legged between her legs. "Breathe deeply, and relax."

"How can I? You're turning me on so much I can hardly breathe, let alone relax."

"Just try." He trickled a minute quantity of lubricant on the outer lips of her vagina.

"What's that?"

"Shh, just enjoy." He massaged, stroked and squeezed, his touch intensifying, driving her into a frenzy. He began exploring her inside, varying the depth and speed of his touch.

"Sanjay, I—"

"Relax. Breathe."

He continued to massage her with one hand, stroking her breasts and stomach with the other. Dawn's used and abused body, the one she had sold for the highest negotiable price, responded to Sanjay's loving and caring touch. Overwhelmed with emotions more powerful than she had ever experienced, she began to sob.

"That's it, let it out, my angel. Your sexual and sensual desires have transformed from ordinary and common to divine, leading to *ananda*, heavenly delight."

Unable to control herself any longer, she exploded with orgasms, one after the other, riding the Tantric wave of intense pleasure. After she was spent, Sanjay lifted away his hands with utmost gentleness and let her relish the after-effects. He held and cuddled her for an infinite moment. Neither one spoke, until Dawn sat up and gazed at him.

"I was right about you, Sanjay."

"Right? About what?"

"When we first met, I said you were generous. Now I know you are, but in ways I never imagined."

"It's because I love you. I wouldn't do this for just anyone. I'm satisfied to be a giver."

"Yes. I know." She began stroking his chest. "Now it's my turn."

Slowly, and with the same loving he had shown to her, Dawn made sure Sanjay, her giver of unprecedented pleasure, was a receiver as well.

22

Sanjay had to force himself out of bed at his usual early hour the next morning. The previous night's sex, plus the excessive amounts of liquor he and Dawn had consumed in the process, made him feel groggy and out of sorts. Dawn was picking him up to take him to the airport in a few hours, and the thought of seeing her excited him. But a run on Mont Royal was the only way to circulate some oxygen and refresh his stale body parts. Unlike last time, however, the damp coldness in the air chilled him to the bone. In Winnipeg, frigid air never prevented him, or any other obsessed runner, from training outdoors in winter. It was a "dry cold" there. But here in Montréal, the dampness went right through him, compelling him to give up his run and return to the welcoming warmth of the hotel lobby. Once there, he decided to opt for the health club and had a brisk run on the treadmill. He hated those machines, but with the present weather conditions, they represented his only alternative for speed training. He kept cranking up the speed until he reached twelve miles per hour. A "personal best" for him.

Must be all that oxytocin floating around from last night.

Determined not to be late for Dawn, he cut short both his workout and his cool down. By 10 am he was in the lobby waiting for her. He knew he could depend on her to be prompt, and she didn't disappoint. Her presence lit up the lobby like a full moon illuminating a heady summer night. It was a spiritual experience for Sanjay.

He leaned over and kissed her cheek. "How about some coffee? I need perking up after my hard run on the treadmill." Her perfume intoxicated him. Or maybe it was just the fragrance of her.

In the coffee shop, they sat side-by-side, lost in each other's gaze. Sanjay imagined her eyes, the deep azure color of the crystal-clear Caribbean, as inviting pools he could jump into and never emerge from.

"Shouldn't you be studying for your courses?" He ran his fingers over her thigh.

She lifted his hand from her thigh, raised it to her lips and kissed it. "Well, actually, Sanjay, I was wondering." She hesitated. "I'm behind in my tuition payments. Any chance you could help me out?"

He frowned, puzzled. "But it's already the middle of the academic year. How can you be attending classes without paying?"

"No big deal. They don't care, as long as you pay up before the end of the school semester. Of course, they charge you a 15% administrative fee."

"How much is it? In total?"

"Ah . . ." She squeezed his hand. "$4,500. Plus the fee."

"I'll send you a check for the whole amount when I get back to Winnipeg."

"You will? Oh, you are such a generous man." She held both his hands to her cheek. "I love you."

His heart jumped.

She's never said that to me before.

"You promised to tell me about your childhood, Dawn, how your family got to New Brunswick."

Dawn squirmed. Despite her self-avowal not to reveal any further information about her background, she was tempted to confide in him. His manner was so persuasive.

Maybe he should have been a shrink. He's so good at listening.

And he was genuinely interested in her. Too interested in her. Nonetheless, she gave in.

"Well, if you insist."

He kissed her cheek. "Yes, I do."

"Okay, so this Frenchman, François Guitard, came to the Bay of Chaleur in 1824 to farm and fish. The beaches and dunes were so pretty that he named the place . . . Well, I can't really tell you the name. Anyway, after my father finished med school in the 60s, he decided to move back to our ancestral home and practice there."

"Wait a moment, I lost you. How was this 'nameless' place your ancestral home?"

"Too complicated, Sanjay, I'll explain that some other time. The important thing is, the place was beginning to thrive. The first few years were hard, especially with my two older brothers being born, but Dad was the only MD in the town, and he had plenty of people competing for his services. I came along at the perfect time, of course."

"Of course."

"With the boys, he was still busy with his studies. When my younger sisters arrived, he was taking more work all the time to support all of us. But when I was born, he had time to devote his full attention to me. And he lavished it on me without limit."

Sanjay gazed at her, mesmerized. "And what father in his right mind wouldn't?"

Dawn's expression became wistful. "I was his favorite. I was so attached to him I never wanted to let him out of my sight. The first thing he did when he came home at the end of the day was look for me. He hugged me, kissed me, played games with me. My siblings were all jealous, but he told me not to pay any mind to them, that I was special. He still thinks I am."

"A wise man."

"I loved going camping the most, outside the town where *Papa* grew up. I used to walk along the trails and daydream about being as free as the wild animals there. But when I got older I thought more about coming back there with my own children."

"You'd make a wonderful mother, Dawn."

"You think so?" She gave him a grateful kiss. "My mom was an Anglophone, of Scottish descent. We were raised bilingual. Our homework was in French, so we taught her that and she taught us English. It was truly a beautiful childhood, Sanjay."

"And what was your favorite part?"

"Girl Guides. I made it all the way to Pathfinder. I still remember the 'Promise,' to be true to myself, my God and Canada. Of course, that all changed when I was fourteen."

"Hormones?"

"Yep."

They cuddled close to each other, luxuriating in their body heat. Dawn looked at her watch. "But it's getting late. How about you bag your flight, take a later one?"

"I'd like nothing, better, but I really can't."

She leaned her head on his shoulder. "We could go back to the room."

"I've already checked out."

"Just tell them you left something in there. We don't have to stay long. Just long enough for a quickie."

"Ah, how you tempt me, angel. If I didn't know better, I would say you're in league with the Devil."

She responded with an enigmatic smile. "Nope. I'm not in league with the Devil. I'm an angel. You told me so yourself."

Dawn rose and pulled Sanjay to his feet. Hand in hand, they walked through the lobby. She waited by the elevators as he explained to the clerk that he needed the key back for a few moments to look for something he had left there. Since he was one of their best customers, there was no problem and within minutes they were back in the room.

Sanjay drew back the curtains on the expansive picture window. "I want to see you, every inch of you, to see your pleasure illuminated in the sunlight as we make love."

They undressed with haste, as much from their eagerness for each other as from their limited time. In the bright daylight, her skin, milky white and smooth, was a stark contrast to his.

"I wish my skin was your color." She touched him with extreme gentleness. "I love dark skin."

"I can think of no color more beautiful than yours."

He kissed her eyes, her lips, her neck, and began to explore her with his tongue. But when he came to her thighs, she pushed him away.

"Not there. I have to shower before I let anyone lick me there."

"I don't care. You smell wonderful, no matter what."

Sanjay respected her wishes and didn't persist. He was happy just to be with her in the act of love. He only wished the moment could last forever.

*

On the way to the airport, they were both relaxed from their tryst but overwrought with emotion at having to part. Dawn extracted two cigarettes from her purse, put them in her mouth and lit them both. She offered one to Sanjay. He hesitated for a moment and took it. As they puffed away, Sanjay looked around for an ashtray. Dawn shrugged.

"Just roll down the window and flick the ashes out."

He obeyed, finished the smoke in a few puffs and tossed it out the window. "I've never felt this way about anyone, Dawn."

"No? What about your wife?"

"I love her, of course, in my own way. But my love for you is different. It's a true love, and a powerful one. Like a tsunami that destroys everything in its path." He paused, surprised at the intensity of his own description. "Do you love me, Dawn?"

"Yes. Yes, I'm afraid I do."

The drive to Mirabal Airport felt much too short. They picked a secluded spot to stop the car and fell all over each other with fervent kisses. Sanjay kissed Dawn's eyes over and over, until he realized time had run out. Finally, he wrenched himself away, grabbed his suitcase from the back seat and strode into the terminal, his tears blinding him to the activity around him. Whether tears of joy or sadness, he wasn't sure. He only knew his feelings were more intense than any he had thought himself capable of. The degree of emotion she had awakened in him was exciting and frightening.

When he reached the gate, he felt a sudden pang of remembrance at something she had said to him in the car.

A true friend is someone who reaches for your hand and touches your heart. To the world you may be one person, but to one person you may be the world.

As of the moment he first met Dawn, he may have been just one person in this world, and he probably still was. But there was no doubt in his mind she had become the entire world to him.

January 22

Who knew the ICU could be such a hotbed of sexual intrigue? Most people think of it as a place where critically ill patients are looked after, a serious, somber, gloomy kind of environment. Actually, it's quite the opposite. All this care for dying patients, dealing with life and death on a daily basis, creates an ironically contrary effect on the caregivers. Most of us have a more relaxed, pragmatic outlook on life and death. Just like 'normal' people, we look for fun in our surroundings. Where else would we be able to look for that? And flirtations are a part of that package. Strangely enough, it's the doctors who are the most emotional among us, unlike the nurses, who are more 'in tune' with life in the ICU and life in general. Sure, we have a reputation for being cold and distant. But nothing could be further from the truth.

In any case, George filled me in on the latest hot gossip this morning. I must say I was rather surprised. Well, maybe not surprised, but he caught me off guard. I was still living my daydream of being with Dawn. In fact, I couldn't stop thinking about her. My office window affords me a view of the Forks, where the Assiniboine and Red Rivers join into each other "in eternal love." The rivers flow north into Lake Winnipeg, rather than the usual south. How symbolic of the mystery that is love. So when George sauntered into my office, I was staring out the window, all caught up in thoughts of . . . her. Dawn. Her smoldering lips, her touch, her fragrance, her body, her sweet, enchanting voice. It's been days since I've seen her but I taste her all the time, her rosy scent constantly fills my nostrils.

In any case, George's mischievous smile brought me out of my fog. I could see he was just dying to spew forth some intriguing news.

"Hey, what do you think of the latest?"

"What . . . latest?" *I was still emerging from my fog.*

"The whole hospital is abuzz with the news. Where have you been? Montréal is not exactly another planet."

If only he knew. "So what is it?"

He lowered his voice. "Dr. Goldstein walked into the research office without knocking and got the shock of his life." *He paused for effect.* "Dr. MacDowell and Kendra were getting it on, right there, and all the patients within ear shot next door. Amazing none of them heard the screaming and carrying on."

"Well, now we know the rumors are true."

I have a lot of respect for my boss Dr. MacDowell, head of Critical Care Medicine here. We call him Dr. Big Mac out of love and respect, but I'm not sure he knows his nickname yet. Known as the 'father of Critical Care Medicine' in Canada, he's a respected national figure. A true 'Renaissance man' who has over 300 scientific articles listed in his curriculum vitae, he can come to the ICU, take care of his rounds, make life-altering decisions, and give crystal clear lectures on complexities of human physiology, without breaking a sweat. He also knows as much about fine wines as he does about medicine, though it's rumored his wine cellar can't keep up with his consumption. But only a privileged few know of his weakness for the taste of women's flesh, especially hot young babes like Kendra the recently hired research nurse. And here he was, caught 'in flagrante' with the woman who had taken over all the critical care activities, who struck awe in the hearts of her underlings. Seems the nurse in question is ruling more than her roost with an iron fist.

"Yeah, this whole place is pretty messed up."

In the course of our conversation, I thought about the subject of Sophie and George's meeting. He had gone for the idea in a big way, and we even booked our flights together. But afterwards, I had second thoughts. George had always been a ladykiller. He might steal Dawn away from me. I'm not exaggerating. He's done this to me before, several years ago, over Mandy. I learned my lesson back then. I couldn't take another chance. So at the last-minute, I scheduled him for work on the weekend we were planning to go to Montréal. I am his boss, after all. It's my prerogative. He lost a bundle on his plane ticket. I guess I'll be buying his beers for the foreseeable future. Dawn is going to be furious, too. It's worth it, though. I can't afford to lose sleep over such worries. I'm a jealous man, I admit.

After George left, I found myself thinking about love and sex and how I was just as messed up, if not more, than my ICU colleagues. Humans are born with the urge to mate and the drive to seek romance, both of which cause our dopamine receptors to proliferate. In times of heightened romantic awareness, we lose our desire for sleep or food. That certainly describes my present state, the focusing on the exquisite details of Dawn's delights, the addiction I have opened myself to in loving her.

But I'm also aware of the downside of romance, the inevitable loss of the initial fanatical interest, the realization of possible bad choices. Sometimes I'm quite sure that's what has happened in my marriage. But will it happen with Dawn? Will she break my heart, or I hers?

If so, then seeing romance as a biologically based, drug-like state can at least provide some balm for the situation. "The highs don't last, but neither does the withdrawal," so says the drug addict. With time the craving and pain go away, and the brain, deprived of the neural mechanisms of romantic attraction and still reeling from its chemically induced stupor, returns to normal.

Small consolation indeed.

23

Sanjay, on his way to the Emergency Department with Justin, was preparing to interview a patient he knew well from a previous admission. The woman's repeat episode of respiratory failure was a condition Sanjay knew did not require the services of the ICU. She was not going to be happy about that.

"She remembers you from last time." Justin, as ever, was trying to score points with his personal skills. "Said you were very nice."

"That's what most people say, but they just don't know me." Sanjay chuckled.

An examination revealed what Sanjay suspected, severe chronic obstructive pulmonary disease. Years of smoking had left the patient's lungs riddled with holes, her floppy lungs and collapsed airways allowing for inhaling but not exhaling. Her condition had worsened since the last time, and her excruciating discomfort and breathlessness saddened him. She might live on like this, her every breath a chore, wishing for the final respite of death, for an indefinite amount of time. Respiratory support only served to prolong a life of suffering, shortened as it was by the disease.

Sanjay's thoughts wandered to Dawn, whose excessive smoking worried him. The prospect of her suffering the same fate later in life drove him into a frenzy of anxiety. He shook off his fears and immersed himself into the treating of the problem at hand. If he couldn't restore the patient's pulmonary function, at least he could find some way of giving her relief.

But once his duties were done, he felt restless. He was a fish out of water, a lover without his beloved. He decided he had to talk to Dawn and dialed her number from his office.

"What's the matter, Dawn?" He perceived her nervousness the moment she picked up the phone.

"Nothing." She hesitated, her voice muted. "It's just . . . I can't really talk right now. Someone's here."

"Ah. I see. But I thought you weren't, you know, 'working.'"

"I'm not. It's someone from Opus Dei. We're about to go to a meeting."

Sanjay paused. He still didn't know how he felt about her activities with this bizarre group. "I was just thinking of you at lunch, wondering if you've eaten. Last time we talked you didn't have any groceries at home. Why don't you take my Visa number?"

She lowered her voice to a whisper. "I can't do that, Sanjay. I just can't handle that responsibility."

"Fine, I'll FedEx you the money. Would $2500 be enough to hold you for a while?"

"Yes, yes, that's perfect. But I really have to go."

Sanjay hung up, feeling dissatisfied. He really needed more than a cursory exchange with Dawn. But his concern for her outweighed his frustration. The girl had to eat, and no one else was going to look out for her. Throwing on his coat, he headed out into the frigid air to the FedEx Center on Prospect Avenue.

*

Dawn was not about to reveal to Sanjay that her lack of groceries was due to her vows of obedience as an assistant numerary with Opus Dei. Celibacy was not her thing, but to make up for it she was more than willing to forgo food when necessary. She fasted when it was required, took her coffee without milk or sugar, didn't butter her toast and turned down second helpings at restaurants. That, in her mind, compensated for her weakness for eating dessert, a practice frowned upon by the Brotherhood. No matter. They didn't need to know everything. The other practices, cold showers, disciplines like the *cilice* and the macramé whips, silences after Holy Mass at night, confession, she left for the most devoted members. She counted her sado-masochistic encounters with men like the Judge to be enough corporal mortification. And there was no way she could practice "the heroic minute." It was all she could do to get out of bed in the morning, let alone jump out of bed and kiss the floor first thing upon awakening.

To her mind, her fervent belief in the "Spirit of Opus Dei" qualified her for membership. That counted for a lot. Her recruitment of her colleague from the English Montréal School Board, Chantal Laframboise, fulfilled Dawn's most recent yearly obligation to bring at least one new member to the fold. Sophie was this year's potential candidate.

Dawn didn't reveal the details of her reasons for bringing Sophie to tonight's meeting. Instead, she provided a running commentary, informed by her many years' association with the sect, as they walked along Doctor Penfield Avenue towards the Riverview Meditation Center.

"I already told you about the Founder, right?"

"Uh, that guy called, uh . . . Echevarria?" Sophie tripped over the unfamiliar name.

Dawn corrected her. "No, that's the current prelate's name. The Founder was Escriva. Josemaria Escriva de Balaguer. He was canonized thirty years ago, too."

Sophie whistled. "Gee, how do you remember all that, let alone pronounce it?"

Dawn ignored her cohort's ineptitude. "It's good to know their aim, too. So you won't be totally lost during the meeting." She paused, looking for some recognition of purpose from Sophie. "'To spread throughout society a profound awareness of the universal call to holiness and apostolate through one's professional work carried out with freedom and personal responsibility.'"

"Okay, Dawn, now I'm really lost." Sophie peered at her. "And, 'holiness through professional work?' How do we handle that?"

Again, Dawn chose to bypass Sophie's natural inquisitiveness. "My professional life is apart from Opus Dei."

"Yeah. Right." Sophie suppressed a smile. "Okay, what else? Lay it on me."

Dawn chose not to reveal the celibacy angle, the potential alienation from one's family, and the corporal mortification. "They're always looking for promising recruits to help them with their work."

"That's me, right?" Sophie was exhibiting intelligence beyond what Dawn had expected.

"Right. They're looking for idealistic young people, usually affiliated with Catholic groups from schools. If they like you, then you get to go to Rome and see the Vatican."

"Whoa. I've always wanted to go there."

"And if you're really on their short list, you can become a member. It all happens during Easter Week. Really beautiful. It's like God's calling you."

"Well, what if you don't want to accept their . . . 'calling?'"

"Then . . ." Dawn hesitated for emphasis. "You are on the wrong track and will never receive God's grace."

Sophie grinned. "I'm already on the 'wrong track,' Dawn."

"Be serious, Sophie."

Sophie's expression turned sober. "Tell me more, I'm fascinated."

"Well, I was recruited as a co-operator and have been promoted to assistant numerary. I meditate every day, go to weekly spiritual sessions, eat very lightly. Sometimes I skip meals . . ."

"Ooh, I don't think I could do that."

"You'd be surprised, once you get into the groove. It's all for the greater good."

Dawn watched as Sophie contemplated the beauties of membership. There was no need to reveal the downside of being a member. The fasting, the pain, the invasion of privacy at having one's mail read by the Directors, the sacrifice of one's personal bank accounts.

After all, no one had revealed these to her when she was recruited. She just accepted her calling, like everyone else. With some notable exceptions.

24

After a couple of pages, Sanjay gave up writing in his journal. In spite of the myriad of activities of the day, he felt too distracted by his Dawn-related reveries to keep the pen to paper any longer. He berated himself for being weak. After all, he wanted to write, more than anything. He wished to chronicle the constant race of his emotions, his experiences, his ideas, his daily struggle in the battle between life and death. He wanted to put down on paper his desire to experience the emotional extremes of life, love, joy, sorrow, the fullness of it. And he wanted to live it with the kind of wildness and craziness that Dawn represented. But this time his mind was dried up, and his hand wouldn't take him any further.

Sighing in frustration, he locked away the journal in a cabinet and tossed on his coat. A drink would do him some good.

Norwood Groves, or the "Woods" as its most passionate aficionados called it, was a mere stone's throw from the hospital. Sanjay was unwinding with a beer when George and his fiancée Irene waltzed in. He envied their youth, their energy. They sat down with the older MD, who ordered beers for them.

If I could be with Dawn and be their age, I'd sell my soul.

"Isn't it true, Sanjay?" George's query interrupted Sanjay's contemplation.

"Is what true?"

"That we're getting fewer and fewer weeks of work in the ICU? They are hiring a bunch of Americans. Doesn't it bother you?"

"Yes, of course it does. But there's very little we can do about it."

"There must be something." George sipped his brew with one hand and held Irene's hand in the other. "Man, I love working there. It's what I was trained to do. And the money, well, you know."

"That's why they're phasing us out." Sanjay frowned. "The Winnipeg Free Press didn't do us any favors by publishing those 'ten thousand dollars a week MD' statistics."

"You got that right. If you ask me, we're worth more. Saving people's lives everyday, bringing them back from the dead. We work hard, use all our skills to make sure they survive, and all we get is a measly ten grand?"

Sanjay exchanged ironic smiles with Irene, who was smart enough to stay out of the fray. "Frankly, I enjoy the extra work. I thrive on it, in fact."

"Spoken like a true overachiever, Sanjay."

"You have to understand. I have nothing else but work to look forward to."

George narrowed his eyes, his expression skeptical. "Oh, come on, man, you're not exactly leading the life of Dr. Gene Dell. You have your money, your souped-up Beemer, your . . ." He lowered his voice to a whisper. "Your GFE's."

"You're right. I always live my life on the edge. I'm addicted to that."

"See what I mean?" George tossed down the dregs of his beer and grinned. "Well, thanks for the brewskis. We gotta split."

Irene smiled her thanks and allowed George to pull her out of her seat. Watching them head for the exit, Sanjay mused on the conversation. He had had many addictions in his life. On the mental plane were his medical studies, his work as a doctor, his research. On the physical were food, coffee, exercise, and in the past, even cigarettes and marijuana. His disciplined nature helped him manage all of these and eliminate the harmful cravings. But now he had a new addiction, another human being. This one was more powerful than any of the others, and it made him uneasy.

What did science know about addiction, about the reasons for becoming obsessed with another person? The answer was, there was no answer. All Sanjay's knowledge of hormones, of dopamine and serotonin and their powers to elicit pleasure, did nothing to explain the heartache resulting from obsession and its compulsive needs. Thinking about Dawn, who was unreachable in his daily life—his "real" life—brought more pain than pleasure. Where was the explanation for that?

*

Dawn was feeling bored, an unusual occurrence for her. She had nothing to do. Her schoolwork was up to date, and Sanjay couldn't come to town because of his weekend education lectures. When Mario Materazzi called, she jumped at the chance to fill her empty hours with her favorite pastime without having to give half of her take to Tom.

"Yo, Dawn. You busy tonight?"

"Mario? Hey, how are you?" Dawn was thrilled to hear from him. A night with Mario was always an exciting prospect.

"How 'bout meeting me at Bruno's for some rock n' roll?"

"Oh, yeah? What's the occasion?"

"I just had a major deal go through. I reserved the whole place."

Dawn knew a "major deal" probably meant he had whacked someone and was celebrating. "Congratulations. I'll be there."

"Cool."

Mario's ties to the underworld, not to mention his link to the Hell's Angels group that held the city of Montréal in a tight grip, made any evening with him an exciting event to Dawn. Tall and husky but muscular, he sported a long, flowing beard that Dawn thought gave him an air of mystery and intrigue. When she arrived at the restaurant, Dawn waved to Mario and noticed he was holding court at a well-placed table. His thugs were falling all over themselves trying to light his cigarette. She had never met anyone who exuded such power and inspired such awe in others. Two immense tables in the middle of the room sagged under the weight of copious amounts of steak, chicken, pasta and assorted Italian side dishes. Wine flowed from a fountain at an adjacent table. At almost every other table, black-clad "associates" snorted cocaine.

He motioned at her to join him. "What's your pleasure? Wine? Pot? Coke?"

"Thanks, but I don't do drugs." She displayed a knowing smile. "I do everything else, though."

"You hear that? This chick's the best." His colleagues replicated his broad smile.

Dawn took a puff of his cigarette and bolted down a half-glass of wine. She pulled Mario to the dance floor, where they gyrated to the thumping beat of heavy metal. Despite the sexy appeal of her sinewy dance movements, no other guy asked her to dance. They wouldn't dare. Mario, drunk and drugged, was lost in the music. Or so Dawn thought, until his phone rang. At that point, he made a one hundred-eighty degree turn, barking orders at an underling. A moment later, he answered again, this time playing the role of yes-man to a boss.

The many facets of Mario's character fascinated Dawn. While he was on the phone she made sure to drink plenty of liquids, for she knew what he wanted from her later, thought it wasn't easy to resist the urge to run to the restroom. When he had hung up for the third time, he trained his gaze on her. She knew what that meant. Mario had plenty of other girls for sex. What he wanted from Dawn was company. And a "golden shower."

"Let's go to the back."

Mario led her to a room out of earshot of the music and boisterous shouts and laughs of the main party. Closing the door, he locked it, made sure it was secure and started to get undressed. The dead silence spooked Dawn, but she followed his lead and removed her clothing, watching as he lay down on a large desk in the middle of the room. She climbed on the desk and squatted over him.

His order was familiar. "Okay, babe. You can begin now."

Dawn knew what to do. No kissing, no touching. "I can see you're getting excited, baby."

She made sure the urine flowed where she knew he wanted it, from his face to his chest to his belly, using her considerable skills to make the stream last until Mario reached his climax. It was all she could do to keep her bladder from bursting after all the wine she had consumed, but she held off until after he had paid her the $1200 she had earned that night.

Dawn recognized the happy smile on Mario's face. "Did you have good time, baby?"

"Oh, yeah, baby. It's better to be pissed on than pissed off, right?"

She responded with the expected chuckle. "Better believe it, sweetie."

"*Ciao, mia carissima . . . mio amore.*" "It's better to be pissed on that pissed off."

Relieved to see she had fulfilled Mario's particular desire for pleasure, Dawn collected her due, dressed and raced to the restroom. She sat on the toilet, sighing with relief, counted the bills and contemplated her evening's activities. It wasn't easy, drinking and drinking and not being able to pee for so many hours. But the rewards made the whole thing worthwhile.

Twelve hundred bucks. And no one took a dime of it from me.

Yes. It had been time well spent.

25

As a schoolteacher, Dawn was exemplary. She often quoted Gail Godwin, one of her favorite authors, on the subject.

"Good teaching is one-fourth preparation and three-fourths theatre."

From her first day on the job, Dawn tried to incorporate Godwin's message, along with all the principals she had learned during her training, in her work. She came well prepared for her lessons but also wanted to make math as much fun as possible for her students and establish a rapport with them from the moment they arrived in the classroom. To introduce herself and her approach, Dawn began each new semester by playing a game. She numbered the classroom seats from 1 to 30 and wrote simple math problems, such as "how many bulletin boards are in the room" on strips of colored construction paper, the answers to which corresponded to a seat number. As the children entered the classroom, they drew a strip of paper and seated themselves according to the number of the answer to their problem. The game worked on many levels. It gave the kids a chance to use their previous math skills right away, taught them math could be enjoyable, and most of all showed them Dawn was eager to connect with them.

Except for the inevitable class bully or two, Dawn knew she could expect keen participation from the children, and by the time March fourteenth, or "Pi Day", rolled around each year, most of the students were eating out of her hand. She created a celebration on this day to reward the kids for their efforts and brought in a home-baked apple pie to serve up to the students.

"Mireille, tell me why we celebrate 'Pi Day' on this date."

The freckle-face brunette answered through her mouth full of apple. "The digits of this date correspond with the first three digits of Pi."

"And what are those digits?" Hands shot up in the classroom. "Étienne?"

"Three-point-one-four."

"Excellent. And whose birthday do we celebrate today?"

"Einstein!" The unison shout filled the room.

"Good. Now let's explore the ratio of the circumference of this *tarte aux pommes* to the diameter."

The kids' enjoyment gave her pleasure. She was committed to being the best possible teacher for them, not only in making them feel comfortable with math but in her personal relationships with them. That meant learning their names from the get-go, keeping an information sheet with their parents' names, hobbies, and their own opinion of their strengths and weaknesses, and in the case of ESL students, knowing how much English they spoke. By the end of a school year, the students knew Dawn cared about them. They reciprocated the attention and respect she paid to them and looked up to her as someone who was fair in discipline and grading and didn't talk down to them. Most of all, they shared her passion for mathematics. To her, that was the greatest reward.

"Okay, now let's do our Problem of the Day. Remember, each correct response within the time limit is worth two extra points on your next quiz." She pulled out a box of flash cards from her desk drawer. "Who would like to be first?"

Dawn scanned the waving arms and smiled, knowing she had succeeded in making an impact on their young minds. Only one non-participant in the class. That was a far cry from her first day of school four years before, when she suffered from new-teacher jitters and struggled to make an impression on her charges. She started out determined to be the best teacher in the school, and by the time the first Parent-Teacher conferences rolled around, she was well on her way.

"When parents come in, anything can happen, especially when a child is not progressing academically, or has had discipline problems." As mentor, Mrs. Nelly felt it her responsibility to advise Dawn on how to handle the conferences. "So make sure you plan ahead and have all the materials assembled well in advance."

"Understood, Mrs. Nelly."

"Our conferences can be the first opportunity in an academic year for the parents to take time to focus on their children's education." Mrs. Nelly's tone became more severe. "Tensions may be high, and tempers may flare from their disappointment in their children's grades. So be prepared."

Dawn took her mentor's advice to heart. She gathered her students' work samples, consisting of "best" and "daily" work in a folder, was meticulous about setting up, and made sure to place sign-in and homework info sheets outside the door for easy access to parents. She kept the conference table inside the room bare except for a notebook and pen and arranged the students' texts and grade books nearby. With that, and a quick smoking break behind the school, she felt ready for her first meeting.

"Good morning, Mr. and Mrs. Fournier." Dawn smiled a welcome and got down to business without idle chitchat. "Jean is a delightful child, and I'm anxious to show you how much he's improved in math."

Seeing her approach pleased the couple, she showed them the textbooks, samples of his work and his report card. "He has good work habits. As you can see, he writes well but math is a bit of a weakness for him."

Mrs. Fournier turned to her husband. "*Tu vois? Je t'ai déjà dit.* Didn't I tell you?"

Dawn was quick to respond to the husband's frown. "However, the work with his peer tutor has brought his grade up from a D to a C. He may want something better, but I keep encouraging him to do his best."

This brought a nod of approval from the father. Dawn continued. "But his attendance and promptness have been excellent. And he is a great asset to our class. Did you know he makes sure the plants are pruned and watered?"

Mme. Fournier nodded to her husband as if encouraging his approval. "*Ah, c'est vrai?* Really?"

Dawn nodded back with a smile. She kept careful track of the 15-minute limit, and after handing the parents a list of things to help their son at home, she brought the meeting to a close.

"Thank you again for coming. Please feel free to call me at the school if you have any questions or concerns. You have a lovely child."

Dawn honed her conferencing skills at every opportunity, and each year she polished her performance to a shine. By the end of a conference day, she was ready to reward herself with a beer and a soak in a hot bubble bath, as she did on Pi days. This particular March fourteenth, her most challenging pupil, Étienne, had shown great improvement in math. That was worth celebrating, as was her upcoming Best Teacher award. She had worked hard to fulfill the requirements for that honor, and this year her efforts were to be recognized in a ceremony that was soon to take place.

Only one teacher in each district was eligible for the accolade, and in order to achieve it, a number of requirements had to be fulfilled. Qualities other than classroom teaching were taken into account for the award. These included mentoring students, volunteering in the community, and helping out other members of both humanity and the animal kingdom. She relished the thought of the next morning's event.

I worked hard for it, and I deserve it.

In teaching, as in her night-time activities, she was determined to be the best. As far as she was concerned, she had achieved both.

Sinking back in her tub, Dawn savored another sip of beer, swishing it around her mouth and letting it trickle down her throat. She thought about how her entire being had changed between the time she was about her own students' age and the years when her hormones kicked in and took control. She had always been one of the most beautiful girls in her village and had endured the leers and unwanted physical advances of adolescent males wherever she went. She ignored them without a problem, until two tragedies struck that year. The first was when her brother Julian lost his right hand in a farm accident. The second was her father's transfer to a hospital to Georgia in the US.

Dawn knew Pierre had taken the new position to make up for the notoriously low salaries New Brunswick's paid its physicians, but his absence devastated her nonetheless. She cried herself to sleep most nights, until she started dating to distract herself from her distress. The boys she preferred were older than she, most of them 12th graders. Of these she preferred Marcel, a handsome, dark-skinned Métis of mixed French and Indian heritage, and Jock, a spoiled French boy from Bellesable's richest family. A number of Dawn's friends were having sex on a regular basis. She, however, kept in mind her mother's advice.

"The Church tells us to save your virginity until marriage. I say you should wait until you fall in love, really, truly in love."

Since Dawn wasn't sure what it felt like to be in love, she figured it wasn't yet time to act on her hormonal urges. She didn't realize opportunity played as much a role in a young girl's ultimate deflowering as emotions did. She was more attracted to Marcel than to Jock, but she shied away from physical contact with either of them. Jock, however, was determined to find a way to woo her. Always having money to spare, he began with small gifts of jewelry, and when Dawn started to respond to his demands for affection, he upped the ante with offerings of ever-increasing value. Gradually she felt comfortable enough to ask him for money.

"My class is going to Greece this summer," she confided to him. "My mom doesn't want me to go."

"Are you kidding? Greece is awesome, I mean, the Acropolis alone is worth the trip."

"Yeah, I know. And we're supposed to go to Crete, too. I hear the beaches there are gorgeous." Dawn sighed. "My dad gave me about half the money, $1,000, but I just don't know where I'll get the rest. My allowance is minuscule." She didn't tell Jock she'd spent every penny of her allowance at the mall.

"No problem, I can spring for the rest."

"You can? Oh, Jock, that's fantastic. Thank you."

On Canada Day in 1991, when everyone was expected to attend the annual celebrations and picnics, Dawn faked illness to stay home and be with Jock. She disclosed this secret to her best girlfriends at school. They were excited for her, but she was apprehensive.

"You're a loving person, and such a fun girl. It'll be easy."

"It's the day after your fifteenth birthday. How could it be anything but wonderful?"

"The best first time ever."

Dawn wanted to believe them. "Well, he is sexy and sweet, and a really kind person, too. He's helping me out with my trip, after all. And he says he loves me."

"There, you see? Just relax, it'll be awesome."

After Dawn's family left for the day, she lit a candle in her bedroom and waited nervously for Jock to arrive. As much as she wanted their encounter to be special, Jock was in a hurry. Within minutes, he had coaxed her to the bedroom and out of her clothes. As he kissed her, Dawn tried to imitate the sexy sounds she had heard in love scenes from the movies. It wasn't long before Jock pulled her onto the bed.

"Get on top, Dawn."

Dawn was hesitant. "I . . . I've heard it hurts more in that position, at least the first time."

"Fine." He was irritated. "I'll be on top."

When he started thrusting inside her, though, Dawn realized she'd made a mistake.

"Oh, God, it hurts. I'm not ready. Jock, please . . . please slow down."

He's not listening. I asked him to look into my eyes, but he's just staring at the wall. How could he act this way if he loves me? Oh, this is wrong, so wrong . . . Afterwards, Dawn told herself everything was all right, but she was not convinced. She tried not to think about the fact that she didn't come, that she had felt better masturbating than she did having sex with Jock. With great effort, she made her way to the bathroom, tried to stop the bleeding and waited until the pain subsided a bit. When she came back, she gave him a hug and lay down next to him. He looked at her but didn't smile or show any signs of affection.

"Whatever happens after this, I was the right person to lose your virginity to, you know."

"That's a strange thing to say and so insensitive. What's that supposed to mean, Jock?"

"Nothing. I'm tired." He rolled over, turning his back to her.

"But can't we cuddle? I just want you to love me."

He was asleep before Dawn finished uttering the words. Confused and insecure, Dawn wept silently.

The next day in school, Jock avoided Dawn. He refused to speak to her, her efforts to call him were futile, and he didn't respond to the notes she sent him. Finally she sent him an angry letter.

I guess it's over with us. How could you not even speak to me? I wanted my first time to be special, but instead I feel used."

All she got in return was a note. "It's over and done with. Don't talk to me ever again!"

Oh, God. What have I done?

26

The ringing phone interrupted Dawn's musing. She hesitated, wanting not to disturb the peaceful atmosphere, but decided it might be someone important.

"Hey, D., what's happenin'?" Sophie's lively voice came through loud and clear.

"Just relaxing, Sophie. You off tonight?"

"Yeah. You?"

"Umm." Dawn took another sip of beer. "Big day tomorrow. Psyching myself up for the awards ceremony."

"Oh, right, it's that time already? Awesome."

"Thanks. So what's up?"

"Nothing." Sophie hesitated. "Can I ask you something? It's about work."

"Sure. Shoot."

"Well, I was just wondering. Do you like your work? Our work, I mean."

"Yeah, I do. It's a great adventure, makes me feel special. The clients come from all over, and it's fun to learn about other cultures from them. Plus, they treat me like a princess and shower me with gifts. What's not to like?"

"But don't you feel bad sometimes?" Sophie's disturbed tone of voice was beginning to worry Dawn. "I mean, about selling your body?"

"I'm not selling my body, I'm selling my time, my companionship. Making them happy with my body is just part of the deal." Thoughts of her double life excited Dawn to a point where she felt a familiar warmth and moisture between her legs. Her heart raced. "I sell fantasies."

"I never thought of it that way."

Dawn took another gulp of beer to calm her mental and physical arousal. "I'm gonna write a book about it someday, about my adventures living on the edge."

Sophie giggled. "Yeah? What would you call it?"

"'Dawnsearlylite.'"

"Oh. Cool. But doesn't your, well, double life . . . doesn't it bother you that they don't know at your day job what you're doing after hours?"

"It's none of their business. They'd kill to have lives as interesting as mine. Besides, I work hard. I'm always prepared. I'm there before anyone else. And I get results."

Sophie's silence signaled her contemplation of Dawn's statement.

"I mean, just think of it, Sophie. I can pick my own clients. I've met hundreds of men, all of them in relationships with other women. They sit in their meetings all day long, making deals, get drunk afterwards and go back to their rooms horny as hell. So I give them hot sex, they sleep like babies and go back to the same routine the next day. It's all good."

"What about the ones who want more?"

"You mean the ones who think they're in love? You're not falling for that, are you, Sophie?"

"No, of course not. But you and Sanjay—"

"Forget that. Listen. There are two types of clients, businessmen and lovers. Businessmen treat you like an escort, make sure they get their money's worth. They're tightwads, not emotional at all. All they want is to spread their seed, like they're programmed for, to propagate the human race. Get it?"

"Yeah, that makes sense."

"Whereas the lovers act all affectionate and pretend to fall in love with you. They buy you drinks, take you out for dinner. But eventually they want more. Something their wives or girlfriends can't give them. Those are the ones to be careful of."

"But aren't you . . ." Sophie stumbled over her words, reluctant to criticize her friend. "Are you being a little, I mean, careless?"

"Hey, not to worry. I've been in this business longer than you. Tom, and all the others at the agency, they like me. I've brought them shitloads of business. And honestly, I like the intimacy. And the sex, too."

"You do?"

Dawn couldn't help but chuckle at Sophie's astonishment. Tom too, had been surprised when she confessed her enjoyment to him. "Do you want to know the image I like to sell? My idea of the 'perfect escort?'"

"Sure, it might come in handy."

"Okay, you got it." Dawn drained the last few drops of her beer. "Here's my credo. Look like a model, provide companionship like a girlfriend, screw like a porn star. Give 'em what they pay for and no less. Got that?"

"Wow. Awesome. Thanks, Dawn."

"Anytime."

After Dawn hung up, she smiled to herself. She had neglected to reveal the last and most important detail of her doctrine to Sophie.

Give them more than they bargained for.

That's why they came back to her again and again. Every time she fulfilled their fantasies, she upped the ante and they needed one more time. And then another.

If you want to do it bad, do it good.

No question. She was the best.

Dawn was so relaxed she had to will herself out of the tub. She didn't want to leave the comforting womb of warm, soothing water. Toweling herself off, she thought about her transition from a teenager dependent on her parents' benevolence to a "woman of the world."

*

"But where will you stay in Montréal? You've never lived away from home."

Pierre was dead set against his daughter's leaving the nest for the big city, as was Deanna. "She's still a little girl, Pierre. Why don't we send her to Moncton, or Fredericton? They're closer to home and much smaller cities."

"But I want to go to Montréal, Mom. The University is great, and they have the best teacher education there." Dawn turned her protests to her father's attention. "I want to see the world, *Papa*. And you promised me two years of university. I've saved some money, and I can work my way through the rest."

"Yes, *chérie*, I'm aware of that." Pierre, who knew Dawn had worked hard at her summer jobs all during high school, turned to his wife. "Let her go wherever she likes. I trust her, Deanna. I'll take her there myself."

Since leaving his family behind in Bellesable, Pierre had made the most of the high salaries and low rate of malpractice suits available to him in rural Georgia. Except for the snow and winter temperatures of twenty below, the atmosphere in Statesville was similar to that of New Brunswick. He made sure to find time for frequent visits home. Their family was close-knit, and he was determined to keep it that way.

Dawn regretted having to leave her childhood behind in Bellesable. On some levels, she wished she could always be a little girl, but her excitement about being on her own in Montréal took precedence. The University itself, one of the top French-speaking universities in the world and one of Canada's leaders in research, had been founded as an autonomous Roman Catholic institution. Its setting was lovely, both in its architecture and numerous green spaces, and its academic reputation was exceptional. Dawn looked forward to exploring the nearby Côte des Neiges neighborhood, one of the city's most cosmopolitan and vibrant districts, with its darling boutiques and cafés.

And, oh, the restaurants.

Gaining entrance into the University was no problem for Dawn. She had applied herself at school and her academic achievements were more than adequate for admission. The main difficulty was finding accommodations Pierre deemed "proper" for a young lady of Dawn's age, religious upbringing and social status. Fonteneige, a women's residence operated by Opus Dei within walking distance of the University and not far from downtown Montréal, proved the perfect solution. Only students registered in full-time academic programs leading to a degree were allowed to live there. Reading the brochure sent from Fonteneige, Dawn's eager eyes and mind took in the descriptions of life at the residence.

"'A setting characterized by openness and friendship, rooted in the dignity of personal and Christian values, where a young woman can enhance her academic, cultural and spiritual backgrounds.'" Dawn couldn't hide her excitement in relaying the information to her parents. "There's a library, a computer room with Internet access, a living room with a piano where you can hang out with your friends, a roof terrace with a garden. Oh, *Papa*, it sounds wonderful, doesn't it?"

Pierre tended to share Dawn's enthusiasm, but he wanted to make sure his daughter's spiritual life was covered as well.

"No problem, *Papa*. It says, 'monthly opportunity to reflect on your everyday life in light of basic Christian principles is provided.'"

"And how is that done?"

"Chaplain Garcia is available for the Sacrament of Reconciliation each month, and Father Pedro directs Holy Mass every Sunday. Then there's Meditations to deepen our personal relationship with God, and—"

"*C'est bien, ma petite.* You've convinced me."

"Oh, thank you, *Papa.*" Dawn threw her arms around Pierre and hugged him with affection. "*Merci, merci bien.*"

Unknown to the L'andrys and most of the other students, Fonteneige actually operated as a recruitment center for Opus Dei's ranks. Negative press had affected their conscription numbers, and offering inexpensive accommodations for female students functioned as a perfect setup for swelling the ranks. But as far as the L'andrys were concerned, Dawn and Fonteneige were made for each other. Now that she and her parents had found a place for her to stay that met with their approval, Dawn was ready to take the lively city head-on.

The initial years were difficult. Aside from her academic curriculum, Dawn felt obligated to participate in religious retreats the priests conducted. In addition, there were conferences aimed at expanding students' knowledge of the Catholic faith, Holy Mass to attend, Rosary prayers and individual prayer and reflection. The students were also taken for visits with elderly or ill people who lived in nearby neighborhoods. It was a packed schedule. Dawn, who was excited about being chosen to attend Opus Dei's annual conference to Rome at the end of the school year, began to wonder when she would have a chance to indulge in the legendary social life Montréal had to offer.

No need to worry about that, as it turned out.

Dawn smiled to herself, tossed her towel in the hamper and wrapped up in a soft, cushiony terry robe. Memories were fun, but sleep was more important. Her upcoming award ceremony was only a day away. Looking well rested for that occasion was going to be *de rigueur.*

27

The next escort call Dawn received came as a surprise. She'd been to the Four Seasons Hotel on several occasions, mostly to service single men on business trips who had drunk themselves into near-oblivion after a hard day's work. This time, instead of a client, she was meeting "clients," a young newlywed couple.

Oh well, 'à chacun son goût.'

Dawn had done threesomes before, with Sophie and other girls from the agency. Sex with a woman satisfied her in ways that masturbation never did, though she didn't consider herself a lesbian. She preferred men, but most of the time her encounters with them left her unsatisfied. Her orgasms with women were more frequent and intense. Making love to a woman was like eating Beluga caviar, a treat that rarely presented itself.

When she was at the University, and the strict atmosphere of the Fonteneige sometimes became too much to bear, she and the girls escaped the confines of the school to scuttle across the street to the local dive. Father Garcia, the Opus Dei caretaker of the residence, made sure the rules limiting male visitors to visits only up until eight pm were adhered to. He also monitored the sexual activity at the school, but he had no clue the girls were using the cubicles at the bar to have sex with each other. They kissed, fondled and touched each other in their own playful, adolescent manner, exploring their own and each other's bodies, arousing each other to a frenzied climax. Dawn's sexual experiences with Eun Sun Mah, the South Korean pre-med student, and Chantal Laframboise, who was to become Dawn's schoolteacher colleague, were memorable to the point they spoiled her for any man.

Dawn was especially close with Sophie. They shared their intimate secrets and experiences with each other but didn't consider their relationship that of lovers. Dawn could count on one hand the number of times she made love to Sophie, but if either one of them was feeling depressed, or heartbroken from a break-up with a boyfriend, she sought consolation in the other girl's embrace. That's exactly what happened years later after they had left Fonteneige, when Dawn's long-time boyfriend Olivier left her bereft.

Olivier had moved out of his rundown apartment to live with Dawn in her upscale condo on Avenue Victoria and stayed with her for nearly a year. During that time, she was careful about her moonlighting. Olivier was French Québecois, the same ancestry as Dawn, but two years younger than her and immature. She accepted that. In her experience, most men stayed childish until they were in their 40's. His wildness attracted her, and being with him made her happy.

"I do love you, Olivier." Even then, Dawn had thought twice about risking those words.

"And I love you, baby." She was happy her declaration didn't scare him. "You know you're the only one I ever trusted."

Not wanting to jeopardize their relationship with her night-time activities, Dawn was careful to keep her "work" to a minimum. Olivier had a cushy job with the Province of Québec, but he spent his money on partying and booze, and for all she knew, other women. She hoped her commitment to him would make him mend his wild habits. But after many months, she found herself wanting more. He was the only man she'd ever been with who made her consider marriage. She dreamed of settling down with him, with a comfy home, and a family.

That made his sudden departure all the more difficult for her. In her paranoia, Dawn thought maybe he left because he had found out about her night-time's occupation. She learned later he was a scam artist. He bilked her of her savings, the $5,000 she had earned from months of hard work. He also stole most of her best linens, kitchenware and upscale accessories when he left.

Now Dawn was heartbroken, alone, and out of cash. She knew Jesus would forgive her, but she made sure to seek forgiveness from Father Escriva, her spiritual leader, and from Father José. To expiate her sins, she was glad to accept their discipline and committed herself to fasting one day a week, sleeping on a board from time to time, eliminating sugar from her coffee, and meditating. She saw these directives as helpful in keeping her weight down and firming her body, two ways of counteracting the aging, over-indulgence, and overuse stemming from her work.

Olivier's occasional calls to ask if she wanted to "party" with him put Dawn over the edge. She was determined to get back at him, to teach him a lesson and try to recoup her money. The only way to do that was with a lawsuit, but she knew she couldn't afford to hire a lawyer. With Sophie's encouragement, Dawn filed a case in Small Claims Court. The sole proof she had was a canceled check from Olivier, evidence of their living together. Other than that, it was her word against Olivier's. She knew she had little hope of winning, but the thought of hauling the jerk's ass in front of a judge helped her keep her sanity.

After Olivier's untimely departure, Dawn sublet her second bedroom to a dentistry student to help defray her expenses. She spent much of her time reading *The Alchemist* and *Rich Dad, Poor Dad*, and daydreaming of becoming filthy rich one day. On one of these occasions, she heard the downstairs buzzer and was pleased to find Sophie at the other end of the speaker. Eager for some company and solace, Dawn buzzed in her friend.

Sophie breezed in like a spring wind off the St. Lawrence, clean and sensual. Her black tights and short black tank top emphasized her fresh good looks, and her long dark hair pulled back into a ponytail gave her a youthful appeal that Dawn found a complete turn-on. Still in her p.j.'s, hair unbrushed, no make-up, she wondered what Sophie was thinking of her. Happy to see each other, they hugged with affection.

"I've missed you." Dawn kissed Sophie on the lips. "How did you know you were just what I needed right now?"

"Just a hunch." Sophie returned Dawn's embrace.

Dawn drew Sophie into the bedroom and made sure the door was locked tight. "Let's get comfy."

They wasted no time in undressing each other and assaulting each other with searing kisses. Dawn, the aggressor, shifted Sophie onto the bed and began licking her skin, starting with her neck and moving down towards her breasts. Her gentle touch to Sophie's pubic area elicited a moan of ecstasy.

"Shh, Sophie, my roommate will hear you."

"I don't care."

Sophie moved on top of Dawn and returned the lovemaking with a vengeance, licking and penetrating, until Dawn came to a rippling climax.

"Only a woman knows how to do that to another woman. And so fast." Dawn beamed at Sophie. "Now my turn."

Reaching into the night table drawer, Dawn extracted her silver vibrator and began to pleasure Sophie until she cried out for mercy. Afterwards, they held each other and fell into a deep sleep. Sophie's cell phone ring woke them.

"Tom?" Sophie looked at Dawn, who made motions indicating she didn't want Tom to know the two women were together. "Okay, I'll be there."

Dawn watched her friend dress. "Can we do this again? Soon?" She accepted Sophie's farewell kiss.

Sophie smiled. "You better believe it, babe."

After Sophie ran off, Dawn cozied up to her favorite blanket and let her mind wander. Sex with Sophie was satisfying, but was it more so than with Sanjay?

What would he think if he knew about Sophie and me?

*

Dawn's own phone ring interrupted her reverie. Her first thought was that it was Sanjay. Instead, it turned out to be the man who wanted her to meet him at the Four Seasons. She dressed quickly and arrived at the hotel in record time. '*Quatre Saisons*' was one of the most upscale addresses in the city, and she imagined this job to be one of her most lucrative. Finding the newlywed couple in the penthouse suite came as a pleasant surprise. They were young, in their thirties, and in town for a convention.

The man answered Dawn's knock with a friendly smile and welcomed her inside.

"I'm Jim. This is my wife, Stephanie."

"Dawn." She returned his smile and flashed one to the wife. "What would you like tonight?"

"Here's the deal." Jim motioned Dawn to the sofa, where she made herself comfortable. "Two hours. We'll all have some drinks, a light supper. Then you go to work."

In a corner behind the door, Dawn noticed a table with a white tablecloth and a luscious spread. A bottle of *Jouet Perrier* on ice completed the picture. "And you want me to . . . ?"

Jim looked back and forth from Stephanie to Dawn. "You and Stephanie make love. I'll watch. From the closet."

"Ooh, that's kinky." Dawn glanced at Stephanie, who was checking her out. "But are you sure you don't want to participate?"

"Just pretend I'm not there. I'm happy with that."

"Okay, but no pictures." Dawn was firm. "And no video."

"No, nothing like that. Just a peek." Jim pulled a wad of cash from his wallet. "A thousand bucks. Do we have a deal?"

Dawn shook hands with Jim, and Stephanie poured three glasses of champagne. After they had consumed drinks and the cold salmon supper, Jim retired to the closet. Dawn began by kissing Stephanie and removing her clothing. Soon they were both stretched out on the bed. Despite her protests, Stephanie insisted on pleasuring Dawn, who fantasized Sophie making love to her. As the two women were getting dressed, Jim emerged from the closet. Dawn saw from his face he was a happy camper.

"I don't know if you girls had any fun tonight. But I had the time of my life."

Dawn headed out of the room with ten one-hundred-dollar bills squirreled away in her panties. It was a satisfying result for an evening's work. Good money, and a pleasant surprise to service only one member of a couple. But what astonished her most was finding her mind filled with thoughts of Sanjay.

What would he say about my evening?

In the taxi on the way home, she also mused over what her staid school colleagues would think of her evening's escapades. She thought of the money she had made and reflected on the contrast between her present line of work and her means of earning extra cash during her first years at the University.

Studies were difficult, and Dawn had little in the way of spending money that year, since her parents had given her only enough for her tuition and necessities. She was lonely, too. Her two older brothers had stayed back in Bellesable, but Pierre and Deanna had moved to Georgia with the younger girls. Dawn found the city boys from rich families arrogant and selfish. As far as she could tell, they were interested in sex rather than friendship. She liked sex, but good male friends were more important to her. She wasn't looking for lasting relationships and indulged in some discreet short-term dating. Knowing her parents had delegated Father Pedro to keep an eye on her in that regard kept her from going overboard. But when she started dating Armando, everything changed.

Armando's parents owned Ristorante Da Vinci, a small but pricey restaurant, whose expert Milanese chef attracted well-heeled patrons. Dawn had no trouble becoming intimate with Armando. He was good-looking and intelligent, but most of all his Continental upbringing made him a savvy enough partner to treat Dawn as an equal. After they had been seeing each other for a year, he expressed his concern that Dawn was wasting her energy and time trying to earn extra money working at a fast-food restaurant.

"You're much too good for that, Renée."

"But I have to do something. My parents give me so little spending money."

"I'll talk to my dad about hiring you at Da Vinci."

Dawn was incredulous. "You will? Oh, Armando, that would be so great."

"Are you kidding? It'll be fantastic. The hourly wage is only $8, but on a good weekend you could clear tips of $100 to $150 for the evening shift."

"But how could I ever repay you for such a favor?"

"You won't owe me anything in return, I promise. It's time you earned what you're worth."

He was true to his promise. It wasn't long before Dawn joined the wait staff at Armando's family restaurant. The guests rewarded her pleasant manner and efficiency with generous tips. Soon Dawn found herself with discretionary income. But she worked harder than she had imagined for it. The customers were demanding, and the waitresses had to smile and be polite in their manner no matter what or how much crap the patrons dealt out. Any rudeness or unpleasantness on Dawn's part meant a huge cut in her potential income. She found some of the men receptive to flirting, especially after a few drinks, and she learned how to make a little playful interaction go a long way, both in the amount of tips she garnered and in making the hours pass more quickly. But between long shifts, her aching feet, and keeping up with her studies and religious activities, Dawn felt as if her life was one long treadmill. With her schedule, any social life was out of the question. She had no time to be with Armando anymore. Not that she missed sex. Mostly she wanted to find the "right person" to settle down with. Unlike the other girls at school, who were looking for a Prince Charming, preferably a rich one, Dawn just sought her "Mr. Right."

Someone I can settle down with and have kids. That's all I ask. Is that so much?

Her friends and classmates at home were already married, with a child or two in tow. None of them had ever left Bellesable, and they all seemed content to stay there and raise their families. Dawn, about to turn twenty-four, felt her biological clock ticking. She was ready to find a man and tie the knot. Then she met Marie, and all bets were off.

Despite working only occasional shifts at Da Vinci, Marie somehow appeared to be loaded with extra cash. Dawn couldn't help but notice Marie's nice clothes and expensive jewelry, and even though the two girls were not exactly close friends, Dawn finally worked up the courage to ask her waitressing colleague how she managed it.

"I work as an escort."

Dawn's mouth dropped in astonishment. She wasn't naïve and knew what an escort was, but the information still shocked her. "Oh my God, you're a . . . a hooker?"

"It's not what you think, Dawn. It's actually fun. And the money is great."

Dawn was puzzled. "Then why do you work here? As a waitress? You obviously don't need the money."

Marie lowered her voice. "It gives me a front. You know, a cover. So people won't know about the escorting. No one's suspicious, since everyone knows we get good tips here. Plus as a waitress I have better chances of meeting someone nice and getting married."

"But isn't it dangerous?" Dawn found the thought of Marie's line of work scary.

"Well, you do have to be careful. But if you use your intuition, you're fine."

Dawn contemplated what Marie had told her. "So you lead a double life."

"Yeah." Marie grinned and raised her voice. "So what?"

Dawn agreed, grinning back. "Right. So what?"

Marie's voice returned to a whisper. "So. You interested?"

"I . . . I have to think about it."

"Well, just let me know. I've got this great contact, Tom. He runs a service, Passion Escorts. I'll introduce you."

"Okay."

Dawn never anticipated taking Marie up on her offer. One night, however, after a grueling shift that brought her to her knees, she broke down and called Marie.

"Cool. We can work together, Dawn. I'll tell Tom."

"Are you sure? I mean, do you really think I can do this?"

"No problem. I have a feeling you'll be one of the best of the best in Montréal. You wait and see."

Marie's prediction turned out to be spot on for Dawn. She took to escorting as if born to it, and when she reflected on her new life from time to time she remembered her experience at age five, when she and her father had come across the hookers peddling their wares near the Halifax waterfront. Her sixth sense told the little girl she had unlimited love to offer. She realized now how accurate her hunch had been . . .

Dawn paid the cab driver, entered her building and got in the elevator. She felt the crisp bills in her panties, rubbing up against her pubic hair. It was a tickling feeling, one that didn't bother her in the least. In fact, she was getting used to it.

28

"Welcome, teachers, principals and guests."

Director General Ian White, of the Montréal School Board (MSB), addressed the gathering of dignitaries, school board politicians and bureaucrats who were happy to exert their influence on the teaching communities of the city, along with the other attendees dressed in formal attire who had garnered special invitations to the auditorium of the Laurier School reserved for such events.

Dawn looked around at the crowd of "best teacher" awardees, their beaming principals and their guests. The sparkle of sequins and sheen of rented tuxes filled the immense hall. Dawn herself was happy with her choice of gown, an elegant black column of silk that accentuated her slender form. Her parents Paul and Deanna sat by her side. She felt a warm glow of happiness at their proud smiles. She didn't see them often, but she was always conscious of making an effort to please them.

"This evening represents an important opportunity for MSB commissioners to learn more about the concerns of our teachers and reward the best educators among us, the role models and heroes of our organization." Dawn smiled, knowing he was referring to her. "It's also the occasion for parents, staff, commissioners and some representatives from other boards to come together as one."

Mr. White paused for effect and continued. "The English community of Montréal is getting smaller by the day. But despite any shortfalls in our system or facilities, we have implemented enriched programs that are the envy of some private schools. We do not choose our students. Rather, it is our policy to educate all comers. It is in this spirit of empowerment that we commend tonight's award recipients. These outstanding teachers provide Canada's youth the foundation for lifelong learning, which is vital to our economic and social success."

Dawn watched as The Director General relinquished the podium to Mr. Dryden, chairman of the Board of Commissionaires. Sensing her excitement, her father squeezed her hand.

"With these awards, the School Board recognizes these individuals' excellence in teaching, creativity, innovation, as well as in their daily lives. These teachers shape the future by inspiring, educating and mentoring the children who are the promising wealth of our country."

Dawn daydreamed while the speaker went on as usual about the teacher's role in society and enumerated the criteria for the selection process. She'd heard it all before: fostering the students' intellectual, social, emotional and physical growth; motivating them to exceed their own expectations; working collaboratively with colleagues; demonstrating in-depth knowledge of curriculum; being involved in personal growth activities; contributing to a positive school climate.

Get to the good part already. If it were me, I'd cut to the chase.

*

As an honored guest of Pfizer Pharmaceuticals for a symposium on emergency medicine, Pierre was invited to bring his family along for an all-expense paid trip to Cancun. Dawn was on spring break from the university, and Pierre insisted on bringing her along, despite the protests of Dawn's younger sister Erin, who had hoped for some undivided attention from Pierre.

"You've always gone on trips with Dad. This was supposed to be my trip." Erin glared at her older sister. "What's the matter, don't you have any boyfriends in Montréal?"

Dawn wasn't exactly thrilled to have Erin's bratty behavior to deal with. "I've been working like a dog, both at school and at the restaurant. I deserve a break. Besides, you know I'm Dad's favorite." She wasn't about to confide in Erin about the four boys she was dating at the same time, all of them different nationalities.

"Yeah. So?" Erin bristled at her sister's remark, which had only made her jealousy of Dawn more pointed.

"So, if you wanna meet boys, why don't you lose weight, Erin?"

"At least I don't starve myself."

"Look, let's call a truce, okay? Just make it a fun time for everyone. Deal?"

Erin agreed, though with reluctance. "Okay. Deal."

Soon, courtesy of the drug company, the family winged its way over the azure Atlantic and were treated to a stretch limo ride to the Grand Amelia Cancun, the jewel of the northern Yucatan. The hotel, built to resemble an ancient Mayan temple, greeted the family with deluxe rooms, with ocean view for the parents and lagoon view for the daughters. Dawn, anxious to get to the beach, picked at her lunch, declined a siesta and opted for sun and surf. While her family slept, she changed into her one-piece magenta maillot, studying her sylph-like reflection in the mirror before she took off for the sand. Unhappy with her small but firm breasts, she ached for bigger ones.

When I have enough money, I'm going for implants.

Warm sun, cool breezes and the music of waves crashing on the sand conspired to relax Dawn's soul and dissolve her tension. She chose a spot at the edge of the water and let the soft caress of a breaker massage her toes and feet. A second wave reached the area between her legs to her upper thighs and up to her navel, and a third wet her nipples. The retreating waves, each one higher and more ferocious, left her feeling more aroused. She resisted an urge to reach her hand under her swimsuit and stimulate herself.

Maybe later tonight, when there are no voyeurs lurking about.

The L'andry women showered and changed while Pierre attended a brief welcoming reception for the delegates. Then they all met at the area's finest Mexican restaurant, where bottomless Margaritas and the aroma of Caribbean Bouillabaisse enticed their appetites. Dawn and Erin allowed their parents a romantic moonlight walk on the beach and checked out the local disco bar. The raucous, thumping music had attracted a gaggle of male students from Québec City. Young studs, thrilled to find two attractive girls sitting alone, did their best to entertain them. Dawn and Alain, a tall, good-looking redhead, generated extra heat in the sultry Mexican night, rubbing their bodies together to the tune of "Hot, hot, hot." Unlike Erin, who went off for a moonlight walk with Philippe, Dawn was anxious to get back to her room. As hot as Alain was, she had her own techniques, practiced over years of self-experimentation, to finish what he had started.

*

A day of sightseeing Mayan ruins and indulging in wasteful buffets left Dawn wondering how five million Mexicans could starve each day while any single American tourist ate enough food for three Mexicans at one sitting.

"I hate wasting food," she complained to her father. "One of these tourists can waste what five Mexicans need to stay alive."

"Nothing we can do about that, *ma chérie*. It doesn't mean you shouldn't eat."

"I'm not hungry."

Dawn glanced around and noticed a curly-haired man who looked Middle Eastern staring at her. Unlike most men who ogled her, this one did not turn away when their eyes met. Not content to eyeball her from top to bottom, he got up and approached the L'andry table.

"Allow me to introduce myself. Zobair Ahmad, from Atlanta." Zobair's eyes never left Dawn, even when shaking hands with Pierre.

"What a coincidence, we are from Statesville." Pierre's eyes twinkled. Zobair had a cultured, moneyed look about him. "Dr. Pierre L'andry. This is my wife, Deanna, and my daughter Renée, who is studying in Montréal to become a teacher."

"Our other daughter, Erin, is otherwise engaged," Deanna explained.

"Ah. I understand. A pleasure to meet you all." Zobair took Dawn's hand in his. "Especially you, Renée."

"Would you care to join us?"

Zobair lost no time in accepting Pierre's invitation. Without hesitation, he launched into a discussion about his ethnic background. His Afghan father married an American, and the couple inherited a sizeable estate from his wife's relatives. He was also forthcoming about his prestigious Oxford education. Dawn thought Zobair to be about fifty. Dark hair, tolerable features. What mattered was that he reeked of money. And since she hadn't "worked" for weeks, she already felt the familiar moist, tingly warmth between her legs.

"Business or pleasure?"

Zobair returned Pierre's friendly smile. "A bit of both. I'm here to recruit models for my agency, Atlanta Modeling, Inc."

"Oh?" Now Dawn was fascinated. "What kind of models?"

"All kinds. Magazines, TV, commercials. We do shows in Paris, Milan, Amsterdam and New York."

During drinks, appetizers and entrées, Zobair regaled the L'andrys with stories of his agency, his profitable and expanding business, and his frequent vacations to luxury resorts. When dessert came, he made them an astonishing offer.

"I think Renée shows potential for a modeling career. I'm off to Paris next week. Would you be willing to bring her there for some interviews and auditions?"

"We'll have to think about it." Pierre wanted to accept but didn't want to seem too eager. "You understand."

"Of course." Zobair flashed a gracious smile. "But you wouldn't mind if Renée and I discuss the details of her possible contract?"

"Not at all." Pierre rose and helped Deanna up. "We always take a walk after dinner."

Pierre and Deanna excused themselves and, and in hand, headed towards the beach. Zobair led Dawn to his penthouse suite, where the setting sun illuminated the tasteful furnishings with a burnished glow. He poured two Cognacs, took out his check book from the desk drawer and wrote a check.

"This is your retainer, the standard five thousand dollars. I trust it will be adequate?"

"Thank you, yes. More than generous."

Zobair sipped his drink. Dawn approached him and began to unbutton his shirt. Finishing off his glass, he put it down and led her to the bedroom. She took off her blouse and skirt and, stiletto heels still on, crawled to the center of the bed on her hands and knees. She looked so sexy in her skimpy panties, it was all Zobair could do to keep from jumping her from behind. Standing motionless, he allowed himself a moment to admire her beauty, then undressed and crept onto the bed, running his hands over her buttocks, thighs and breasts, finally lying on his back. Dawn, now an expert from countless escorting experiences, knew exactly what to do. Still on her knees, she moved in between Zobair's legs and kissed his nipples. Then she moved down, kissing his stomach, groin, and penis. Her soft lips and firm tongue worked wonders for Zobair. His body tensed, then relaxed, in quick succession. She had been like a much-needed sleeping pill for him.

"Goodnight, my darling. See you in Paris."

"Goodnight, Zobair."

"No. From now on, you must call me your 'Majnoon.'"

"Goodnight, and thank you, my 'Majnoon.'"

Dawn kissed him goodbye, dressed, and slipped out of the room, the check safe in her purse.

That night, Dawn went to sleep and dreamt of being a super model strutting down the catwalk, ultimate body and fresh features aglow, displaying the energy and attitude of a Petra Němcová.

29

Paris was first-class all the way for the L'andrys, from the royal treatment on Air France to the luxury suite at the Ritz. Dawn glued her eyes on the sights through the limo window. She had heard about the impressive Eiffel Tower, the Arc de Triomphe, the elegant Champs-Elysées, and the Louvre, but seeing them for real made her heart leap. She had second thoughts about ditching her dream of a teaching career after all the obstacles she had overcome thus far. But she was too excited about the new possibilities awaiting her to dwell on what she had left behind.

Over a typical Parisian dinner of escargot and sauced veal, Zobair explained in detail what Dawn was to expect in pursuing modeling. Rather than training, emphasis was on physical attractiveness.

"The agencies will pick girls who have 'the look' that will sell products. That's the bottom line."

Between Zobair's descriptions and her daydreams of photo shoots in Maui, Dawn decided breasts implants were an absolute must.

Maybe Tom will foot the bill.

"I am meeting with some potential clients tomorrow, while you have your photo shoot. A good portfolio is all-important."

Dawn had sudden doubts. "But isn't that expensive? I mean . . . I'm still a student, working part-time in a restaurant. I don't know if I can afford—"

"Don't worry about a thing, I'll be there to help you every step of the way."

Despite his assurances, Dawn felt completely intimidated the next day when she walked into the ballroom filled with the most gorgeous women she had ever seen. The first thing she noticed was that all of them smoked like they were about to be guillotined any moment. Dawn, nervous, opted for the mouth-watering buttered croissants available in every corner of the room. Zobair moved through the crowd like a celebrity, swarmed by young beauties vying for his attention. Nonetheless, his interest focused on Dawn.

"This is our top photographer, Henri, a model's best friend. If he can't make you into an internationally acclaimed model, no one can." He plucked the pastry from Dawn's fingers. "And none of that. You have to starve yourself to make it in this business."

Dawn found the photo shoot tiring and overwhelming. Henri's request for nude photographs startled and confused her. "But I thought I was just going for fashion modeling."

"*Thees* is what Zobair ordered."

Even for Dawn, Henri's thick French accent was difficult to discern. She wasn't about to tell him she spoke French, however. Finally they compromised on Dawn's posing in lingerie and skimpy dresses. The last thing she wanted was her nude body plastered on billboards and magazine covers. She still wanted to be a teacher at some point in the future.

To make up for her frustrating day, Zobair took Dawn back to his room, promising a surprise. Her fatigue and disappointment dissipated when he presented her with a velvet jewel box with two exquisite pearl earrings nestled inside.

"None of this cheap jewelry. From now on, my dearest, you will be wearing pearls, diamonds and platinum—and nothing else."

"Oh, Zobair, you are so generous."

"And I'll get you a matching ring when we come home."

She wasn't sure if her passionate lovemaking resulted from love or gratitude, but it didn't matter. She enjoyed the intimacy, and calling him 'Majnoon' did wonders for both of them. As they both fell into a contented slumber, she resolved to make Zobair proud of her. She had learned enough about his tastes to realize he was only interested in the best of everything.

A phone call from Pierre awakened them. "Yes, Dr. L'andry, she is here. We were discussing tomorrow's auditions. We'll join you shortly."

Dawn felt guilty about not spending more time with her parents, but they were more than understanding about her need to learn as much as possible about her new career in a short period of time. However, sleep did not come to her that night. Worries besieged her instead.

What if they don't choose me? . . . No, Zobair will make sure I get in. Worst-case scenario, I can go back to school, graduate and find a job. It's all good.

Dawn joined the ranks of smokers in the ballroom the next morning, as they all waited for agency execs to call them in for the verdicts on their portfolios and interviews. When Dawn's turn came, she strode with confidence into the office, with no other thoughts in mind except to be hired. Her self-assurance took an immediate plunge.

"Your profile looks good but we don't have a contract for you right now. If something comes up in the future, we'll get in touch."

Crushed, Dawn fought back tears. "Does . . . does Mr. Ahmad know about this?"

"Yes, he does. He'll speak to you later."

Swallowing her disappointment, Dawn walked out of the office, oblivious to the beautiful faces staring at her, and went straight to the lobby lounge. After downing two champagnes and starting on a glass of Bordeaux, she spied Zobair coming towards her.

"My darling, you did so well for a first try."

"Thanks, I appreciate your effort to boost me up, but—"

He interrupted her with a kiss. "I have a confession to make. I don't want you to be a model."

Dawn was incredulous. "What? But the trip to Paris, all the preparation. Why?"

"I planned all this so we could become closer, my dear. You see . . . I want children, a beautiful home, a nice life, with the right person. I want you to be my wife."

"I don't know what to say."

Zobair drew her close. "Just say yes."

She gave in to his embrace, ecstatic but overwhelmed with doubt.

Could he the one? Would she be forced to convert to Islam? Would they require her to wear top-to-toe airless burka? Would I become so repellently sexual that as a Muslim woman I would be relegated to a sullying object too disgusting to be seen in public? What would happen to her own religious beliefs? And my Papa? All Papa wants is for me to be happy and well provided for. But how would he handle a son-in-law who is so foreign? How would rest of the family in New Brunswick relate to an Afghan after ghastly events of 9/11?

Zobair cut short her thoughts by pulling a page from the Real Estate section of the Montréal newspaper from his breast pocket. "And here is your engagement present." He opened the paper and pointed out a sparkling-new condo listing in an upscale neighborhood. "I've already taken care of the paperwork. The deed has been transferred to your name."

"Oh, Zobair, is it true?" She threw her arms around him. "I love you!"

"Of course, I would like you to move to Atlanta to finish your studies. We have a an elite, women's only college there—"

"Why don't you come to Montréal while I finish my degree? Then I could move after I graduate."

He gave her a disapproving look. She backed down.

"Well then, yes. Yes, of course, my Majnoon. Whatever you say."

She covered him with kisses. He smiled, accepting them.

*

After she had moved in to her new condo, Zobair told Dawn he wanted to take her on a whirlwind trip to Vegas and the MGM Grand. She imagined his plan was to wine and dine her in a luxurious setting to firm up their commitment. She was right. Once immersed in the glamour and excitement of the sophisticated shows, the gourmet, the hip nightclubs, the wonders of the African Lion Habitat, and the lavish accommodations of the Sky lofts, a luxury Boutique Hotel located on the top of the Grand, Dawn was sure she would say yes to anything. Within reason.

They arrived from their respective airports and met at Shibuya, the apotheosis of elegant Japanese dining, at the Grand. After an exquisite lunch of the most delicious miso soup, sushi and tempura Dawn had ever tasted, an entourage of waiters escorted her and Zobair to their lavish suite. Once ensconced there, Dawn felt like she was in heaven. The luxury surrounding them took her breath away.

Thank you, Lord, for answering my prayers.

For Zobair, the impeccable suite was the perfect place to discuss his marriage plans with Dawn. He was looking for ideal atmosphere in which to place a three-karat diamond on Dawn's slender finger. He had gotten tickets for *La Femme* that night, and planned an intimate dinner at The Mansion afterwards. Zobair also promised her a facial at the Grand Spa.

After she had taken in her plush accommodations, Zobair insisted on giving her $3,000 to shop at the exclusive boutiques at the hotel. Instead, she felt drawn to the Lions' Habitat. The King of Beasts had always fascinated her, and she wanted to get a close-up look at the noble creature. But within the see-through passageway, with the animals virtually inches above or below her, Dawn saw the lions were still captives, held against their will. She realized she, too, would be in captivity, under his control all her life, if she married him. Discomforting thoughts assaulted her brain.

He wants me to live in Atlanta and go to a girls' school so I wouldn't be around guys . . . That's the sign of a possessive person . . . He tricked me into thinking I could become a model . . . Do I want someone to own me? I want to be free, to be wild again. To be my own self.

She chased all such thoughts from her mind, however, when she looked at the time and knew she would be late for her spa appointment. Rushing away from the scene of her near-epiphany, she sprinted through the vast hallways and arrived, panting, at the salon, where the staff gave her the kind of treatment she had always wanted.

*

Dawn and Zobair both relished every moment of *La Femme*, which combined light effects, film, and projections to create dramatic effects, some subtle, some humorous and all sensual. Since they had a small window of time before their Mansion reservation, Zobair suggested a small diversion.

"Tonight we will celebrate. At the Grand Casino. You'll love it. It's my favorite of all Casinos in the world."

Again, Zobair was true to his word. Dawn tried not to stare at the luxurious arrival hall, with its plush carpeting and red velvet draperies, the crystal chandeliers of the main hall, the resplendent flower arrangements in the chambers outside the gaming rooms.

Zobair led her to the main gaming hall and ensconced her next to him at the Blackjack table. "I always set a limit for myself, no more than $50,000 at a sitting."

Dawn gasped. "Fifty-thousand!"

"But tonight I might bet more." He squeezed her tightly to quell her fears. "Don't worry, Fate is on my side tonight. As long as I have you by my side."

Dawn felt a sudden unease. She had not been aware of his trait of Zobair's, and the thought of having a husband with a gambling habit worried her. This night, to her disbelief, he was on a roll. He warmed up with hundred-dollar chips, easily traded those for thousand-dollar ones, then ten thousand-dollar chips. He won hand after hand. Soon the game became a back-and-forth battle between him and the dealer, with stakes so high no one else dared to do anything but stand back and watch.

Dawn's heart was in her stomach. "Please, Zobair, you're so far ahead of the game. Can't you stop now?"

Zobair, dead set on winning the entire house, ignored her. With $300,000 worth of chips in hand, winning by $100,000, and a 3-karat diamond in his pocket that he planned to slip onto Dawn's finger after the game, he went for broke. He didn't notice the Manager's arrival at the table, but Dawn did. It was a bad sign.

"Zobair, please, let's just go. Please, Majnoon."

He refused to listen and placed all his chips on the table. It came down to either he or the dealer getting an Ace. He planned to double his bet if the dealer did not. "Ooh's" and "aah's" from the crowd heightened Dawn's worries and almost made Zobair's heart stop. As if out of nowhere, an Ace of Hearts appeared on the dealer's side of the table.

"Three hundred thousand to the Bank."

The dealer pulled in all the chips. Dawn rose and fled from of the room. Thoughts cascaded through her head, the remembrances of previous conversations she had thought of when she was in the Lions' Habitat.

Zobair caught up with her and took her arm. She wheeled around to face him.

"$300,000? You lost all that?" Her voice escalated in volume. "You're a compulsive gambler, and you didn't even tell me."

"Shh, my darling, people will hear you."

"I don't care. My God, what am I doing here?"

"It's only money. I'll win it back another time."

"That's what all addicts say. They just keep at it, over and over. It never stops."

Her nagging tone angered Zobair. "It's my money. It's not for you to tell me what to do with it."

"You're right, it's not. Now that we're over."

She pulled her arm away and strode towards the door and into the main hall.

He ran after her. "What do you mean, 'we're over?'"

"You heard me. I'm out of here. I'm going back to Montréal."

Dawn looked at him, hoping for a sign he would relent, or at least say something, anything, as a response. He remained silent, fingering the diamond ring in his pocket. She turned, walked through the French doors into the warm evening air, and asked the Concierge to hail a taxi. Whatever happened next, she knew her "real" life awaited her back home in Canada.

Yes. I will be free. And I'll still be a rich woman. Someday.

30

"Today, we honor the youngest teacher to receive this award. Renée L'andry."

At the moment her name was finally called, Dawn felt her phone vibrate. She was incensed.

Who the hell could be calling me at a time like this?

Ignoring it, Dawn made her way to the stage, where she accepted a certificate and commemorative gold pin from Mr. Dryden. She acknowledged her parents' smiles of delight as she crossed the stage and returned to her seat. She accompanied them to the gym, where the Board had spared no expense in presenting a lavish spread of champagne and hors d'oeuvres. She introduced her parents to her colleagues and the board members and circulated among the crowd, her head held high, her face glowing with pride and gratification. Then she excused herself to take her call.

"Do you want to work tonight?"

Dawn snapped at Tom, speaking under her breath to minimize the echo in the women's restroom. "No. I'm busy. An important event."

He softened his tone to a persuasive murmur. "The Judge wants you."

"Read my lips through the fiber optics, Tom. No." She paused to restrain her fury. "My parents are here, for God's sake, all the way from Statesville. I have a life, you know."

Tom's voice turned sheepish. "Yeah, you're right. I guess."

"No more calls, okay? I'll let you know when I'm available."

"Right. Have a nice evening."

She could tell he was pissed, but she didn't care. She clicked off and headed back to the party. The phone vibrated again.

"Who is it?" Her anger subsided as soon as she heard the voice. "Oh, sorry, I didn't know it was you, Sanjay."

"Is everything okay, Dawn?"

"Yeah. Sure. How are you?"

"Fine, I'm fine. I hope I'm not disturbing you."

"Of course not. What's up?"

I'm coming there next weekend. I know it's short notice, but . . ." He hesitated. "Well, can we get together?"

Dawn thought for a moment. Her parents were staying through Friday. "I can see you on Saturday and Sunday."

The happy relief in his voice broadcast through the phone wire like a trumpet fanfare. "Oh. Wonderful. Of course I'd like to see you before then, but if you can't . . ." He paused, hoping she would reconsider. She didn't say a word. "Meet me at the Delta Centreville at 11 am on Saturday. I'll skip my last meeting, and we can be together."

"Sure. Same arrangement as before, one thousand per day, right?"

"Yes, my angel. And expect a gift. An expensive one."

"Ah, you know me too well, Sanjay."

"No such thing, my darling. Till then. I can't wait to see you."

"Me, too."

She hung up the phone and cursed under her breath. Two phone calls on an evening when she wanted to savor her moment in the limelight, be the center of attraction. It sucked.

Oh well, at least one of them was nice.

Glad to escape the confines of the bathroom, Dawn hurried back to the gym. She still had time to enjoy her much-deserved special evening. She could hear an Acadian folk song blasting through the speakers as she approached the celebration. Despite the serious nature of the ditty's lyrics, its lilting phrases and upbeat rhythms reflected her cheery mood. There was a lot to be happy about.

*

Dawn and Sanjay's tryst lasted all day, from late morning until dinnertime. The more he had of her, the more he wanted. Her credo in action.

She had always wondered why *Les Caprices de Nicholas* was such an expensive restaurant. Maybe it was the food and wine. Certainly not the décor, which was mediocre for a high-end establishment. Not that she didn't feel comfortable in the Garden Room, where she had been numerous times before.

"Maybe you can tell me why this place is so pricey, Sanjay."

"I don't know." He checked out their surroundings, the small windows, the worn floors. "It definitely doesn't look the part. Average at best. Yet it has a reputation as one of the best in the city. What do you think?"

"I've heard it's the waiters. If they're young men, the restaurant is moderately expensive. If they're middle-aged, the place is very expensive. And if they're women, the place is more or less irrelevant."

"Hmm. I've never thought of it that way." Sanjay took another look around. "If the food and wine are as good as the waiters are ugly, I'm willing to put up with that."

Dawn giggled and extracted a cigarette from her purse. "You're funny, Sanjay. I like that in a man."

Noting his pleased expression, she lit the cigarette. She wondered what he would say if she told him about her previous weekend's exploits as an escort. She suspected he'd be annoyed. Sanjay was paying all her expenses in exchange for her promise to stop working for Tom, whom he perceived as a glorified pimp who sold Dawn to ugly, horny men. She had fulfilled her end of that bargain. But how to explain her addiction for the thrill of that line of work?

"While you were away, I . . . I worked."

Sanjay's eyes narrowed. "What do you mean? You promised me—"

"Oh, it's not for Tom. I'm on my own."

"I don't understand. I'm covering your expenses, you don't need to work. Even on your own."

"I know, but, well, you get addicted to it. I'm trying to stop, really I am, but it's not easy."

His disgruntled expression made her wonder if she should have said anything. It was too late now, so she plunged ahead. "You're a doctor. You must understand cravings."

"Yes, I do, but this is different."

"No, Sanjay, it's not. Just like men get addicted to hookers, we get addicted to you guys."

"But that doesn't make sense. I thought you . . . they . . . did it for money."

"It starts out that way, but over time you meet different people, you start to like it. And before you know it, you're hooked."

Sanjay was both distressed and fascinated. "Tell me more."

Dawn tried to gather her thoughts. She wasn't sure how to describe her behavior to Sanjay without offending him. "It's this excitement that starts with the call from Tom, then I get this adrenaline rush when I'm walking down the corridor and my pulse quickens when I knock on the door. I never know who's going to be there. Sex with a stranger, money, excitement. All highly addictive."

"I never knew hookers thought that way."

"Well, what did you think? That we're emotionless robots who lie down on your bed, spread our legs and just let you have at it?" She watched his face for a reaction. "We're not lifeless mannequins, we're human beings with feelings. FYI, most of us enjoy what we do. Why wouldn't we?"

Sanjay was flabbergasted. Dawn was right. In spite of his vast experience with escorts, hookers and GFE's, he did tend to think of prostitutes as professional women who functioned only to put out the fire in men's loins. If Dawn hadn't enlightened him with her point of view, he would still think of them as objects. Now that he was in love with one, his viewpoint had changed, and he saw her in a different light.

"Thank you for being honest with me." He grasped her hand and squeezed it. "My angel."

Dawn snatched her hand away. "I've already told you, Sanjay, I'm not an angel. I'm dangerous, like a fire. If you kept my hand there, it would burn you."

He took back her hand. "I love to play with fire. And I love danger."

"Be careful, then. Fire destroys all it touches."

"Dawn . . ." He hesitated, worried about upsetting her, but decided to continue. "What would your father think if he knew about your . . . 'work'?"

She glared at him, suspicious. "Why are you asking me that?"

"I don't know why. It just suddenly occurred to me." He squirmed in his seat, uncomfortable. "You don't have to respond."

Dawn thought for a long moment. "He'd be devastated. He loves me most of all his children, you know."

"Of course he does. How not?"

"And it would cause him such pain to know about me, my real life. I can't imagine what he'd go through." She was silent for another minute. "If he ever found out, I'd kill myself."

"Come now, aren't you exaggerating a bit?"

"Sanjay, you don't know how much I love him. I couldn't bear to see him suffer the way he would if he found out. I'd rather die."

Despite the enticing look of the specially prepared Vegan dish their "middle-aged" waiter brought and set on the table, Sanjay just pushed it around on his plate. Finally he took small bites and washed them down with wine, holding her gaze as he did so.

Her mind wandered. A feeling of dread overcame the tender feelings rushing through her veins. Something wasn't right. She shuddered.

Is he going to betray me? Oh, God, what have I done?

"You wouldn't do that to me."

"Do what, my darling?"

"Never mind."

She couldn't tell him what was gnawing at her consciousness, terrifying fantasies that he would ultimately destroy her once he knew more about the sordid side of her life. She had already opened up to him far too much, shared too many secrets. That alone was dangerous.

After an awkward silence, Sanjay tried to lighten the atmosphere. "So tell me about what you did last weekend."

She wriggled in her seat, uncomfortable. "You really want me to?"

Sanjay was both repelled and intrigued, but he wanted to show her his tolerant side. "Yes, I do. I'm sure it's fascinating."

Dawn recounted her experience with Mario, watching Sanjay's expression as he listened. She sensed his repulsion and regretted her decision to tell him about the evening's activities. To his credit, he didn't criticize her, but instead encouraged her to go on.

"Tell me more escort stories, I like them."

She peered at him, skeptical. His words belied his true feelings, which, she was convinced, were jealousy and hurt. Outside, he was pretending understanding and tolerance. Inside, she was sure he felt incredulity that his beloved could be doing such depraved things to other men, and, on occasion, women. How could he not?

"Maybe some other time."

She didn't tell him about the threesome at the Four Seasons Hotel with the young Anglophone couple. She kept to herself all talk of her sexual exploits with Sophie. She certainly wasn't ready to tell him about the episode with the man in his fifties with the grown son, who had her parade around his hotel room naked while he wrapped himself in a baby blanket and sobbed like an infant, crying, "Don't leave me mama, I will be a good boy, don't hit me mama, take me with you mama." That really shook her, especially when he started playing with himself and screaming "Forgive me, mama," until he climaxed. Strangely, all she could do when she went back to her condo on that particular night was lie in bed and dream about having children of her own.

No, she couldn't tell Sanjay about any of those incidents. It would all have to wait until she knew him better. Much better.

31

The annual "St. Paul's Day" at the school gave students and teachers the opportunity to demonstrate their extra-curricular skills. The administration considered singing, dancing, and acting just as important as academic aptitude in a child's educational development. All teachers were expected to help unearth the talented students, and to encourage them to put on a celebration worthy of the school's pride, one that included both athletic activities and theatrical performances. Dawn was always at the forefront of the group of teachers organizing and creating each year's theater production.

The previous year, she had received kudos across the board for her French dance sequence. This year, she was eager to do something different and decided to direct a play entitled "Street Gangs and Juvenile Prostitution," based on an interactive drama Sergeant Jacques Bisson of the Montréal Police Service created. The intent of "*Le Prince Serpent*" was to teach youth about the dangers of street gangs and juvenile prostitution, and to target children between the ages of twelve and fifteen, who were most vulnerable to the lures of gangs and selling sex for money. Dawn was aware of the social and legal problems juvenile prostitution and gang violence had posed in recent years. The police arrests of these youths made the front page of the local newspaper with increasing frequency.

To be sure she was interpreting the play according to his intentions, Dawn paid a visit to Sgt. Bisson. He was happy to help her understand the issues.

"In today's world, we need a new approach to get through to young people."

"I thoroughly agree. How do you manage to accomplish that, Sergeant?"

"The play familiarizes them with the strategies gang members use to recruit victims, and the consequences of a prostitute's lifestyle on young girls."

Dawn was impressed. "And the source of this information?"

"I've spoken with groups that go into the community to help juveniles, youths who fall victim to gangs and prostitution, and show them how to break free of their way of living."

"I really admire that, Sergeant. More power to you."

Along with the theater group that had first popularized the play, Sergeant Bisson attended rehearsals and assisted Dawn in directing the production and supporting the pupils' efforts. She was happy to spend her weekday evenings working with the students, thus having an excuse to confine her "work" activities to the weekends.

On the prescribed day, the students' two months of hard work paid off to everyone's great satisfaction. After a morning and afternoon filled with races and other sport events, the children and staff transformed the school gym into a makeshift theater. Non-participating students, staff and parents gathered along with school board members and several commissioners planning to present awards to deserving students. The evening's first event was the requisite French Québecois musical culture presentation. On the dot of 8 pm, the curtain opened on "Street Gangs." Filled with anticipation, Dawn sent her two stars onstage. She knew the action and dialogue by heart.

First, teenage boy Chad approaches 13-year-old Christie at the local shopping mall. "Hey, want to go out for Chinese food?"

Chad's attention flatters Christie. His lanky frame and flame-red hair attract her as well. "Uh, yeah, sure."

Dinner turns into a movie, and after a few "dates" Christie finds herself heading to the mall everyday after school. Chad treats her to meals, buys her jewelry and doles out small bits of cash to her every so often. Not realizing Chad doesn't attend school but instead works for a pimp, she becomes dependent on his company and his gifts. It's not long before he introduces her to the pleasures of cigarettes, marijuana and crystal meth.

One day, Chad asks her if she'd like to meet a friend. "His name is 'Daddy.' A real nice guy, you'll like him."

Christie follows Chad to a hotel room, where she meets the pimp who sizes her up. "She's a real pretty girl, right, Chad?"

Christie looks to Chad for approval and accepts the man's offer of a cigarette. "Thanks."

After this encounter, Christie begins to skip class and lies to her parents about doing homework at a friend's house after school. She spends her days having sex with men procured by "Daddy." When Chad gets a prescription for the STD she contracts, she hides the medicine from her parents. Before too long, she runs away from home to live with Chad, who forces her to turn tricks all night, every night. She's too addicted to the drugs to escape his clutches.

In the play's final act, Christie and her hooker friends are working their usual corners. Police officers posing as johns conduct a Sweep Operation, arresting the young girls. Christie is handcuffed and led off to the Police Station.

Dawn watched from the wings, enthralled, as her student actors mesmerized the audience. When the curtain fell, the deafening applause told her she had done her job as director with astonishing ability. Her pride in the students' performance was confirmed during the gathering after the show.

"Well directed, Miss L'andry." The Director of the School Board commended her. "Very realistic depiction of Montréal street life and its dangers. Is that really how they . . . those men . . . approach young girls and recruit them?"

She nodded with assurance and flashed a smile at Sergeant Bisson, who was across the room chatting with the Commissioner. "Just ask Sergeant Bisson."

"Thank you, I think I will."

Dawn excused herself and poured a cup of punch. She sipped slowly, watching the students take in the congratulations and praise from parents and staff.

They deserve it.

At that moment, she realized she had turned her phone off and was expecting an important call. She raced down the corridor to the staff room to check her cell phone log. As expected, there were two messages, both from Tucker, a Hollywood producer she had seen on several occasions. She accessed the first one.

Hey, Dawn, I just blew into town for the weekend.

She smiled with anticipation. She really liked Tucker.

We're doing shoots at the Museum of Civilization and Mont Royal. Want to get together?

The next message brought another smile.

Me again. Forgot to tell you, I'm busy till nine pm. How about after? Four Seasons, I'm booked under the company name, Room 1534. See you then. Let's have some fun.

Dawn sent him a brief reply, "I'll be there at ten."

Resisting the urge to dash outside for a smoke, she walked back to the gym. The school had a "No Smoking" policy, and though some teachers did indulge in the habit behind the building, Dawn never joined them. When she did smoke, it was when nobody was around. No one, not one colleague, knew she smoked, and she preferred to keep it that way. She had an image to protect, an ideal one, and she wasn't about to compromise it. Her eager anticipation helped her overcome her craving for nicotine. It wasn't everyday she could hang out with an A-list Hollywood director. Tucker was great for partying with, and he told her lots of stories about life on a movie set. Plus, he paid her well.

What more could a girl ask?

"Where have you been, Renée?" Chantal, her erstwhile lover and present colleague, was curious as usual. Dawn had observed that Chantal's curiosity was the one thing more insatiable than her sex drive. "We were about to head over to Bistro *L'Intrigue* for wine and mussels. How about it?"

"Thanks, but I already have plans. Sorry."

"You're always busy." Chantal half-smirked. "So who is he?"

"Nothing serious, just a friend from out of town."

"Yeah, right."

"Gotta go. See ya."

Dawn threw on her coat, waved to the other teachers and dashed off before Chantal could blink. She had just enough time to drive home, freshen up, leave her Tercel in the garage and hop a cab downtown.

And I thought the evening couldn't get any better.

32

Tucker Wilson had told Dawn all about Hollywood's love affair with Québec, the "Hollywood of the North." The Film Industry loved everything about Canada. Directors looked at Québec through their camera lenses and saw old world Europe. Montréal doubled for any American city but was much safer and more affordable. The place was heaven for Producers. From low-budget indie to blockbuster, anything could be filmed there. The unique climate and geography replicated that of any location or weather condition, and studio facilities were Hollywood caliber, with dedicated, highly professional crews and technicians. To add to Montréal's appeal, the tax credits and financial incentives were unparalleled.

"Hey, what's not to like?" Tucker had asked Dawn during their first encounter.

Dawn had just launched her school teaching career, but free weekends and school holidays afforded her enough time for GFE activities.

When Tucker first met Dawn, he was an Assistant Producer on the film "The Day After Tomorrow." Lying naked on the bed in his hotel room, they shared their backgrounds with each other, along with a bottle of *Dom Perignon*.

"I already staked out the location and persuaded them to film here."

"Them? Who?" Dawn ran her finger up his leg. "You'll have to explain everything. I don't know the first thing about films."

"You watch them, don't you?"

"Yeah. But I don't tell anybody which ones are my favorites."

"Not anybody?"

"Well, not until I get to know them better." She held his gaze. "So who are 'they' and what do 'they' do?"

"'They' are the financiers who control the purse strings. I practically have to lick their asses to convince them what's in their best interests. Cheap bastards."

Dawn flashed him a provocative smile. "Unlike you."

Gradually Tucker revealed his insider secrets to her. His job was to make sure his chosen location worked for the director and to see to it the shooting went well.

"I thought mine was the most important job. I was dead wrong."

"Oh, really? How'd you find out?"

"After shooting began, I discovered everyone who was anyone stayed at the Fairmont or Four Seasons, not the cheaper Crowne Plaza they dumped me at. Sure, the staff looked after the small, inconsequential details. But I was the one who made sure everything ran smoothly and as planned. And I got hardly any credit for it. That had to change."

"Ya got that right, baby." Dawn smoothed back a stray hair from his forehead.

"Next time I came to Montréal, I went first class all the way. I was finally getting my due. That's where you came into the picture."

"Which meant your wife was out of the picture?"

Tucker frowned. "Brenda hated living out of a suitcase. Which left me without company away from home, except when she was willing to cross the continent to join me. That almost never happened."

"So you took advantage of your freedom."

"Yep. I developed a taste." He downed the rest of his glass and leaned over to lick her nipple. "For French Canadian chicks who just happen to be GFE's."

"Umm." She pulled away, teasing him. "Thank goodness for Google. Nothing like some T&A to warm those cold Montréal nights, right?"

"'Twenty-six-year-old French-Canadian with long blonde hair, blue eyes, 34-24-34, available to provide a true 'girlfriend experience.' I prefer Anglophones and tourists, two hundred dollars an hour for my companionship.'" Growling like a bear, he attacked her other nipple.

"'Whatever else may occur between the two consenting adults is nobody's business. Please email your request to Dawnsearlylite76@aol.com.'"

Dawn saw Tucker as one of those lonely men, away from home on business, who craved more than a business arrangement. He wanted more than the women who came in and out the door like they were punching a time clock. And he was willing to pay for what he wanted. That was just to her liking. She generally didn't care how a guy looked or how old he was. As long as he had a wallet full of cash, she was happy to service him. In Tucker's case, the package was a bargain. Though he appeared older than his 42 years, a result, she was sure, of his stressful life style, he was not bad looking. His pockets were deep, very deep. And he always paid in advance.

He took a breather from her bosom and poured more champagne for both of them. "I knew from your description you knew what you wanted, and how to deliver it. I hardly had time to call the wife before you showed up."

"And what did you talk about?" Dawn enjoyed teasing him. "We didn't have time to go over that."

"'How are you honey, it's cold here, everything's going according to plan, I miss you.' Like that. You know the drill, right?"

"Hardly. I've never been married. Or even in love."

"Poor baby." He licked her ear and headed down towards her neck. "She's a good wife, takes care of the house, the finances. What more could I ask?"

Tucker talked on, sharing the most intimate details of the movie shoot with Dawn. She envied his exalted position, being responsible for making a mega blockbuster, a film unlike any ever made in Montréal. She could tell from his weary sigh he was beginning to fade.

Time to get to work.

Dawn pried the champagne glass from his grip and set it on the night table. "Now just lie on your stomach and relax, baby. I'll take care of everything."

Eyes closed, he obeyed her. She massaged his back with a slow, gentle touch, moving her fingers over his buttocks and legs, up to his thighs. When she tickled his scrotum, he smiled.

"Feel good, baby?" Dawn turned him over on his back, stroked his chest, teased his nipples with her fingers, and aroused him to the point of panting. She reached into her purse and unwrapped a condom with expertise. Placing it on his penis, she let her lips work their magic. Within a minute or two, she could feel him ready to explode. "How long has it been, baby?"

His breath came in short gasps. "A . . . whole . . . month . . . O-oh, I feel so good."

"So that's why you got off so fast."

She rose, walked to the bathroom and came back with a wet washcloth. Removing the condom, she wrapped the moist cloth around his penis. Seeing he was on his way to profound and much-needed sleep, she kissed him, got dressed and crept to the door.

He murmured through his drowsiness. "You'll take care of the lights, right, baby?"

She obeyed. She could hear his sleepy voice, now in a whisper, as he closed the door.

"Call you tomorrow."

33

Dawn was too busy at school the next day to think about Tucker and their encounter of the previous night. Besides her classroom duties, marking the math tests for grades seven and eight, and the mission statement she had to prepare for St. Paul's required by the city School Board, her hands were full. Mrs. Nelly had also called for a staff meeting. Dawn was behind on the write-up of her plan to help students excel in math. Concerned over the school's recent low placement in the province-wide math quiz, as well as the usual parent complaints, the no-nonsense principal insisted on the teachers' completing assignments in a timely manner. She expected even more from Dawn, whom she considered the most promising young instructor on the staff.

"I'm sorry, Mrs. Nelly." Dawn couched her failure in an abject tone. "If you give me another day or so—"

"I'm willing to do that, Dawn. I know I can trust you to come through." Mrs. Nelly's voice was firm.

"Yes, absolutely." Dawn breathed a sigh of relief.

"And keep those homework assignments coming. We like parents to complain." The principal smiled. "It means you're doing a good job, and it forces the parents to take a keen interest. It is, after all, their responsibility."

The meeting came to a merciful end, and Dawn remembered she hadn't had time to check her email. She hurried to the staff room and logged on to the computer. Not one, but three, emails from Tucker were waiting for her, and she saw he was online.

Le Chandelice, 8 pm tonight?

She salivated at the thought of meeting him at one of the top-rated restaurants in the city but frowned in disappointment when she realized she was not available.

Can't make it Friday or Saturday, and the restaurant is closed Sunday. Would Monday work?

My wife is coming to town. How about next weekend?

"I'll check my calendar.

Dawn sighed. What a shame she had made a date with Raj for Friday. It was a necessary evil, though. Things were getting too close with him. He considered himself her boyfriend, and she was worried he was getting too serious. That would not do. She planned on breaking up with him.

But only after sex. It'll be easier to break it off with him after he's had a piece of tail.

She also found the prospect of breaking up easier with a few beers under her belt. Raj made sure the fridge of his nicely refurbished warehouse condo in Old Montréal was well stocked and his kitchen table filled with spicy Indian food. His hospitality pleased Dawn, but her guilty feelings about her post-sex bombshell made her let her guard down and she drank too fast. The first beer went down nice and smooth, but the second one tasted strange. For some reason, she was getting high much sooner than she usual. She was confident in her ability to handle several beers. This time it was different.

*There's something in this beer, something funny tasting. What did he put in here?...*By the time Dawn realized what was happening, it was too late. She felt drunk, but not sleepy, and out of control. Her inhibitions flew out the window, and she accosted Raj with the vengeance of a woman who had not had sex in decades and wanted a hot, raunchy roll in the hay. She was too foggy to be aware of what was happening between them, only the feeling of spiraling downward into a dark, deep morass and crashing at the bottom. As fast as she plummeted, she came out of her haze when she felt something dripping from between her legs. She wasn't surprised at that, but she was shocked when she spied the webcam on top of the computer across from the bed, her nakedness in full display in the monitor.

"Did you tape me?" She shrieked in fury. "How dare you! You motherf—"

Not waiting for a reply, Dawn threw on her clothes, snatched up her belongings and stormed out. Thoughts of Internet screenings of the unauthorized video assailed her.

What's he going to do with it? Son of a bitch.

Upset and sick to her stomach, she canceled her escorting date later that night, as well as her Saturday one. Sunday was a total wash out, since she had to work on her school report. The loss of income infuriated her.

That S.O.B. It's all his fault.

Thinking about Tucker consoled her. There was a lot of potential there. It was obvious he liked her. Otherwise he would not keep coming back to her. The experience with Raj made her realize she needed to limit her work and get rid of any potential boyfriends. Being with Tucker gave her that freedom. She wasn't attracted to him in a physical way, but she liked talking to him. Besides, he was a Hollywood hot shot. It was all good.

When Dawn arrived home, she raced to the computer and sent off an email.

I missed you. Planning on seeing you next weekend. XOX... Putting aside all thoughts of her disastrous encounter with Raj, Dawn sank into a hot bubble bath, but without her usual beer. As far as she was concerned, the evening never happened.

*

Dawn welcomed the shortened school week. In-service Fridays provided a long-awaited respite from the treadmill of schoolwork and shouting at rowdy kids. Most teachers were happy to sit in a darkened auditorium all morning and listen to formal talks about improving school discipline, the psychology of learning, and the most recent research literature on education. The "Teacher as a Role Model" workshops, where the whole group divided up into subgroups of eight to ten teachers, took place in the afternoon. Known as a mover and shaker among her colleagues, Dawn was chosen as leader of her group. She was in charge of the brainstorming sessions on how to lead a personal life students could emulate and was responsible for presenting a summary of their discussion to the entire gathering. She was brilliant at fielding the divergent opinions between the members, which were usually divided according to age.

Dawn was aware this younger teacher and the others in his age range partied on weekends and smoked and drank without restraint. A number of them indulged in sex with multiple partners on a regular basis. She let the discussion continue without comment.

A young woman affirmed the first opinion. "He's right. We should be able to lead our private lives the way we want to."

The older instructors took issue. "On the contrary." A man in his fifties offered his view. "We all must set an example in our personal lives as well as in the school."

Another woman agreed. "Society expects that of us."

"I just want to know how to get onto the set for *Day After Tomorrow*. A youthful woman showed her lack of ability to concentrate on the matters at hand. "I thought I might try to bump into Dennis Quaid."

"Or Jake Gyllenhaal." Another young woman piped up. "He's so hot."

"Shall we keep to our topic?" Dawn had to suppress a knowing smirk. Tucker was sure to introduce her to either or both of the stars if she asked him.

The heated discussion resulted in no conclusion. Dawn was not surprised.

This discussion could go on for sixty minutes or sixty years.

Dawn had no problem presenting her summary to the group-at-large afterwards, but her mind was occupied elsewhere. Namely, on what she would wear to *Le Chandelice*, and whether or not Tucker would go for her proposal.

34

Tucker had called Dawn to say he was running late. No matter. The expensive champagne was a worthy stand-in. She was happy to sip from the elegant flute and gaze around her. The restaurant's décor looked nice enough, but the aroma of the food and the bouquet of fine wines wafting in the air confirmed its exclusivity. Dawn sighed with contentment.

I could get used to this.

Tucker rushed in. "Sorry, usual production hang-ups." A waiter, middle-aged, Dawn noted with interest, appeared and filled Tucker's champagne flute with a deft flick of the wrist.

Dawn took another sip. "How was your week with 'Wifey'? Lots of hot sex, I gather?"

"Her name's Brenda. We had a lot of catching up to do. Household stuff, you know." Tucker swallowed a large taste and nodded with approval. "She likes Ste. Catherine Street. It reminds her of Europe. And the shopping on Sherbrooke and Ste. Denise is not too shabby, either."

"Hmm. I can relate to that." Dawn put down her glass and studied his face. "Tell me more about your film. What's it about?"

"You mean the premise?"

"Yeah. Right."

Her fascinated gaze egged him on. "It's about global warming, with a twist."

"What kind of twist?"

"There's evidence that global warming causes cooling."

"I've heard about that. How do you show it in the film?"

"Okay, here it is. Melting polar ice caps disrupt the Gulf Stream, and the ocean current circulates warm water from the tropics to the Northern

Hemisphere, thus leading to the catastrophic changes in the earth's climate. As a result, three hurricane-shaped storms spread across the entire Northern Hemisphere. The initial predictions are for these storms to build over six to eight weeks. But they all combine in just over a week to form a huge planet-wide storm system that sucks super cooled air from the upper troposphere. Anyone caught in it is flash frozen."

"Wow. That's a fantastic plot. Tell me more." She took off one shoe and tickled his leg under the table with her naked toes.

"That's privileged information." He saw the disappointment in her expression. "But hey, you're family, right?"

Over *foie gras* and lobster laced with cognac, Tucker went into a lengthy explanation of the story. He gave her details of the story's origins, from the book *Global Superstorm*, and explained about the author's paranormal-themed talk show discussions about life after human destruction of the earth's environment. He described superstorms in Los Angeles, hailstones falling on Tokyo and rainwater pounding the Atlantic until it floods Manhattan. Dawn was mesmerized.

"And Dennis Quaid rescues everybody." Dawn sighed. "I love him, he's so hot. All my female colleagues are wild about him."

"Is he sexier than me?"

Dawn grinned. "Not by a long shot." It was a lie, but she knew he expected it. "You know, I almost became a model."

"I can believe that, baby." He gave her body an appreciative look. "You gotta be careful about exploitation in that industry."

"Just like in any industry, right?"

Tucker polished off the last of his *île flottante*. The bill appeared, as did a wad of cash from his wallet. Dawn noticed he added a generous tip to his payment. That was a good omen for the plan she was going to propose later that evening.

*

In the comfort of Tucker's hotel suite, Dawn waited until they were both nude and lying side by side on the bed to reintroduce the subject of his wife.

"How long have you been together?"

"Ten years. Married five."

"And are you happy?"

"Would I leave her, you mean?" He reached over and stroked Dawn's nipple. "No way. She'd take half of what I have."

"Ah." Dawn shivered from his touch. "What do your personal assistants think of her?"

"They know what a control freak she is."

"Do they know about me?"

"That's none of their business."

Dawn rolled on top of Tucker and began to rub her breasts over his chest. She mustered up her courage for her next question. "Would you like me to be your mistress?"

Tucker was flabbergasted. "I . . . I never thought of that."

She leaned closer into him. "Just think. We could see each other on a regular basis when you're in Montréal."

"What's involved, exactly?"

Dawn went in for the kill. "Just a monthly allowance. $5,000 would do. I make myself available to you whenever you want me. I could even come to L.A. sometimes."

"That's tempting."

"We could get closer." She rubbed her lower body up against his groin. "What do you think?"

He hesitated. "My wife does all our accounting. I'd have to find a way of paying you so she doesn't find out."

"I'm sure you'll think of something."

His turned-on expression told her she had conquered his resistance. Gratified, she set about making him happy. She knew he was not into exotic lovemaking. From what he had confided to her, his work life was crammed with adventure, and he had to use whatever ingenuity was left to satisfy his wife's demands in the bedroom. All he wanted from Dawn was relaxation at the end of a hard day's work and fulfillment of his biological needs.

For five thousand a month, she could deliver that. No problem.

35

During the filming of *Day After Tomorrow* Dawn and Tucker continued to see each other. On weekends when he flew back to L.A. to see Brenda, or she came to town to see him, Dawn made herself available to other clients. She didn't feel pressured to overdo, however, since the money from Tucker gave her the financial freedom to pick and choose her customers. Sleeping with Tucker did nothing to fulfill her sexual needs, but she was able to satisfy herself when needed. Masturbating was a fair trade off for the monetary advantages of being a kept woman without financial restraint. And Sophie's twice monthly visits from Ottawa gave Dawn enough sexual activity to keep her happy, at least most of the time.

On the rare occasion when she needed something more, Dawn visited the Orchid Night Club on Laurent Boulevard, where the hottest young studs hung out looking for equally hot chicks. In this freewheeling atmosphere, Dawn let her hair down, getting drunk and dancing all night. All of the guys drooled over her, and she picked up the sexiest one to take home with her. She didn't ask them to pay her. "Having fun" off the clock made her feel like she had the best of both worlds. Some of these encounters were memorable, but most of the time the guys were more interested in their own needs rather than hers. It didn't matter. She got plenty of that kind of attention from Sophie.

Being Tucker's mistress had its advantages. The steady flow of cash enabled Dawn to live off her four hundred-fifty dollar per week schoolteacher's salary and squirrel away everything else into Québec Government Bonds. While not lucrative, these investments were secure and guaranteed a decent return. Fine restaurants were part of the bargain with Tucker, and if he was not available Dawn had an abundance of requests from businessmen who were glad to squire her to expensive dinners as long as she provided the "R&R" afterwards. With her nest egg increasing, she continued to study the newspapers' business sections and resolved to learn the techniques of stock market investing. She considered herself a smart woman, not a typical hooker who spent money on drugs and expensive clothing. She had ambitions, and the most important of these was to be rich.

Sophie understood that ambition, but she didn't comprehend why Dawn wanted to focus so much effort on her day job. Dawn tried to set her straight one evening over beers at the local pub.

"I need a challenge outside the bedroom, Sophie."

Sophie was puzzled. "Why? If I made the kind of money you're making, I'd just take it and run."

Dawn had infinite patience when it came to Sophie. "It gives me a sense of accomplishment, dignity, self-respect. And teaching is more difficult than you think. I trained five years to learn the communication skills I need to keep the students happy."

"Keep them happy?" Sophie giggled. "Like you do your johns?"

"Maybe, in a way. They have to like you, and you have to be entertaining, or else there's no way they'll learn anything from you."

"Plus you have your looks and fashion sense going for you, right?" Sophie cast an admiring glance at Dawn's tailored suit, carefully made-up face and neatly done hair. "Did you get yourself gussied up like that to teach?"

"Sure. Even sixth graders can appreciate an attractive, well-dressed teacher. If they're girls, they admire you. If they're boys, well, they want to be close to you." Dawn winked. "If you get my drift."

"Is that what your mother taught you?"

"She taught me how to make up my face like an artist. Let's leave it at that."

"Oh. Sorry." Sophie knew Dawn was touchy when it came to discussing her mother.

"And frankly, Sophie, I think it's better to have something to fall back on. That's why I'm training to be a Geriatric Nurse's Aide."

Sophie rolled her eyes. "Oh, brother. What are you, nuts?"

"Look, we're not going to be young and beautiful forever, right?" Dawn searched Sophie's face for signs of recognition. "My little bubble can burst someday. I want to be prepared."

Sophie shrugged. "I suppose you're right."

"Besides, it's not that time-consuming. All I have to do is take a few courses part-time, like medical terminology, anatomy and physiology. The rest I can do by correspondence or online, and the practical stuff by volunteering at the nursing home down the street."

"Okay, how much of this is you wanting to please your dad. I mean, didn't he wish for you to be a doctor like him?"

Sophie's comment astonished Dawn. This girl was smarter than most people gave her credit for. "I was a bio major at University, remember? I could've been a doc. I was smart enough."

"But boys got in the way." Sophie smirked.

Dawn ignored the tease. "My dad's happy I'm a schoolteacher, even if it doesn't pay that well. But we have a plan for the future."

Sophie motioned to the waitress for another beer. "You astonish me, girl. Details, please."

"He's thrilled I'm in training for a new career. He even offered to pay my tuition, but I wanted to do this on my own. He wants to open a nursing home in the States, in Hilton Head, South Carolina."

"The resort town for the rich and famous?"

"Exactly. With all these rich Americans getting old and sick, and their children too busy to look after them, it would be a win-win. Profitable, lucrative and worthy."

"But old people? Ugh. How can you handle that?"

"You forget, Sophie. I come from a small town, where big extended families were the norm. My grandparents pretty much raised me, since my mom was trying to run a household with six kids. I know the drill."

"Whew." Sophie whistled. "Dawn, I am impressed. Any room for me in this scheme?"

Dawn smiled. "Sure, why not? I'll be the chief administrator. By then we'll both be married with kids."

"Whoa, I'm not sure that's in my horoscope."

"Don't you want kids?"

"Nope."

"I want four, I think."

"Girl, you amaze me." Sophie lifted her beer and smiled at Dawn. "Here's to you making all your whacky dreams come true. And me going along for the ride."

36

That year's cold, hard winter was a mixed blessing for Tucker's film shoot. The frigid weather was ideal for the blizzard scenes, but the cast and crew were reaching their limit in coping with the constant freezing temps and endless mounds of snow that accumulated on a daily basis. They were ready for a change and anxious to return to Southern California's balmy clime.

None of this mattered to Dawn and Tucker, who were keeping each other warm. Their friendship became comfortable and close but had no danger of developing into a passionate love affair. They had a contract, and Dawn especially was happy to deliver her portion of it. She desired no more or no less than what she was getting from the relationship. From Tucker's glowing demeanor, she gathered he, too, was content with the arrangement. By the time spring thaw came around, they had dispensed with emails and were calling each other on their cell phones. They both decided it was more practical.

Dawn planned to spend Easter break with relatives in her hometown of Bellesable, and Tucker was scheduled to go back to Los Angeles. To take advantage of their last days together, they decided on a mini-vacation to Québec City, where Dawn had spent a year doing her practice teaching. She was thrilled to go back and visit, and to show her lover the sights of this charming European city, with its rich history. She was not, however, prepared for the surprise that awaited her when they arrived.

"Château Frontenac! Oh, I've always wanted to stay here." Dawn gazed around at the elegant lobby, taking in the richness of its furnishings, and threw her arms around Tucker. "You're the best."

He smiled. "The company's paying for it, babe. Deluxe all the way."

Dawn was overjoyed with their suite, decorated with tasteful Persian rugs, Aubusson tapestries, a generous-sized bed fit for a French monarch and luxurious velvet tapestry curtains and bedspread. She was more thrilled, however, at the prospect of taking off to explore the city she had missed so much since she had left several years before.

"That bed's tempting." She beamed at Tucker. "But there's a whole new world out there waiting for us."

Tucker agreed. "Anything you want, babe. This is your special time."

"And yours."

She gave him an affectionate kiss. "You're the best. Have I told you that?"

He kissed her back. "Yes. You have."

Hand in hand, they strolled through the city. Dawn was excited to show Tucker everything and tell him all she knew about the city and its history. She couldn't keep herself from racing through her explanations and was unaware he had trouble keeping up with her rapid speech.

"There's almost no way to tell if you're in France or North America. Except, of course, by the language. French in Québec is spoken differently than in France. The Québecois have coined descriptive terminology for the city depending whether it's topography, history, day-to-day life, archaeology, or culture. Plus they've made up phrases out of English-based words but with a French twist, like '*magasiner*, which is the French word for 'warehousing' bastardized into a verb meaning 'to go shopping.' And they have different names for each section, Old City, Old Capital, Lower-Town, Upper-Town, Old Québec—"

"Hey, slow down, will you? We've got all weekend."

"Oh, sorry." She squeezed his hand. "Can I tell you where the name 'Québec' comes from?"

"Sure, babe, bring it on."

"Well, Québec's earliest population included Native Americans, so "Kebec" comes from the Algonquin language and means 'Where the river narrows.' The St. Lawrence, of course. Isn't that cool?"

His amused smile encouraged her to go on. "Settlers came from France and England, too, which probably explains why the Québécois are so warm and welcoming."

"So that's where you get it, huh?"

She tossed him a mock pout. "You know where my favorite place is?"

"No, but I'm just dying to."

"The *Quartier Petit-Champlain*, next to the Old Port. It's the oldest commercial district in the city. It has the oldest church, the oldest street . . ." She winked. "And the best boutiques."

He grinned. "Now why does that not surprise me?"

In spite of his teasing tone, she could tell the *Quartier* charmed him as much as it did her, with history seeping from every corner of its narrow, cobblestone streets and centuries-old houses. Each boutique was one-of-a-kind. Glass-blowing factories. Confectioneries with hand-made candies in pastels colors. Locally designed clothing shops. Dawn was pleased at Tucker's astonished reaction to the bounty surrounding them.

"It's ideal for finding that one perfect gift for that special someone, Tucker, an *objet d'art* or distinctive piece of clothing. Something original."

"Is that a hint?"

She laughed. "Well, maybe. How about something exceptional for each of the ladies in your life?"

"Sold."

Their exploration of the clothing boutiques yielded several one-of-a-kind silk blouses and a hammered silver belt for Brenda, but Dawn was unable to find anything that spoke to her until she and Tucker peered into the window of a crafts store that featured unique ceramics. She tugged him inside and fixed her eyes on at the colorful displays and settled her gaze on a ceramic clock perched high on a wall, square-shaped and enameled in bold blue. On it were painted a table and chairs, one of which held a black cat with eyes peering out at the viewer. Underneath the table was a pastiche depicting beige sand and turquoise water. The tabletop held a large fish skeleton, its bones picked of every morsel of flesh, which explained the cat's secretive expression.

"Ooh, look at that. I've never seen anything like it." She caught the eye of the shopkeeper. "May we see it?"

"Of course." The woman ascended a ladder, removed the item and brought it down for the couple to inspect. "Hand-painted, as I'm sure you know."

Dawn's eyes widened with delight. "It's perfect. Isn't it, Tucker?"

"Yeah. I must admit I've never seen anything like it."

"Can we get it?" She turned over the clock and checked the price. "I know one hundred-fifty is a bit steep, but it is unique. Right?"

"Right, babe. Anything you want."

She threw her arms around him. "You're the best."

They shopped to the point of collapse and stopped in a café for sustenance before heading to the Plains of Abraham for a quick trip back in time. Dawn loved this lush, grassy knoll with its mile-high 360-degree views of the city and the St. Lawrence. They positioned themselves on a bench and gazed out over the river.

"The British and French fought three battles here between 1759 and 1775. The French lost." She shuddered. "Hard to imagine all that bloodshed in such an exquisite setting."

"I can't believe how much you know about history."

"It fascinates me."

He pulled her close. "Not as much as you fascinate me."

Dawn was content. Safe in Tucker's affectionate grasp, she savored the moment. Their relationship was about to end, but she had enjoyed the ride. They had planned well and made the most of their arrangement. Now it was time to move on.

Tant mieux. Change is good. All good.

"I'll miss you, babe."

"Me, too, Tucker."

But she wasn't sure if she would miss him or the money more.

37

"It's hard to say goodbye."

Dawn wasn't in love with Tucker, but their friendship had developed into a powerful bond. To her astonishment, she found their arrangement, convenient at first, difficult to break in the end. Their physical connection, and their compatibility with each other, had brought them closer than they had anticipated. She wanted to make sure their final session was memorable and summoned up a degree of passion she had not hit upon in her former encounters with him.

Afterwards, Tucker cuddled with her, stroking her hair. "I'm gonna miss you, babe. Montréal would never have been the same without you."

"It's been great for me, too." Dawn was surprised to find her voice trembling from emotion. "You've been so generous, Tucker."

"No other way to be, with someone as wonderful as you."

Dawn felt her face redden, atypical for her. "I wish you luck for 'Day After Tomorrow.' It'll be a huge hit, no doubt."

"Thanks, kid. I have faith in you, too. Whatever you do, you'll always be the best."

That was just what she wanted to hear. "I have every intention of fulfilling that prediction. Maybe I'll even come to L.A. someday."

He grinned. "You know where to find me."

Dawn knew he was just trying to placate her. They were both ready to move on. She was sure he wouldn't miss her, and she was happy to consider doing something new and different, even if it meant going back to work for Tom.

The next month passed quickly for Dawn. The approaching finish to the school year meant escalating pressure on students and teachers in advance of their release for the summer holiday. Dawn was busy preparing extra exams, and she spent long evenings and weekends grading them. In order to make sure all her classes performed well on the tests, she met with the few weaker students before or after school to coach them. Helping them feel better about themselves made her feel better as well.

Mrs. Nelly took note of Dawn's extra efforts. One day towards the end of the semester, she called dawn into her office. "Your commitment to your students and to the school remains laudable, Dawn. I have high hopes for you."

"Thank you, Mrs. Nelly."

Elated, Dawn rushed home and rewarded herself with a beer. Collapsing in front of the TV, she groaned when her cell phone rang.

"Forget it, I'm not working tonight. No way."

The ringing stopped, but a minute later the phone rang again. Dawn jumped up and answered it. An irate female voice assaulted her ears.

"This is Dawn, I gather?"

The angry tone gave Dawn an immediate feeling of unease. "Yes, this is Dawn."

"I'm Brenda Wilson. You know, the wife of Tucker Wilson. The one you were having an affair with."

Brenda broke Dawn's dazed silence. "I'm sure you're wondering how I know. Well, I'm no dummy, Missy. I could tell something was up, starting with our sex life, which was fantastic, by the way. Until you came along."

"I . . . I don't know what you're talking about."

"Oh, please. I saw your number on the bills and called the phone company to find out whose number it was. Bingo. Calls at all hours, all of them to you. Solid proof."

Dawn was speechless.

"Of course, he denied it when I confronted him. I tried to get him to say what it was about you, younger, better looking, more satisfying in bed? He didn't have an answer. He just tried the lovey-dovey approach. Maybe that worked with you, but it just didn't cut it with me. Bastard."

"Look, Mrs. Wilson, I never intended—"

"He finally admitted it." Brenda, now incensed, interrupted. "Told me your name. As if I didn't already know. Tried to buy me off with a dinner at my favorite restaurant, said he loved me. Then the prick tried to tell me it was only a few times. A few times?" Dawn thought she heard the woman spit into the phone. "Try two hundred-eighteen phone calls. I'll show you a few times. He didn't have a leg to stand on."

Dawn considered hanging up on her.

"What exactly do you want from me, Brenda?"

Brenda ignored the question. "What did you do to him that I couldn't do? Oral sex?" Angry tears caused her voice to tremble. "Blow jobs? You put his dick in your mouth?"

Dawn was beginning to lose patience. "I don't have to listen to this."

"No, you don't. But Tucker will. So will his lawyer. And I'm naming you co-respondent." She waited for Dawn's gasp of distress. "It's over, a marriage of ten years.

And it's your fault, Missy. Are you happy now?"

With that, Brenda slammed down the phone. Dawn shuddered, hoping Brenda's furious wrath was spent. It wasn't. Brenda assailed her with phone calls, sometimes in the middle of the night. Dawn felt like she was living in a nightmare.

Tucker called her only once, while she was on her way to see a client. "Dawn, is that you?" The sound of his voice distressed her. "Dawn, I've left my wife."

"I know. She called me."

"Oh my God, I'm so sorry." He paused, breathing heavily. "She was just too smart. She got a lawyer right away. And she went to some of those feminist group meetings. I'm sure they nailed me to the wall."

"You should have known, Tucker. You should have gotten one of those disposable cell phones or something to cover you. I thought you were smarter than that."

The awkward silence made him uncomfortable, but he pressed on, desperate.

"Can we . . . could we get back together? I miss you so."

His pleading tone left her cold. "Our contract is finished, Tucker. I did appreciate your generosity, believe me, but I have a boyfriend now, and I'm not working anymore. As an escort, I mean." She had a momentary twinge of regret at lying to him, but it passed. "I'm sorry about what happened with your wife, but maybe you can still work things out. Goodbye, Tucker."

She could hear him sob as she hung up the phone. Her mind raced.

I just want it to be over. It was just a contract, not a relationship. How did I get myself mixed up in this? Thank God the bitch doesn't live here and doesn't know I'm a teacher. That would really screw me.

In her psyche, however, Dawn felt guilty. She had caused pain to another woman and knew if she were in Brenda's position she would be devastated. She tried to put the whole business behind her, but Brenda's incessant phone calls came as a constant reminder of her indiscretion. She didn't know whether to be rude to the woman, to be sympathetic, or to try and comfort her. One thing Dawn couldn't do was to hang up on her. The final call, a non-stop diatribe, put Dawn over the edge.

"What are you, Satan in a woman's form? Is that what you do, ruin people's marriages? Are those the values you parents gave you? Is this what you learned in school? Do you do it for fun, or for money, or for what?"

Dawn wanted to hang up the phone but couldn't. The woman was right. She deserved to be yelled at, to be punished.

"It's because of you that I'm going through all this pain. It's your callous actions that have caused my suffering. I only wish you could feel my grief. I hope you go through the same thing yourself one day. You don't sell sex or pleasure. You sell pain and hurt, you dirty whore."

Unable to take another second of abuse, Dawn clicked off. The next day she changed her number for an unlisted one, even though it meant notifying each individual client and relative. She called Tom to let him know she was going out of town, and she didn't respond to her emails. The lure of money and her addiction to her "work" had lost their luster.

It's not worth it.

Dawn L'andry, schoolteacher *par excellence,* educator and role model to young children, had learned her own powerful lesson. From the grieving Mrs. Wilson.

38

Dawn and Sophie sat over a cup of coffee on Dawn's balcony, watching the sun come up. Saturday mornings afforded Dawn this leisure. Since her school exams were marked and her lessons prepared, she felt little pressure to do anything except appreciate the glow of the sun reflecting off the tower of the University of Montréal campus in the distance. After enduring the cold, grey specter of winter's light, Dawn welcomed the appearance of the golden orb of warmth as a sign that things would be looking up for her.

"How are things with Amran?" Dawn pretended interest in Sophie's new Moroccan boyfriend, a resident in urology at the University.

Sophie peered at Dawn, suspicious. "Get real, Dawn. I know you. There's something else on your mind."

"Yes, you do know me. Too well." Dawn sighed. "Here's the thing, Sophie. I need to make some decisions, and I need to run them by you."

"Shoot."

"Okay. But first I have to tell you about my experience last night."

"Ooh, do tell. Details, please."

"That's just it Sophie. There weren't any."

"What?"

"Well, hardly. I did it as a special favor for Tom." She grimaced. "I didn't want to, but I also didn't want to get on his bad side."

"Good idea."

Dawn continued. "So we're on our way to the Fairmont, and he tells me my customer is a Francophone. Well, I went ballistic."

Sophie pretended ignorance. "And why was that?"

"Oh, please." Dawn wadded up a paper napkin and lobbed it at her companion. "You know I don't do Francophones. So does Tom. But he just kept begging me."

"So that means it must have been some big shot."

"Yeah. Turns out Tom owed the guy favors. Bailing him out of jail, among others."

"What kind of person would do something like that?" Sophie gasped. "You're not telling me—"

Dawn nodded. "Yep. None other than the Minister of Justice, François Boucher."

"Holy crap!"

"And then Tom has the nerve to tell me to be extra hush-hush about it. Didn't want any scandals. Like I would ever."

"Right. You're more discreet than any of the other girls." Sophie thought for a moment. "So what did you do?"

"I told Tom I'd do it just this once. It's not like I'd ever see the guy again. Then I told Tom I was quitting."

"Is that what you wanted to talk to me about?"

"I want a life, Sophie. I can't keep doing this stuff."

"I hear you. What did he say?"

"He went on about how this is the busiest season for the service, that I was giving up piles of money. The usual."

"Well, he's right. And so are you." Sophie drained her cup and poured another. "So what did he do?"

"Gave up. He knows my leaving will devastate his business, but there wasn't a damn thing he could do."

"And you're telling me this because?"

Dawn gave Sophie a sober look. "I'm not sure if I'm I doing the right thing. I mean, will I really be able to have a life of my own if I quit?"

Sophie grasped Dawn's hand and squeezed it. "Baby, you can do anything you want to do. I believe in you."

"Thanks, Sophie." Dawn's eyes glistened with grateful tears. "You're the best."

"I know." Sophie grinned. "So how was he? The Minister, I mean."

Dawn giggled. "Oh, really lame. He didn't even want sex, just a nude massage. Well, that worked for me. So did his fifty buck tip."

Sophie whistled. "Not bad for a night's work. Why didn't the guy just call a masseuse?"

"That's what I was wondering."

The two women shared a laugh. Dawn's expression sobered. "After I finished, I got into Tom's car, handed him the cash—the hourly, not the tip—and gave him a farewell kiss. Then I walked home." She frowned. "Am I doing the right thing?"

Sophie contemplated Dawn's conflicted face. "Do what makes you happy, Dawn. Life is short."

*

Mrs. Nelly gave one of her rare house parties that night to celebrate the successful school year. Dawn never missed one of these. She was trying to stay on the principal's good side, and she also used the opportunity to ingratiate herself with her colleagues. A discussion about *The Day After Tomorrow* brought back discomfiting thoughts of Tucker and his wife, however, and Dawn was hesitant to share her insider information.

"The 'global super storm' depicted in the movie is not only implausible, but impossible." The science teacher was just shy of his PhD and wanted to show off his expertise. "The premise relies on chaos theory instead of meteorology or climatology."

"But it makes for great entertainment, doesn't it, Harold?" Dawn couldn't resist throwing a wet blanket on the teacher's theory.

"Besides, it's my favorite movie." Mrs. Nelly was always up for a debate between her charges.

"Really? Me, too." Dawn said this with a straight face, though she repressed an urge to blurt out the reason why.

Mrs. Nelly's smiled showed she was pleased with Dawn's view. "Why don't we see what Larry King had to say?"

The older woman slid a tape into her VCR and motioned to the teachers to gather around the TV. Dawn watched and listened, fascinated, as scientists thrashed about their theories on the movie's scientific merit.

"Even if an increase in fresh water caused a slowdown or stopped the thermohaline circulation, that would more likely cause regional rather than global cooling," theorized one expert.

"What?" The non-science teachers, among them Chantal, were lost.

Another onscreen expert agreed. "And it would take decades, not a few days."

"It is blatantly wrong that the descending stratospheric air would be cold, because the air descending faster will heat faster, too." The first scientist furthered his opinion. "A great movie but lousy science."

Dawn suppressed a chuckle.

I wonder what Tucker would think of all this?

She was even more curious about the reaction she would cause if she revealed what had transpired behind the scenes, but she refrained from sharing that information.

Infidelity, adultery, a broken marriage. The ingredients of success. Who knew?

She wasn't up for arguing the merits of the movie's premise, or the accuracy of its scientific pros and cons. On the other hand she had played a small, if key, role in its production. That counted for something, at least in her mind. Her thoughts wandered away from the heated discussion and towards her next encounter with Sanjay. She wondered what he'd thought of the film.

On second thought, maybe it's better not to bring it up at all.

Yes. That was the safe choice. Dawn mused about the subject of safety. She had spent her life taking chances. Now it had blown up in her face. She wasn't about to risk that again. The lesson learned from the Tucker fiasco was a hard one. Sanjay was too important to her. A conversation about the movie might lead to talk of Tucker, and then the whole nasty marriage break-up business. Dangerous territory. She didn't want to frighten Sanjay with the prospect of anything similar.

No. Definitely not a good idea.

*

Dear Sanjay,

I'm sorry, but I have to bail out of the Vegas trip. I accepted your invite before I had a chance to think things through. I hate to think of you alone there during your weekend meeting. But I have to admit your constant questions about my identity had me spooked. I know you said you needed my real name to book our suite at the Mandalay Bay, but somehow it doesn't make sense. Really, Sanjay, your demands are beginning to get to me. We talked about this when we first met. Remember? I don't have to remind you what I said about not seeing you anymore.

Having said that, I can see you have a big heart. I get goose bumps just reading your sweet letters. It's so nice of you to offer to help me financially. I feel truly blessed to have your support, in every way. It's a shame there are so few people like you in this world. You're a wonderful human being.

I'm sorry if I caused you any inconvenience in the Vegas trip. I hope you can find it in your heart to forgive me. In any case, I'll see you soon!

xox

Dawn

39

Sanjay loved the cozy womb of his favorite Winnipeg Indian restaurant on a Sunday evening and enjoyed the company of his kids. His wife's constant carping, however, negated most of his pleasure.

"You've been going to Montréal an awful lot lately. It's hard being here without you."

He knew she was trying not to sound bitchy, but the nature of her statement made it impossible. "It's not exactly fun, you know."

"We miss you." Eight-year-old Chandra gazed at him with intense, dark eyes.

"Yeah, Dad." Anil spoke with the authority of an elder brother. "What do you do there, anyway?"

"I go to meetings, sit in a dark cold room, all day long, everyday. Sometimes I network over dinner or in the evening." He tried to banish sudden thoughts of Dawn, her soft, firm body, her sweet voice, the things they did together. "That's about it. Very boring."

"I'll say. Can I have another coke?"

Sanjay ordered the coke for his son and watched his children chew their food in silence. "By the way, Vinita, something has come up next week."

"What is it?"

"A Critical Care convention."

"Isn't that short notice?" Vinita frowned.

"They needed someone at the last minute to do a series of talks on acute lung injury." He paused. Vinita wouldn't like this. "In New Delhi."

"Delhi?" She gasped. "Why couldn't they let you know sooner? I want to come this time."

"What about the kids?" Having anticipated her reaction, Sanjay had prepared a response. "We couldn't leave them behind. Besides, it's a very short trip. I'll hardly be leaving the hotel."

Vinita pouted. "I want to see the Taj Mahal. It's only three hours from Delhi."

"How about we all go this summer?" Sanjay knew how to placate her. "The kids will be out of school. We could make it a family expedition."

"Yay!"

The children's unison shouts of joy silenced any further comment from Vinita. Sanjay patted her hand. "There, you see? Isn't that a good solution? Now everybody's happy."

Nibbling the curry on her plate, she avoided Sanjay's glance.

*

In spite of his love for his work in the ICU, Mondays were always tough. This particular one was taking its toll on Sanjay more than usual. Too many critical cases, too much death hanging over. He knew he needed to focus on the nurses' systems reports, but he was distracted. The previous evening's discussion with Vinita nagged at him. Before long, she was going to suspect he wasn't telling the complete truth about his out-of-town forays. He dreaded that. But he was too hooked on Dawn to contemplate making any changes in his routine.

He went about his rounds, formulating plans for transferring out patients who had been there for the requisite amount of time and for admitting new ones.

"Did it ever occur to you how strange it is that people don't fall ill between 9 and 5 but prefer to do so in the wee hours of the night?"

His attempt at humor brought soft chuckles from the residents, whom he had gathered together in the hallway.

"Now about today's issue. As you know, euthanasia is illegal in Canada. However, withdrawal of care, done with compassion, affords both patient and family members autonomy and dignity. If a patient is unlikely to survive critical care without significant disability resulting . . ."

Sanjay had been through it countless times. The family meetings, the consultations with other medical personnel, the soul-searching thought process required to come to a decision affecting a person's life. And death. Most physicians avoided this process if at all possible. Sanjay thrived on it, at least most days. By the end of this day, however, he felt drained of energy and purpose. When he spied his colleague George in the hallway outside their respective offices, he realized he needed a respite.

"Bailey's, Dr. Rosen?" Sanjay raised his eyebrows at George.

The other doctor smiled. "You read my mind, Dr. Kaul."

"But no hitting on her, right?"

"Yeah, right. And no staring."

Sanjay and George changed quickly and headed to the bar lounge. The two of them had nicknamed Earl's Restaurant in honor of a waitress who was hot enough to turn their heads in a major way. They flashed broad smiles to each other when they spied the gorgeous young girl approach their table.

Sanjay was the first to greet her. "How's the modeling trade these days, Bailey?"

"Not too busy to keep me from taking care of you guys." Her smile melted any vestige of their resolve not to stare.

"Large Kokanee with chips and salsa." George tried not to gape at the cleavage created by her low-cut red Henley, its buttons unfastened from the neck to just above her bra.

"Make that two."

"Sure thing."

Bailey scurried off to get the order. George fixed his eyes on her until she was out of sight. "Great ass."

"Yep."

"I could marry her."

"Every beautiful woman you meet, you want to marry her."

"Don't you?" George chuckled. We're both the same, Sanjay."

Meanwhile the comely waitress had set their order down and gone off to the next table, the two doctors clinked bottles and drank.

"Awesome stuff. Too bad they don't make a bigger bottle."

"Just as well, George. You never know if or when we might be called back tonight."

"Since when is that a problem? 'You can't be an Intensivist if you can't handle booze.'" George imitated Dr. 'Big Mac's" self-important tone of voice.

"At least according to our esteemed colleague."

"Yeah, if he wasn't head of critical care he'd have blown it by now."

"Oh, I don't think so. When it comes to booze, no one can beat him." Sanjay took another gulp of his beer. "He can imbibe the entire St. Lawrence River."

"Did you see him at the last house party?" George grinned. "He drank all his guests under the table, and then some."

Sanjay nodded. "Not a drop remained in the house once he was done."

They clinked again. George winked at Sanjay. "So who are you doing these days?"

"Why is it our conversations always come down to girls and money, George?"

"What else is there?"

Sanjay chuckled. "So who are you doing?"

"Man, you wouldn't believe it. I'm engaged to Irene, Shelley is text messaging me, Noreen emailed me about going out to lunch, and Krista wants me to do her. She's a real sweetie."

"Ah, the Great Womanizer."

"How about you? What, or should I say who, did you do in Montréal?"

"Nothing and no one. Just me and the bed, alone."

"Yeah, right."

Several large Kokanees later, Sanjay and George made their way out of the bar.

Bailey waved to them. "Drive careful, boys."

"You bet." Sanjay smiled in Bailey's direction and turned to George. "By the way, I'm going to Delhi tomorrow for a few days. Can you cover my calls?"

George raised his eyebrows. "Sweet. Who's the GFE?"

40

Dawn and Sanjay boarded their Air Canada flight to India with excitement running through their veins. It was their first trip together. The prospect of visiting the Taj Mahal had both of them in a state of exhilaration. Sanjay was a man of his word. He had promised to show Dawn the monument of eternal love. Now he was fulfilling that pledge.

"Do they really call it 'the greatest place on earth,' Sanjay?" Dawn buckled herself into her Executive Class seat.

"Yes, and for a reason. One man spent his lifetime creating it for his one true love." He gazed at her with fondness. "It's a wonder, a masterpiece. Like you."

Dawn smiled at the compliment and sighed. "I've always dreamed of seeing it. I can't believe you've never been there before."

"I never had the desire. It's a place only lovers would go. And I've never found true love before I met you."

The intensity in his eyes sent shivers down her spine. "I read it was built at the same time the Acadians were exploring my native terrain."

"That's true, in the 1600s. The Taj was created when all of Europe was entrenched in the Dark Ages and people were fighting each other for no reason. How's that for contrast?"

Dawn flipped through the airline magazine. "fourteen hours and thirty-five minutes. I've never been on such a long flight."

"Crossing ten-plus time zones is no small feat."

"I guess I'll catch up on sleep. What else is there to do?"

Sanjay smiled. "I'm sure we'll think of something."

"Would you care for orange juice, sir?" The flight attendant, in an elegant long flowing blue dress with a red scarf trailing behind her, gave Sanjay and Dawn a welcoming smile. Dawn looked up in admiration.

"Oh, what a beautiful dress."

"Thank you, miss."

The attendant leaned over to serve Dawn and Sanjay and moved on. Dawn watched Sanjay pull out *The Da Vinci Code* and *Eleven Minutes* from his briefcase.

"A little light reading, Sanjay?"

"I can never sleep on a plane. These will occupy my time and attention."

Dawn smiled to herself.

Ironically, they both tell stories of sex and prostitution.

Dinner arrived with the usual trappings of upper class air travel. Dawn ordered a steak and salad to go along with the velvety Bordeaux Sanjay ordered. The three glasses of wine they each consumed went down with ease. Before long they both felt a pleasant buzz.

"I don't know how you can survive on just salad." Dawn was enjoying every bite of her meat. "I'm impressed."

"You don't need more than thirty grams of protein a day."

"You may not, but I do." She grinned. "Maybe that's why you're such a great lover. No protein, no fat, just carbs and loads of energy."

"Right." Sanjay's mouth turned up in a mischievous smile.

By two am Toronto time, the cabin lights had been turned off and the atmosphere was hushed. Sanjay glanced around at his fellow passengers, who all looked asleep or drunk. The flight attendants sat together, eating and chatting about their boyfriends and husbands. Dawn lay back in her reclining seat underneath a blanket, eyes closed, but she sensed something was about to happen. She knew she was right when Sanjay touched her right leg for a moment and moved his hand up to her waist and breast.

He whispered in her ear. "Let's go to the restroom."

"I don't need to. You go ahead." She whispered back.

"No, I meant both of us. Together."

"What?" Opening her eyes, she sat up and frowned at him. "I don't know what you have in mind, but whatever it is I'm not doing it on a plane."

"Come on, Dawn, it'll be a unique experience. I've always fantasized about having sex on a plane. Did you know the low oxygen levels in a plane enhance orgasm?"

"Is that true?"

"Well, it's never been scientifically proven. But it's worth a try."

"What if we get caught?"

"Doesn't that prospect make it all the more exciting?"

The more Dawn thought about Sanjay's proposal, the more it intrigued and aroused her. "Okay. I'm game."

Sanjay was ecstatic. "We'll use the one reserved for Executive Class." He kept his voice low. "I'll go first and leave the door unlocked. You wait a moment and walk in after me."

"Are you sure about this?"

"No one will notice. They're all asleep or drunk. Or both."

Dawn looked around, confirmed Sanjay's statement was accurate, and nodded her agreement. Sanjay got up and moved towards the back of the cabin and into the restroom. Dawn waited a minute and followed him. The cubicle was barely large enough for one person, but since both Dawn and Sanjay were slight of build they were able to fit inside with little effort. Their hearts racing, the two lovers began to envelop each other with frantic kisses, their tongues licking and probing their mouths, becoming more aroused with every stroke of the tongue.

Dawn gasped, breathless. "How are we going to do this?" She glanced at the tiny space. "This is impossible. What position?"

"Don't worry." Sanjay carefully placed the lid down on the toilet, pulled off one leg of his jeans and sat down. "Just sit in my lap."

Dawn removed her skirt and obeyed. "Okay, but there's not a lot of room in here. I'm going to have to do all the work."

But Sanjay wasn't listening. Dawn's movements, cramped as they were, brought him to a state of near-ecstasy. He groaned with pleasure. "Oh, Dawn, my love. I can't believe you are fulfilling yet another of my fantasies."

The plane's sudden pitching movements and the announcement from the cockpit only heightened their pleasure.

"Ladies and gentlemen, we are experiencing some turbulence. Please return to your seats and fasten your seatbelts." The warning came from the P.A. system.

"I don't care if the plane crashes, I have to come." Dawn thrust at Sanjay with increased fervor.

In the cabin, the flight attendant checked to make sure the passengers were awake and had buckled themselves in. Noticing Dawn and Sanjay's seats unoccupied, she strode to the restrooms and discovered the first two were empty. She heard the soft sighs and moans of Dawn and Sanjay's mutual climax coming from the third one and knocked on the door.

"Please return to your seats. We are having turbulence."

Embarrassed, the flight attendant moved away. An instant later, Dawn emerged from the restroom and calmly walked back to her seat. Sanjay followed a moment afterward. The curious stares of their fellow passengers did not concern them. When they were both buckled in, the two exhilarated lovers whispered to each other.

"It's not like we were smoking." Dawn giggled. "No law against making love at thirty-five thousand feet."

"Low oxygen, excessive alcohol, fear of getting caught. Sounds like a recipe for the experience of a lifetime."

They sealed their agreement with a kiss. And Sanjay slept all the way to Delhi.

41

Dawn was amazed at the atmosphere of magic and mystery in the air when she and Sanjay landed in Delhi. Accustomed to airports where masses of people rushed about, she fixed her eyes on the unhurried individuals around her, who all looked as if they had no stresses in their lives, and gaped.

"I feel like I've landed in Oz." She grasped Sanjay's arm. "What is it about this place?"

"India's spirituality pervades the surroundings, as well as the soul of everyone who comes here."

"So you feel it, too?"

"There is little stress here compared to our world, Dawn, no deadlines, no worry. Yet the nation manages to govern itself. It's enough to make an atheist like me become a believer." He smiled. "Well, almost."

The Immigration Officer inspected their passports and glanced at them. "Are you related?"

They looked at each other. Sanjay held Dawn's gaze. "Are we related?"

She returned his look. "I don't know. Are we?"

Content to leave the question unanswered, they headed outside and hired a Tata Safari to take them to Agra, where their hotel awaited them. The taxi crept through the congested streets of Delhi, with its wall-to-wall people and general confusion, and made its way onto the Agra Expressway.

"How far is it?" Dawn suppressed a yawn.

"Three hours' drive. It was the capital of the Mughal Empire during the 16th and early 17th centuries, you know."

Sanjay smiled. Dawn was already fast asleep. He contented himself with viewing the countryside from the window, holding her close as she dozed, until the cab pulled up in front of the Jaypee Palace Hotel.

Dawn jerked awake. "Are we there yet?"

"Yes, my darling."

She looked up at the red sandstone building, perched on a slight incline and surrounded with a sprawl of well-manicured gardens. "Ooh, this is beautiful."

"It's unlike any other luxury resort in the world, with a first-class spa. We'll be treated like royalty here."

"Umm, just my style."

"I thought as much. What would you like to try first? Rejuvenating longevity treatment, signature massage therapy, hot oil treatment, body wrap . . ."

"I'd like to wrap my body around you."

"You have four whole days to do it."

She planted a tender kiss on his cheek. "How far are we from the Taj? I can't wait to see it."

"About two miles. Why don't we rest a bit and visit it this evening after supper? The beauty of the Taj by moonlight is something not to be missed."

"Whatever you say, my beloved."

"Now you're thinking like a true Indian."

"Am I?" She sighed. "It's only to please you."

*

"The Taj is an architectural wonder, shrouded with poetry and romance. Rabindranath Tagore described it as 'a teardrop on the cheek of time.'"

Even though he and Dawn had hired Mohammed, a local from Agra, to escort them to their place of enchantment, Sanjay was luxuriating in his role as Dawn's personal guide and historian.

"The English poet Sir Edwin Arnold called it 'not a piece of architecture, but a proud passion of an emperor's love, wrought in living stones.'" He held her chin in his hand. "'A celebration of a woman's love, exquisitely portrayed in marble.'"

Dawn sighed. "How romantic. What does 'Taj Mahal' mean?"

"'Crown Palace.' And you are my queen."

At her first glimpse of the stunning edifice, Dawn gasped, awestruck. "Oh, my God, it's magical."

Sanjay glowed with pleasure. "Just wait till you come closer."

Mohammed glanced back at the couple. "May I add to that, Sahib?"

Sanjay drank in Dawn's enthralled expression as she craned her neck to see more of the apparition on the banks of the river Yamuna coming into view. "Yes, go ahead." He sat back to observe the dialogue between her and Mohammed.

"Persian princess Mumtaz Mahal was Shah Jahan's second wife. He gave her this name, which meant 'beloved ornament of the palace.'"

"How romantic. Isn't that romantic, Sanjay?"

Sanjay nodded. Mohammed continued.

"She died giving birth to their fourteenth child."

"Uh-oh, not so romantic."

"He was so crushed he went into mourning for a year. When he appeared again, his hair and beard had turned white and his back was bent like an old man's."

Dawn frowned. "Oh, how sad."

"Building the Taj fulfilled his first promise to her while she was alive."

"What were the other promises?"

"Second, that he marry again. Third, to be kind to their children. Fourth, to visit her tomb on the anniversary of her death."

"And did he keep all of those?"

"Yes, the first two. Only seven of the children survived. But he remained devoted to her memory all his life. The Taj was meant as a symbol of eternal love. It took twenty thousand people twenty-two years to build."

He paused, while Dawn gasped. "It is best appreciated when the architecture and its adornments are linked to the passion that inspired it. If you understand my meaning."

The loving glance between Dawn and Sanjay confirmed their understanding.

Mohammed pulled the car as close as possible to the building and led the couple to the entrance. "The Queen's jewel-inlaid cenotaph lies within the dome."

Dawn drew in a sharp breath, taking in the sight before her. The celebrated dome, flanked by four tapering minarets, rose from a high, rectangular red sandstone base topped by an immense white marble terrace.

"The workmanship, it's so perfectly proportioned."

Mohammed nodded. "So exquisite, in fact, it has been described as 'designed by giants and finished by jewelers.' The only asymmetrical object is the casket of the Emperor, which was built beside the Queen's, as an afterthought."

Sanjay added, "The Shah's son deposed him and imprisoned him in the Great Red Fort for eight years."

"Oh, how unfair."

"Yes, my darling, it was. During that time he was not allowed to visit the Taj. Only in the minute reflection of a diamond could he have a view of his 'symbol of eternal love.' After his death, he was buried alongside his beloved wife."

The sobering explanation gave Dawn pause.

I've never imagined any love to be so strong.

The couple and their guide hovered by the main gate, where Mohammed resumed his monologue. "The base symbolizes the different ways of viewing a beautiful woman. The main gate is like the veil of a bride's face on her wedding night, lifted slowly and gently to reveal her beauty, as is the Indian tradition. Observe the arch above and the crypt inside."

Following Mohammed's instruction, Dawn and Sanjay directed their eyes upward and glimpsed the tomb inside, set against the background of the river.

"The reflection of the water transforms the view with magical colors. The semi-precious stones set into the tomb change their hue as they catch the glow of the rising moon. The pink tint in the morning light, the milky white color in the evening and the golden glow in the moonlight depict the changing moods of a woman."

Sanjay smiled at Dawn, squeezing her hand. "That explains a lot about you."

"It's always good to know, right?" Dawn returned his look.

Mohammed led them to the octagonal central chamber. "It is said the Shah intended to build another Taj across the river, this one of black marble. That is only legend and has never been proved."

Dawn moved for a closer look at the tomb's inscription and turned to Mohammed. "What does it say?"

"Translated, it reads, 'the illustrious sepulchre of Arjuman Banu Begum, called Mumtaz Mahal. God is everlasting. God is sufficient. He knoweth what is concealed and what is manifest. He is merciful and compassionate. Nearer unto him are those who say: Our Lord is God.'"

Dawn was impressed. "Wow. That's so beautiful. Isn't it, Sanjay?"

"Yes." He leaned over, lowering his voice. "But I think he must have meant 'love' rather than 'God.' At least that's how an atheist like me tends to think of it."

Mohammed remained in place while Sanjay led Dawn around the perimeter of the monument. Together the lovers lingered by the river, holding each other close, staring wide-eyed at the inspiring scenery. Sanjay kissed Dawn for a long moment.

"I love you as much as Jahan loved Mumtaz."

She returned his embrace. "Then would you build me a Taj, too?"

Sanjay gave a soft laugh. "If I could, I would build you ten of them. But I'm afraid you'll have to be content with a book."

"A book?"

"I promise you I will write a book, the book of Dawn. It will be the emblem of our love."

"'The Book of Dawn.' I like the sound of it. Or maybe, 'Dawnsearlylite?'"

"I'll name it whatever you want, my darling."

There, as the Taj had bore witness four hundred years before to the eternal love between Mumtaz and Shah Jahan, the embodiment of their devoted passion entered the souls of Dawn and Sanjay.

42

Dawn and Sanjay's retreat into the tranquility of India proved an idyllic time for the lovers. In the mornings after breakfast, they strolled through the gardens, and then went to the fitness room to work out. Later in the day, they tried the spa, indulging in the hotel's signature couples massage. For dinners, they sampled all five restaurants in the resort. Sanjay introduced Dawn to the delights of exotic and spicy South Indian Vegetarian cuisine at the Deccan Pavilion.

For a full day, they toured Agra Fort, originally built as a military installation and converted into a palace for the emperor and his queen. The Sheesh, or "glass palace" inside the fort delighted Dawn. She loved the idea of the oversized tub for the queen's bathing. She also noticed how the special harem intrigued Sanjay and teased him about it.

"You men and your harems."

"I don't really need it as long as I have you."

"Yeah, right." But she still smiled.

After four blissful days in Agra, the lovers headed to Delhi for some sightseeing and shopping. Sanjay thought he detected a softening in Dawn's demeanor. He hoped the magical atmosphere of the Taj had mellowed her heart. Dawn was made of steel, but he was convinced the awe and beauty they had experienced, coupled with his blind infatuation for her, would do wonders for her determination not to abandon her heart to him. Dawn tried to resist the romantic pull of the "symbol of eternal love" the Taj represented. Ultimately she gave in to it and allowed herself to love Sanjay to the extent her stubborn nature allowed her.

Sanjay and Dawn both found the contrasts in Delhi fascinating. Its extremes between old and new, riches and poverty, were typical of large

Asian cities. They both coughed up black soot by the second day from the pollution in the air, but they felt the limitless shopping and diversity in choice of food were worth the trade-off. Dawn loved jewelry, especially diamonds and pearls, and the shops in Connaught Place stuffed with gems and sparkling gold gave her plenty of eye candy.

"I can't believe how much gold there is in India."

"This country is almost single-handedly responsible for the high demand for the metal. Though I don't know why Indian women are so enamored of it. I don't find it very pretty at all."

Dawn fingered a delicate gold filigree necklace, holding it up against her creamy skin. "Are you sure?"

"On you, my angel, even stainless steel would be beautiful."

Dawn's energy was beginning to flag from all the excitement of their adventure. Between sightseeing, shopping and trying different restaurants day and night, she became too exhausted to make love. Sanjay didn't mind. He was love-struck and couldn't think of anything else than trying to get through to the heart and soul underneath Dawn's defenses, though he had no illusions about succeeding.

Even the gods can't do that. And I'm only one measly human.

At the Embassy Restaurant in Connaught Place, the two lovers shared a scrumptious vegetarian meal of succotash, blackeye dumplings, and the Indian dessert, Kheer. Sanjay watched, concerned, as Dawn picked at her food. "Not hungry, dearest?"

"I'm sorry, Sanjay. This has been one exhausting trip. I'm going to need a vacation when we get home."

He laughed. "We've hardly scratched the surface. There's so much more to see in this huge country."

"Oh, no." She groaned. "Don't even think about it."

"But someday, my love, I want to take you to the place where I was born. I grew up in a small village, just like you. This one is nestled in the Himalayas."

"You did? Cool. What's it called?"

"Simla. I've been all over the world, but to me Simla is the most beautiful place."

"What makes it so special?"

"During British rule, people went there to escape the summer heat, so it became quite a social magnet. Even Kipling went there for excitement. He found the social life scandalous."

"Ooh, sounds steamy. Just my style."

"You'd be interested in the education there, too."

Her guard went up. Why did he think she was interested in education? She suppressed a shudder and pretended not to identify with the subject.

"The oldest private school in Asia, the Bishop Cotton School, is there. The Brits established it to educate their children."

"Fascinating."

"Its former students have contributed to professional life all over the world, for close to two hundred years."

"I'm impressed, Sanjay."

"But mostly it's like heaven there, Dawn, high in the mountains, with gorgeous soaring green vistas everywhere. Those meadows, like a balcony to the sky, would tempt even the gods to come down and frolic" He sighed. "I'd go back in a heartbeat."

She eyed him. "But not this trip, right?"

"Don't worry." He flashed her a tender smile. "We did what we came to do. We saw the world's only monument to eternal love. That's all that counts."

"Yeah, like a pilgrimage, right? Vatican City for Catholics, or Israel for Jews, or Mecca for Muslims."

"And Yatra."

"Yatra?"

"It's the ultimate holy place for Hindus, the shrine they travel to so they can pray at all four Dhams of Hinduism." He thought for a moment. "Just like those once-in-a-lifetime trips for religion's sake, lovers like us have to make a trip to the Taj. That's our religion, Dawn."

All of a sudden, Dawn began to laugh so hard tears streamed down her face.

"What is so funny?"

Dawn had to use all her strength to stop herself from laughing. "Nothing. I think your idea is fantastic. We should start a new trend, the 'Taj Mahal.' Kind of a 'must-do' for lovers."

Sanjay's eyes lit up. "Yes. People could say to each other, 'Have you done your Taj Mahal yet?' And if they haven't, they would say, 'you haven't? What kind of lover are you?'"

"Awesome, Sanjay. We've just created a whole new invention. Are we clever or what?"

The evening of their midnight flight back to Canada, Sanjay suggested a romantic "last supper" at Parikrama, an upscale revolving restaurant perched high atop the tallest building in the city. Dawn gawked at the view from their window-side table, with the carpet of lights at their feet and the Red Fort at the center of their sightline. "This is fabulous." She gazed around at the ancient Indian art and artifacts making up the décor. "It's almost more like a museum than an eating place."

"You're absolutely right." Sanjay paused. "I have something to ask you, Dawn."

Dawn swallowed hard. The ominous tone of his voice made her uneasy. "Let's have a beer first."

"Of course."

Two Kingfisher beers appeared almost as soon as Sanjay ordered them. He clinked bottles with Dawn. "Did you know this beer is made in England and imported back here?"

"Nope."

Dawn drank at a rapid pace, in nervous anticipation of what Sanjay had to say. He did the same in order to quell the butterflies in his stomach. The restaurant revolved to reveal a view of the India Gate, a kind of Indian *Arc de Triomphe* located in the middle of a crossroads at the center of the city. The one hundred-forty-foot structure was a war memorial containing the names of Indian soldiers who died fighting for the British in World War I and Indian and British soldiers killed in the Afghan War of 1919. War was the last thing Sanjay wanted to think of at that moment. Like Shah Jahan, he had love on his mind and in his heart.

Dawn's spicy chicken curry and Sanjay's chickpea entrée arrived. Dawn was hungry, but she could no longer wait to hear what Sanjay had to say.

"Okay, spill it. The suspense is killing me."

Sanjay was having serious doubts, but he summoned up his courage and forged ahead. "Let's get married."

Dawn looked down, not knowing how to react.

"Here, in India. An Indian style wedding." He grasped her hands and pressed them to his lips. "Make me the happiest man on earth, Dawn."

Shocked, but not surprised, she chose her words with caution. "But, Sanjay, you're already married. You have a wife. Can you have two wives here in India?"

"I want you, Dawn, just you. You are the only one I want for a wife."

She looked at the luscious plate of curry. Her appetite vanished. "In that case, you'll just have to get a divorce."

Sanjay furrowed his brow. "That's a long, tedious process. And a painful one."

"Then I'll just continue to be your mistress. What's the difference, anyway? You can have me whenever you want."

"I know, Dawn, I'm aware of that. But you deserve more. You're beautiful, educated, sophisticated. An angel." He searched her faces for a sign of recognition. "I can't just keep you as my mistress. I want you as my wife."

Dawn shook her head. "Sanjay, you're not being rational. It's just not possible. And even if it were, the whole thing about my identity would come up again. You know how I feel about—" The arrival of their server with a tray full of spicy side dishes interrupted her protest. She breathed a silent sigh of relief. "Let's talk about it another time, okay?"

Extracting her hands from his grasp, Dawn picked up her fork and tasted her food. The piquant flavor of the chicken reawakened her hunger. Life had its perks, after all.

43

Getting back to reality at home was more difficult than usual for Sanjay. He protracted his already late rising from bed with a self-indulgent extra fifteen minutes of daydreaming about Dawn. His habitual routine, ear-curling Jamaican coffee and perusing the screaming headlines about the madness in Iraq, did nothing to divert his thoughts away from her. As it had done so many times before, the image of a patient with lung cancer whose disease metastasized through the entire body and ravaged the brain assailed his consciousness. It paralleled his obsession with Dawn. Visions of predator cells, choking off the oxygen supply to his vital organs, ruled his being. Memories of her suffused his grey matter like lethal blue cancer organisms breaking off from the tissue and flying with rapidity through the bloodstream, attaching to the struggling red and white cells. The video of Dawn remained on auto play, repeating without end.

The scene waiting for him at the hospital, however, wrenched him out of his fog.

"Code Blue, ER, Code Blue, ER!"

The paging system shrieked, its insistent repetition producing a rush of adrenaline in Sanjay's consciousness. It coincided with the arrival of a racing ambulance with lights flashing and sirens blaring. Sanjay found the ER already in motion. Two nurses, an emergency room physician, and two ICU residents awaited the code blue arrival with impatience. The respiratory technologists, middle-aged Edward and twenty-four-year-old Tanya, were readying the resuscitation kit. Sanjay strode in and flashed an approving glance at Tanya, who had opened the intubation kit and was selecting a size eight endotracheal tube. Tanya did good work. And she was easy on the eyes.

The patient was wheeled in. The resident filled in Sanjay on the usual details. "Romeo Charlie, thirty-eight-year-old male, unconscious, no pulse, probably brain-dead."

"Married?" Sanjay addressed the resident.

"Yes, doctor, a Mr. McTaggert. His wife came in with him. Said he complained of a nagging pain in his chest and left arm all morning. Keeled over at the breakfast table. She thought it was a heart attack, but he insisted he was too young."

"Yes, that story is all too familiar."

The resident continued. "Tried to get up. Didn't want to waste a beautiful Saturday morning in a stinky, overcrowded ER, the wife said."

The emergency technician compressed the patient's chest, while Tanya masked and bagged his oral and nasal orifices. Sanjay checked the rhythm and pulse and calculated the down time of the resuscitation records. He looked down at the patient. It was over for the guy, no question.

"Modern medicine can't save him now. Neither could Jesus Christ, God the Father or the supreme Allah."

The tech frowned, continuing his futile attempts at resuscitation. "Don't you want to take over, doctor?"

Sanjay shook his head. "He's dead. Let's leave him in peace." He hated pronouncing those words, as necessary as they were.

What modern sciences are not, and what God's powers are not. Shame he had to die so young.

Leaving the ER personnel to take over, Sanjay made his way from the room. His first thought was of the deceased's wife, whose grief he needed to console. He hated doing that even more than the act of pronouncing someone dead. His next thought was of the living. He hadn't had yet time to check his email for a message from Dawn. He strode into his office and found one waiting.

Hi Sanjay,

I was pouring bubble bath under a stream of warm running water and thought of you. I just wanted to send you a short note thanking you for your last email

Thanks in advance for offering to send me a check. That was so thoughtful of you. It's not necessary to send it by express mail. Regular mail is fine, though you could send it Priority if you like, no problem. Your call.

My bath is ready now. I really need to relax my muscles. I've been doing some really intense workouts at the gym all week. I plan to take a break from that tomorrow.

Hope you're having a nice day. Talk to you soon.

Dawn

P.S. I keep reminiscing about our visit to India, what an amazing country! One moment you are like, 'Get me out of here, this place is crazy.' And an hour later you see the sunset or hear the sounds of local music and you're like, 'This is the most beautiful thing I have ever seen or heard.' You're awesome.

The email read like a business letter. No words of endearment, not even a hint of affection. Sanjay was disappointed, but upon further reflection he realized he wasn't surprised.

Well, yes. It is a "business arrangement" after all.

Clicking on the screen to minimize the message, he went off to make the acquaintance of Mrs. McTaggert.

44

Compared to the rest of Canada, Spring break in the Québec schools came early. Dawn took advantage of her vacation to spend some time with her parents in the States. The contrast between the still-nippy Montréal air and the searing Georgia heat knocked her over the instant she stood under the large sunroof in the airport's main terminal. Vienne was not the bustling hub Atlanta was, but the beautifully renovated airport reflected an increasing faith in the city's burgeoning commercial potential.

Dawn's early flight arrival gave her some time to explore the airport shops and gulp down a cappuccino from Starbuck's. Her father, Dr. Pierre L'andry, was tied up with his ER duties that day. His wife Deanna took on the task of picking up their daughter. Glancing at her watch, Dawn gulped the rest of her coffee and headed out to the curb. Her mother had a habit of being prompt and disliked waiting. As she had suspected, the Nissan Pathfinder was parked at the curbside. Dawn walked over to her mother and hugged her.

"Welcome home, dear."

"Thanks, Mom."

Deanna loaded Dawn's suitcase in the SUV. "Well, shall we?"

It didn't take long, in the light afternoon traffic, to exit the airport and be on the Interstate for the hour's drive to Statesville, or for Deanna to reveal what was on her mind.

"So how are things in Montréal?"

"Same old, same old."

"How's school? Still love teaching?"

"Yeah, of course. Why wouldn't I?"

"I'm glad, dear. We were so proud of you when you received the award. And Sophie? Do you see her often? And your other girlfriends?"

"Sophie? Sure. She visits from Ottawa whenever she can."

Deanna paused. Dawn was uncomfortable. A silence often meant her mother had something on her mind.

"Seeing anyone? Since breaking up with Olivier, I mean."

"No. Why?" Deanna lit a cigarette and offered one to Dawn, who shook her head.

"Thanks, but I just quit smoking, you know. I don't want to fall off the wagon so soon."

"Go ahead, you might need it."

Dawn frowned at her mother, taken aback. "What do you mean, Mom?"

"Well . . ." Deanna took a long drag. "I have something serious to talk to you about."

Oh, Lord, I knew it. What could it be? Did she find out about Sanjay? How is that possible?

"Couldn't it wait till we get home?" Dawn took the proffered cigarette, lit it and cracked open the window.

"Yeah, I thought so, but I can't wait that long." Deanna took the exit to Interstate 301 North and pulled the car into a Texaco station soon afterwards.

Dawn looked around, puzzled. "Why are we stopping here? Are we going to visit Lorie?" Dawn was fond of her sister, and especially her two little boys, who despite their autism were cuter than Easter chicks.

"No, she's on shift at the operating room today. She'd love to see you tomorrow, though." Deanna pulled up next to a Dunkin' Donuts. "Let's sit down for some coffee and chat."

Dawn followed her mother into the cramped area near a checkout counter. The place smelled like hot oil and sugar. The two women chose a table as far away from the door as possible and sat down with their comfort food, large coffees, an apple fritter and a French cruller.

"Umm, good pastry." Deanna broke off small pieces of her fritter and chewed on them, savoring each morsel. "Want another ciggie?"

Nervous, Dawn gave in. "Sure. Now what's up?"

Heaving a sigh, Deanna gazed at her daughter. "Dad and I are worried about you, hon. You're turning twenty-nine in a few months, you're still single, and nothing is on the horizon. At least as far as I can tell."

"So?"

"So. When are you going to get married? When are you going to have children?"

Dawn shrugged. She had been thinking of Sanjay all day. Deanna's pointed questions brought feelings of guilt and remorse to the surface.

If she only knew I'm a mistress to someone. It is a kind of marriage after all. God, if mom and dad find out about this, or my double life, they'll kill me.

Her daughter's silence didn't stop Deanna from pursuing the subject. "Listen to me, Renée. When you're young it's okay to have fun, meet lots of boys, experiment. But there comes a point in your life when you have to be serious."

"Mom—"

"I was only eighteen when I married your dad, and I had your brother Jean at nineteen. I know the times are different now, but your reproductive years are passing you by. You don't want to be damaged goods. Then no one will marry you."

"You know I've always dreamed of having a family, but I've never even had a long-term relationship except with Olivier. And we both know he wasn't the right person for me."

Whether or not he knew about my "work." And the lure of money and hot sex was more important than—

Deanna began to cough and gasp for air. She dug out a blue inhaler from her purse and sucked in two quick puffs from it.

Dawn frowned with concern. "Someone with chronic obstructive pulmonary disease shouldn't be smoking."

"I know, I know. I just can't stop. I wish I could. Believe me, I've tried."

They each lit another cigarette and took a deep drag. Deanna bit her lip, nervous, finally finding the courage to come out with her statement.

"I hope you're not doing anything, you know, bad."

Dawn was shaken.

You have no idea.

"Like what, Mom?" She gazed at her mother's anxious face. "I don't know what you mean. What could I be doing? Don't you trust me?"

"Of course, hon, you're my daughter. You and your siblings are the best kids in the world, just like Dad and I raised you. I'd feel awful if you thought I suspected you of . . . well . . . it's just . . ." She crushed out her cigarette and lit another. "You have all these nice clothes and expensive jewelry and you're always going on trips. I just wonder sometimes, that's all."

"I told you before, Mom, I do private tutoring, which pays really well. And I make great tips at that fancy restaurant in downtown Montréal on weekends." She peered at Deanna. "Is that what you wanted to talk to me about? Money?"

"No, sweetie."

"Then what?"

"Well, both Dad and I, we both wanted to talk to you about marriage."

"Marriage? What about marriage? I don't understand."

"We'll discuss it tonight, with Dad, after dinner."

"I can't wait till tonight. I want you to tell me now. Come on, out with it."

"Let's go before your father gets home." Deanna rose. "By the way, I'm cooking your favorite, pasta al forno Siciliano and Caesar salad."

Before Dawn could protest, Deanna was striding towards the exit. Dawn had no choice but to follow her.

45

Dawn was pleased when her mother took the Main Street exit of the highway and passed by the Statesville City Hall. It may not have been Montréal, but Dawn had a soft spot for the small city. It had a pleasant atmosphere, as small towns go, and she had often thought of spending the rest of her life there.

Deanna tried to lighten up the tense atmosphere between her and her daughter. "Remember how much you enjoyed studying our town's history when you were in school?"

Dawn glimpsed the statues of General Sherman and the plaques commemorating his 1864 march through Georgia that had decimated most of the state. "'Statesville, incorporated 1866, only city of that name in the U.S., probably named after the state of Georgia.' You see, I still remember."

"Did you know Georgia Southern has more than fourteen thousand students now? It made U.S. News and World Reports' list of the South's top five up-and-coming regional universities."

Dawn whistled. "Wow, that's pretty cool."

"Too bad you didn't want to go there."

"I wasn't about to give up a scholarship to the Université de Montréal, even for a place with Botanical Gardens, a Raptor Center and a Bald Eagle Sanctuary."

"No, I guess not. Remember how you always said you could live here for the rest of your life?"

"Is that a hint, Mom?"

Pierre was already home when his wife and favorite daughter arrived. "Renée, I can't believe you're really here. You made my day." He gave her a quick hug. She followed as he heaved her suitcase up the stairs to the guest room.

Dawn studied his face. "Hard day in the ER?"

"Well, since you asked, yes. A bit." He placed her suitcase on a rack by the door and hugged her again. "Why don't you rest a bit before dinner?"

"Thanks, Dad, I think I really need it."

He turned to go. "By the way, we're having a guest. So dress up nice, okay? That's my girl."

Okay, there's definitely something up with them. But whatever it is, I need a nap first.

Pierre tiptoed out the door and closed it. She was fast asleep before he reached the bottom of the stairs.

*

Dawn awoke at seven pm. Daylight still bathed the view out her window.

I wish our days grew longer in Montréal as soon as they do here.

She put on her navy blue Mandarin collar dress and matching pumps. Not knowing the mystery guest's identity, she wanted to present a conservative image. He was waiting when she came downstairs.

"This is my daughter, Renée." Pierre gestured to the boyish young man sitting on the living room sofa.

"Nice to meet you, Dawn, I'm John." He rose and extended his hand. "John Kriarakis."

Dawn eyed the guy, who looked as if he was straight out of high school, and shook his hand. "Nice to meet you, too."

"I've heard a lot about you from your parents."

"All good, I hope."

The two young people laughed. Pierre brought them each a glass of red wine.

"Why don't you two get acquainted while Mom gets supper ready? I have some calls to make to the hospital."

Dawn watched as her father turned and left the room. She eyed the newcomer.

Oh, now I get it. So this is the "surprise." A suitor. He's not half-bad.

They sat on the sofa, sipping their wine.

"So, John, what's your story?"

"It's a long one. Sure you're up for it?"

"We have all evening. And you already know all about me."

"Okay, here goes." He took a long swallow. "My father came from just north of Athens. My mom is second generation."

"Ah, I thought your name sounded Greek."

"My dad came through New England first. He did every kind of odd job you can imagine, from driving a cab to working in restaurants, finally settling for work in a steel foundry. It paid decently, and with my mom's income from working at a pizza parlor, they were able to buy a small house and raise my two siblings and me."

"I always admire immigrants who can make a life from so little."

John smiled. "It's nice to know you appreciate that."

"Oh, totally. So how did you get here?"

"My folks wanted to find a place with lots of job opportunities, less expensive than Massachusetts, with a large Greek community. We found it in Vienne."

"I didn't know there were so many Greeks here."

"Oh, yes. The first one came over to Vienne in 1881 to work for Jean Lafitte."

"The pirate?" Dawn was incredulous.

"Yep. That guy and his family ended up in Galveston. Other Greeks followed. They did everything from selling fish and flowers to hauling charcoal and washing dishes in restaurants. Some of them eventually became restaurateurs and real estate moguls."

"And your dad?"

He emptied his glass. "My dad's dream was to open a pizza place."

"Do you want me to get you another red wine?" Dawn rose.

"No, thanks, Renée. That was fine. I don't want to stagger into the dining room." He chuckled. "Please. Sit."

Dawn obeyed. She was beginning to warm to him. "So you spent your childhood hanging around, helping your folks with their 'mom and pop' enterprise."

"Yeah. How did you know?"

"I guess my parents didn't tell you how smart I am." She smiled.

He returned the look. "Oh, yes. They did."

Their eyes locked. Dawn gestured. "Go on, tell me more. I'm fascinated."

"Well, it wasn't easy. Competition was fierce, and we struggled to keep our heads above water. We survived because we all pitched in."

"And especially you."

"How did you know?"

"I told you, I'm smart." She smiled. "So what was it like for you and your siblings?"

"We did our homework in between serving customers and delivering pizza."

"I'll bet it was tough working and trying to do schoolwork."

"Yeah, but I survived. My brother and sister chose other occupations, but I was happy to stay and work with my dad. We opened a place in Statesville 17 years ago. We've known your family for ages. Your dad stops in for lunch all the time."

"Oh, is that why he's getting that little paunch?"

Deanna strolled in, interrupting their laughter. "Still talking, you two? Come, let's eat."

Dawn eyed the dining room table, groaning with a feast of baked parmesan chicken, home-made pasta al forno Siciliano, Caesar salad and homemade bread. It outshone anything in her recent memory. The bread was a surefire tip-off to Dawn that her mother meant business. Deanna made bread from scratch only on the most important occasions.

The two couples took their time eating to savor every bit of Deanna's exquisite cooking. Dawn could not believe how hungry she was and had to restrain herself to avoid wolfing down her food.

"This is luscious, Mrs. L'andry."

"Please, John, call me Deanna."

"It's delicious, Deanna." John turned to Dawn. "I hear you just came back from India. How was it? Where did you go?"

"Agra and Delhi. It was a fabulous trip. What an amazing country. It draws you in. You love it and hate it all at once, and then you just can't wait to go back."

"What did you like best?"

"The Taj Mahal, no question." She sighed. "So beautiful. And romantic."

"Did you go by yourself, or with a friend?"

Dawn thought quickly. "Ah, with my girlfriend, Chantal. She's one of my teaching buddies. We had a great time."

Deanna appeared with dessert. Dawn sighed with relief. She was not about to blame John for all his questions. Still, that one was too close for comfort.

"*Crème brûlée.*" Deanna made her announcement with pride. "And baklava. Courtesy of Vacation Pizza."

John blushed at Deanna's shameless endorsement, which didn't stop him from scraping all the tiny morsels from the bottom of the dessert ramekin.

At 11 pm, he excused himself. "I have to go back and help my mom close the restaurant. Mrs. L'andry, I mean, Deanna, it was a delightful evening. Thank you." He took Dawn's hand. "And it was a pleasure meeting you, Dawn. I really enjoyed talking to you."

"Me, too."

Deanna insisted on doing the clean up. Pierre couldn't wait to pick Dawn's brain about John.

"So? Did you like him?"

"He's nice enough, I guess."

"'Nice enough?' He's the nicest young man in town."

Dawn looked at her father with suspicion. "Why do you ask, Dad?"

"Why? Because he's the best catch in Statesville."

"And by 'best catch' you mean?"

"I know him well from when he helped out at the hospital. John's a hard worker and helps out his parents in their business. He and his mother are taking care of it single-handed. His father is quite ill." He paused. "And he's still not married."

Dawn grimaced. "Oh? Aren't there any nice girls here?"

"Don't be rude, Renée."

"Sorry, Dad."

Having finished the kitchen work, Deanna, who had been eavesdropping behind the kitchen door, sauntered in.

"Your father and I think John would be an ideal husband for you, Renée. Would you consider marrying him?"

Dawn looked at them, incensed. They were ganging up on her. How could they have conspired to rope her into this?

What is this, a third world country? Like India, where they arrange marriages?

She took a deep breath to curb her outrage. "Look, Mom and Dad, you know I've always loved and respected you. But I never imagined you'd go behind my back to find a husband for me."

Deanna looked hurt. "We haven't gone behind your back, Renée, we—"

"Yes. You have. How dare you put me in such a position, inviting over a prospective suitor without asking me first?"

Pierre interjected. "Renée, I think you're being a bit hasty."

"I'm being hasty? What about you? Talking about marriage, when I hardly know the guy?" She bit her lip to quell her anger. "I can't marry him. I don't even love him. And I'm not ready for marriage."

Dawn wasn't prepared for the barrage that followed from both parents, who came forth with both barrels blazing.

"Are you in love with someone else?"

"We know your relationship with Olivier fell through, but—"

"What are you going to do, wait for Prince Charming?"

Dawn didn't respond. Her heart still ached for Olivier, in spite of his betrayal and the lawsuit pending against him at small claims court. She thought about Sanjay, who had entered her life, and maybe her heart. He had already proposed to her, at least in his fashion. Through all her soul-searching, her parents still hammered away at her. They were nothing if not persistent. She was sure they would continue to hold out hope of her yielding to their wishes. But what her father said next bowled her over.

"Why don't you and John go to Vienne together while you're here, maybe to Hilton Head? You can charge the whole thing on my Visa. See if you can grow to like him." She watched his expression, which looked sincere. "He's a very nice guy, Renée, the best for you. Trust me. You'll see."

Dawn shrugged. "I'll think about it, Dad. Right now, I think I need to go to bed."

Pierre smiled. "Of course, darling. We all can use some rest."

The three family members hugged and went off to their respective rooms. Dawn lay down on her bed, thinking about how devoted she felt to her father. She loved him too much not to make an effort at pleasing him. Maybe he was right. Maybe she needed to give a relationship with John a fighting chance.

After all, what have I got to lose?

46

Deanna arranged for Dawn and John to meet at the French Quarter Café on their first date.

"Just a nice evening, to get to know each other better."

Underneath that innocent assertion was Deanna's hope that the fine Cajun cuisine, live music and cozy atmosphere would conspire to make the two young people warm to each other. She reserved a cozy table for two far enough away from the musicians to allow intimate conversation and afford a view of the red brick City Hall building across the street. Deanna wanted to set the stage for serious relationship potential between her daughter and the "best catch in Statesville." She took care of all the details, including prepayment with Pierre's Visa card.

Dawn and John ensconced themselves at their table. She gazed at the City Hall, her mind wandering to Sanjay.

"Have you been here before?" John's query interrupted her reverie.

"Yeah, once, I think. You?"

"I come here a lot. It's a nice place to bring a date, with the music and all. Food's great, too."

"Umm." Dawn pulled her gaze from the window and back to her companion. "So tell me what else you've done besides help out your dad."

"I studied nursing."

"Wow, I didn't know guys were into that."

"Yep. It's been the trend lately."

"So what happened?"

"Well, between my studies and working at the pizza restaurant and football practice—"

"You played football?" Dawn pictured rippling muscles. "Awesome."

"Yeah. I guess I was good at it."

Dawn laughed. "I guess so."

"Anyway, I didn't have time for the full course of study. That required two to four years at Southern Georgia U. So I went for a part-time certified nursing assistant training course. It usually takes twelve weeks, but it took me a year."

"Then did you actually work in hospitals and stuff?"

"Yeah, and at nursing homes."

"Cool. Did my mom tell you I'm a qualified geriatric attendant?"

"No kidding." John gave Dawn an admiring look. "I loved the work. You know, helping people who can't help themselves, really satisfying. I couldn't keep it up, though."

"Why not? Too little pay?"

"Yeah, plus the emotional demands of caring for old people gets to you after a while. And dealing with the young people isn't easy, either. Alcoholism and drug dependency, really harsh."

Dawn gave him a look of sympathy. "Yeah, my dad's told me about how hard nurses work."

"Can you believe doctors get mega bucks for spending five minutes with a patient, and the nurses get decent salary, but the assistants who do the real work get next to nothing." He frowned. "Oh, sorry, no offense to your dad."

"None taken. I know what happens in those situations."

"Anyway, after my dad's stroke, I had to devote full time to helping my mom. I'm the one who really manages the place. I'll own it someday."

"Yes, I figured that."

Dawn pictured John's muscular arms lifting heavy cartons. The image was enticing. And he was trying to impress her with his eventual earning potential.

"We make a good profit. Immigrant labor is cheap here in Georgia, so we can keep our costs low." He searched her face for signs of recognition. There was none, so he changed the subject. "I'd love to visit Montréal. Don't think I could live there, though. Too many memories of shivering my way through childhood in Massachusetts."

"I hear you. I pretty much hibernate all winter. I loved the warm humid weather when I lived here."

"Oh? So you think you might come back here to live?"

Dawn smiled. "You never know."

"I think you'd really like my house. Why not come for a visit tomorrow?"

"Sure, why not?"

On her way home, Dawn mused about John and what he meant to her future. She needed an escape hatch in case her double life became exposed one day. As careful as she was to cover her tracks, her woman's intuition nagged at the back of her mind.

I'll be outed someday. How, I don't know. But if I ever have to get out of Montréal, John could be my ticket.

Dawn managed to maintain a positive spin on her thoughts over breakfast with her parents at breakfast the next morning.

"So? How did it go? Do you like him?" Deanna hardly looked at her eggs.

"Yeah, he's a nice guy. He likes taking care of old people, just like me."

"He's going to be very successful at his business. He'll make you very happy, without doubt. You won't regret choosing him for a mate. His family history in our area is impressive."

Dawn glimpsed Pierre nodding in agreement behind his morning newspaper. "Yeah, I know all that. But I don't know if I'm ready."

Deanna cut short Dawn's protest. "Don't drag your feet, my dear. He's already had offers from Greek girls, from here to Athens. If you're smart, you'll jump at the chance. Immediately." She searched Dawn's conflicted face. "He's good looking and he owns a restaurant. What more do you want?"

My parents are trying to trap me into an arranged marriage. Me, the most beautiful "catch" in history. I can't believe this.

Dawn tried to mollify her parents. "We're meeting tomorrow night, at his house. That should make you happy."

Her parents' pleased expressions lighting up the kitchen, Dawn sipped her coffee and thought again about her difficult position. Deanna and Pierre knew nothing about her secret life. Prostitution, like the stock market, was something easy to get into, but difficult to disentangle from. Sanjay knew about it. She had nothing to fear from him in that regard. He was handsome and athletic and enjoyed money, titles and fame. And he had offered her marriage, of a sort. But he was older than she, older than John. And he was married.

That can put a real crimp in a relationship.

*

Dawn was familiar with Miramichi Drive, where John's house was located. The setting was rural, the neighborhood much less upscale than her parents'. She pulled the Pathfinder into the driveway and glanced at the dwelling. The lot was large, but the abode was average and uninspiring. No comparison between this and her own condo in Montréal.

I could never live in this. Unless I were desperate.

John greeted her at the door, helped her off with her jacket and led her to the living room. A paint bucket, roller and brushes set on newspapers occupied one corner of the room. The walls sported oversized posters of rock stars like Chris Pierson, Van Morrison and Sade and other music talents, and one of football's "bigboy," Tom Brady.

Dawn suppressed her dismay at the plainness of the décor. "Nice house, John. I really like it."

She watched his smile of pleasure and focused on her excitement at the thought of an evening of lovemaking. Whether or not the marriage became a *fait accompli*, the prospect of sex was no different with this man than any other. It didn't matter where, or with whom.

"Wine or Ouzo?"

"Which has a higher proof?"

"Ouzo."

"Then bring it on."

John poured two glasses and clinked with Dawn. "Ouzo is to Greeks what vodka is to Russians. With all the Greeks in Vienne, it's pretty much available anywhere."

Dawn sipped. The taste of the spicy drink made her wish she had opted for wine. But she needed the high alcohol content to relax her. "So tell me what else you like, besides restaurants . . ." She gestured at the wall posters. "And sports."

"Watching TV, traveling. And just taking it easy." He motioned her to the sofa, where they both sat down.

"Me, too. Life is for having fun, right?" She smiled. "Have you brought many girls here? Had many relationships?"

"A few. How about you?"

"Yeah. A few."

The awkward silence between them made them move on with the conversation.

Dawn broke the quietness. "So, read any good books lately?"

"Oh, no, actually I hate reading. It's a waste of time. I only read what I have to. For my business, you know?"

Her heart sank. "Oh. That's too bad. I love books."

Good thing I'm feeling drunk.

The front doorbell rang. John leapt up. "That must be the pizza."

"Pizza? Gee, I thought you were cooking tonight." She winked and flashed him a jocular smile.

"Nope."

Dawn watched, incredulous, as he ran to the door. She thought it impolite, even gauche, to invite a prospective bride for dinner and serve pizza.

Oh well, what the hell. As long as he's good in bed.

After John had bolted down most of the box's contents, they segued to the bedroom. Dawn didn't resist the pull of his hand. Most of the men she slept with were older. Her mouth watered at the notion of having sex with a strapping young man.

A hard man is good to find.

In the bedroom, they undressed. Dawn was surprised.

"Don't you want to kiss first?"

John blushed. "Oh. Yeah. Sorry. I haven't been with a woman in a long time."

She tried to make light of the problem. "Oh? Tough getting laid in a small town?"

He smiled, sheepish. "Yeah, actually."

"It's okay." Dawn thought about John getting off on pornographic satellite TV movies. "We'll take care of you. Not to worry."

John kissed her lips. She responded, pulling his tongue into her mouth. Encouraged, he moved to her neck and breasts.

"I . . . I can't wait, Dawn."

"I can't either." She pulled him down on the bed.

"French Acadian women turn me on." He was on top of her and inside her in within a second.

"Really?"

His thrusting became more urgent. She fantasized about Sanjay.

If only all my encounters could be as hot as with him.

Not wanting to seem too "professional," Dawn moaned and screamed enough to show John her pleasure. She wasn't surprised when he came after a moment. Men who are deprived of sex for long periods of time were expected to do so. She didn't reach climax, but she did enjoy the feeling of his hard, young, thirty-one-year-old body pressing against hers.

Spent, John lay back on the bed. "When do you go back to Montréal?"

"In two days."

"Oh. So soon?"

Dawn brought her attention back from Sanjay. "March break is short." She read the disappointment in his face. "Plus I have to prepare lessons for next semester. Teaching math is hard. You have to know it inside out but be able to make it simple enough to drill it into the kids' heads."

"I have a lot of respect for that. I don't know how you do it, Renée."

"Thanks."

Dawn got up and started to dress. John gazed at her body, admiring it. "You know, I've had a lot of, uh, proposals. From Greek girls."

"I know. My mom told me."

"But you're different, Renée. You're sophisticated, educated, savvy. And I've always had a thing for French-Canadian women. I never thought I'd meet one and . . . well, get to know her."

"Really? I'm flattered."

"I like you, Renée. I really do."

"I like you, too, John."

Dawn thought about her parents. They were indeed trying to arrange a marriage for her, but she couldn't blame them. They worried about her, about her future, living alone in a hostile, dangerous city, and they wanted her to live closer to them. John was an eligible bachelor, easy on the eyes, who owned a thriving business. She understood why they thought him a logical choice. Her heart of steel kicked in, thinking about what a relationship with John held in store. She didn't feel great enthusiasm for him, especially as a lover, but he had potential. The possibility of instructing him in the fine art of lovemaking motivated her to consider his proposal, which she was sure was forthcoming. She wasn't about to dismiss him without careful consideration. She could grow to like him. Two words occurred to her when she thought of John, embodying her thoughts when it came to a relationship with him.

Safety net.

47

Dawn found the pressure at St. Paul Junior High after spring break unbearable. Most of the students had forgotten what she had taught them, and she had less than a month to prepare them for final exams. The extra classes required in order to accomplish this meant little time for her own needs. Compounding this problem was her inability to focus on her classroom work or prepare her lessons as well as she had in the past. Since her visit to the Taj Mahal and her subsequent introduction to John, Dawn felt distracted. Her outlook on life had changed. She was unable to see herself staying with her chosen lifestyle indefinitely. Worse, she couldn't hide the alteration in her demeanor from the children. Observant little creatures that they are, they noticed the difference and became restless and less productive in class. Their parents were not happy about this, but Dawn didn't know what to do to improve the situation.

Dawn tried everything possible to pull herself out of her funk. She sought counseling from her Opus Dei priest. Although Sanjay had fulfilled her monetary needs for some time, she even tried escorting one weekend, rationalizing altruistic contributions to the school as her financial motivation. Nothing helped. She decided to look for consolation in the arms of her friend Sophie, whom she hadn't seen in months.

The May weekend was spring-like and balmy. Tulips and chicks appeared all over Montréal out of nowhere. Dawn invited her friend and teaching colleague Chantal to join her at the Japanese restaurant to await Sophie's late arrival from Ottawa on Friday evening. Over sake and sushi, the two women watched Sophie dash into the restaurant. Dawn ran over to greet her friend.

"Sorry, Dawn, traffic was horrendous. Montréal is getting as bad as New York."

Dawn welcomed Sophie with a hug and a smile. "You've never been to New York."

Sophie grinned. "Yeah, but that's what I've heard."

"Come on, Chantal's waiting." Dawn leaned over to whisper in Sophie's ear. "FYI, she only knows me as Renée, so discretion, please."

"I'm nothing if not discreet, *ma chère* 'Renée.'"

Laughing, Dawn drew Sophie over to the table and introduced her to Chantal. The three women chatted with easy camaraderie, but Dawn was restless. She needed to be alone with Sophie. They had a lot of catching up to do. After seeing Chantal off, Dawn and Sophie went back to Dawn's condo, where they could not keep their hands off each other. They hadn't made love in a long time, and their desire for each other took a back seat to Dawn's need to talk. She decided to leave the talking for Saturday morning and abandoned herself to her friend's tender caresses for the rest of the evening.

Sophie was gazing out over the early morning sunlight on the balcony when Dawn brought out the coffee. She took a sip of the brew and sighed. "Great stuff."

"Sanjay brought it from Jamaica."

"Okay, enough chitchat. Tell me about Statesville. How did you and John get along? Did you get it on?"

"Yes, we did." Dawn squirmed, uncomfortable. "My parents like him."

"Your parents aren't marrying him." Sophie furrowed her brow. "The important thing is, could you live with him the rest of your life?"

"If I had to. He's a nice, guy, Sophie. Stable, with good prospects. He's been looking for a wife for a long time." She avoided Sophie's gaze. "I want to move closer to my parents. I miss them."

The women drank their coffee in silence, until Dawn changed the subject.

"Tell me about Amran. Any sign he wants something permanent?"

Sophie frowned. "Not. He's applied for a fellowship in the States."

"Oh, sweetie. That's too bad. I thought things were going in a positive direction."

"Well, they were. Until I told him about my work."

"Sophie! You didn't! Are you insane?"

"I didn't want to. He just kept pushing me to tell him something 'private' about my life." She used her fingers like quotation marks around the word *private* and took a large gulp of coffee. "He almost fell off the chair when I did."

"Big mistake, Sophie. You know men can't imagine sharing their girlfriend with someone else. Especially strange men."

"I know." Sophie heaved a sigh. "Hey, enough about that. Where's that photo of John you were talking about?"

Dawn brought more coffee from the kitchen and retrieved the photo Deanna had given her to take with her. Sophie studied the image of the average looking youth with dark complexion, his hair combed straight back.

"He looks awfully young, Dawn."

"Yeah, he's really more like a boy than a man. I guess his mom babies him. He's very close to her."

Sophie scrutinized Dawn's face. "How is he in bed?"

"He's okay."

"Just 'okay?'"

"Yeah. No fireworks. He's no Sanjay." At the mention of Sanjay, Dawn began to choke on her coffee.

Sophie couldn't restrain her amusement. "You mention Sanjay and you start choking. What's with that?"

"He wants to marry me."

This time Sophie choked. "Oh? That's a real trick for a married man, even if he is madly in love with you."

"That's the thing, Sophie, he is. And he's too much. Too much in love with me, too much of an intellectual, too much of an athlete."

"And the sex?"

"That's too much, too. My God, he's a maniac. Even if he divorced his wife and we married, I'd never satisfy him. He'd still be going after escorts."

"That is a definite drawback." Sophie thought for a moment. "But he's got lots of money, and titles and social position. Overall, he'd make you happier than John."

"I'll never be happy in life. It's over. All those years of splurging, indulging myself with sex, money, and fancy trips. I had it all." She gazed at Sophie with a beseeching expression. "I want a stable relationship, a home, a family. I'd be such a good mother. You know that, Sophie."

"But what does John do for a living? Can he support you in the manner you're accustomed?"

"He's about to take over the family pizza restaurant. His parents bought him a house. He's set for life."

"Let's see, a family pizza parlor versus a guy with a couple of mills. You do the math."

Dawn shook her head, hopeless. "Sanjay would have to divorce his wife. Plus he knows I'm an escort."

"*Was* an escort."

"Okay, you're right about that. And, sure, he loves me now, but who knows if in a few years he'll start calling me a slut. Or a whore."

"So." Sophie drained her coffee cup and stood up facing Dawn. "You'd marry an average looking guy you don't love who flips pizzas over a handsome, wealthy one who is head over heels in love with you?"

Dawn rose and paced across the small balcony. "I don't know. I'm still thinking about it. But there's something else." She hesitated. "I just have this feeling."

"What feeling?" Sophie placed a supportive arm around Dawn's shoulder. "Okay, girl. Out with it."

"The bubble I live in is about to burst. I'll be exposed. The school board and everyone else I know will find out about my . . . my other life. Media will start snooping around, waiting to pounce on me."

"Don't be ridiculous, Dawn. Whatever gave you that idea?"

"Woman's intuition." Dawn reached for Sophie's hand. "Actually, a good deal more than woman's intuition. A reporter from the Montréal Gazette called to talk to me about a story she was doing on teachers. What if she found out what I do after school hours? What if she already knew?"

Sophie shrugged. "Aren't you being just a bit paranoid?"

"And Sanjay keeps asking me about my background, who my father is."

"So?"

"So maybe he knows more than he should know. Maybe the whole school board knows. Maybe all of Montréal knows."

Dawn burst into tears, unresponsive to Sophie's caring hugs.

"I worked so hard to get an education, Sophie. I can't give up my career in disgrace. I thought about moving to Winnipeg to be with Sanjay, but it's even colder than here. And how can I deal with an irate ex-wife and two pre-pubescent kids?"

Sophie rocked Dawn in her arms. "It's okay, sweetie, it's okay."

Dawn spoke through her sobs. "Marrying John would get me out of the cold, far away from here and closer to my folks. He's nothing special." She pulled away from Sophie and looked into her eyes. "But I'm not, either."

The sun disappeared behind a bank of clouds. Dawn let Sophie lead her back into the apartment away from the sudden chill permeating the air. She lit the fireplace and settled in front of it with Sophie holding her close and thought about her options. After a few minutes, she realized there was nothing more to think about.

Her mind was already made up. She wanted to be an average woman.

*

Deanna and Pierre reacted to Dawn's news with absolute joy. They assured her marrying John and moving home was the right thing to do. With John's experience and hard work, the pizza restaurant had gold mine potential. Dawn's future would be secure, and even better, she'd be living close by.

"We'll help you in any way possible to get on your feet. Dad will find you a position as secretary or assistant in his clinic, or as a geriatric attendant in a nursing home."

"Thanks, Mom. I really appreciate it."

Dawn still had her doubts, but the School Board approved her application for a one-year sabbatical without difficulty. With her credentials and track record as a teacher supporting her, they agreed to pay her wages for the entire year, on the condition she return to her school armed with additional skills. She satisfied this requirement by stating her intention to study language teaching.

All that remained for Dawn was to get to know John better. She was too clever to leap into the marriage waters without a life vest. Having promised to call him, she decided to test his mettle on the phone before making a final decision.

"Renée, where have you been? I've been frantic waiting for your call."

"I'm sorry, John, I had one crisis after another to deal with at school." She waited to see if he was satisfied with her explanation. "Anyway, I've really missed you. Have you missed me?"

"Of course, Dawn."

"I'd much rather be there with you than in Montréal. It's so cold here. And lonely."

"Me, too. But what's stopping you from coming here? Your dad said you were willing to marry me."

"Oh, yes, John, I am." She tried to find the right words, so as not to scare him off. "But I need more time."

His reaction did not surprise her. "More time? What do you mean?"

"Well, we don't really know each other yet. Why don't we move in together, maybe for a year? Then we can get married."

"That's fine with me, but my mom would never, ever allow me to live in sin with a woman. She's traditional, you know? Old-country family values."

"But we barely know each other, John. It would be silly to—"

"I'm sure you know my mom still controls everything. She even owns my house. I don't want to get on her bad side. Besides . . ." John paused to let this truth to sink into Dawn's consciousness. "She's found girls for me on both sides of the Atlantic. Any of them would marry me in a heartbeat."

Dawn fumed. How could he hold this over her? "Here's the deal, John. We've only been together twice. I can't just up and marry someone I've only been with twice. I need time. To fall in love."

"You don't think you could love me?"

Dawn heard the hurt in his voice. "Oh, yes, John, I'm sure I will love you, but not until I know you better. Do you understand?"

He grumbled under his breath. "Yeah, I guess so. But I feel I know you from knowing your family so long. I like them, and I like you. I'll make you happy."

"I know you will, John." She thought for a moment. "Give me a few more days. I'll think about it and we can talk some more, okay?"

"Okay."

Dawn breathed a sigh of relief after they hung up. The conversation had been difficult, but she knew she could handle John. He was a puppy dog. The real, stomach-churning problem lay with Sanjay. She was going to break his heart. Not that she hadn't done that before, most notably to Tucker. But Sanjay was different. He was dynamic, intriguing. In her own way, she had true affection for him. She wasn't sure how to break up with him, but she knew it was the only way to move on with her life.

If only Sanjay and I got married, it would solve everything . . . She thought about him, her mind filling with bittersweet memories. The notion of seeing him in person, or even calling him, tormented her soul. Worse, it was impossible to predict his reaction to her news. She decided email was better, nothing too serious, just something to make him smile. Yes, that was the best choice.

I can do that, right?

Once she overcame this last obstacle to her new life, she could contemplate her future with a clear conscience. Someone was willing and able to marry her. A respite from the frigid clime of Canada, and the study of Language Arts, awaited her. She set her mind to planning out the details. Life was good.

48

An increasing number of Canadian schools were encouraging teachers to form book clubs outside of school. The Montréal School Board was no exception. Principal Nelly required the St. Paul teachers to convene their book club five times a year in exchange for in-service credit hours. The School Board provided a reading list, plus reviews and additional literature for the teachers to consider, as well as a number of questions to guide selections. How would students react to a certain book? Would it be recommended for the classroom, or for individual reading? Mrs. Nelly was convinced the St. Paul Book Club created positive changes in the curriculum, enhanced the teachers' working relationships, and established a forum for exploring new ideas.

Dawn's deliberations over Sanjay distracted her from her extra school activities as well as her teaching obligations. Aware she had to maintain at least the appearance of fulfilling her principal's extracurricular requirements, Dawn volunteered to hold a meeting of female teachers at her condo. She tried to focus on welcoming her colleagues, acknowledging their comments about her living space, but her mind was on Sanjay and how she was going to break her life-altering news to him.

"Awesome place, Renée."

"Oh. Thanks. It's just a condo."

"What a view. Mont Royal is right there. How do you afford this on a teacher's salary?"

"What?" Dawn came back to reality. "Oh." She looked around at the luxurious furniture, Berber carpeting and original artwork. "My uncle left me some inheritance, you know, he didn't have any kids of his own. Plus my dad helps me out a bit."

"You're a lucky woman, Renée."

Yeah. And I work my butt off, so I deserve it.

The woman served themselves the fruit punch Dawn had prepared and settled in to start the discussion. Dawn guessed only she and Jacqueline had done their homework, as usual. Jacqueline made eye contact with Dawn, who gave her a nod to go ahead.

"*Eleven Minutes* opens with a striking sentence: 'Once upon a time there was a prostitute called Maria.' Rather than fairy tale or sexual saga, this book tells the story of how a young girl tumbles into a life of prostitution. Ultimately she ends up falling in love, but is unsure whether her dual personality will ever allow her to find fulfillment with one man. The story points up the fact that most women are dissatisfied with their sex lives."

Dawn, who had read the novel during a trip to Rome for an Opus Dei convention, shuddered at the parallels between her own life and that of the book's protagonist but felt calm enough to comment. "The book brings up the issue of sacred sex, whether it is attainable or just a utopian ideal." She looked around at the other women's raised eyebrows. "I liked Coelho's first novel, *The Alchemist*, better. But the heroines in both books have a similar view of themselves. They've failed to live their dreams and see themselves as either victims or adventurers. There's no doubt the author inspires the reader's compassion for both characters."

"Very impressive, Renée." Jacqueline smiled. "You definitely understood the subtleties of the book's message."

"Thanks, Jacqueline. Now the book I'd like to discuss is—" Her ringing cell phone interrupted Dawn's statement. "Oh, excuse me. I'd better take that. Be right back."

Flipping the phone open, Dawn hurried from the room. When she heard the voice at the other end, her heart sank. She wasn't ready to talk to Sanjay. Not yet.

"Hi, Sanjay."

"I missed you."

"Oh, me, too. Are you here?"

"No, in Winnipeg. I just had to hear your voice."

"That's sweet. But I can't talk right now."

"What a shame." She perceived the disappointment in his voice. "You're busy?"

"Would you believe I'm having a book club meeting? Six young females discussing *Eleven Minutes*."

"Hmm, sounds intriguing."

"Yeah, they really liked my analysis. And get this. I'm just about to discuss one of your favorite books, *Toxin*."

"Really?"

"Yeah. It made me think of you. Those scenes in the slaughterhouse are enough to make even me a vegetarian." She suppressed a shiver. "All those deadly bacteria."

Sanjay laughed. "That's not the reason I'm Vegan, though. It's because of the cruelty to animals."

"I knew that."

The sound of a shrieking tea kettle in the background interrupted the awkward silence.

"Uh-oh, do you hear that? Time to make tea for the ladies."

"Oh, well, in that case, I'll let you go."

"Call me soon, okay?"

"I will, my darling. Thinking of you day and night."

"Me, too, Sanjay. 'Bye."

Dawn clicked the phone shut, sighing with relief. The seconds of her life were ticking away like grains of sand trickling from the top of an hourglass. The conversation confirmed what she knew she had to do but couldn't find the courage to carry out. She needed to end it with him, without another hour of delay. As soon as the meeting was over, she planned to sit down at the computer and send him her last email.

"Renée, the kettle's boiling." Jacqueline called out from the living room.

"I'm on it."

She raced to the kitchen to silence the offending noise. A cup of tea sounded good right now. She chose a tin of the strongest, blackest tea she could find.

If this doesn't give me courage, I don't know what will.

What she really needed was a good, strong Scotch. But the ladies would never approve.

Later, baby, later.

Humming a soft tune, she set about playing hostess to her gathering. Before long, such obligations would be history, at least for this group.

As Mrs. John Kriarakis, though, I'll be serving plenty of tea and biscuits to my friends.

That thought motivated her. To get to that goal, she had a few more steps to take care of. Then she was a free woman.

49

Hi Dawn,

It's been crazy busy at the ICU this week. An extremely ill 28-year-old woman, with a 4-month-old baby, is fighting for her life. We are doing our best, and I have every confidence she will pull through, but it's been a real trial. And the fact she is so close to your age . . . well, you can only imagine how deeply that affects me.

Do you have any idea how special you are to me? In spite of all the heartache, since I met you everything in my life has gotten better. I've discovered a side of myself I didn't even know existed. Plus I'm being more productive in my career than ever. Several of my manuscripts have been accepted for publication in addition to the ones already published, and my research projects have taken off. They may be only medical writings, but I swear I will dedicate the next book to you, my darling, whatever it may be. Perhaps someday I'll write something else, something about you.

I'm so glad I finally got you to laugh from my last email. If I made you feel special, I can only say you make me feel special, too. You are my dream come true, a fairytale princess sprung to life. I would become your humble servant and wait on you for the rest of my life, if I could. I have never begged anyone for anything, Dawn, but at this moment I would sink to my knees, imploring you to be mine and all mine. PLEASE email me back soon. I'm on my knees at this very moment. I miss you!

Sanjay

Dear Sanjay,

Thank you for your latest email. I could tell every word came straight from the heart. You are a kind and generous man, and your friendship means a lot to me. Your desire to help me out without wanting anything but my friendship in return demonstrates your true compassion. I thank you for that, and for having gotten a chance to meet you. I am even more grateful for having found a place in your heart.

I thought your message about getting down on your knees and begging was a funny one. I can't imagine that. No matter what anyone's title is in life, I always treat everyone equally. I wouldn't even kiss a prince's hand, nor would I expect any person to kiss mine. You and I are like anyone else, and we should treat each other in the same way no matter what. I don't believe in being put on a pedestal, or looking down on people. No need to bow for me. I am just like any other normal person. Thanks, though, you make me feel special.

You were so generous to offer me the gift of diamonds. You know how much I love diamonds! Just be sure and read up a little on how to search for quality, since there is so much variation. Color and clarity are the two most important things to look for, the whiter and clearer the better. And you absolutely must insist on getting a certificate stating its authenticity. A ring is not necessary. I'd gladly accept a nice pair of earrings. However, it would be best if you took care of this soon, as I am moving in a month. Yes, I'm leaving Montréal. After my graduation next week, I will be gone for good. I have to get away from my past, sinful life. I've decided to take a sabbatical from the school to travel with my church group.

I know the above news must be a shock to you. I have been thinking long and hard about our relationship, and I now realize you and I were not meant to be together. I know you are in love with me, but I also know you're frightened of letting this love go. I'm afraid if we continue to see each other, I, too, will fall more deeply and hopelessly in love with you. And since you're married, that isn't fair to me. Plus I will only interfere with your life and distract you from the sharp focus you have achieved in your work. Therefore, I don't wish to see you anymore. It is for the best. We both need to start new lives, peaceful and happy lives independent of each other, and thus will have to sacrifice our love for that end.

Don't worry, Sanjay, I will never, ever, go back to escort work again. I promised you that, and once I swear to something I don't renege on it. I credit you for influencing me to change my life in that way, and for that I'll always be grateful to you.

Everyone who crosses our path in life does so for a special reason. The reason I met you is clear in my mind. You've called me an angel. If that is so, then I am an angel that came into your life to make you realize you have fallen. The teachings of Opus Dei have shown me this. I hope the memories of our beautiful encounters will give you the strength you need to pull yourself back up and lead a life that creates hope for others. Our meetings, I feel, have brought a sense of peace and serenity into both of our lives. I am honored to be the one who has allowed you to see your true way more clearly.

I will always appreciate what you have done for me.

Yours,
Dawn

Dawn,
I read your message at work, and my day became horrid after that. How could you do this to me, the person who has devoted body and soul to you? It couldn't have come at a worse time, now that I'm finally getting on with my life. After all we've been through together, after all I've done for you and given you, I don't deserve to be treated this way.

Sanjay

Sanjay,

I'm sorry you feel that way, but it doesn't change the fact I can't see you anymore. Your tone was very hurtful, and I feel you are trying to exploit my vulnerabilities. This is a terrible thing to do to someone you supposedly love and cherish.

Dawn

Dawn,

Your tone was insulting and made me do a slow burn. Not even a dog deserves to be put down the way you did me. I've NEVER done anything to 'exploit' your 'vulnerabilities.' How, in good conscience, could you EVER accuse me of such a thing? You have really wounded me to the core. I've ALWAYS kept my promises to you. Have you EVER kept your commitments to me? Because of you, I've suffered immensely, financially and personally. I don't know if I'll ever recover. Do you care at all about anyone's feelings but your own? I don't think so.

And speaking of commitments, I promised you diamond, and I stand by that promise. I looked into top quality diamond earrings, VVI flawless ones, and they are $15,000 US, a steep price, to say the least. I only ask that you allow me to present them to you personally. I work hard for my money, Dawn. Sixteen hour days, seven days a week, twelve months of the year. Believe me, I've never given anyone a gift like this before. It might be a nice parting gesture if you would see me one more time.

As I write this, I have tears in my eyes. You have hurt me so deeply. I hope you're happy now.

Sanjay

Sanjay,

I don't wish to see you anymore. It's as simple as that. It would only make me feel worse than I do now. I have no need of money or presents from you, either. I will try to get by with what I have, and to erase the memory of you from my mind. I hope you will be able to do the same. What we had was nice, but it's just a memory now. I only made your heart ache, but remember, I warned you, didn't I? From the beginning, I said I was dangerous. You didn't believe me. You said you thrived on danger. Forgive me for bringing up this painful point, but I'm not the only guilty party here.

If you want some 'spice' in your life, please seek it elsewhere. I cannot make your dreams come true. If you prefer to see me as a waste of your time and money, feel free to do so. Just please respect my wishes.

Go on with your life, Sanjay. You fell in love with a fantasy, a shooting star that streaked across the heavens and burnt itself out in a flash. I'm sorry if I hurt you.

Hoping you understand,
Dawn

Dawn,

What you said hit me below the belt. My emotions and experiences belong to me, and I can write about them as I choose. Unlike you, who have caused me such pain, I didn't wish to wound you in any way. Now I am hurting so much I can no longer waste time writing to you or about you.

Adieu!
Sanjay

50

The minute he clicked on his last hurtful email to Dawn, Sanjay felt a huge wave of regret. He had to see her, to persuade her to change her mind. The gifts he had purchased for her were the perfect excuse to beg for a meeting. Quaking with trepidation, he picked up the phone and dialed. He shivered when he heard her voice.

"Dawn? It's me. Please don't hang up."

Her voice was tinged with anger. "Why shouldn't I?"

"I just called to say I . . . I'm sorry, I'm so sorry."

"That's not enough, Sanjay. You've hurt me. I want to put everything related to you behind me."

"You've hurt me, too."

"Then we have nothing to talk about. I'm hanging up now."

"Please, Dawn. Don't. I'm begging you." He choked back a sob. "Couldn't we see each other again? Just one more time?"

"What for? Haven't we said our goodbyes?"

"No, we haven't. I need to see you. I have something for you. A gift for your graduation."

"Whatever it is, I'm not accepting it. Give it to your wife."

"Dawn, please."

"I want a new life now, Sanjay, a normal life. I want to forget my past, that I was ever a hooker or a GFE. Or a mistress."

Dawn thought about John and the promise of a fresh, unsullied life with him. He was nice, easy to get along with, and most of all a naïve and innocent man who would never be suspicious of her or dig into her past. So what if he was not an intellectual? She had enough contact with Sanjay, with Wilson, with the judge and many more of that ilk, to know what motivated type 'A' men. They always wanted more out of life, too much in fact, and were never happy. They focused their energies on furthering their knowledge, pushing boundaries, going higher and higher in life in order to outclass others. And, indefatigable, they always wanted more sex. Sanjay was living proof of that.

"I want a simple life, the kind the Bible and Father Garcia taught me, a pious life like my mother's." She paused, imagining the look of hurt on Sanjay's face. "Can you understand that?"

"Yes. I can. And I respect you for it." Sanjay sighed. "But after all we've been through together, well, I need closure, my angel. I need to say goodbye to you."

Dawn thought about how her life had changed since she met Sanjay. The effect of his love was more powerful than she had ever imagined possible. Money was still her weakness, but the excitement, novelty and adrenaline rush of sex with strangers had worn off. She knew Sanjay was madly in love with her, and she loved him too, in her fashion. But she had to move on.

"You're not trying to change my mind, are you, Sanjay? Because if you are, I swear, it's a waste of energy."

"No, my darling, that's not it at all. I just need to see your face in front of me. One more time."

Dawn's softer side, what there was of it, started to emerge. What Sanjay was telling her pulled at the one, small fraction of her heart that was open to receiving emotions. He was an unfortunate, unhappy intellectual caught between a loveless marriage and a marriage less love. Her precipitous break-up had devastated him, broken his heart. His pitiful, pleading tone was more than she could bear. She actually felt sorry for him.

"Okay, Sanjay, you win. Just make sure to behave yourself, okay? I don't want to talk about us, or love, or any of that. Promise me."

"I promise." Sanjay was flooded with relief. "Thank you. Thank you, my angel."

"But it will have to be soon. I have a lot of loose ends to tie up before I leave Montréal."

"Of course, darling. I have to be in Ottawa on Tuesday for meetings. I can come to Montréal to meet you for dinner. How about *Chez Queux*. 6 pm?"

Dawn knew about the restaurant, renowned for its wine cellar and considered the best in Montréal. It was a perfect milieu for a final send-off, for sure. "Okay. I'll wait for you there."

"You won't regret it."
"No love talk?"
"None. I swear."

Dawn hung up, biting her lip. She hoped he was right, that he wasn't going to go ballistic on her. She was all too familiar with his unpredictable side.

51

Dawn sipped her *Dom Pérignon*, lost in thought. Sanjay was never late, although if he was flying in from Ottawa there might have been some delays. Still, it wasn't a good sign. She tried to focus on the positive. Her lifelong dream was close to being fulfilled. Marriage, children, family and friends close by, were all she craved. A normal life. It wasn't too much to ask. She wanted to put the past behind her, to emulate her mom by bearing and raising kids, going to church and managing a household. Her maternal instincts dominated her entire psyche. It was all falling into place. The School Board had accepted her sabbatical proposal and application. At the prospect of marrying her, John was happier than a newborn babe suckling its mother's breast.

So what if I don't love him? I'll learn to, after we marry, and if not then certainly after we have kids together.

The waiter, older and not at all good-looking, Dawn was happy to note, appeared at her side to pour her another glass.

These Québécois have class. Almost makes me regret leaving Montréal, winters notwithstanding.

Halfway through her second glass, the pleasant buzz she was feeling gave her second thoughts.

What am I doing, giving this all up to marry a pizza guy?

The contrast between this atmosphere and John's pizza parlor was almost too funny to contemplate. She chuckled to herself.

Well, at least he's the owner. A 'restaurateur.' I'm doing the right thing. Aren't I?

Spying Sanjay coming towards her, Dawn gulped the last of her champagne and took a deep breath. As he came closer, she could see the details of the bouquet he carried, a stunning arrangement of ten white orchids surrounding a chocolate and a pink one. It was a not very subtle reminder of the subject always on his mind.

"Sorry I'm late." He leaned over and kissed her forehead. "These special orchids are hard to find. I had to shop around quite a bit."

"They're beautiful."

"As are you." Sanjay slid into the chair opposite her at the secluded, candle-lit table. "I missed you, my angel."

Dawn bristled. "Let's not go there, Sanjay, okay? You promised to behave."

"I know, I know. You're right. I'll be good." He gazed with admiration at the sight of her in her impeccable business suit. "So tell me what you've been doing. I want to know everything."

The waiter hurried over, filled Sanjay's glass and looked to him for approval. Sanjay sipped and nodded. Bowing, the waiter disappeared.

"Everything?" Dawn hesitated, thinking. "Well, since I haven't been working for Tom, I've had time to help out at the Humane Society. And I aced my exams for graduation."

"I knew you would." He smiled, proud. "What else?"

"Nothing, just packing and sorting stuff I'm not taking with me. Tell me about you."

"Me? The usual. Before Ottawa, I went to a leadership meeting in Hilton Head."

She peered at his dark skin, which had a glow she had never seen before. "Yeah, I thought you looked pretty tan. For an Indian, that is. Healthy."

"It was so glorious there. I wish you could have been with me."

"Now, Sanjay, I just said not to—"

"Sorry, I couldn't help it." He shot her a look of repentance. "After Hilton Head, I had a chance to go to Vienne."

"You went to . . . Vienne?" A bead of sweat broke out on her forehead. She dug around in her bag for her makeup and touched up the spot.

"Yes. The plantations, the countryside around it, all exquisite. You're familiar with the area, of course. Didn't you once mention you have family there?"

"Did I?"

She reached for the champagne bottle. The waiter hustled to her side and filled her glass before she could even touch it. She nodded her thanks to his retreating form.

Sanjay continued his query. "What was the name of your hometown? State something?"

Oh Lord, when did I let him on to that? I must have been drunk or something.

Squirming, Dawn hastened to change the subject. "So, did you remember to bring my graduation gift?"

"Yes, of course." He patted his jacket pocket. "I'm sure you'll like it. Sparkling and shiny."

Her eyes shone. "I can't wait to see it."

Dawn waited for Sanjay to produce a box, but he just gazed at her. "Dawn, I have something to say to you. Something important."

"Sanjay, you promised not to bring up—"

He took her hand, kissed it, and let it go. "Yes, I did. But I must say this to you. Please forgive me."

Frowning, Dawn extracted a pack of cigarettes from her bag and lit one. "Okay. I'm listening."

"Dawn, I'm in love with you. I always have been. You know that, right?"

She nodded. "Yes, but what good will it do to—"

"Just hear me out. I can't fathom life without you. I am ready and willing to give up everything, my career, my work, my family, and go with you wherever you go."

"Sanjay, this is insane. Why even talk about it? You can't give up your work, healing people's pain and suffering, saving lives. It's too important."

"None of it is important to me anymore, certainly not as important as you are."

"Me? I've been nothing but a distraction for you. You have to let me go." He said nothing. "And what about your wife?"

"I don't love her."

"But you need to be there for your kids."

"All I want in life is you, Dawn. All I choose is you. I will leave everything and everybody for you. I will even give up vegetarianism and eat animals. I'll join Opus Dei. There's nothing I wouldn't do for you." He paused to watch her expression, hoping her armor was breaking down in some small way. "You love me, too, at least a little. Don't you?"

She lowered her eyes, murmuring. "Yes. I suppose I do."

He let out a deep breath, joy and relief cascading over his face. "Then marry me."

"I can't, you know that." She tamped out her cigarette and lit another. "You wouldn't want to marry a hooker. Hundreds, no, thousands, of men have been inside my body. I am not made for you and neither are you for me."

"I don't care about your past, it doesn't matter to me. For me, you are pure as an angel. My guiding light."

"I'm not. I'm just a fleeting fantasy that touched your life and vanished in an instant, like a comet, or a meteor."

"Don't talk like that, Dawn you're breaking my heart."

"You asked for this, Sanjay, not me."

The waiter arrived with a bottle of ruby red Bordeaux, opened it with a flourish, and dribbled a taste into Sanjay's balloon goblet. Sanjay tasted and nodded to the waiter, who poured for both Sanjay and Dawn and scuttled away.

"Without you, I'll be crushed, devastated. I'll die a horrible death." Sanjay took a deep swallow of the crimson liquid. "My love for you is all encompassing. I need your love. Desperately."

Dawn fidgeted with the cork the waiter had left behind. "Your love is infatuation, obsession. It's a sick love."

"It's not sick." Hurt flooded his face. "And it's not ordinary, either. It is a very special, unique love, a love as yet unnamed, not experienced by any one else. A 'supreme love.'"

"You always do things in extremes, Sanjay. What you described is a fantasy. I'm not capable of fulfilling your daydreams. I've told you that a million times." She drained her glass in one long swallow.

"Yes. You can. You already have." Sanjay turned away from her and stared into space. "I've been holding this back, but now I'm just going to come out with it. I have a proposal for you."

Dawn crushed out her cigarette and rose. "I'm sorry, Sanjay. I can't do this. I have to go."

He turned to her, reached out for her arm, holding her back. "Just listen to me. If it doesn't suit you, I'll let you go."

She snatched her am back and sat down. "Okay. What is it?"

"It's simple. I'll give you a million dollars if you marry me for five years. That's all. No strings attached, all cash."

Sanjay pulled a brokerage statement from his pocket and thrust it under her gaze. Dawn glanced over it, her eyes widening at the bottom line: three-point five million dollars. She summoned up every shred of her willpower.

"Sanjay, I've learned a great deal from you, and I have you to thank for getting me out of hooking. But now I realize money isn't everything. I don't splurge anymore. All I want is peace and quiet and the ordinary life of a housewife, and kids."

"Then give me a baby."

"What?"

"I want a beautiful little girl just like you, with your angel's face and blue eyes, and my dark complexion."

"Are you out of your mind? Who would keep it, take care of it?"

"I will. I'll tell my wife I'm adopting the child of some young woman who died in the ER. She'll believe me. And you can keep the money, all of it."

"You can't be serious."

Dawn was struck by the irony of Sanjay's proposal. After a lifetime of wanting to be rich and bear a child, he was offering her all she had wished for but in a cruel, distorted way. Shaking her head in disbelief, she poured herself another glass of wine and drank it in one long, drawn-out mouthful.

"This is a dangerous game you're playing, Sanjay."

Sanjay watched her, concerned. "Be careful, Dawn, you haven't eaten anything."

"Don't worry. I can hold my liquor."

Sanjay gestured to the waiter, who rushed over to them. "Check, please."

"But Monsieur, you have not ordered yet."

"Another time, perhaps. Thank you."

"*Oui, Monsieur.*"

The check appeared in an instant. Without looking at it, Sanjay pulled out a roll of bills and placed them on the table. He turned to Dawn. "Would you be willing to talk about this some more?"

Her head was pounding from the alcohol she had consumed and the intensity of her reaction to Sanjay's proposal. "Okay. I guess so."

With a gentle gesture, Sanjay took her arm. She didn't pull back.

52

Sanjay gazed at Dawn, worried. She lay on the bed in Sanjay's hotel room, clutching her head.

"I'm sorry, Dawn, this is my fault."

"No, Sanjay, it's not. I take responsibility for my actions. I'm a big girl now."

Sanjay called the Concierge's desk to request some Advil. He sat down next to Dawn and massaged her head with gentle strokes. Her furrowed brow relaxed.

"I'm your humble servant, Dawn. If I could take care of you like this for the rest of my life, I will feel I've accomplished my purpose."

A small envelope of Advil appeared under the door. Sanjay retrieved it, filled a glass with water in the bathroom, and helped Dawn take the capsules. Soon her headache subsided. She sat bolt upright in bed and began to sob.

"How do I know if I can trust you, Sanjay? What if you tell someone about me, my former life? It would devastate me."

"I would never . . . I could never do that to you, my love." He caressed her shoulder, massaging out the knots tightening her tense muscles. "Your secret will never come out, I promise you."

"Swear you'll never, ever hurt me."

"I swear."

"If my dad ever found out, I would kill myself, I swear."

"If you hurt yourself, it would hurt me, too. If you kill yourself, I will take my own life."

Sanjay reached into his pocket and pulled out a small box. Opening it, he placed it in front of Dawn. Inside were two one-carat diamond earrings and a five-carat heart-shaped diamond necklace with platinum lace filigree. The sparkle of the precious stones dazzled her.

"Oh, Sanjay, they're exquisite." She put the jewels on, all anxious thoughts dissolving from her mind. "Thank you. I love them."

"They're no less than you deserve, my love." He leaned over her glowing face and kissed her lips. "Diamonds can soothe a woman's pain like nothing else on this earth."

"Let's fantasize this is our wedding night, Sanjay, a night to remember for the rest of our lives. You always wanted to marry me. For tonight, I am your new bride and you are my groom, and our love is special."

Sanjay was mesmerized. "Yes, my darling, a sacred love, a pure and beautiful love."

She looked up at him, eyes shining. "Kiss my eyes, like you used to."

Sanjay obeyed, kissing her eyes, her lips, her entire face, over and over. Soon their two bodies were entwined in a ballet of ecstasy. He loved her with his mouth, with his tongue, with his entire being. Her low moan of enjoyment intensified until she cried out in pleasure and erupted into a volcano of fulfillment. She closed her eyes and gasped.

"Yes, my love, yes. Love me."

"Yes, yes, I will." With a tormented cry, he replicated her blissful release. "The way God intended."

Dawn opened her eyes and stared at him. "'God?' But you don't believe in God."

"I do now."

He cradled her in his arms, caressing her and showering her with kisses, until she pulled away and rose from the bed. Reality had set in. She had a whole other life to go back to.

"I have to go. I'm leaving for my parents' house tomorrow morning."

Watching her dress, Sanjay felt his chest cave in with pain. "Yes, my darling. I know." He reached into the night table drawer and pulled out a small, black velvet pouch. "But before you go, well, I wanted you to have this."

She looked at the bag, flabbergasted. "Sanjay, you've already given me—"

"Shh, just let me show you." He reached inside the bag and extracted a gold medal. "I won it a couple of years ago, in the Boston Marathon. It's my most precious possession. Worthless in term of monetary value, but earned through a lot of blood, sweat, hard work and devotion."

Its sparkle caught the light. Dawn gazed at it, filled with remorse. "I . . . I can't accept it, Sanjay. It wouldn't be right."

"Oh, but you must. I had it engraved for you."

He turned the medallion over. Dawn read the inscription aloud. "*From Sanjay to Dawn with Love.*" Oh, Sanjay! I'll cherish it always."

"That's all I ask." He kissed her eyes one more time. "I love you."

Holding the medallion to her heart, she turned and walked slowly to the door. "I love you, too."

He couldn't bear to watch her go. Instead, he sat cross-legged on the bed and willed himself into a meditative state. In his condition, only one thought penetrated his consciousness and infiltrated his mind.

The saddest moment in life is not when someone dies, but when hearts are broken.

53

Sanjay needed to rest from a long, dreary day of meetings at the Royal College of Physicians and Surgeons in Ottawa. Instead, he paced back and forth in his room at the Westin, like a caged panther. Much as he appreciated the mixture of old and new in the architecture of this Catholic Seminary transformed into a present-day Mecca for medical education, all Sanjay could do was brood over Dawn. He knew his only hope for dealing with his current frame of mind was to hire a girl, any girl, to talk with. Someone who understood his predicament.

He found Nicole on Ottawaescorts.com. Her description sounded enticing. Twenty-two years old, brunette, medium build, very friendly. The photographs appealed to him. He hoped she bore at least some resemblance to them. Within half an hour, she appeared at his door.

"Your looks actually match your photographs. That's a pleasant surprise."

She smiled. "We aim to please."

Her manner is as engaging as her looks.

"Won't you come in?"

She responded to his gesture. "Thank you. I'm Nicole. Why don't we get the finances out of the way first?"

"Of course."

Sanjay told her his name, handed her some cash, and lay down on the bed. She joined him and started to remove her blouse. He stopped her.

"This may sound strange, Nicole, but I'm not really up for sex. I just wanted to talk."

She didn't look surprised. "Sure. Whatever twists your top, Sanjay."

"Thank you for being so understanding." He studied her attractive face. "Tell me something about yourself."

"Well . . ." Nicole adjusted her position to a more comfortable one. "I'm studying journalism at the University of Ottawa, waitressing part-time. I only work as a GFE every so often. And I want to emphasize I am a GFE and not a prostitute."

"Then this is my lucky day."

"You're sweet. So. What kind of name is Sanjay? Indian?"

"Kind of obvious, isn't it?" He grinned. "I'm always interested in heritage. What's yours?"

"Italian. You can tell, right?"

Sanjay watched as she shook out her long, chestnut hair and regarded him with sultry dark eyes.

"Actually, yes. My parents are in the States, though." She lifted her blouse to show the small of her back. "D'ya like my tattoo? It's in Greek."

He studied the lettering. "Yes, I know. It means, Aphrodite, the Goddess of love and beauty."

"You're dead on. How come you're so smart?"

"I'm a doctor. I was required to study Greek and Latin."

"Oh." Nicole peered at Sanjay's face, trying to read his expression. "I have the feeling you didn't exactly ask me here to talk about the weather, right?"

"Right."

"Okay, so we're on the same page. Start talking."

Sanjay let out a deep breath. "I've become deeply involved with an escort."

Nicole shook her head. "Uh-oh, I have a feeling this isn't going to be a fun story."

"Are you sure you want to hear it?"

"Absolutely. But don't judge me if I give you my honest opinion."

"That's fine with me."

"Fire away."

Sanjay recounted his history with Dawn, the meeting and his "love at first sight" reaction, her resistance to falling for him.

"I upped the ante by sending grocery and tuition money, and one extravagant gift after another. She upped the ante as well."

"Oh? How?"

"I can't really discuss that." He avoided her gaze. "Anyway, we kept it going like that for a while. It worked for both of us. I was having the most incredible ride of my life. Of course, she wouldn't reveal her true identity to me. She was very protective of that. Her close relationship with her father . . ."

"Of course. I understand."

"But at least she was getting out of hooking. I guess I had that effect on her. She must have felt secure. On the other hand, there were conflicts."

"Surprise, surprise."

He frowned at Nicole. She made an apologetic gesture. "I wanted her all the time but couldn't have her. She wanted me, too, but it was not realistic. My marriage and all."

Nicole nodded in agreement. "Yes, that does tend to get in the way."

"She hinted about my being married and that maybe I should divorce if I thought we had any future together. It's not that easy, I mean, how do people do that?"

"They just do it. Fifty percent of the time, as it turns out."

He ignored her barb. "Meanwhile, she didn't know what to do with my deepening infatuation. And then . . ."

"And then?"

"She broke up with me."

"Well, what did you expect? It was bound to happen eventually."

"But it was the way she did it." He gritted his teeth in fury. "By email."

"Ooh, that's not very cool."

"No, it's not. She said some very nasty things."

"In that case, I don't blame you for being pissed."

"More than that. I want to hurt her. Where it hurts most."

Nicole stared at him, alarmed. "Hurt her? How?"

"Not in a physical way. I meant by exposing her double life to her father."

"Oh, no. You can't be serious."

"She exploited me. Not so much financially, but my emotions."

"Don't do this, Sanjay. You will ruin her life forever. If her dad finds out, well, we're talking major damage here." She shot him a look of genuine concern. "I don't know her, but I do know she'll feel guilty for the rest of her life. Do you really want to do that?"

"Yes. No." He jumped up and began pacing. "I don't know."

She rose from the bed and caught his arm with a gentle motion. "If you do this, you'll not only be hurting her. You'll hurt yourself, too. The guilt will eat away at you. Forever."

Sanjay looked at Nicole, scrutinizing her anxious expression. Perhaps she was right. "Thank you, my dear, for listening and offering your advice." He extracted some bills from his wallet. "I want you to know how much I appreciate it."

Nicole accepted the "tip" as a sign Sanjay was ready to bid her farewell. "Thank *you*, Sanjay." She turned to go. "I hope you'll think more about what I said before you—"

"Good night, Nicole."

He closed the door behind her and sank down on the bed, head in hands. Instead of calming him down as he had hoped, the conversation had left him more agitated. Much as Nicole had meant well, he realized she could not feel his pain. Since she herself was not suffering, her sympathy only made his worse. His mind reeled with the stabbing pain of what Dawn had perpetrated, and he found himself wishing he could inflict the same anguish on her she had caused in him. His ambivalence took the form of a two-way inner conversation between his battling selves.

I will hurt her.

No, you won't. How will it help you?

By making her realize how much she's made me endure.

She already does. Exposing her will only make you miserable. You shouldn't.

Yes. I should.

Unanswered questions plagued him. Why was he in love? Why with this person? What could he do to rid himself of his confusion and agony? He knew he would never come up with answers in his agitated state. The only solution was to consult someone else. His hypnotherapist friend, Fred Lupul, was sure to offer some advice. He seated himself at the desk, extracted pen and paper from the drawer, and poured out his soul.

54

You are asking me hard questions, Sanjay.

First of all, why love for this person and not for another one? What is the special chemistry existing between the two of you? Neurologists will tell you love is a "chemical thing," that the brain creates peptides, etc., that circulate through the body setting up some sort of magnetic resonance that attracts certain individuals. I'm sorry to say I have no training in this area.

Others say the attractive forces are set up through past-life energies. This, of course, is theory, but it is based upon collected empirical and anecdotal evidence. Unfortunately, this hypothesis, formulated by those who believe in reincarnation, will likely remain improvable. At least this is more familiar territory to me

Here is what I believe. Before we enter into this "Earth Dimension" we have an opportunity to establish what sort of lessons or learning we should absorb. Therefore we establish a script, a plan where we set up certain challenges, so we can experience those feelings the script generates. Then we come here and play out the established part. Our purpose is to determine whether we have the fortitude to play our chosen role despite any distractions we have chosen to complicate the process.

Your preferred path is that of teacher and healer, as is mine. Yet we repeatedly test ourselves to see if we can perform our task in spite of whatever personal occurrences tend to distract us.

These kinds of events have occurred in my life three times. As I look back on them, I realize they consumed most of my attention, especially in my quiet times. But as each day passed, the intensity became less, especially when I reiterated to myself exactly what my role was. (I was really stupid to let it happen three times. I must be a slow learner!)

In retrospect, I think it would have been disastrous to give in to my fantasies and desires. I know now all of these flights of fancy were unsound, and I would have been unhappy had I implemented any of them. Of course I'm talking about relationships, Sanjay, as you may have guessed. I do not regret having these experiences. Because of them I am a better counselor and a better person. I know I am a better person because I was able to overcome the temptation. It was not easy. I have become stronger because of the experiences. It would be different if we made our relationships our careers. I now know we learn more through our careers than through any relationship.

Now, the problem with the Reincarnation Theory, as far as I am concerned, is the karmic component. We are told this sort of attraction exists because of connections made in other lifetimes. You may have been intimately connected to her in another existence, where she loved you and yet you did not return her affection and now you are paying for your actions. You may have rejected her outright. Frankly, I think all that karmic stuff is gibberish.

Another theory, that each of us is connected to a group or organization that has a large project to work on, makes more sense to me. There may be hundreds of individuals in your group. The plan is to work together and accomplish this task, though it may take thousands of years to complete. An example would be nuclear energy, where people like Niels Bohr, Einstein, Pauli, Heisenberg, the Curries, etc., came together to solve the problem. They may have been working towards the solution for hundreds of years in other lifetimes. So, when we enter a physical life we may run into the same characters. Again, to test our mettle, we place distractions and diversions in our way, but we should not allow these things to divert us from our "big plan." If the same feelings are not shared with the individuals concerned, it is probably not going to work out, and is truly a distraction. Just move on.

So how is that done? Not by trying to put her out of your mind. That just makes it worse. Who knows, in some way she may be part of your group. She may even be teaching intimate members of your group in her classroom, as we speak! But she may be the one who plays a minor role in your life who wakes you up to the dangers of being distracted. Honor her for her role in some of your meditations, with the understanding that at some future date all will be resolved. In the meantime, continue with your routine, with the anticipation of better things just over the horizon.

If you do not settle this in your consciousness, continually viewing this as a bad situation, your body will eventually break down. That is what psychosomatic medicine is all about. Embrace all that has happened between the two of you. It has had its purpose. No regrets, no remorse. Most of all, no contact. Remain focused, at this particular moment, on your life-paths diverging.

Last week I had a client who ran the South African Marathon a few years ago at a time of 10:30 hours. He said it was a wonderful experience. Focus on something similar as the center of your attention. You excel at this. It is something only you can do.

I hope this answers some of your concerns. Just remember, Sanjay. It's all a test.

Fred

Dr. Lupul's advice was sound, but Sanjay was beyond accepting it, or any other counsel, rationally. His obsession over whether or not to expose Dawn dominated his consciousness. Unable to focus on work, he sat at the desk in his office, his work emails opened and unanswered in front of him, his mind in turmoil. One question controlled his thoughts.
Should I expose her?

He knew revealing the truth about Dawn to the public meant disaster for her potential career as a physiotherapist. No Medical Board would hire her. She would be rejected without hesitation, no questions asked. The issue of her father's likely reaction posed another conundrum.

Would she really kill herself?

As before, a two-way inner battle took hold of his psyche.

She is a hooker, with no scruples. She breaks people's hearts, takes their money. There is no way she would end her own life.

But what if she does? Do I want to feel responsible for that for the rest of my life?

She is lying. She always lies. That's been her whole life, to lie about everything to everybody. She will never kill herself.

Realizing his mental treadmill would never leave him in peace, Sanjay decided to seek solace elsewhere.

55

Unlike Dawn, Victoria, a GFE from Newfoundland, led a triple life. She worked for a credit card company during the day, spent two or three nights a week as a GFE, and claimed to be in a full-time relationship with someone. Sanjay never asked how serious the commitment was, but he imagined Victoria and her Significant Other were probably engaged. He could not fathom how a woman was able to sustain such a relationship and still sell her body for pay, unless somehow the money strengthened the bond. Maybe she bought him presents, or romantic dinners.

It's probably just like any other job, where you sell your time and skills. As long as you don't involve the emotions, it doesn't really matter what you do.

Sanjay didn't really believe that, but he was aware how close he had come to becoming involved with the sick and dying patients under his care. As an Intensivist, he could not help but show empathy to them and their loved ones. It was difficult not to attach himself to a sick person, to avoid feeling their physical and mental pain. He had to remind himself countless times how contrary this was to his medical training and spent a huge amount of effort on maintaining an emotional detachment. Insulating himself from the death and suffering was a major necessity. Somehow he had to stay sensitive while remaining unaffected personally. A tough job, under any circumstances.

Maybe escorts develop the same kind of conflicting state, selling sex but avoiding emotional involvement with their clients, even if they spend more time with that person than with their own lovers.

Sanjay arrived at The Garden of Eden to find Victoria on her shift. He enjoyed her company and was happy to link up with her. She was mature for a twenty four-year-old, perhaps because she had had extensive experience traveling, and although her physical attributes were average, her enjoyment of sex was clear. Instead of just lying down and opening her legs, she preferred chatting and connecting with her clients. Sanjay appreciated that. He often came to see her for conversation rather than sex. Her perspective on life was refreshing. He was willing to pay top dollar to be with her.

"My day job is not so different from my night shift." Victoria lit a cigarette, took a puff, and offered it to Sanjay.

"How so?"

"The credit card business is booming. My company's making a killing, recruiting all the time. They offer money to people so they can shop, fulfill their desires and be happy." She giggled. "The pain only comes afterwards, when the bills arrive."

Sanjay acknowledged his agreement with a sardonic grin.

"I just got my tongue pierced." She stuck her tongue out to show him. "Do you like it?"

"Not really." He placed one hand around her buttock and squeezed. "I like this much better. Why would you do that, anyway?"

"It's good for giving head."

"Ah."

Victoria peered at his expression. "You look sad tonight. What gives?"

"I need to ask you a question."

She cuddled closer to him. "Okay, I'm comfy. Go for it."

Sanjay related the story of Dawn, as he had with Nicole. "What would you think if I told her parents about her real life? I mean, hypothetically."

Victoria was appalled. "I would wonder why you'd want to do this to her. What do you gain from such an act?"

"I need to get back at her for what she did to me."

"If you really loved her as you say, if you cared about her, you wouldn't even consider it."

"But if I did . . ." He paused. "I mean, if it happened to you, how would you react? What would you do?"

"If someone hurt me that way, I wouldn't take it lying down. I wouldn't be afraid to hurt him back." Her anger rose. "I'd go to the police, accuse him of rape, whatever it takes. I'd never leave him alone."

"It was only a question. I don't know why you're so angry."

Wrenching herself away from him, she lit another cigarette and sucked in a deep inhalation. "Some question."

Sanjay went back to his office more agitated than ever. The meeting with Victoria gave him answers, but not the ones he sought. He tortured himself with a string of probing questions.

What do I really feel towards Dawn? Love, infatuation, jealousy, pain? Some other indescribable emotion? What do I want from this? Vengeance? Abject apology? Has anyone else ever had such an experience? Am I just sick? Is this why some people pour their hearts out into writing books?

Other than those required for medical and scientific articles, Sanjay had no writing skills. He ached to express his pain in a piece of fiction, perhaps a novel of love, romance, sex and betrayal. Accomplishing such a project was out of the question, beyond his abilities.

I'm doomed to eternal agony. All because I fell in love.

Mad with anguish, he knew he had to do something before his personal demons tortured him to death. He dialed the phone.

"Tom? This is Sanjay Kaul." He waited for some sign of recognition. "Yes, from Winnipeg. I'm looking for Dawn, Dawn L'andry. Do you know of her whereabouts?"

"Sorry, pal, she stopped working for me ages ago. Can't help you."

"So . . . she's not back at the agency?"

Tom made no effort to conceal his resentment. "I already told you, no. Don't call me again."

After Tom hung up, Sanjay wracked his brain. He didn't know why the guy had been so angry. But he had to find Dawn. He called every phone number he could find, asking whoever answered if they knew where she was. He tried her number, and finding it disconnected sent her an email, which bounced back. Desperate, he went online and Googled every town in the state of Georgia with the word 'state' in its name, but without knowing Dawn's real name he realized he was unlikely to find anything but dead ends. He was beside himself.

I'm not thinking clearly. I must focus.

Lucidity returned after a brief meditation in which he visualized a broom sweeping the cobwebs from his mind. Accomplishing his goal of finding Dawn without knowing her real name was too daunting for him. To cope with this problem, Sanjay needed a Private Investigator. In his usual meticulous manner, he researched all the PI companies in Montréal and chose the most topnotch and most expensive of them all, Begley and Co.

Ethan Begley hit a brick wall, however, when it came to probing the confidential life of a person whose real name Sanjay did not know, and whose phone was listed under a phantom address. Even a buyout of Dawn's former employer Tom led to a dead end. Tom knew the address of the condo unit where he picked her up, but not the apartment number.

"What else you got?" Ethan's style of speech tended towards the monosyllabic. "Car?"

"I can't recall the license number. It's under her sister's name, anyway."

"That gets us squat. What else?"

Sanjay wracked his brain. "There's a brokerage account."

"Now you're talking."

"But she wouldn't go for a joint one. That would have required revealing her identity."

"Aw, jeez. This gal's smart."

"Yes. She is." Sanjay thought for a moment. "I gave her my login and password, so she could trade. The deal was she would trade under my supervision but take all the profit."

"You call that a deal?"

Sanjay sighed. Ethan was right. "But you're not allowed to take cash out, so . . ."

"She must be transferring money into her bank account. Bingo."

Soon Ethan was hot on Dawn's trail. Having found out Dawn's real name, he looked up her condo registration and driver's license, which she had kept under her former New Brunswick address. But his search for Dawn herself turned up a number of false leads. Her skill at dodging Ethan and his team of assistants was evidence she suspected she was being followed. Their mettle proved too persistent even for Dawn, however, and they finally caught up with her at St. Paul's. Ethan reported back to Sanjay.

"Real name's Renée, same last name as you told me, L'andry. We watched her teach. She's really good at it." Ethan waited for a reaction from Sanjay. His client's silence worried him. "You okay, Sir?"

"Yes. I'm just a bit confused. She's a . . . schoolteacher?"

"Yeah, actually, teacher by day, hooker by night. Who would' a guessed it?"

Sanjay shook off his disbelief, focusing on other questions that kept cropping up in his mind. "What about physiotherapy school? She claimed she needed money for her tuition, her expenses."

"Sorry, Sir, no evidence of her being enrolled in any school. Seems she made that one up."

Sanjay had to take a full minute to let the information sink in. "She's a schoolteacher!" He breathed outrage for another several seconds. "She has a day job? And I was sending her money?"

"Yeah." Ethan paused, expecting some praise from Sanjay for the extent of work he had done. Sanjay was too shocked to come up with any words at all, never mind laudatory ones. "Then we surveiled her at home. She's not doing any escort work, just so you know."

Sanjay contemplated Dawn's name. Renée suited her somehow. Very pretty, he had to admit, even in his infuriated state. Finally, he found his voice again. "She doesn't have to. I can't imagine what she's done with all the money I've sent her. I've never seen anyone so desperate for cash. The way she was always begging me for it, I thought she had to be doing drugs."

"Nope. She's clean."

Sanjay was relieved. "So what now?"

"We keep going. That is, if you want us to."

56

Sanjay's heart skipped a beat when he heard Ethan's voice over the phone.

"We've got something for you."

"Yes? What did you find?"

"I don't think you're gonna like it."

"No, I'm sure I won't." Sanjay made an effort to keep his simmering impatience below the boiling point. "Just tell me."

"Okay. Well, I found out her hometown's called Statesville, so I checked the newspapers, clicked on the Statesville Herald link and input her name in the search column."

"And?"

"I found an article about her. In the Wedding announcements."

Sanjay felt as if a poison dart had lodged in his heart. "What? Are you sure?"

"Yep, it's her all right, picture and all. I'm faxing it to you as we speak."

Sanjay turned and watched as a page started its way through his office fax machine.

"Is it coming through, Sir?"

"Yes . . . yes, it is."

"Fine. Take a look and make sure it's readable."

Trembling, Sanjay removed the page from the machine. What he saw shook him to the core.

Weddings and Engagements
"Renée L'Andry and John Kriarakis

"*Dr. and Mrs. Pierre L'andry of Statesville announce the engagement of their daughter, Renée Dawn, an award-winning schoolteacher from Montréal, Canada, to John Kriarakis, son of Mr. and Mrs. Christos Kriarakis of Statesville . . .*

The rest of the announcement disappeared into the haze of Sanjay's fury and disbelief. His eyes blurred over the photo of a radiant Dawn on the arm of a young man whose bland, ordinary looks paled in comparison to her beauty.

The couple has planned to wed . . . St. John's Greek Orthodox Church . . . Vienne . . . All friends and relatives invited to attend . . . Please RSVP to . . .

Sanjay was stunned.

Cold-hearted bitch. Slut. Whore. She'll be sorry.

Overcome with jealousy and reeling from shock, Sanjay tried to process all the information Ethan had provided him. He had been devoted to Dawn, plied her with money and gifts, put up with her abusive emails. Now she had thrown him over for another man, the final insult. Her claims of needing money for her physiotherapy school were a complete fabrication. She had slashed him to ribbons. He would never get over the pain and the grief.

"I'll let you look it over yourself in privacy, if you know what I mean. Call me if you have any questions."

"All right. Thank you."

Sanjay hung up and studied the horrific page once more, his rage boiling over like red-hot lava spewing from a roaring volcano.

Let her roast in hell. I don't care.

But he did care. He cared very much. Enough to ruin her life.

Sanjay suddenly remembered a quotation from Shakespeare's *Othello* he had been required to memorize in high school:

> "O, beware, my lord, of jealousy;
> It is the green-eyed monster which doth mock
> The meat it feeds on"

Like Iago, Dawn had stabbed Sanjay to the heart, put her finger in the wound and twisted it. His torture had barely begun.

*

If I can't have her, no one can.

Jealousy is not only inbred in human nature, it is the most basic, all-pervasive emotion touching all aspects of human relationship. The difference between love and jealousy, according to scientists, is that love evolved to bind two people together for a long time, and jealousy to protect the integrity of their bond. A destructive emotion, perhaps, but also functional and normal, until it causes irrational behavior. Jealousy has no boundaries but penetrates on all levels, social, intellectual, age-related, racial, and economic. Sociobiological theory views female jealousy as fear over losing a relationship or anxiety over a rival relationship. Male jealousy, focusing on the sexual threat of the rival, is marked by competitiveness and aggression, suggesting the mate is still interested in maintaining the primary bond.

Jealousy exists in every culture and religion. God, by definition, tolerates no other gods beside Him, and is so jealous as to visit the sins of the fathers upon the children unto the third or fourth generation. The *Mirabilis Dei* implies a duality of God's jealousy as both awful and wonderful. Stories of jealousy and the havoc it wreaks abound in mythological tales. Greek Gods took revenge upon those mortals unfortunate enough to be romantically involved with their mates. Hera transformed women into animals for mating with Zeus. Troy and Greece fought a war over Helen. Tristan died from a broken heart over his tragic love for Iseult. Mélisande perished from the sorrow caused by Golaud, whose jealous sword pierced the heart of Pelléas.

Crazed with jealousy and rage, Sanjay made it his life's work to ruin Dawn. He realized how much he cared and how betrayed he felt. His initial indifference spawned a determination to wreak vengeance, no matter what it cost him in money or grief. He knew the media enjoyed feasting on human suffering, and he placed anonymous phone calls to the Montréal newspapers, alerting them of Dawn's double life. The more sordid the story, the more intrigued they were. From the research he had done on the English Montréal School Board, he learned they were under constant fire from the French Québécois government over funding issues. At any given moment, they were ready to act on whatever indiscretion may have been committed by any member of its army of schoolteachers.

To her detriment and my gain.

*

Sanjay,

What on earth are you trying to do, have me killed? Or would you rather I take my own life? Do you have any idea how dangerous Tom is? You are causing havoc in my world, and for what, some sort of sick revenge? I've lost my teaching license, thanks to you. I'll never be able to teach again. Are you happy now?

This game you are playing is deceitful and underhanded. The waiters at my favorite restaurant tipped me off to your little PI friend. And would you believe, he hit on me? Trying to do me with your money. How do you feel about that? What an asshole.

By the way, Tom told me you were asking him for 14-year-old girls. That is disgusting. How do you sleep at night? I have a mind to phone in an anonymous tip to the Police about you.

Get out of my life, you sick bastard. Just leave me alone and stop harassing me. And find some help for your pedophilia before it gets out of hand.

Dawn

Sanjay read the email, distressed. He wasn't sure what upset him most, being found out by Dawn, being lied about by Tom, or discovering his PI was trying to screw him over. Probably all three. He reread the email countless times, in shock and outrage, going over its details in his head.

Why did she do this? Makes me fall in love with her, takes my money, breaks my heart, and then threatens me? The whore! She deceives the school, the students, her parents, an unsuspecting young man she promises to marry in order to escape? The world must be coming to an end for such behavior to be tolerated.

He tried to think. What should he do? With the email from Dawn, he now had her email address. At the very least, he could pen a reply of protest.

Dawn,

I don't know what you are talking about. I never asked Tom to supply me with 14-year-old girls. He is a liar, a sick, perverse liar. I just called him to find out where you were. When he couldn't tell me, I hired the Investigator to search for you. That's all.

After all I've done for you, I don't deserve to be treated so poorly, or to be described with such foul language.

Sanjay

He was in total denial, blinded by his jealousy of Dawn and his outrage at her ingratitude. Even though he had instigated a vengeful investigation to get back at her for hurting him, he had considered himself guiltless in the whole mess. Now, he was in more pain. And he had no one to blame but himself.

57

The reward for a hard day's work saving lives and stamping out disease was several rounds of Sanjay and George's favorite drink, Kokanee Gold, at their favorite restaurant, Bailey's, served to them by their favorite waitress, Natasha. She was the darling of every patron who came in to partake of the food, drink, and ambiance. In an establishment famous for its exquisite servers, "favorite" was a generous compliment.

"She must work as a GFE on the side." George admired Natasha from behind as she took off to obtain a second round for the MDs. "All the beautiful girls do."

"Why don't you ask her if she'll do you?" Still stinging from Dawn's cutting attack, Sanjay may not have been crying in his beer but was more than ready to drown himself in it. "Wait a minute, aren't you getting married soon?"

"You should talk. Married, with two kids."

"Married, but not buried."

The two men chortled and focused their gaze on the stunning scenery outside their window.

"A view like that makes me almost believe in God."

George pretended to be scandalized. "You, the atheist? What is the world coming to?" He peered at Sanjay's troubled expression but decided not to ask what was bothering him. "For me, a beautiful woman is a lot more inspiring than trees and lakes."

"Why am I not surprised?"

"No, really, Sanjay. When I see a woman, I want to have sex with her. It's healthy, normal."

"That's not normal, George. It's sick."

"Don't you?"

"Don't I what?"

"Want to have sex with women who attract you?"

"Just the pretty ones. The others are for you."

They drank in silence for a while. George finished his beer and gestured to Natasha to bring another round. "You ever hear anything about that Montréal bitch, what's her name . . . Dawn?"

"No. Nothing at all. *Nada*."

"Whatever happened, anyway?"

Sanjay gazed into the bottom of his glass. "She broke my heart, took my money, and disappeared."

"That's really harsh. You handling it okay?"

"No, George, I'm not. In fact, I'll never get over it." He looked up, misery etched in his face. "She even hit me once."

George gasped. "No way. Is that for real?" He watched as Sanjay confirmed this with a nod. "Jesus . . . Just be glad she didn't ask you to divorce your wife."

"She did."

George gulped. "Good thing you didn't. She would' a left you hanging high and dry."

"And manipulated me any way she pleased."

"Ya' got that right."

"I hope she burns in hell." Sanjay looked up at George. "Why did she do it?"

"Gee, I don't know, Sanjay. Women make no sense to me. Love doesn't, either."

Two more beers appeared on the table. George took several long gulps. "We all get rejected sometimes, but most of us find someone sooner or later who'll return our love. It's the natural order of things, right?"

"And what if you're obsessed with someone? Did you know in the States over a million women are victims of stalkers?"

"Whew." George let out a deep breath. "Good thing you aren't one of those guys."

"Right you are, George. Right you are."

George didn't know Sanjay had videoed one of his sessions with Dawn at the hotel, his own version of *Sex, Lies and Videotape*. The footage included some of her soliciting and asking him for tuition money. Ironically, he had gotten the idea from her.

The more he drank, the deeper Sanjay plunged into the abyss of his tortured mind.

She shouldn't have told me about that ex-boyfriend, the Indian one, who did that to her before. Tuition? My ass. She was never a student. It was all lies. Lies intended to pull the wool over my eyes. Why is it so impossible for man and a woman to love each other?

Sanjay's rage overcame his reason. He was determined to bring Dawn plummeting to her ruin. And if that meant bringing himself down with her, he was resigned to that.

Well, you just have to serve Revenge like a frosty tankard of beer, cold and delicious.

58

Dawn awoke early on her wedding day to find her father hunched over the kitchen table, an untouched cup of coffee in front of him. Hearing her come in, he glanced up for a moment, caught her gaze and cast his eyes downward again.

She sat down next to him, stroking his shoulder with one gentle hand. "Dad, what is it?"

"*Rien, ma petite.* Nothing at all."

"Come now, you can't dismiss me that easily." She turned his face towards her. "You don't exactly look like a proud papa who is finally marrying off his daughter to her premier suitor."

Pierre shook his head, hopeless. "You know me too well, *ma chérie,* but you couldn't possibly be interested in my . . . nightmares."

"You're my father. Of course I'm interested. Just try me."

"*Vraiment? Tu es sûre?*" She nodded. *"Eh bien, écoute, ma fille . . ."*

*

It was supposed to be an easy day for Dr. L'andry. One of the most well respected radiologists at Victoria General in Halifax, he was expected to interpret the 50 or so x-rays mounted on the view box without breaking a sweat. He had gotten to number 34 with little problem, recounting each one into his Dictaphone.

"Postero-anterior chest X-ray demonstrates normal cardiac size, normal mediastinum, normal lung fields but minor blunting of the costophrenic angles."

Radiographic images fascinated Pierre, who was trained to scrutinize depictions of human organs and appendages in a way that differed from that of his colleagues. His canny eye revealed signs of disease to him that would escape the recognition of any other physician at the hospital. One look into his view box with his skilled eye and the most minuscule tumor lost all hope of escape.

Today, however, he had trouble concentrating. Thoughts of meeting up with the newest young nubile beauty at the local massage parlor distracted him, whipping his psyche into a frenzy of arousal he was unable to ignore. It wasn't the mere thought of a massage that excited Pierre. A veteran of more than 1,500 massages, he needed more than that to twist his top. Ginger, owner of the Bluenose Massage Studio in town, had made sure to describe her newest model, Lucinda, to Pierre in scintillating detail. Now that the local police force had cracked down on prostitution, it was getting more difficult for new girls to enter the profession. But City Hall sanctioned the studios, which were covered under a "recreational massage" clause in the local bylaws. As much as he deplored the sight of hookers offering their wares on Main Street, City Councillor Alex Bolden wanted to avail himself of a "massage attendant" whenever he felt the need, especially if she was attractive.

"Forty-two down, eight more to go." Pierre sighed. It was not going as quickly as he had hoped, but the next x-ray got his attention. "Whew, that's got to be a C cup, if not more."

The sight of the shapely breast was almost too much for him to take. He felt a surge of sexual excitement rush from his chest to his groin. Anxious not to let the view sidetrack him from completing his work, he focused on the clinical report.

"Twenty-eight-year-old female with history of hemoptysis."

He knew there was more to it than that. Using his uncanny ability to feel vibrations from a black and white picture, he extended his ultra-sensitive fingers close to the image, where he could see a subtle 5 mm nodule in the lower left lobe behind the heart. The two faint blood vessels that appeared to be connecting the module to the hilum resembled a small round stone and necklace hung from the left pulmonary artery, like a walking stick with a round handle. He recognized immediately the presence of a rare disorder.

"Very likely suggestive of pulmonary arterio-venous malformation. A contrast enhanced computerized axial Scan (CAT) is recommended to confirm the diagnosis."

He gave himself a virtual pat on the back for formulating the difficult analysis, but the full-breasted image had awakened his insatiable hunger for female flesh. His thoughts shifted to Ginger's description of yet another beauty, Sussex, who was 5'7", 32-26-34, 120 pounds of nubile, alluring flesh. Just his style. The memory of it made his mouth water. Without wasting another second, he dialed Bluenose Studios.

"When will Danielle be working?"

"She should be here by five."

Pierre recognized the high-pitched voice of Maria, a stunning 25-year-old brunette with whom he had had 50 or more encounters. "What does she look like?"

Maria knew Pierre's voice as well. "Twenty-two years old, Pierre, pretty as a magnolia in spring bloom."

"She's that pretty? Are you sure?"

"Yes, of course. Would I exaggerate to you? Believe me, she's just your type. Call back at five to see if she's here."

Pierre hung up, eyeing the piles of work awaiting him. Yesterday's dictated reports had been transcribed but needed signing. There were urgent phone messages from residents clamoring for his attention. More work was needed on the manuscript he had submitted to RADIOLOGY. He had to call the General Electric salesperson to fulfill the radiology department's urgent need for another 16 detector CT scan machine. Would it never end?

I hate paperwork.

His thoughts drifted to his evening's hoped-for meeting with Danielle, or better yet the young and beautiful Sussex, whose acquaintance he had not yet made. He hadn't met anyone new in weeks. He was tired of Maya, Stacey, Brittany, Desiree, Jennifer, Ivy, Serena, Amber, Bronwyn, and . . . He had seen so many of them the previous month. He couldn't remember them all. The studios knew his taste. Aside from being young, beautiful and well proportioned, he liked them to be nice. Money was no object, and he didn't care about skin or hair color. He wanted, and deserved, to be treated well.

Pierre checked his watch: ten minutes to five. Electricity surged through his body, ending at the growing bulge between his legs. No use trying to concentrate any longer. With rush hour traffic, the drive to the studio would take at least fifteen minutes.

He dialed the phone. "Is Danielle there yet?"

This time Ginger answered the phone. She also recognized his voice. "Maria already told you. She'll be here at five. Try to keep it in your pants, Dick."

"I'm just checking, don't jump down my throat. Are you sure she's a beauty?"

Ginger sighed with impatience. "For the thirtieth time, she's gorgeous. Petite and blonde, just your type."

Blonde. I love blondes. They're my fantasy.

Pierre booked her for 6 pm. That gave him time to finish his calls, head over to Salty's Best Catch on the Waterfront for a few quick beers and get to the Studio in plenty of time. He immersed himself in reverie. Young, beautiful bodies titillated him to the point where he couldn't get enough. Each tryst made him want more. That scared him, but he still couldn't control his cravings. Thanks to the new mayor's policy, the supply of *filles de joie* was not exactly infinite. He was willing to take the luck of the draw. Tonight, with providence on his side, his ship would come in, big time.

When he parked his car by the pawnshop next to Bluenose Studios, his heart was pounding with such force he could barely keep the endorphins from making his brain explode. Adrenaline and dopamine flooded his consciousness, giving his body the intense need for release. The orgasm he experienced from touching, kissing and caressing a nubile body was all he needed to satisfy his addiction. He treated the girls well, gave them the same pleasure he received, and tipped generously.

He paid Ginger $125 and followed her to Room #1, his favorite. Seating himself on the soft black leather couch, he glanced around at the surroundings. Intimate, romantic lighting and muted pink walls added to his feelings of arousal, witnessed by his swollen penis as he undressed.

I want this to be my last, most intensely powerful orgasm.

The thoughts were always the same. Each experience was supposed to be his last, but it only made him hornier. He made a conscious effort to restrain his anticipation long enough to avoid ejaculating too soon. That was always a danger.

The next five minutes felt like five years. Pierre waited, willing himself to hold off his excitement, until he heard the soft knock at the door. After a brief moment, Danielle tiptoed into the room. Pierre looked at her, horrified, and gasped.

"Renée?"

"*Papa?*"

Pierre screamed, holding his heart, afraid he was going into cardiac arrest. It couldn't be true! He had to wake up from this nightmare . . .

*

"Oh my God, *Papa*." Dawn's face turned pale. "Is this true? Do you . . . ?"

"No, *ma chérie*, of course not. I've never in my life visited one of these . . . these places."

"But it sounded real. Terribly, terribly real." Her shoulders began to shake. "How . . . why would you have such a dream?"

Pierre rose and put his arms around her. "I don't know why, *ma petite*. Believe me, I am as repulsed as you are." He tightened his grasp, comforting her. "I feel terrible, having such a nightmare the very eve of your wedding. It seems so ominous."

Dawn took a deep breath to quell her hyperventilating. "I'm sure it will be okay, Dad." She turned to him. "Won't it?"

59

The newly minted Mr. and Mrs. John Kriarakis put off their honeymoon to the island of Crete until things quieted down at the pizza parlor. Dawn, who was eager to enjoy this side benefit of marriage soon as possible, had agreed to help her mother-in-law at the store in hopes of moving things along at a faster pace. She couldn't wait to meet her new relatives on the other side of the Atlantic. To her, Greece, and the islands in particular, represented romance and civilization in one attractive package. If her children were going to be half-Greek, she wanted to know something about their heritage even before they were conceived.

She returned home from work one day to the sound of her phone ringing. Her intuition told her not to answer. Her duty as a housewife dictated otherwise.

It could be someone for John, a business contact.

Against her better judgment, she picked up the phone. Within an instant she knew it was a mistake.

"Mrs. Kriarakis?" A female voice echoed through the line.

"Yes." Dawn enjoyed being called John's wife.

"I'm from *Le Journal du Montréal*. We're doing a project on the hypocritical attitude of our lawmakers towards the issue of prostitution."

"What?" Dawn practically dropped the phone. "Who are you? How did you get my number?"

The faceless voice ignored Dawn's query. "We feel the public ignores the fact that prostitutes are real individuals, with genuine feelings, who are often made to suffer unfairly, and have even had their lives destroyed. We feel you may be able to offer some insight into this subject."

Dawn became increasingly agitated. "Who told you about me?"

"I'm sorry, I'm not allowed to reveal my source. I only know you have information that could help in our study. Your contribution would be most valuable."

"I have no idea how you know that, but I can't help you. Goodbye."

She reached for the disconnect button, but the woman was too quick. "Mrs. Kriarakis, please don't hang up."

"Why should I talk to you?"

"Don't you feel that women who turn to a life of prostitution should get a fair shake? Wouldn't you like to expose the unreasonable attitudes of politicians and other officials who exact excessive penalties on prostitutes? Don't you think the public should be offered a more sympathetic view of what these women endure, the damage that bad publicity can do to their lives?"

Dawn was torn. After what she had been through with Tom and Sanjay and other difficult clients, she was tempted to agree to the interview. The woman was right. Someone had to air the issue, to give people a chance to judge for themselves whether or not hookers were getting fair treatment by the press and by the government.

"Yes. I do."

"And would you be willing to share your experiences?"

"I . . . I guess so."

"That's wonderful, Mrs. Kriarakis. You won't be sorry."

"But you can't reveal my name. If you do, I'll hit you with the lawsuit of the century."

"Of course. We maintain strict anonymity."

"Well, you'd better." Dawn's tone was threatening.

"Yes. Thank you, Mrs. Kriarakis."

"Be aware I still have to think about this. I'm not quite ready to make a final decision. I'll be in touch."

"Thank you."

The woman hung up. Dawn felt uncomfortable. She wasn't sure she was doing the right thing, but she wasn't about to take another step until she found herself a savvy lawyer. For the most part, the wheels were in motion.

No going back. It's too late now.

*

"Dr. Kaul?"

"Yes."

"Jeanne-Marie DeNeault, from *Le Journal du Montréal*."

The hair on Sanjay's arms stood on end. "Yes, Ms. DeNeault. How are you?"

"Fine, thank you. I just wanted to let you know I was able to interest our chief editor in your story."

"Oh. That's . . . excellent news."

"Yes, notwithstanding your extensive contacts with the media, your credentials speak for themselves. Your medical stories have always been in much demand with the press here in Montréal."

"Thank you, I'm very flattered. I'm glad you were able to convince your editor."

"By the way, Ms. L'andry agreed to an interview."

"Oh . . . really?"

"Yes, we here at *Le Journal* are all very excited. I know you were adamant she not be interviewed, but we believe the story will be so much more compelling if we included that."

"Yes . . . I see . . . I'm curious, how did she react?"

"At first she denied everything, of course, but once I pointed out that we had solid evidence, she changed her mind."

"Yes. I'm not surprised."

"However, she insisted on doing the interview in French, from her lawyer's office."

Sanjay's guard went up. "Her lawyer?"

"Yes, sir. After I spoke with her, she promised to call me back. It was actually her lawyer who did so and informed us she agreed to be interviewed only after the legal agreement was drawn up and signed, by me and by our publisher."

"Ah. I see."

"The agreement stipulates she will give a truthful interview on condition the paper not publish the photographs you provided us. But even without those, our follow up to your suggestion we contact the School Board and Ministry of Education will help the story ring true, I'm certain."

"Yes. I'm sure it will."

"I'm so glad you convinced me to pursue the story. It will be a most thought provoking feature. Thank you."

"You're quite welcome. The pleasure is all mine."

As soon as Sanjay hung up the phone, he broke out in a cold sweat.

What have I done? Dawn is a beautiful person. I am a terrible person, an evil person. Everyone told me not to hurt her. What am I doing?

Unable to get his mind away from what he had done, Sanjay tormented himself with such thoughts for days on end. Underneath it all he had an unnerving feeling that all the people he had confided in, George and the two escorts, were right. In hurting Dawn, he was only hurting himself. And he was prepared to pay the price.

60

Dr. L'andry was awash in more chaos than usual in the ER when an orderly told him about the FedEx package notice waiting in his office. He couldn't afford to take time out to retrieve it, too much was happening at once, and not only the typical "bread and butter" cases. A never-ending cavalcade of ambulances had been dropping off critical cases since the wee morning hours, like a continuous barrage of crossfire in a World War II battle. In the midst of all this mayhem, he tried his best to maintain order and life.

"It can't be the full moon. It's only 9 am."

Pierre glanced at the redheaded nurse who had made the comment loud enough for everyone to hear over the pandemonium, thinking her body had seen better days before the effects of gravity and abuse had set in. He managed a quick nod of agreement to the nurse.

"Vienne must be on the wrong side of God today. Looks like people have been trying to die and kill each other or themselves with a vengeance all morning."

"You got that right, Doc. Gunshot wounds, stabbings, motor vehicle accidents, overdoses, you name it. We have it all."

The next time Pierre had a moment to look up at the clock, it showed 2 pm. His shift ended at 3, time enough to get to the FedEx office on Emory Street and pick up the mystery package.

Pierre turned to the nurse. "I've got to have coffee, or I'll never get through this." He ducked out in haste and rushed to the cafeteria, where he grabbed a large cup of caffeine-laced brew. His break was short-lived.

"Code Blue, ER, Code Blue ER." The paging system whooped its cry of alarm as yet another ambulance raced to the Emergency Department with its lights flashing and sirens screeching.

"Dammit."

Leaving the coffee on the cashier's counter, Pierre raced back to the ER. Despite the repeated blaring of the P.A. system, he couldn't keep thoughts of what awaited him at the FedEx office from assailing his mind.

Who could be sending me a package? All my official mail comes to the office address on Westminster Lane. It must be something personal, but what?

Within minutes the ER's resuscitation room had filled to capacity with life-saving professionals. Pierre darted in to find two respiratory technologists, two nurses, and two orderlies awaiting the code blue to arrive. Another orderly wheeled in a bald middle-aged male named Louis. His wife, a young female in her twenties with pale complexion and long flowing auburn hair, followed behind the gurney, her expression terrified.

The orderly explained the situation. "Forty-four-year-old male, cardiac arrest."

"That's awfully young to go into sudden death. When and how?" Pierre watched the technologists prepare a jolt of cheap hydro imported from Canada.

"At home while eating lunch with his wife."

"It was a late lunch." The wife offered a worried explanation. "Thank God I knew CPR. I compressed his chest for what seemed like a half hour before the paramedics arrived, but it was only four minutes. I . . . I was afraid he was dead."

Pierre turned to her. "Technically, he probably was. You breathed life into him."

The young woman bit her lip and focused on the staff's efforts. Once the hydro had regulated the patient's chaotic cardiac activity, the techs secured his airway with a tube and initiated amiodarone to prevent any further arrhythmias.

"Looks like a classic myocardial infarction." Dr. L'andry addressed one of the nurses. "Initiate T&K." He turned to the young wife, whose puzzled look called for an explanation. "It's a clot busting drug, Mrs . . ."

"Savage."

"Mrs. Savage. Primary percutaneous angioplasty is the state of the art in these cases. Unfortunately, Vienne is too far from a center where it's done. This drug is the next best thing."

She looked doubtful. "Is he . . . is he going to be all right?"

"We'll do everything we can to see that your husband lives to tell the tale. Meanwhile, rest assured you've played a major part in his potential survival."

"Thank you, Doctor."

Waving aside her acknowledgment, Pierre strode from the room to the ER desk, where he signed out of his shift. It was past 3 pm, time for the next emergency physician to take over. Within minutes, he jumped in his Pathfinder, sped to the FedEx office and signed for the parcel. Tucked inside the FedEx packet, with a sender's name he did not recognize, he found a #10 business-size envelope, unsealed, with no return address. Anxiety spreading through his brain, he locked himself in the SUV and scrutinized the skinny white envelope. Instinct told him it was a ticking bomb waiting to explode. His heart raced. His inner voice screamed at him not to open it.

He disobeyed. The simple hand-printed one-page letter from a woman who signed only her first name struck him like a two-ton missile. He read the missive, reeling with disbelief and shock, then reread it just to make sure he had understood its contents.

Dr. Pierre L'andry,

I am the unfortunate wife of an individual, my husband, whom I left after I found out about his affair with a woman named Renée L'andry, a.k.a. "Dawn." I happened to come across all the emails and other information about their affair and copies of the checks my husband gave to her. That is where I found your address. It's unlikely you are aware that in addition to her day job as schoolteacher in Montréal, she works as a prostitute. My husband met her through an escort agency in that city, where she worked as "Dawn" for a number of years. After meeting my husband she carried out the above-mentioned intimate relationship with him to take money from him, as she found him to be quite vulnerable.

Dawn/ Renée told my husband she was a physiotherapy student and needed to work as an escort in order to pay for her tuition and living expenses. After reading their emails, and the reports from a Private Investigation company he hired to discover her true identity, it became quite clear to me that my husband did indeed give her money so she could complete her studies. She misrepresented herself in this way for quite some time until he found out about her subterfuge, after which she terminated this relationship with him. This break-up led to a bout of severe depression for him and other difficulties between us, ultimately causing our subsequent separation and divorce. I found out from my husband that Renée L'andry previously had been mistress to many other men, including a CEO from Atlanta, a Hollywood producer and a Montréal judge, and often took large sums of money from them. My husband gave her a large amount of our money as well.

You may be wondering why I am sending you this note. Rest assured it has nothing to do with vengeance on my part. My marriage is over, but I can only hope "Dawn" does not destroy other marriages, and hearts, in the future. I am sorry to be the one to break the bad news to you. Believe me, I've done so in hopes your daughter will stop ruining other people's lives.

Vinita

Pierre dropped the letter onto the passenger seat. His mind lurched with confusion and anger. How was this possible? Was the woman lying? What reason did she have to do so? Somehow he had to get to the bottom of this. The trouble was, once he did manage to discover the truth in the situation, he had no earthly idea what he was going to do about it.

*

Deanna retrieved the afternoon newspapers from her front porch. She looked forward to winding down from her day by devouring the contents of *Le Journal de Montréal* and the Toronto Sun before starting dinner preparations. She had special arrangements with publishers to send her the papers so she could remain in touch with her English and French Canadian heritage.

Opening the *Journal*, she scanned the front-page headlines, her eyes agape.

'*Professeur le jour, Escorte la nuit*'—double life of an award-winning schoolteacher . . . Uttering a cry of anguish, she held onto the chair by the front door to keep from falling over and quickly unfolded the Toronto paper. Yet another headline assaulted her consciousness.

'*Dawn's secret sex life*'. . . *Montréal teacher profits from her school holidays to supplement her low wages working as . . . an escort."*

Shattered, Deanna sank into the chair, eyes wide with horror, as she perused the article.

Unbeknownst to her family in Statesville, Georgia, US, the schoolteacher known only as Dawn in her second life . . .Deanna fumbled in her pocket for her pack of cigarettes and lit one, hands trembling. Then, extracting her cell phone from her other pocket, she called Pierre.

61

Rather than confront Dawn at home, Dr. and Mrs. L'andry waited for her in the living room of their daughter Lorraine's house in Vienne. They thought it best for her to be a distance away from John during the meeting. That way if she became distraught, which they were certain she would, she still had the time and space to collect herself before facing her husband.

They sat in silence, lighting each other's cigarettes, until Deanna spoke. "How do you think she'll take it?"

"What do you think? Two furious, disappointed parents ganging up on her?" Pierre crushed out his cigarette and lit another.

"We're not ganging up on her, we're just . . ." Deanna seized Pierre's cigarette and lit a fresh one with it. "We still love her, no matter what. We have to make sure she understands that."

"She should have thought of that before she sold her body."

Deanna blanched. "Please, Pierre. No parent wants to see their child grow up to be a prostitute, but she's married now and trying to be respectable. She's still our daughter."

"It's the ultimate travesty. What if the local papers find out, or John, or our friends and my work colleagues? Jesus Chr—"

"Pierre!" Deanna avoided taking the Lord's name in vain at all costs. "Look, we haven't slept in two days, we're both very tense. We have to try and be a bit calmer about this."

"Oh? After she's jeopardized our relationship with the entire Kriakis family, not to mention our own circle of friends? Our reputation is at stake."

"And what about Renée's reputation?"

Pierre fixed his eyes on Deanna. "As I said, she should have thought about that before."

The silence between husband and wife darkened the already austere atmosphere. Deanna made an effort to soothe her husband.

"Let's just see how it goes, all right?"

Pierre bristled but stayed quiet when he heard Dawn's car pulling up in the driveway.

Dawn's instincts told her something was amiss when her parents asked her to meet them in her sister's house in Vienne instead of at home in Statesville. They hadn't wanted to discuss whatever was on their minds over the phone, and if they were planning a social visit, they would have all driven to Lorraine's together. When she noticed only her parents' Pathfinder, and not either of Lorraine's cars, parked in the driveway, she became agitated. Quaking with fear, she walked up the front steps. The heaviness in the atmosphere hit her like a slap with a wet dishrag. The expression on her parents' faces confirmed, to her dismay, that her trepidation was justified. She sat down opposite them, trying to affect a cheerful manner.

"Hello, *Maman*, hello, *Papa*. I'm sorry I'm a bit late. The traffic was—"

Pierre interrupted her. "Tell me, Renée, how did you . . . leave things in Montréal?"

"How did I 'leave things?' What do you mean, *Papa*?"

Deanna, anxious her husband would lose control of his emotions, interjected before he could respond. "Well, dear, we were just concerned that nothing . . . untoward happened there."

Dawn's heart sank. She knew too well what they were talking about but was determined not to let her guard down.

"How could anything 'untoward' happen, Mother? I did only what I told you, teaching at the school during the day, volunteering at the nursing home after hours and at the Humane Society on weekends."

"You didn't do anything . . . wrong?"

"Never, *Maman*. Surely you know me better than that." She glanced back and forth between Pierre's hardened expression and Deanna's distressed one. "You have no reason not to trust me as you always have."

Trying to quell her panic, she changed the subject. "Did I tell you John and I are leaving for Crete in a couple of weeks? Finally, we get our honeymoon. His family over there is so eager to meet . . ."

The look of hatred on her father's face told her there was no use in continuing her charade. She wasn't distracting them. On the contrary, the anguish in their faces increased with her every word. Dread flowed through her veins. Only one thing could be causing this reaction. They knew about her double life.

How? Who told them? It couldn't have been Sanjay . . . Tom? . . . No, he wouldn't . . . The reporter signed an agreement not to disclose my name. How did this happen!

She had no time to contemplate further. Pierre extracted a piece of paper from his briefcase and thrust it in front of Dawn. It was Vinita's letter. Dawn read it, her mind reeling with remorse. She didn't even know this person who had poured out her agony in writing, but now as a wife, Dawn identified with this woman's pain. Not willing to abandon her resistance to the horrific truth, she persisted with her defense.

"I have no idea who this is. Is that an Indian name? I don't know any East Indians. I did date that Indian guy from McGill, maybe he's trying to harass me." She paused, taking in her parents' grim stares. "I never worked as a prostitute in my life. I've never been anyone's mistress. All of this is completely false!"

Deanna was losing patience. "You're lying through your teeth, Renée. Why don't you simply admit the truth?"

"But I'm not lying, *Maman,* I'm telling you the truth."

Dawn's tearful protests did not distract Deanna from her mission to upbraid her daughter. "Is this what we taught you as a child? We raised you so religiously, gave you everything you wanted, and you return our love with . . . this? How could you?"

Dawn cast a regretful eye at her father's expression of misery. Deanna continued her litany.

" You were always your Dad's favorite child. He loved you more than all the others, Renée. Just look what you did with his love and trust. You hurt us, you wounded our love, our trust that we placed in you, and you still don't have courage to tell the truth? Tell me. Give us some answers."

"You trust this letter from a stranger more than you do me?" Dawn turned her tear-stained face to her father's. "*Papa?*"

Maintaining a controlled silence, Pierre reached into his briefcase, pulled out some pages torn from a newspaper and held them in front of his daughter. The color drained from her face. Her father's livid expression commanded she read what was before her. She did so, but silently.

'Dawn' (not her real name), a Montréal math teacher, has been hiding her 'second occupation' from family, friends and colleagues. She agreed to be interviewed by Le Journal on condition of anonymity.

Constrained by her low salary and attracted by the prospect of 'easy money,' she entered the underworld of high-end prostitution and sold her 'talents'—for a price. The agency employing her took half her earnings as commission, but she was still able to clear $125 an hour. She enjoyed dinners at upscale restaurants, sumptuous suites at luxury hotels from Québec to Las Vegas. She admits to developing a taste for expensive clothes and jewelry and fancy cars. When one of her clients, from whom she extorted $20,000 and an unknown number of 'perks,' hired a private detective to find out her real identity, 'Dawn' went underground with her métier.

She wasn't satisfied with her job as a (math) teacher. 'It wasn't stimulating enough for me,' she explained. 'I was literally treated like a real princess.'

The paper published other quotations from her interview.

'For four years, I shared my time between schoolrooms and hotel rooms. But I only worked on weekends so as not to compromise my teaching,' she says. 'I'm daring by nature and wanted to see what that other world was like. All I can say is, it's dangerous. But the risks attracted me. And I felt I was helping those poor guys who couldn't find love. It is all about love, after all' . . . 'My boss at the agency liked me because he rarely has educated girls.

'With my clients, I was a real actress. I had my story down pat. I said I was studying physiotherapy and was working as an escort to pay for my studies.

'The most I charged a client was $300 an hour for 3 hours.

'It didn't bother me to sleep with men for money. If I had not been an escort, I probably would have met someone in a bar and had relations with him. And I wouldn't have been paid . . . 'Working as an escort, I made several hundreds of thousands of dollars.'

Dawn let the paper flutter to the floor. "I . . . I don't know anything about this. It's not me." Trembling, she stood up. "I don't want to discuss it."

Pierre seized her arm, sat her down, and placed another page in front of her. "*Lisez,*" he demanded.

"*Papa,* please . . ."

His menacing face silenced her. She glanced at the print, her eyes misting over. There were quotes from the Minister of Education about dismissal protocol, from the President of the Federation of Parents' Committees about possible legal action, distressed opinions coming from the Teachers' Alliance, the School Boards and even direct quotes from her students.

> *The President of the Fédération des Comités de Parents finds it 'difficult to accept' the idea of a teacher also working as an escort . . . This is not in accordance with the values promoted in the public school system.*

> *The Association of Anglophone School Boards of Québec calls the situation 'serious' and 'striking.'*

> *'You can say that there is a moral problem in allowing a teacher to work as an escort,' says the Chairman. 'The link of confidence between the school and the teacher is broken.'*

But the quotes from her students on ratemyteacher.com brought Dawn to her knees.

> *'She's the best. She's young, pretty, and she has style like no other teacher. But it's true that she gives a lot of homework.'*

> *'She's really nice, but she gives too much homework and she thinks we can do everything.'*

> *'She's really mean and she thinks she's perfect!'*

> *'She's really cool and makes learning math enjoyable.'*

> *'She really has style . . . maybe too much.'*

And, to her horror, a series of scathing statements from Sanjay, and an extended listing of *Free Republic* and other blog entries that beat her character to a pulp.

'Ho' teacher . . . at least she wasn't canoodling any students . . .'

'Nah, they couldn't afford her . . .'

'Homework was never quite like this . . . She should be premierette of Québec . . . Better a hooker than buggering the boys . . .'

'. . . Retired as a teacher at the ripe old age of 29? I'm studying for the wrong profession . . .'

'Sample word problem from one of her math exams: if Dawn charges her johns $250 for straight sex or $200 for oral sex, and her pimp takes a 30% commission, how many counseling sessions in Bill Clinton's office will she need to make in order to net $1,400?'

'Does she have a Columbus Day special? . . .'

The stream of quotes was relentless. And there were more on the next page.

'She wouldn't encourage women to work as prostitutes? Well, how generous of her . . .'

'Prostitution is treated differently by the law in The Great White North. Plus, it would be a cash business, untaxed. It's a shame that some skunk of a client decided to check up on her. Frankly, I think that both professions are far more noble and legitimate, as they provide a useful service, than (in some cases) politician or lawyer.'

'The angle of the story should not be math teacher moonlights as prostitute but prostitute daylights as math teacher . . . Many teachers can sell their bodies as she does, but few prostitutes can sell their minds as she also does.'

'The former teacher, who now works as a waitress in a restaurant, hasn't told her family or partner of her experience. So, this teacher was not only moonlighting as an escort, she was also stepping out on her partner, whoever he/she is . . . '

Dawn, mortified, struggled to find words. "I . . . I'd better go now. John is waiting for me at home."

Pierre had never rained his anger upon his beloved daughter. He had remained quiet through all of Deanna's accusations and Dawn's protests, but was no longer able to hold back the volcano simmering in his consciousness. He rose from his chair, his face beet red, his eyes bulging, sweat pouring from his baldpate, and loomed over Dawn. His menacing expression, a confusion of disappointment, rage and insanity, terrified her. She had never seen him like this.

"You are a liar, a deceitful backstabber." His anger escalated as he spoke, his voice increasing in volume. "Get out of my sight, you dirty whore!"

Raising his hand, Pierre struck her face with colossal force, sending her reeling onto the floor. Deanna gasped, horrified. Pierre's words were deadly, but his actions had a destructive effect on both of the women in his life, most of all Dawn. In one stroke, a loving relationship of 29 years was smashed to bits.

Deanna moved to help Dawn, but Pierre held his wife back. Dawn, feeling the life sucked out of her from her father's blow, struggled to her feet. Thorns of deep hurt stabbed at her heart. Fighting to catch her breath, she took one last look at the parents who had been her lifeline of support for three decades and staggered out the door.

62

Dawn wrenched her Passat out of the driveway and started to drive, but she had no idea where. Her mind spun out of control like the wheels of a car hydroplaning on a rain-slicked highway. Her father's words and actions stung her in ways she had never felt before. She thought she had developed a thick hide, impervious to such deep pain. She had never been so wrong. Panicked thoughts assailed her in rapid succession, as her driving speed accelerated.

Why did he have to call me a whore, why not just . . . kill me? Yes, I did work as an escort, I sold my body, but I had my reasons. It was my choice, my decision. Everybody has a past, don't they? Why did this have to happen to me now, when I was trying to make a new start in life? Oh, I want to go away from everyone, far away, and not ever return.

Oblivious to the climbing numbers on her speedometer, Dawn followed Highway 516 southbound and within minutes found herself at the junction leading to the Alabama border. Instead of turning left towards Statesville, some unknown impulse compelled her to make a right and continue north on Highway 16.

Where am I going?

There was no answer to her self-query. She had no idea how fast the car was going, but her mind was exceeding 100,000 m.p.h. Her thoughts fast-forwarded to Talmadge Memorial Bridge, only a few miles ahead, where she and John had stood for their wedding pictures after their church ceremony. She had not asked him why he insisted on having their photos taken in the middle of this cabled 50-year-old bridge suspended over the Vienne River, which had been replaced with a taller bridge of a similar design in 1991. Whether it was a construction project he had worked on as a teenager, she wasn't sure. She just remembered glancing down at the river 250 feet below and having a sudden puzzling thought.

A nice place to die.

Dawn knew know that her speed was excessive, but despite the State of Georgia's strict speed limit enforcement policy, she did not attract any attention from the Police. Under normal circumstances, this lack would have struck her as strange. This time, she was too absorbed in her thoughts to notice. All she thought of was Sanjay, what a sick bastard he was, and how much she detested him for wrecking her chances for a happy life.

Because of him and his sick campaign of vengeance, I got fired by that despicable School Board, lost my license, and had to quit teaching forever. It was his fault I had to marry a pizza maker and run away from the city I adored. If he had been willing to leave his wife, none of this would have ever happened . . . She whacked the steering wheel with her hand, crying out in agony. The passing scenery was only a blur, the salt from her tearful outrage biting at her tongue.

Why, Sanjay, why did you do it? I told you I wasn't the right one for you. What did you want from me? What will you get from this vendetta? You are ruining not only my life but also the lives of my parents and my poor, innocent husband. They will grieve forever.

Tears blinding her, Dawn spoke aloud, as if Sanjay were sitting beside her. "You promised not to interfere with my life, Sanjay, or hurt me. Ever. Why didn't you just come after me, kill me, if that would satisfy your sick mind? Why hurt my dad, who loved me so much? What good does it do to make him suffer? He didn't deserve this."

During all her years as an escort, she had kept in mind an escape plan if her parents ever found out her horrendous truth. Now she realized the time had come to implement it. She knew what to do. Catching a glimpse of the speedometer, she pressed the pedal to the floor and increased the car's speed to its maximum. Approaching the bridge, she focused her thoughts on the center of the span, where she and John had stood, smiling and posing, less than a month before. Seeing her goal looming in front of her, she uttered a hurried prayer.

Oh, Lord, please forgive me. Don't make my dad suffer for my sins.

In an instant, if God were merciful, it would all be over. Her last thought was of the man who was responsible for her torment.

"Sanjay, you perverted sicko, I hate you!" She shouted at top volume. "I hate you so much, I want you to feel it all the way to Winnipeg!"

Dawn unbuckled her seat belt. With one last tortured cry, she declared her readiness to meet her creator. *"Seigneur, je te rejoins!"*

With full force, the small automobile collided with the light standard at the entrance to the bridge. The impact sheared the car in half.

A State paratrooper trying desperately to catch up with Dawn's speeding vehicle had already alerted other police cars, ambulances in the area, and the local Emergency Room, of a probable motor vehicle disaster with possible fatalities. He watched the carnage ahead of him, horrified. He had seen it time and time again, these people gunning their cars to the max, so anxious to win some kind of unknown race, spinning out of control and needlessly extinguishing lives. When would they ever learn?

63

Sanjay finished his morning ICU rounds with a visit to the ER. Nothing was more exciting to him than bringing back patients from the jaws of death. That, to his mind, was the entire *raison d'être* for going into medicine. The latest victim was Donny Fontaine, a twenty-four-year-old male who had gone into un-witnessed cardiac arrest. His aunt had found him slumped on the floor with no pulse and no sign of breathing, by all appearances dead, but still warm. The EMS personnel resuscitated him with the standard asystolic cardiac arrest protocol.

The tech filled Sanjay in on the details. "It only took two doses of epinephrine and five minutes of cardiac compressions along with bagging via endotracheal intubation to get him going again."

"Perhaps because he's so young." Sanjay scrutinized the youth's form. "Possible cause?"

"May have had something to do with the empty morphine sulfate and Valium bottles we collected at the scene."

"Ah." Sanjay was well versed in the occurrence of drug overdose in young males.

"You know who he is, Doctor?"

"The name sounds familiar. Where would I have seen it?"

"In the papers. He just got released from prison. Member of the Indian Posse gang, you know, the guys who would break your knee if you looked at them cross-eyed?"

"Yes, I think I remember. From what I read, this one had a life full of danger and a constant dread of dying. Ironic he would perpetrate his own demise."

Having saved a "businessman" whose methods of money making were questionable at best, Sanjay turned his attention to the Code Blue blaring through the P.A. system. The task of tending to these cases normally fell to residents rotating through the ICUs, or the ICU fellow rather than attending physicians. Sanjay was incapable of passing up the excitement of running a code. It was yet another opportunity to save another poor slob from the brink of nothingness.

A fourth year med student, who was known for his single-minded intent to save the entire world, accompanied Sanjay. "I'm going to do my first live intubation today." His announcement broke the uncomfortable silence in the room.

Sanjay suppressed a sardonic smile. The youth's ingenuous enthusiasm reminded him of his own impetuous tendencies during his student days. His smile turned serious, however, when a messenger brought him an envelope marked "URGENT." He relinquished charge of the ICU to the fellow whose usual task was running the codes, slipped out of the room, and ripped open the message. It was from Ethan, his PI.

Dawn believed killed in fatal car crash at Talmadge Bridge in Vienne.

The crushing news confirmed Sanjay's worst nightmares. He trudged down the hall to his office, entered and shut the door, and looked at the deadly missive again. Not ready to believe the message, he dialed a number in Montréal that he knew by heart. Tom kept abreast of the news of his girls, past or present. He would know if something terrible happened to one of them.

"I hope you're happy now." Sanjay could picture Tom sneering. "It's unforgivable, you reporting her to the media. Why'd you do it, anyway? What did you get out of it?"

"How do you know I—"

"Oh, please. Sophie called to tell me. Dawn was distraught. She was always worried you'd snitch on her. Obviously, you did."

Sanjay was speechless. Good thing Tom didn't know about Vinita's letter and his own complaint to the School Board.

"You go to hell, you bastard. You'll meet her there, no doubt."

"That's a lie, Tom, she couldn't. She's . . . she's an angel."

"She may have been my favorite girl, but she was no angel. She'll go to hell, and so will you."

Sanjay winced from the clatter of the phone slamming down. Tom blamed him for Dawn's demise, and with good reason. It was indeed

Sanjay's fault. Miserable, he slumped in his chair and contemplated the reality. Thoughts of Dawn played like a film screening before his eyes. She had given him so many chances over the last six months to bring about an amicable closure to their relationship, but his perennial stubbornness prevented him from doing so. He might as well have snuffed out her life by his own hand, that beautiful life of his lover, his angel, now gone forever. He was still alive physically, but his spirit had left him, and he felt he was living on borrowed time.

George pushed his way through the half-open door to Sanjay's office and stopped short when he saw Sanjay's ashen face and watery eyes. "What's the matter?"

"She died."

"What? Who died?"

"Dawn."

"The Montréal bitch? How?"

"Smashed her car on a bridge. Possibly suicide." Sanjay lowered his head. "It was my fault. I killed her."

"No, you didn't. She brought it on herself. Don't blame yourself."

"Oh, but I do. I do blame myself. Totally." Sanjay got up slowly and gestured to his friend. "I think I'd like to be alone now, George."

"Are you sure?"

"Yes. I . . . I'll see you later. Okay?"

"Sanjay, I don't want to leave you by yourse—"

"Please."

"Okay, but . . ."

Sanjay's pleading expression convinced George his presence was not wanted. He acquiesced to his friend's request. Once alone, he unlocked his desk drawer, pulled out his journal from the last surreal months since his breakup with Dawn, and started to read.

June 30

I imagine I have three options for closure. One, to continue pursuing her by phone calls to her school, but she could easily call the police and get them after me. Not a good option. Second, to sue her through the court system. This will necessitate spending a lot of money, it will harass her to the extreme, and her reputation will also go down with the ship. Not a great option overall. Third is to tell her story to the world. That will satisfy my creative urges, make me famous, maybe make her famous, and maybe even make me some money . . . Yes, I think this is the best option of all, a superb option, actually.

July 03

Today I found the fabulous photograph of her on the web from 1999. How ironic. She looks as beautiful as always. What a lucky day! I sent her a birthday card, though I don't know if she will ever open it or see it. Anyway, it feels like life is beautiful and full of beautiful things. As I decided on July 1st, I am going to take her love as a guiding light to make me a stronger, better individual in all respects. I am going to be an athlete, scientist, doctor and writer. The thing is to keep my thoughts under control and stay focused . . . Falling in love with Dawn, what an experience, definitely the best time of my life. I wish other people could go through this too, though of course without the pain and hurt. Most people aren't lucky enough to undergo such a gamut of emotions and feelings in life. If only they knew what they are missing . . .

July 14

It has to get better than this. I am in a constant state of anguish, caught between reporting Dawn to her parents, or leaving her be. There is definitely a risk there. It is quite possible her father will be pissed off and will report her to police. I can't take that chance. I'll just have to cut my losses and move on. There is nothing I can do here, nothing. I just got the experience and the heartache out of it. But what an experience!

My only recourse is to write a book. With that, will come closure. It will give meaning to my life. With that, I can survive anything, even the painful self-retribution for what I have done."

July 18

Why is it I can't let Dawn go, forgive her? Why do I want to get back to her and hurt her in some way? I guess revenge is a basic human trait. If someone hurts us we want to hurt him or her back. She did hurt me and that may be my reason for retaliating. After all she broke my heart, ripped me off, and then discarded me, like a piece of old clothing. But knowing myself, I suppose she is likely off the hook. I can't really hurt anyone. Can I?

July 26

"Interesting that I haven't written for over a week. I guess I fell as far and as low as one can. I suppose ups and downs are the part of life. However, I have gotten up and will be able to walk with my chin held high.

I do regret emailing the School Board and the newspaper. Did I do that because I was depressed, or missed her or was getting over her memories, or I felt powerless and just couldn't stop myself? Or is there some other pain in my life? I think it is a combination of all of the above and more. But the important thing is that I have gotten up and am walking again. No question her memories are some of the best things that ever happened to me. I'll cherish that episode of my life forever.

Life. It goes on but is also too short. Therefore, we need to make the best of it. We need to do our best and also achieve a lot. We need to pursue what we love as long as we enjoy it, whether fantasy or reality. I pursued Dawn but it turned out to be a fantasy. Feeling pretty good today though, meditation session last night went quite well and the workout was excellent yesterday as well."

July 30

I have done the deed now. It did bring me a closure, but I really regret hurting my beloved, my angel and guiding light, my Dawn. I know she will be destroyed and she may not be alive after this ordeal. Will she kill herself?

I don't think she will. I sincerely hope she will escape any damage from this. Nonetheless, I've tortured myself over and over with the ultimate question. Why did I do it? The simple answer is, nothing

> *else was bringing me closure. I tried everything else, nothing worked. For my closure and my peace of mind I destroyed her, and for a while I felt better. Free, the same way Dawn felt (I think) when she wrote her last letter saying she was cutting off all contact with me. But now that it's all sunk in, I feel nothing but remorse. This is the most appalling act I have ever done, and I'm so sorry. How can I live with that, knowing I shattered her life, that I destroyed her? I will never, ever forgive myself.*

Reading his own written explorations of his psyche, Sanjay came to a decision. As cruel and selfish as it was for Dawn to leave him behind, and as angry as he was at her for doing so, he wanted to put an end to his suffering. If she were waiting for him in hell, he was going to go there now, today. What was the point in waiting?

With agonizing slowness, he removed a vial and a syringe from the same drawer where he kept his journal. The label, with its skull and crossbones, showed the letters KCl in bold, frightening yellow letters. No one was sure exactly how much potassium chloride could kill a person, but Sanjay didn't want to take any chances and withdrew the entire contents. The substance was strictly regulated in the hospital, and he was only able to obtain one bottle from the pharmacy. He had to do it right the first time. Carefully laying the implements on his desk, he picked up his journal and pen and wrote one last entry.

> *Dawn my love, my baby. I am coming to be with you now. I am sorry for inflicting all the pain and hurt on you, but I was helpless to stop myself. Believe me, I did not mean to hurt you. How could I, you are the most important thing to me, my love, my life, my guiding light . . . I was sick inside and couldn't recognize the consequences of my actions. I apologize. Please forgive me, my darling. I'll tell you all about it when I see you in hell.*

He applied a tourniquet to his left arm and slapped his veins to make them prominent. Poised to puncture his skin with the needle, his thoughts turned to Dawn. He wanted to join her as soon as possible. He knew he had less than ten seconds once he began to empty the clear liquid into his vein before the KCl entered his bloodstream, targeting the cells of his heart, irreversibly paralyzing them and stopping his heartbeat. He wanted to make every last moment count.

The final earthly thing to enter his consciousness was the sound of his secretary's radio blasting Angels and Lovers:

> *And somehow, right from the start*
> *I'm clear in every part I play;*
> *For the first time I see nothing*
> *That will make more or less of you or me.*
> *So we are here together now, on one soil*
> *And we have seen for ages how,*
> *there's no way on earth, to mix water and oil.*
>
> *But I love you dearly,*
> *As if every breath,*
> *You take is my own;*
> *As if every breath,*
> *Has unending soul.*
> *And you know, you know you're not alone.*
>
> *Because we can't deny that power lies between us;*
> *Without you beside me there's no purpose;*
> *I can't believe if you don't see,*
> *And there's nothing to do;*
> *I'm not even half of me,*
> *Without you.*
>
> *But I see you clearly now,*
> *As if every ray,*
> *Of light is my own;*
> *As if every ray*
> *Has unending sun.*
> *And you know, you know you're one.*
>
> *But I love you dearly . . .*

64

"2005 has been an extraordinary year for Canadian Critical Care Research. Using all the tools medical science had to offer, our research has chronicled the efforts to give patients trapped between life and death a fighting chance to survive. During that period, five important protocols have been completed. Two of them have already been published, one has been submitted to a high-impact journal, and two have been entrusted to the writing committee.

"Since the inception of CCCR in the 1960s, the only significant breakthroughs have been in low volume lung ventilation, a counter-intuitive, revolutionary technique to prevent escalation of organ damage, and the use of activated protein C, a clog-busting drug, to improve blood flow to a septic patient. These two procedures averted the dysfunction and eventual breakdown of the patient's vital organs. But it is Dr. Hebert's discoveries in the area of blood loss that we laud at today's CCCR Convention here in Montréal. In a situation where every organ struggles to survive, blood supply is a critical factor. The University of Ottawa's Dr. Hebert, who believes transfusions cause more damage than good, has proved his hypothesis in a series of randomized clinical trials. Patients who were restricted in the amount of transfusions they received developed fewer complications, survived longer, and eventually were able to leave the hospital."

Sanjay delivered his report without with his usual enthusiasm, but the Critical Care Scientific Community critiqued and accepted Dr. Hebert's findings amidst excitement and fanfare nonetheless. The day's meetings were filled with discussions of more important and innovative ideas and sessions drawing up battle strategies for the difficult task of obtaining research funding for the coming year.

"I am honored to transfer the chair to you, Dr. Hebert. I have great respect for your accomplishments in our field."

"Thank you, Dr. Kaul. The feeling is mutual."

The euphoria of the day's successes dissipated as soon as Sanjay returned to his room in the Hyatt that evening. Ever since George had foiled Sanjay's suicide attempt, the depression Sanjay struggled with stuck with him like a stubborn wasp determined to annoy the human being invading its space. George, whose office was across from Sanjay's, had observed his friend's despondency over a number of weeks. He became suspicious when Sanjay did not answer his "stat" page to the ICU. He had seen Sanjay rushing in to his office with wacky look on his face. Fortunately, all doctors have common keys to all doors in the hospital complex. George panicked when he found the door to Sanjay's office locked. Using his key, he barged in to find Sanjay slumped over his desk with a half-empty syringe still attached to his arm.

"Code Blue, Code Blue!"

George screamed over the P.A. System until a cadre of personnel, nurses, a resident, an intern and two orderlies, rushed to his aid.

The first nurse gasped when she saw Sanjay. "Oh my God, what—"

"KCl overdose, hopefully small enough to stop, if we act quickly." George lost no time in commanding the colleagues surrounding him.

A resident stared, wide-eyed, at Sanjay, shocked to see a full-fledged physician in such a condition. "What do we need, Doctor?"

"Calcium, sodium bicarb, glucose, highest possible concentration. Insulin, too, Stat! We're gonna try the whole kitchen sink."

The nurses and interns rushed to obey George's orders. The resident addressed George, concerned. "What are the chances of surviving a potassium overdose, Doctor?"

"Not thinking about that. Let's just get cracking."

To everyone's relief, Sanjay finally responded, though not without a bombardment of every substance in George's bag of tricks. Five minutes of resuscitative efforts seemed like five hours but good enough to prevent any lasting damage to Sanjay's body.

"Thanks to the blessings of modern science, you're still with us." George smiled with relief at Sanjay, who was returning to consciousness. "But hey, we almost lost you. Don't do that to me again, pal."

"Lost me? I wish you had."

"Don't even go there, Sanjay. And don't do that to me again."

After that, George kept a concerned eye on his friend's behavior and counseled Sanjay to seek treatment. Sanjay, who blamed himself for his situation, was determined to withstand it by immersing himself in writing the story of his agony and ecstasy. Surviving his potential demise was more than he deserved. At least that's how he felt. As for his mental state, it was his responsibility, and his alone.

Being in the Hyatt after such a long absence brought Sanjay a bittersweet *déjà vu*. His affair with Dawn had ended over a year ago. The pain and hurt were ever-present, but his need for sexual gratification was as strong as ever. Something about being at a conference in the city where he had first met Dawn and started their ill-fated liaison made him feel the need for a companion. Against his better judgment, he found himself surfing the Yellow Pages for Passion Escorts. To his chagrin, the listing was nowhere to be found.

They don't just go away, do they?

As he continued to explore the options, he noticed a massive turnover in the name and quantity of businesses and personnel in the sex trade. Aware that those connected to this "vocation" often changed their names and identities, Sanjay chose a few possibilities and made several calls. He couldn't help wondering if he might end up talking to Tom, but chastised himself for even thinking it.

Finally, a full-page photo of a young blond woman in a suggestive position caught Sanjay's eye. She was bent over in such a way that her rounded, perfect buttocks looked like two beautiful moons shimmering in the sky over an otherworldly planet. Turned-on, he dialed the Escort Service's phone number and discussed the available choices with the manager. None of them appealed to him until the man mentioned a 30-year-old French beauty.

"34-24-36, blond hair and blue eyes, very friendly and very nice." The manager paused to let the description sink in. "She's one of our most outstanding escorts, very hot. It'll be a memorable GFE experience, without a doubt."

"All right." Sanjay pictured the prospect. "It sounds like just what I'm looking for."

"Thank you, Sir, you won't be disappointed."

"When can I expect her?"

"Half hour or less. How would that be?"

"Fine."

Sanjay hung up, pulled two Molsons from the mini bar and let the alcohol saturate his stressed out consciousness.

Not much has changed. Ah, how I love Montréal.

The jangling phone interrupted his reveries. "She's on her way. Be there in five minutes."

Well, maybe some things have changed after all. They're more punctual now.

One thing Sanjay hadn't lost in his near-successful attempt on his life was his keenness for punctuality. He still hated being kept waiting. Suddenly Sanjay realized the manager's voice belonged to Tom. Fortunately, Tom had not recognized Sanjay's voice. In any case, he hadn't shown any signs of detecting it.

The knock at the door was nearly inaudible. Sanjay, already stripped down to his underwear and eager for his eye candy, threw the door open without looking through the peephole. What he saw before him shot through his body like a bullet entering his chest and exiting through his torso.

She's dead. I know she's dead, gone to Hell. How could this be?

A thousand thoughts raced through his mind. He had made thorough inquiries. Even his PI had confirmed Dawn's death. This wasn't possible.

Maybe it's a look-alike, or a relative. Or her younger sister, the one she said resembled her so much . . . He took another look, unable to shake the impact of the vision.

A ghost? A dream? A hallucination?

The voice filtering into his mind dispelled any doubt.

"Sanjay, is that you?"

He came back to his senses with a thud. "Dawn? It couldn't be, you died in a car accident, in Georgia."

"They thought I did. I sure came close. They flew me to the ICU at Emory University Hospital in Atlanta, kept me alive until surgeons could repair a tear in my aorta. Look at my scar."

Dawn lifted her vibrant red blouse, revealing a well-healed half-moon scar that Sanjay recognized as the remnants of a thoracotomy.

"But you, Sanjay, how come you're still alive? I heard through the Montréal grapevine you committed suicide by injecting potassium."

"I tried, but my friend George saved me from the brink, Dawn."

"By the way, I'm not Dawn anymore, Sanjay. She died. I go by Renée."

"Ah." Somehow this did not surprise Sanjay.

"And believe it or not, I was pregnant at the time of the accident. They were able to save the baby. I have a three-month-old daughter now. She's beautiful."

"I have no doubt. How could a baby of yours be anything but?" Sanjay tried to picture the exquisite child he had so craved to have with Dawn. "What about John, your marriage?"

"Oh." Dawn's face took on a wistful expression. "That didn't work out. It was too hard for him to handle, the move, the accident, the new baby. But I'm really better off without him."

"Did he ever find out? I mean, about your past life?"

"He probably knew, but we never talked about it."

Sanjay felt sorry for Dawn. Her inner sadness pervaded her aura to the extent she looked almost like a child, a lost waif. "Would you like a beer?"

She accepted, grateful, and they sat down by the window overlooking Mont Royal, taking in the view of the mountaintop Holy Cross, illuminated and glowing in the evening light.

Sanjay, still reeling from the shock of seeing Dawn returned from the dead, knocked back a hefty swallow of the brew, its sharp taste infusing his body with a much-needed kick. "And those self-help books you were reading didn't help you turn your life around? *Healing the Heart of Conflict: 8 Crucial Steps to Making Peace with Yourself and Others . . . ?*"

"I read all those and more." The tinge of irony in her grin was something Sanjay had not seen before. "*Four Agreements: A Practical Guide to Personal Freedom. Ten Days to Self-Esteem.* You name it. I tried it. Nothing worked."

"I told you this self-help movement was mumbo-jumbo, just a big sham. Do you know how many books are on Amazon? Almost 52,000, when you do a search for 'the secret to happiness,' not to mention—"

"Please don't preach to me, Sanjay. I didn't come here for that."

"I apologize. It just angers me to see how these books do more damage than good. All they do is empty the pockets of people who believe them."

"I know, I know. The answers these books offer is simplistic, but I realized after a while that life is much more complex. I kept reading more of them. But in the end, I still wasn't able to dig my way out of my mess."

His heart went out to her. Perhaps she didn't deserve hell after all. "What about Opus Dei?"

Dawn's sadness morphed into sheer despondency. "They found out the truth about me, and they . . ." A tear appeared at the corner of her eye. She wiped it away. "They released me of my vows."

"Oh. I'm sorry."

They paused, looking away from each other, focusing on the view from the window. Finally, she put her beer down on the windowsill and faced him.

"I know you were obsessed with me, Sanjay, but how could you try to end it all? I mean, I thought you just . . . just hated me too much."

"It was the only way I could get over you. I thought if I joined you . . ." He paused to take a large gulp of his brew. "Afterwards, I tried everything, psychotherapy, hypnotherapy. It just made things worse." He turned his gaze on her. "Existence takes its own life. We humans are powerless to alter its course. Life continues. Its flow just carries us along."

Dawn rose, walked to the bed and removed her red blouse, pencil-thin black mini skirt and 4-inch stilettos, down to her black bra and panties. She lay down with her legs dangling almost to the floor, the way Sanjay was used to seeing her. Despite the damage done from the accident and childbirth, to him she looked as beautiful as ever. He began to daydream about things going back to the way they had been.

"What would you like to do?" Her voice was weary, as if life had drained her of her former energy and enthusiasm. "My prices are still the same."

Sanjay shook himself from his reveries, summoning up all his willpower. What he was considering was insane. "I . . . I don't want to do anything now. I can't. You're dead to me, Dawn."

"Oh, so you're still as fucked up as ever." She sat up and glared at him. "I'm not dead. I came back to work, I'm just a normal, ordinary person."

"I didn't expect an 'ordinary person.' Not tonight, or any night. I wanted a fantasy. I need to make love to a fantasy." His thoughts wandered again, back to his daydreams of the woman whose love had turned his world on its ear.

"Are you sure, Sanjay?" She tried to restrain her anger, but it was bubbling to the surface.

"Yes, I am. Here's $200. It should cover your time and Tom's cut. Sorry, no tips tonight." He pulled ten crisp 20-dollar bills from his wallet and offered them to her. "Please leave, Dawn. Or Renée. Whoever you are now."

Dawn got up and dressed hurriedly. Placing the bills in her purse, she strode to the door, opened it and rushed out. Sanjay stood in the middle of the room, unable to get a handle on his feelings. He felt numb. His mind was a blank.

Am I alive or dead?

Suddenly, he felt a warm sensation shoot through his veins. A familiar arousal pervaded his body, from the hair on his head to the nerve cells in his loins. Almost naked, he ran through the door and down the hallway, where Dawn was waiting by the elevator.

"Dawn, I'm sorry. I want you. So much."

She looked at him, puzzled. "But Sanjay—"

"No. Don't say anything." Grabbing her hand, he pulled her back towards his room. She didn't resist.

They had no need for explanations or recriminations. All that existed between them was time, time to love and be loved, until dawn's early light.

The End

Edwards Brothers Malloy
Thorofare, NJ USA
March 7, 2013